Steven Jacob earned his history degree in 2004 from Utah State University. He went on to become a lawyer in Southeast Asia where he works on international corporate matters. He spent five years researching and writing *Nobody's Heroes* and has since written several follow-ups that he hopes to find in publication soon. He currently lives in Vietnam.

Nobody's Heroes is dedicated to my family for all of their support over the years and for their constant love.

Steven Jacob

Nobody's Heroes

Austin Macauley Publishers™
London • Cambridge • New York • Sharjah

A CIP catalogue record for this title is available from the British Library.

ISBN 9781528940740 (Paperback)
ISBN 9781528940757 (Hardback)
ISBN 9781528970464 (ePub e-book)

www.austinmacauley.com

First Published (2019)
Austin Macauley Publishers Ltd
25 Canada Square
Canary Wharf
London
E14 5LQ

Writing a book of this magnitude is never done in isolation. While I did most of the research through books and primary source archives, I must add my gratitude to my mother for her remorseless critiques, and to my law school loans for providing the funds to travel the route of the regiment in France. I worked on this novel for five years, and without the constant support of family and friends, I could not have finished it.

Harlem, Manhattan

New York City, New York
October 1, 1916 – August 30, 1917

Reuben Ayers stepped into the back room—many shady dealings took place in back rooms, especially in Tammany Hall's Manhattan, that great democratic machine that ran the city. Once his eyes adjusted to the quality of the light, he saw two men—both white—sitting in front of him. Good odds: two men white, one man black. Better than a lynching mob.

One man, Asa Bird Gardiner, almost eighty years old, his flesh stretched thin. I knew the name. A lawyer, he wore the scraggly remnants of his white hair short. A Medal of Honor recipient, but dishonored, the award rescinded. Apparently, the supporting documentation was lost or never existed, but there was talk in certain circles, talk that brought shame to the man. Gardiner. A name well known among my people, a racist of consummate capability. I knew that much and more from the name alone.

The other man, Ralph Van Deman, a blank slate. I knew nothing of him. He sat beside Gardiner, thin as a post next to the aging supremacist. Narrow features. Long limbs. A stretched face with the nose of an English aristocrat. He sat quietly, his fingers clasped on the table before him. Every few minutes, he would lift a teacup to his lips and sip the pungent green liquid.

"From China," he said in response to my look. "Ceylon tea. Much better than that black stuff the Brits like."

"Imported?"

"By my own hand. Straight from Peking."

"You've—"

"Many times," Van Deman gave a toothless smile. "It's part of my...passion if you will. Part of why I've asked you..."

He spoke with confidence, with ease, and ignored Gardiner's presence completely. Van Deman commanded the room.

"Intelligence," he continued. "Wars are won with intelligence. Knowledge of the enemy's strength and movements and supply lines. These things inform strategy and...well, they provide the ideas that make great generals and soldiers. Without information, an army—no matter how grand—is lost."

"I understand the concept," I said. "Intelligence is important...but why am I here?"

"The Fifteenth New York," Gardiner croaked.

Van Deman glanced at the Sachem, a Tammany Hall faithful, distaste on his face. "Yes, quite. The Negro regiment. There are people—both locally and at higher levels—concerned that this venture may threaten certain, well-established status quos."

"A thousand men who spend their few spare hours marching about a borrowed theatre?"

"War is inevitable," Van Deman said. "Wilson doesn't want to admit it but within a year, we'll be officially committed...if for no other reason than the man's delusions of influence—he thinks he can talk the bloody Boche into surrender—but we'll be at war. Declared, approved, and properly funded—"

Gardiner leaned forward, "It's certain the...Fifteenth regiment will be tasked...somewhere."

Van Deman waved Gardiner to silence, irritated. "The concern is that…that we have no idea what to expect from such a group. For all we know, they might reach France and defect, or offer themselves as servants to the Boche. We aren't asking for a complete dossier, just a warning. If that regiment takes an action that might endanger our war plans, we need to know beforehand—"

"To avoid another Brownsville?"

"Or something similar. We need an insider to give us the tip if the men…" Van Deman raised his hands, palms open. "We need someone to give us that warning."

I looked between Van Deman and Gardiner. I knew the old man, I knew his reputation, the things he said and did as judge advocate. His participation in the railroading of Johnson Whittaker. One out of two. But Van Deman…

"No disrespect, but who in the hell are you?"

Gardiner sputtered and leaned forward, "Boy, don't you—"

Van Deman put a hand on Gardiner's bicep. "That's a fair question. It's also one that deserves an answer…particularly as regards the nature of my request."

Gardiner leaned back in his chair with a grunt. In the front room, a bell rang, a customer. I heard muffled voices through the door.

"Army War College."

"Authority?"

Van Deman ran the tips of his fingers across the table. "My own."

"With the support of Tammany," Gardiner didn't sound like a Southern plantation owner, just an old man who smoked too much, but in my mind, the vowels lengthened and the drawl thickened.

"Let me explain," Van Deman said. "It is only a matter of a few months before American entry in the war. This much is agreed to be inevitable. By the time Wilson finally pegs to the fact, it will be too late to put effective intelligence networks in place."

"Getting an early—"

"That's right. Some colleagues and I are scouting potential issues and opportunities. When your…" Van Deman glanced at Gardiner, a half glance really, just enough to betray a sense of distaste and distrust, "associates contacted us with information about this new regiment."

"We voiced concerns," Gardiner said. "It's a damn foolish idea to teach Negroes to use guns."

Van Deman waved a hand to acknowledge and dismiss Gardiner's input. "Quite. The point is, there's an opportunity here for us, and for you."

"For me?"

"Gardiner," Van Deman turned in his chair.

The grand old man edged forward. I was half-surprised his foot wasn't in a cast from gout. As it was, he walked his bulk forward inch by inch. First the left, then the right. His face and hands showed liver spots and the skin on his face looked as pale as baker's flour. The sparse hair that tufted his head gave him to look like a discarded rug.

"Your relationship to Tammany…your ability to achieve your goals, however delusional they may be, could be…enhanced." Gardiner paused then, to breathe long, slow, painful breaths. "The likelihood of you receiving the benefit of that association—"

"What do I get?" I said, already on my guard. "More vague promises. I've been promised to death yet seen—"

"Tammany gave you your job. That job gave you your house and you ask what Tammany gave you?"

"That house did not come from Tammany. That house—"

Gardiner scoffed. "Uppity, aren't you? Get a little money in your pocket and all of a sudden—"

"Gentlemen," Van Deman raised his hands between the cracker and me. "I must side with Mr. Ayers here. Nothing you said sounded remotely committal."

"Bullshit."

Van Deman pushed back from the table. "It sounds like your people aren't as behind this as I was told. When you come to an—"

"Mr. Van Deman," Gardiner said. "Do not underestimate the commitment of either myself or Tammany Hall. The Columbian Order is in agreement that this specific assignment is vital to our interests and they are willing to give a great deal…for the right party's involvement."

"Then whence the reticence?"

Gardiner scratched his chin then pulled non-existent whiskers toward his belly. "Any reticence I might express comes not from a lack of desire to commit. No, any reticence at all comes from my serious misgivings in regards to the qualifications of this Negro that sits before us."

The way Gardiner said Negro, he just as well could have said Nigger without the slightest deviation in meaning.

"I've earned everything that Tammany's given me."

"Hardly," Gardiner grunted. "We've given you far more than you think, you've only seen the surface. You owe us, boy, and we know how to—"

"What?" I nearly bolted from my seat. "You know how to collect a debt? More likely lynch a body? No, better than that, you know how to railroad an innocent man—"

"I will not sit here and listen to this boy's disrespectful—"

"Gentlemen," Van Deman slammed a palm on the table. "Let's discard the acrimony, shall we, and sit and talk like the mature adults we are."

Gardiner crossed his arms over his chest.

I settled in my seat. "The sooner he puts a firm offer on the table, the sooner we can—"

"We'll put you up as a district leader. That's as far as we can go. Anything else, you earn on your own."

"Thank you, Mr. Gardiner," Van Deman said. "Now, Mr. Ayers, we will expect regular reports—"

"I haven't said yes."

"Oh, quite."

Gardiner grunted. I thought I heard him mumble 'damn nigger' under his breath.

I held my hands in the air above the table and spread my fingers, counted slowly, one to ten. "The thing is, you're asking me to take several steps I have never contemplated and, to be honest, I'm not sure I want to take."

"How so?" Van Deman said.

"Three things come to mind," I said. "First, the practical considerations. My mother is invalid and my home is just becoming a comfort. Neither of these…issues is readily disposed of. Second, the army. I agree that American entry is only months away, but I had little thought of fighting. When I am accorded the full rights of a citizen—in every corner of this country—then I might think about it. Finally, my race. You want me to spy on my own people, to betray them to you for position and patronage when my very reason to seek that position is to help them."

"Pshaw," Gardiner shook his massive head. "You have no more altruism in your body than any politician born this side of the Roman Republic."

"Gardiner," Van Deman said in warning.

"It's the truth."

Van Deman turned back to me and flashed a grin, this time with teeth. I was almost surprised at how well aligned they were, considering how annoyingly British he was trying to be.

"Mr. Ayers," Van Deman said. "Our proposition is not an easy one, and you are certainly justified in taking some time to make your decision."

"Deals come with deadlines," Gardiner said.

"That is true as well. If you take too long, we may have found another candidate, or our leverage may no longer warrant the same reward."

"Let me think it over," I said, "but next time, bring a different Sachem. I don't enjoy dealing with bigots."

***

I couldn't sleep. I kept thinking of Allie. Her black hair tousled, her eyes deep enough to drown a man, her skin soft and creamy white, her body…I rolled on my side and pulled a pillow to my chest, wrapped my arms around it. A poor substitute for the muscle and flesh and bones. I could still feel her against me. A dream made solid. My amore.

It hurt, the memory. Still fresh the longing. I wanted to find her and knock down her door and take her in my arms and…

Damn Tammany.

No. Damn me. The decision was mine to abandon her in favor of an aspiration. An idiot's choice but…I couldn't go back. To turn away now, to walk away from the investment made over years, escaped reason. Economics required continuation. My sacrifices called for more sacrifices until I could reach my goal. The reason in it, though, did little to salve my broken heart. I made my decision—my decisions—and now, like Macbeth of Shakespeare fame, I must steel my heart and take the battle to the king. Damn Tammany.

And for all my tossing and turning, the reality that had presented in Ralph Van Deman still stole my slumber. One more sacrifice, one more deal. Go to war and return with the assurance of a true political post. Not just patronage anymore, but serious political advancement. Betray my people and in exchange, I receive the greatest boost of my career. True, my cogitations would have ended long ago had the promise been of something more, but still, a district leader in the Tammany machine. The possibilities. It meant an overnight transformation. I would be more recognizable and more important that Frederick Q Morton or Robert Woods ever dreamed. A real-life black politician.

I tossed the pillow aside and rolled across the width of the bed. Allie and I never fell asleep in each other's arms, both of us found it uncomfortable, but her presence alone, the mass of her, caused me to turn in place. If I tried to roll over like I now could, arms flailing, my wrist would have smacked her…and then she would have smacked me back. I smiled in the dark at the thought.

Allie, my love.

Damn it. I threw back the covers and sat up. The carpet—Allie's choice—insulated my feet from the cold hardwood if not the air in the room. I found my robe and slippers and padded quietly downstairs. My mother lay in her bed on the second floor, her breath even, if raspy. I had no idea if she was asleep or awake. For her, one state resembled the other. I glanced in the other direction and saw the narrow bed and nightstand, the trappings of a lie. The cover story with which we clothed Allie's overnight visits, our secret miscegenation. She came as a nurse to care for my ailing mother, not as an angel to arouse my desire, at least that's what we wanted people to believe. The bed stood empty, as it always had, and I felt my longing grow. With a sigh, I kept on down the stairs to the sitting room and the fireplace.

A few embers remained a dim red glow. I grabbed a poker and did my best to stoke life from their dying light. Yesterday's *Times* added immediacy and, in a few moments, I dared place more sturdy fuel on the fire.

Satisfied, I wandered to the kitchen and poured myself a generous portion of Scotch. One sip for the road, I returned to the sitting room and slumped in a chair, stared at the flames before me. The Scotch blurred things, a little, but as I stared into the yellow fire, I could see Allie in the heat. Hot, hot heat. White-hot. Her hips swayed, her hair flicked, her lips puckered. Every disturbance, every gust across the flue, and Allie cat-walked in my mind.

Maybe ten minutes later, two-thirds of the glass down, a strange noise interrupted my fantasies. Knock, knock, knock. I stopped to listen, heard nothing more, dismissed it, and took a slug of Scotch down my throat. Then again, knock, knock, knock. I set my glass on the side table and padded to the front door. Who?

When I opened the door, I suddenly found myself grateful to have left my glass behind. Standing on my front step, dressed in black, a ghost.

Allie.

***

Tears. My Allie, broken into pieces, sobbing on my sofa. I sat beside her, not sure if I could—or if I should—reach out to comfort her. When she first stepped through my door, she fell into my arms. It felt good, her there, close, but it also felt dangerous. I had checked the street for any stray onlookers before I shut the door and led her into the sitting room. She took the offer of a drink and I refreshed mine as well. We sat for a while, together in a bizarre silence, she not ready to volunteer her reasons, I not ready to ask.

She had gained weight since I saw her last. A few pounds that softened her face and enhanced her breasts. The curves drove me wild, to see them under my roof, my bed so close at hand. I wanted to lunge at her and attack her with my passion. Her beauty remained undiminished in my eyes. My love, my muse, my Allie.

"My father," she finally said, "he…he died."

The act of disclosure triggered it. She tried to fight it. Her lip trembled, her jaw. She clamped her teeth together and put her hand to her mouth. Shuddering effort to keep the pain at bay. But it was too powerful. She broke and the tears came. A gasp and then the sobs. Her body wracked. She held on to the arm of the sofa, afraid the rocking would unseat her. She grasped at the upholstery, desperate for grounding, reality, comfort.

My heart ached to watch. I hungered to touch her, hold her, soothe her. A man more at ease than I would not hesitate, yet I…I had to consider the politics. As I write, now, I know the bastard I was. Cold-hearted heel. That I sat there, glass in hand, and watched the woman I loved suffer without the benefit of human contact. Monstrous. I let thoughts of my political benefit prevent me from making the slightest gesture. Justified, in my mind, completely. I could not afford to move, for if I moved to her, if I touched her hand, her hair, her skin, I would be lost. She would turn me forever from Tammany's embrace and steal my life's ambitions. And gladly, I knew, would I bear it. Yet at that moment, at that pivotal moment, I sat frozen in fear. I gave in. I let Tammany win.

Fool.

"My father was the only one…the only one who didn't…he loved me…he didn't care…about any of it."

I stared at her. God, how beautiful.

"I thought you…I thought you would want…to know."

She had realized my perfidy. Already she exerted greater control. The sobs turned to tears to sniffles. It dawned on me then, in my ignorant stupidity, her purpose. She came for comfort. She came to me hoping to be welcomed and held, and told everything would be all right. She had thought my devotion to Tammany could be overcome and that I could stand by her side regardless. She trusted in the humanity she believed lay in my heart. And now, she saw her error.

"I'm sorry," she said. "I'm sorry to have disturbed you."

I opened my mouth, but no sound emerged. How could I defend something so indefensible? I just sat there, silent, as she collected herself, stood to her feet, and walked out of my life…again.

***

The convalescent home was in New Jersey, across the Hudson, and beyond a ways. I took a Sunday, a precious day of rest, and worked my way from Harlem to the seemingly distant resort. Cab, El, foot, ferry, train. An arduous journey that cost more than its worth and left me, a Negro, in the Jim Crow car. Prejudiced by something so basic as an interstate common carrier yet done so with the explicit approval of my government—the same government that would soon ask me to war, to fight the German menace on behalf of its allies. *Supreme hypocrisy*, I thought, seated with half a dozen other Negroes from the city, separate but equal despite the blatantly inferior quality of our facilities. On to New Jersey. *Click-a-clack* went the train.

"Welcome to New Haven Convalescent and Rest Home."

I smiled and accepted the outstretched hand. An administrator of sorts, a face for the institution, led me from the gate toward the main building. As we passed through gardens and walkways, secret outdoor alcoves made private by hedgerows and rose bushes, I could see the care exerted—even through the browned branches covered with snow. Someone spent a great deal of time to manicure the grounds so immaculately.

"We currently have forty-two guests. Three of them are Negroes like yourself."

I nodded and followed the man inside from the cold. It was the reason I had made the journey—not the cold, but the Negro inhabitants—no convalescent homes existed in New York, at least not in the Burroughs, that accepted Negro applications. I had, in my research, heard rumors of this place in New Jersey, this New Haven, where Negro patients were accepted for a price. Separate but equal. I did more research and verified the rumors, obtained an address and references, and solicited an appointment.

"I understand your mother is invalid?"

I nodded, my attention on the half dozen white men and women gathered around a fireplace. They sat in silence and stared blankly at the flames, on their laps quilted covers. One of the men was a child, maybe eighteen years old, the rest ancient and white-haired. New Haven served a dual purpose, not just for the elderly, where those who suffered illness or surgery could come to restore their health and sanity. Those with money, that is.

I gestured to the young man, "What…"

The administrator glanced over and shook his head. "Sad that one. He went to England on a school trip—before the Lusitania, of course. They visited a veterans' ward and talked with the soldiers. Several amputees and others who had suffered serious injury. Some gas victims. When he returned, he was fine until someone told him that it was just a matter of months before America entered the war. He went to bed that night like a normal boy and woke up…"

I stared at the boy, shocked. Could it be so bad that the mere thought of war sent a child into catatonia? And I contemplated voluntary enlistment?

"I'd like to visit with your Negro patients?"

"We prefer to call them guests, and…I'm not sure that will be possible."

"I specified in my letter."

"Yes, yes, I know and I'm sorry. It can't be helped you see."

"Why not?"

"One of them is, as your mother, completely incommunicative. You could visit with him, but it would do no good."

"And the other two?"

"One is on a family visit. His son took him home for a week…the other is in hospital. It was quite sudden. Yesterday, she had an…attack…so, you see, it was quite impossible to inform you on such short notice. While you're here, let me show you—"

"Is there a nurse, someone who works with them, who I could speak with?"

The administrator paused, his eyes darted to the back of the building and back to me. His face reddened. He obviously did not want to allow my request, but he was smart enough to know any more excuses would alert even a dull man's suspicions. Eventually, he nodded. "There is a nurse, yes, you can speak with…Josie is her name."

"I would like to speak with her alone, if possible."

"Uh…I suppose…would you be comfortable walking the grounds? The only other suitable place would be my office and…it's currently in use."

I ignored his lie. "I'm fine outside. Can you fetch her now?"

"Of course, a moment if you will."

He didn't offer me a seat before he disappeared down a corridor. I took one anyway, next to the boy and close to the fire.

I said nothing, only let my eyes see what he saw, watched the flames and imagined. I walked through a veterans' ward, saw the stumps where legs once grew, the bloodstained bandages, the ghosts who once were men. I listened in the night as men succumbed to horrific images conjured by unconscious memory, their voice weak from countless nightmares, heard the whimpers and tears. I smelled the rot, the flesh turned black, and the soldiers who once more faced the surgeon's saw. I saw men—black and white—diminished as they tried to go on, unable to find work, reliant on friends and family, slowly descending to poverty and madness. If I, as a child, had seen this and then learned my fate would send me to face the same, I too might retreat into myself and forever shut out the fears and tragedy. Hell, I was a man now and still I counted this young man privileged—in a way.

"Mr. Ayers?"

I looked up to see a small Negress standing beside me. I smiled, "Yes, are you, Josie?"

"Shall we walk, if you please?"

I followed her to the door and out onto the grounds. I walked behind her a step, enough to give her an appraising once over. Small, yes, but perky. She was maybe thirty years old and swallowed in the heavy coat she wore, but she walked with easy steps that belied her stooped shoulders. Her hair was braided tightly against her skull and dropped at her shoulders in pigtails. An attractive woman but worn down a bit.

She led me a hundred feet from the building proper and behind a hedgerow. Far enough to avoid prying ears. Settled, she spun to face me, hands on hips, and looked me in the eye, "You don't want to bring your momma here."

"I'm sorry?"

"You don't want to leave your momma in this place, no way, no how."

I stared at her.

She got the hint. "The Negroes, they're neglected. Their families pay more than the crackers and get less. Always that way I suppose. Your momma, you send her here, she's going to rot in a back room, get brought out when you all visit."

"What about—"

"And when the high mighty cracker gets angry, Lord, he's liable to go and hit her, especially as she can't say nothing to you later. I try to say something, but I need the pay."

"You've told me what I wanted to know," I stepped toward a gravel path, the snow crunched beneath my feet.

"Wait, mister, what are you going to do with her, your momma?"

I looked back at her, "I don't know."

"You ain't never going to find someplace nice. No place like that exists."

"I'm beginning to see—"

"She been invalid a long time, your momma?"

"Years."

"Never going to get better, is she?"

I shook my head.

Josie glanced around the end of the hedgerow toward the home, then reached in her pocket to retrieve a scrap of paper.

"I'm not one to encourage this, but sometimes, Lord knows, ain't nothin' left in this world good. Sometimes, the best thing to do for a person is to hurry them on to the next," she extended her hand with the paper. "There's a man in your city, he can help if you of a mind."

I took the paper and glanced at the writing, an address somewhere in the Bowery. "Thank you."

"Don't tell no one I said nothing."

I slipped the note in my pocket. Josie didn't say goodbye, just rushed toward the building. I turned and walked the other way. I didn't see the need to go back inside.

***

Amazing Grace, how sweet the sound.

I stood in three inches of snow, cold, and wet, that lapped at my shoes, a frigid invader laying siege to my feet. The wind whipped through the manicured hills; an icy knife full of rage. My coat threatened to fly up on a gust. I wore a tie—Paisley to match my love—and a carefully folded handkerchief in my pocket. A fedora sat firmly on my head. A dapper dandy—with spats to boot. Cold, though, for a strut about town.

That saved a wretch like me.

Alone, I stood in the snow and listened to the voice soar above the white carpet and the hills and the trees taller still. A rich voice, saddened, that did not, nay, knew not how to lift itself from its depression. A deep sorrowful pain emerged with each note. How sweet the sound.

I stood alone and listened to the song cross the hills, my personage hidden by the mounded earth and a yearling tree that shivered through its first Manhattan winter. I listened to the lyrics, flowing so sweetly from my love's throat. Words written by a slaver turned monk, a tragic figure who had lived a life too craven to repent, though he had tried, and in trying written the words she sang through the winter winds.

I once was lost.

But now am found.

I daren't move, though my toes began to numb. To move might reveal my presence, my uninvited attendance, and add shame to her sadness. My motives…my motives remained elusive. I did not know her father, and I had forsaken the opportunity for more forthright support. I could only listen in the chill, listen to her voice, listen to the judgment that rang forth like some fierce fire, burning those who listened with its acrid edge. I longed to walk to the crown of the hill, to look down and see her, to go to her and hold her in my arms. I longed to be with her but I remained frozen. Stood still by the knowledge of my brazen betrayal. I missed her. But for all my heartbroken lusting, I knew I could not.

Was blind.

A bell clanged in the distance, a clattering alarum that warned of danger. A bank robbery, a fire, a riot. The clouds above turned darker, ominous, pregnant. Across the hill, beyond my sight, she began to cry. Her words took on a cracked edge, a tear on the wind. Now, the quality of the song changed from a mocking condemnation to a mournful sorrow song. Reality, an unfortunate anchor that brought her crashing. I longed yet. If only I dared, I would race through the frozen powder and wrap her in my arms and pledge my love to the gasping, gawking gathered. I love you. It will be okay. I love you.

But now I see.

As the last note faded, I turned and walked through the snow, away, trailing a solitary track of shuffled footsteps testimony to my pain.

***

I took the El down Third Avenue to Delancey, in the Bowery. Here, the El split on either side of the street, one line on the left and one on the right. Buildings lined the row, shadowed by the raised tracks, solid fronts from corner to corner, a phalanx of facades aligned against the voices of passing revelers. Rumor said that gardens filled the spaces behind, a virtual paradise hidden by the bricks. I could not confirm the truth of this, I knew only that I had never seen such things. And since my move to Harlem, I had found little reason to visit.

On my left, the El rumbled south.

A few men ambled past. I heard a woman shout somewhere and the sound of laughter. I recoiled at the smell of stale beer. Last night's debauchery still drying in the dim winter light. Maybe fifty feet away a soldier dressed—mostly dressed—in a green army uniform stumbled from a hidden door and cried at the sudden sunlight. He covered his eyes and squinted for the better part of a minute as he finished dressing, took stock and, determining he was still in possession of all his valuables, turned south and then east at the next corner.

The Bowery.

I pulled the scrap of paper—the one from Josie at New Haven Convalescent Home—from my pocket. I dodged a horse and cart on my way across the street and pushed open the heavy wooden door of Big Jim's Apothecary: Pharmaceuticals, Sodas, and Other Healthy Concoctions.

A pair of filtered lights showed a dull green on the place. A bar ran along one wall. A pair of young men sat close to each other, their hands on each other's thighs, their eyes locked in a quiet conversation that was only interrupted when one of them took a sip of the single soda shared between them. Scratchy music played from an aging phonograph: opera. I didn't know enough to recognize it, but I didn't have to.

"Don Giovanni, by Mozart," said a voice from the shadows in the back.

"I'm sorry?"

Then a third light blinked on to reveal a section of the establishment previously hidden in darkness. A low counter ran across the width of the space, covered with various bottles and containers and boxes. Behind this counter stood the owner himself, Big Jim.

"The librettist was Lorenzo Da Ponte."

I stared at the man, oblivious to his words. He was enormous. Shorter than me, he weighed easily four hundred pounds and resembled nothing so much as a life-size pear with legs. And as if to accentuate the effect, he had shaved his head to the skin. The only hair on it, two eyebrows that threatened to sprout furry wings and fly away. Black as midnight, the blue light only accentuated the effect and with each movement of his mass, pools of darkest purple shifted and roiled. He wore a bib about his neck that sloped down his chest. It bore stains and marks the color of blood. Otherwise, he wore a pair of suede overalls and nothing else. His arms and chest visible, with every roll of fat, between the straps. A farmer made urbanite from some unknown background, some unknown past.

"Big Jim?"

The man smiled—at least he still had all his teeth—and waddled forward to extend a massive paw. "Da Ponte, you know, used to run a produce shop from this building. Immigrated in 1806 and sold carrots and apples."

I wiggled my fingers to check for damage.

"What can I do for you?"

I glanced at the lovers on their stools and back at the barely illuminated pharmacy. "I was referred to you by a woman, a nurse, in New Jersey."

"Were you now?"

"Her name is Josie, a little woman, and she works at a conval—"

Big Jim smacked his palm across my mouth and almost knocked me off my feet. "Perhaps we should talk in my office."

I nodded and Big Jim dropped his hand. He banked into a turn and maneuver into the blue gloom. I followed, rubbed my jaw. He waddled us back to a small office with an uncolored bulb—bare, in fact—that dangled from the ceiling. He squeezed around a desk that filled most of the space and dropped into a chair made of rough beam lumber. A smaller chair, dainty by comparison, remained. I closed the door and sat down. The chair creaked under my weight. I felt like laughing.

"How's Josie?"

I shrugged. "Tough."

Big Jim laughed. "That girl is tougher than Harriet Tubman and Teddy Roosevelt combined."

"She—"

Big Jim waved a hand. "You went out there for a reason. Who is it?"

I stared at the man, unsure. All I had so far was a surreptitious recommendation from a complete stranger. But if I didn't…

"My mother."

"I see."

"She's had two strokes now, and invalid. She's been laid in bed unresponsive for—"

"I don't care. Your reasons are your own and my reasons are mine. I am not in business to salve your conscience. That's between you and God."

"Okay."

Big Jim leaned forward, "However, the stroke—or the fact of the stroke—is useful."

"How so?"

Big Jim shook his head. "A stroke can be imitated, and imitated so no one is the wiser."

"Even the coroner?"

"Your mother drinks milk?"

"When I give it to her."

"Then even the coroner."

Big Jim reared forward and lumbered to his feet. I pressed against the back of my chair to give him space—his bulk enough that any movement in the cramped office brought his girth uncomfortably close. "I will give you something—a dairy by-product—that contains certain contaminants. Feed this to your mother with milk and in a few weeks, she will have another stroke."

"But what if she doesn't—"

"Risk assessment. Increased odds come with increased possibilities of detection. If she doesn't…you can come back and I'll give you something else—free of charge."

"Okay."

"No talk of this once I open the door—though those boys don't speak but a lick of English."

Somehow, after he said the words, Big Jim snuck between me and the desk, opened the door, and ventured into the multi-colored gloom beyond. Following, I pulled the door closed after me and turned as the man adjusted a red filtered lamp and added one more color to the rainbow.

I watched as he busied himself about the rows of bottles and containers. I was doubting my resolve. Could I really kill my mother? It seemed sensible, the only thing to do if I was to leave her behind. There were no other relatives. I was it. But to take her life with my hands…

"These boys are poor immigrants, you see, got themselves kicked out by their daddies when…"

I glanced at the boys, the subjects of Big Jim's monologue, and saw how they now sat together—somehow—on a single stool. In the dim light, I couldn't see their hands nor was I sure I wanted to. The Bowery, home to tramps, whores, thieves, and fairies.

"We have an agreement, those boys and I, that's why they're here if you're wondering."

Not particularly.

"It's my weight, that's the thing, difficult to come by an honest fuck when you look like me." Big Jim poured a portion of the white powder into a small paper envelope, tied the clasp, and offered it my way. "Three weeks, like I said, and your problem will be…resolved."

"How much?"

Big Jim grinned, "Either a blow job or two large, whichever you prefer."

I peeled four fifties from my wallet, held them in the air and contemplated the envelope. Could I really take it? I thought not. I dropped the money, though, and turned away. It was enough to know that I had tried. I would find some other way to take care of the problem, to allow me to follow the Army and fulfill my goals, and to occupy my mother in her invalid state.

***

The door opened under my key and I pushed it fully ajar with the toe of my shoe. I took one step and stopped. A smell of rot and putrid garbage, fetid refuse punched me in the face. I put one hand on the door and the other over my nose. God. It was awful. I didn't dare leave the door open, never in Manhattan. I pulled my tie loose from my collar and wrapped it around my face. Shut the door, locked it. I checked the kitchen and bathroom. Nothing. What in God's name…

I took the stairs two at a time, three. The smell got worse. The air settled thick, like a stew made thick by a city's sewage. I gagged and found the window. It stuck at first and I pulled harder, driven by desperation until it scraped the runner and flew open hard against the stops. I shoved my head through the opening and gulped air. Cold now. Freezing. The *Times* called for rain freezing to snow tomorrow. I could see my breath. Steam rose off my arms, crystallized, and floated away. It smelled so clean and pure. Winter crisp. Two minutes, three minutes, four. I gave it five full minutes before I sucked the chilly evening in and ducked back through the window. When I turned, the sight explained everything, every part of the stench.

My mother lay on her side, her legs straight out, her back arched. A pool of vomit soaked the sheets in front of her, matted her hair, damped her gown, and dripped off to the floor. Her legs were soaked, her functions all failed, catastrophically. Urine and feces mixed, a noxious combination. But for all the terror, the thing that struck me most was that I had left her that morning reclined on her back. Now, she lay on her side. Something, or someone, had moved her. It was a second before I moved to her side and put a hand against her mouth, feeling for breath, and finding none.

She was dead.

***

"Poison?" the doctor said. "I suppose there might be something that could cause symptoms similar, but nothing in my experience…though limited as concerns such things."

"But she moved, somehow. She hasn't moved since the first attack."

The doctor clutched at his bag. "The body can do unexpectedly when stressed in such a manner. Your mother, after years of invalidity, it is not inconceivable that she…a body during apoplexy is prone to seizure."

The doctor was a Negro from Philadelphia. More than that, I knew little, of his background, at least. In appearance, he resembled a balding cucumber. Not thin and not fat but straight up and down. His belly didn't protrude nor did it recede and he stood in such a way—with loose-fitting pants that, in dim light, seemed to join together into a single piece of cloth about his legs—to complement the impression.

"You're certain?" I said. "Apoplexy? Again?"

"Not like lightning."

I nodded, not wanting to encourage the man to elaborate in his stilted syntax.

"I should be going…"

I followed him to the door and settled the bill. He shook my hand and disappeared in the direction of Fifth Avenue. I closed the door and finished cleaning. As I shoved the soiled sheets in the trash bin—I would buy new ones tomorrow—my mind played with the idea incessantly. Poison. The doctor's reassurances did little to ease my suspicions, not after my meeting with Van Deman and Gardiner. I did not, unlike many an Irishman in this city, hold Tammany up as incapable of such a heinous act.

***

I poked my head around the jamb of the door and saw Asa Bird Gardiner half reclined in a sofa chair.

"You..."

"Reuben Ayers," I stepped into the room. "If you'll excuse us, miss."

The young woman, a nurse, glared at me, unmoving.

Gardiner waved a hand, "Some of that tea you make, Maud, you know the fruit one, with all that favor...like a summer afternoon on the plantation...a big pitcher of iced tea...hmmm."

"Sir," the girl slipped from the room, one last glare for my sake then closed the door behind her.

Gardiner lived in Suffern, a small village maybe twenty miles inland from the Hudson at the base of the Ramapo Mountains and inches from the New Jersey border. Climb Nordkop Mountain above the village and you could see Manhattan's growing skyline with ease, despite the haze. Only a few thousand inhabitants sullied the earth here, and Gardiner one of them. He owned a flat in the City, too, but inquiry revealed the man hid in Suffern, his face shamed by the army's recent request to return his Medal of Honor.

"You finally made up your lousy mind then, boy?"

I took a breath, a deep one, and fought the distaste that rose like bile after a difficult meal. "I've made up my mind, yes."

"And?"

"And I'll help you. I'll spy for you."

Gardiner struggled forward and teetered from the edge of his sofa to his feet. He lumbered to a sideboard and opened it to reveal several glass decanters filled with dark amber.

"Kentucky bourbon. Great stuff, not something I imagine someone of your...background can properly appreciate."

"Try me."

Gardiner ignored me and continued to pour himself a single glass. He corked the decanter and turned slowly, the whiskey alight in the crystal. "It's the maple...the syrup adds a touch of sweetness you won't find in Scotch or Irish whiskeys."

I said nothing, just stood my ground and watched the bastard slosh his drink about.

"The deal's changed."

"What?"

"You took too long, boy, and you've got competition now. If you want what we've got to give, then you got to work all that much harder."

I wanted to storm out, but I knew that such feelings were triggered by my dislike of the man in front of me more than by any issue with the underlying transaction, or with the potential of reopening negotiations. After another breath, then, I said, "What do you want?"

"Tammany doesn't want this experiment to succeed."

"But—"

"Tammany likes the press that comes from helping our fool darky brethren escape the oppressive jungles of San Juan Hill and Harlem town, but to give your kind a chance to fight, a chance to create a genuine war hero...no one in their right mind wants a Negro able to rally support because he killed a dozen Germans in the heat of battle."

"To read your people's press, we're all going to run the other way, put us five miles of the front."

"You and I both know yellow journalism caters to the lowest common denominator."

"You're scared, then?"

Gardiner laughed. "I'll be dead before it matters, but Tammany would like to hedge its bets. Murphy doesn't want this regiment anywhere near the front. And if they do—he wants the worst showing since Custer led his own massacre."

"A saboteur."

"Exactly. You stop your regiment from reaching the front and give your reports for what's his name—"

"Van Deman."

"Yeah, him," Gardiner sipped his bourbon. "You do these things and Tammany will make you a district leader. Should be easy enough for someone of your predilections."

I wish I could say that these new conditions gave me to hesitate, to rethink my position with serious gravity. I wish I could say that the simple thought of betraying my brethren drove me immediately and irrevocably from that room never to return. Reality, however, prevents me from so saying. Truth be told, in my mind and heart, I had already prepared myself to make a betrayal. This new condition, a question of degree, could not deter me from a decision already taken.

"I'll do it."

"Good," Gardiner downed the rest of his whiskey and coughed a little at the sting. "Now, get the hell out of my house."

***

The Lafayette Theatre glowed in the darkness, Manhattan's night fallen, a beacon against the gloom. Lights spelled the name across the marquee, LAFAYETTE, and illuminated the intersection of Seventh Avenue and 132nd street. There was no performance this evening, the Lafayette Players preparing their next show. But a steady stream of humanity crossed the threshold and darkened the sidewalk outside the door. In the distance, I heard a band blasting, brass, and percussion, as it wound its way through the streets of Harlem. A quiet buzz seemed to fill the street, a woman wrapped her arms around a boy, sobs wracked her body. A mother crying at the anticipated loss of her son.

I removed my hat and crossed the street. The Renaissance facade of the theatre towered above me, its central marquee rising to the top, like a steeple, a church of entertainment, the House Beautiful. A boy laughed and raced down the gutter, dressed in several layers of rags, he seemed immune to the late winter chill. Two more boys chased after until they disappeared down an alley. The band grew louder. I mounted the curb and approached the doors, passed a poster for the last production of *Madame X*, and entered the foyer. The first floor was a mall, a stretch of shops and conveniences, a shoeshine, a newsstand, a candy shop. I turned to the left, where the crowd seemed biggest, and saw through the pressed bodies a flash of green wool.

I approached. The throng was not so great upon closer examination, maybe ten or eleven people, mostly women, a few men, come to sign their lives to the new regiment. I took my place at the edge, waited as a pair of men, brothers, signed their names to the list, and three women burst into tears. I imagined Allie, here, to see me off, to see me take such a momentous decision, but I knew it could not be. I had lost her, lost her to my own intractability.

"You, son, you here to sign up?"

I looked up at a square-jawed officer, clean-cut and full of Rooseveltian fervor.

"Yes," I said. "I've come to sign up for the regiment."

Harlem, Manhattan

New York, New York, USA
November 12, 1919

I could think of little else but Allie. She was on my thoughts and in my heart. The sacrifice that I had made to leave her behind in favor of Tammany Hall's benefaction caused me pain. It was a sin, I knew that now. To leave behind one's love in favor of political power. And from Tammany.

I remembered Gardiner's obese frame and the way he lifted his gouty foot from the floor to set it on a chair seconded for the purpose. And then there was Van Deman. A skinny Brit—well almost—who seemed more at home with his tea and crumpets than with the racist likes of Gardiner himself. It was a confusion, and for all its alien nature, he had agreed. And in agreeing, given up all that he had loved.

Yesterday was Armistice Day. The one-year anniversary of the cease-fire. November 11, 1919. A day that would forever go down in history as the end of the war to end all wars. But had it? Had it taken my heart and ground it down into a poultice of meat and sinew? I knew that this was something that I would have to live with, my sacrifice, but I hated it. I hated the idea of it, and I knew that I needed to do something, to find Allie, to find the love that I once knew. To find forgiveness. To find forgiveness.

I spoke with a priest in Chalons-sur-Marne, during the war, when I was deep in France and filled with the love of a people who did not justify their behavior by the color of my skin. He told me that the priest gained nothing from confession, only that it was a service to the penitent, who needed to ease his heart and to lift the burdens from his shoulders.

I didn't know if that was true, but perhaps…

I needed to confess. I needed to confess my sins and I needed to find Allie and I needed to repent of my wrong decisions. I had put all my life, all my hopes into the uplift of my people through political means. It had been a foolish desire, one that I now saw as blinded by ambition and greed. I had been a foolish man with a foolish goal. I had risked everything for it and came up wanting.

But how does one repent when one is not of a religious bent? I did not know. Only the words of the priest, his cassock tight around his neck, his hat—a strange-looking thing that I still can't describe—atop his balding head. He spoke with confidence and assuredness and he spoke with the ability, or so it seemed, to read into my soul. I don't know how he did it, but he looked me in the eye and told me I was on the wrong road. Perhaps it was my mien. I couldn't have hidden my doubts then, it was too late. Already the white men came to the front, already Pershing had published his decree, already the harm was done.

Yet I knew there had to be hope. God, or fate, or the universe, whatever invention put man into motion, must have some plan for redemption. One cannot simply walk into the future and leave behind the past. It is too simple. There must be retribution. There must be an atonement.

***

I took the notebook in my hand. It was hefty, though not heavy, solid, and powerful. I did not know what I would write in it, only that my confession must be made in secret. That much I knew from the priest. It is not for publicity that one must stand and give account, no, but for the privacy of the confessional, between oneself, the priest, and God.

The notebook was thick, it's binding workmanlike. It was thin paper, though, and had many sheets. I thought it might do. I did not know how much my confession would require, whether I could fit it all in one notebook or whether my sins required a series of small pads, pages pasted together, patterned words filling the path. I turned to the clerk and handed it to him. He wore a patterned tie, and a tall collar that was starched and pristine, and a blue striped shirt. He took the notebook from me and commented on the appropriateness of my selection.

I said nothing.

I moved on.

I needed a pen. A good quality pen. I found a display, several pens behind glass, their quality obvious by their company. I pointed to one, a Schaeffer Lever Filler. The pen was thick at the butt and narrowed at the tip. The cue was tight and pointed. It would do. The clerk retrieved a key and unlocked the case. A moment later he lifted the pen onto the notebook and together I purchased the set. I now had my confessional, all that was lacking was a confession.

***

I sat in the black and tan where I met Allie. I remembered her dancing. It was the fact that she was there at all, a white woman, willing to meet Negro men, willing to associate with people whose skin the color of chocolate. I remembered her hair, her face, her eyes. It all came back to me, the way her breasts pressed at her dress. A modified Mother Hubbard, lower at the bosom, and set to evoke arousal in all types of men.

A picture of Jack Johnson, signed, hung from the wall behind the bar. I drank a whiskey sour. I wasn't in the mood for straight whiskey, not now. I sat at the bar and listened as the piano man played stride. A few couples stood on the dance floor stomping and twirling to the rhythm. I didn't recognize the tune, though that wasn't strange, I did, however, know that it was jazz.

It made me think of Jim Europe, the man who would change my mind. The man who would show me that power over race came not just from politics, or power itself, but from intention and action.

The thought passed and I turned to the open page in front of me. I knew that I had to write, I had to begin. There was no going back. I couldn't look at my past without regret, and that shamed me. I needed to absolve my conscience, and the only way I knew how, guided by an old priest in the middle of a French cathedral, was to confess my sins. So I lifted the lever-filler and set the point of the pen against the page.

Newark, New Jersey

August 15 – October 8, 1917

We stood guard duty against anarchists, Bolshevists, and Germans. Mostly Germans. Our position from the Hudson stretching sixty miles east. Two companies tasked to protect the rails: Pennsylvania, Erie, Lehigh Valley, Delaware Lackawanna and Western, and Central of New Jersey. A state's worth of track and just two hundred men to guard it. The only way to accomplish the objective was to be selective. Men stationed at the highest risk targets.

Twenty-four hours, we stood watch, eight-hour rotations, as trains chugged through the yard, black smoke thick until their exhaust seemed to congeal into a smoggy soup. It settled over our lives and blackened our uniforms. It stuck to our skin and hair and stained our bathwater. It coated our lungs and dusted our food. It hovered thick and ugly. It was a cloud beneath which we choked and gasped with each plodding step.

Check-ins, marches, and challenges. Walk back and forth, across the bridge's mouth, sometimes across its span. Watch the supports. Climb down the slope and examine the superstructure. Check for bombs. Pace the yard until you meet the next patrol. Stay alert. Challenge everyone. If they fail to respond, shoot first, rather a dead innocent than a blown bridge.

Off duty, we slept, lounged in the Negro diners, and gambled.

A few of the men played poker, usually patience—or some variation—and used cigarettes for ante. The rest played craps and used real money to make their bets. Easier than poker. The only equipment two small dice, cubes of bone or wood, carried in a pocket or carved out of scraps from the kitchen. Homemade sets meant loaded dice, accusations, and escalating recriminations. A raft of cheating sons of bitches in the Fifteenth.

The day's wages lost to a seven out.

A dozen men gathered at the top of Military Park in a semi-circle. They squatted on a patch of hardscrabble. A short wall at one end formed a concrete backstop against which the shooter bounced the dice. Coins littered the ground.

A tall Negro stood at the semi-circle's zenith. His hand was balled into a fist over the ivory dice. He crouched low. He raised his arm, bulging muscle straining the seams of his uniform. He shook his hammered fist in the air. "Come on way down, come on, little Joe," he said. "Come on way down to the fields."

"Shoot it."

"Shoot it."

"Shoot the two."

A two meant the shooter could move on to seven, and then if he managed to do that before rolling something sinister, he could gather up the coins littered at the feet of the gathered men. The shooter took a step forward and threw the dice. They bounced hard against the concrete and rolled back. A man scrambled out of the way.

"Yo-leven."

One of the men scooped up the dice and tossed them across. The shooter caught them both in one enormous hand. He cupped them tight, shook them scrambled, and raised the hammer again.

"Shoot the two."

"Shoot it."

"Come on way down. Come on, little Joe. Come on way down to the field."

Another step and another throw, "Seven out."

I was next. I felt the heat of chance on my cheek. As the dice passed, I felt electricity run through my blood, a tingle from my palm to my feet. I was alive and I was lucky. I slapped a five on the ground. "Don't pass."

"Too much, man."

"Fate me."

"No one's gonna fate you for that."

"Fate me."

"'s too much."

"Fate me."

"Split it, we'll split it. We'll fate you, the three of us."

Four dollars and a handful of change hit the ground. The point still two. I felt alive, my whole body thrilled at the risk, the longing for success, the rush. I squeezed the bones. Glanced around the circle. They felt it too. I could see it in their eyes.

"Shoot the two."

"Shoot it. Shoot the two."

I shook my hand, thumped it once against my chest, and let fly.

"Fever five."

"Shoot it."

"Shoot the two."

I threw again.

"Hard ten."

And again.

"Easy six."

Then, as the bones left my hand, I knew it, the surge of success that trilled my spine. This was the one.

"Deuce."

Almost there.

I caught the dice. Hot irons in my hand. They burned me up till I was on fire. Seven out and I won. "Come on seven, seven out."

"Lieutenant, a word," said a voice from behind me.

The voice startled me, caused my hand to unfurl and the dice to drop to the ground at my feet. They bounced once, twice, and settled with quiet clicks against the hardscrabble. Black circles stared up. The dice angered. Cold bones.

Snake eyes.

Wait.

One teetered. It threatened. It rolled. The white bone now darkened with dots. One and six. Seven out.

I won.

"Lieutenant."

I bent to retrieve my winnings. My arm stretched, my fingers spread. A chill hand gripped my shoulder and ice quenched my greed.

From the semi-circle, white eyes watched, hungry.

I let the money lie and stood to my fate.

"Lieutenant," Captain Napoleon Marshall said, "walk with me."

We walked north on Broad Street. Behind us, the four corners, Military Park, and the heart of Newark. We passed Old Paddie's Memorial Church in silence. Its towers of coursed granite guardians of the faith, its dome green-tarnished copper, Tiffany glass windows made eyes, darkly vigilant portals into the soul of Newark. Up Broad Street another block, through a row of shops, small-time retailers: grocers, millers, tailors, cobblers.

At Washington Park, we moved off the street. We walked through the green space, along cultivated paths, and under trees, until we came to Gutzon Borglum's 'Indian and Puritan.' Two bronze figures erected one either side of a towering shaft. A puritan tall, with hat, his eyes vacant as he stared into the distance, his aesthete's life heavy on his stone back. An Indian, with long hair braided back, his body tense, poised to attack.

"It is not right for an officer such as yourself," Marshall opened. He stood still, like the Puritan, but stone. He was not a big man when you saw him, yet when you thought on his memory you recalled a size commensurate with his personality. A presence that compelled attention for its intelligence, passion, and, in no small measure, for the size of his nose.

It dominated his face, and, from its base, a neatly trimmed mustache sprouted, black in contrast to the graying hair on his temples and above his ears. Occasionally, he would scratch at the joint of nose and lip as if some small insect lived among the bristles and tickled his skin, an annoyance but not reason enough to shave, then he would huff through his nostrils and rub his nose along the back of his hand.

"I know, sir," I said.

"Then why?"

"To learn, sir, to become acquainted with the men…and for them to become acquainted with me."

"By looting their pocketbooks?"

"By taking part in their pastime."

"Gambling."

I shook my head, "A game of chance."

Marshall laughed, then, and rubbed his nose with the back of his hand. His mouth opened to reveal the teeth of a cultured man, well-groomed, clean.

"I've been a lawyer as long as you've been able to piss on your own. I would advise you *not* to play games with words. It only makes you look foolish."

"You assume I care."

"The only people who are impressed by a fool are those more foolish still. And as I am not a fool—"

"Again, you mistakenly think I care to impress you."

"Then you are a fool," Marshall said.

"Respectfully, sir," I said. "I think you take pleasure in calling me a fool. I resent this. If you would make your point and let me be about my business."

Marshall ran a finger down a mustache. He gazed up at Borglum's 'Puritan' and only after a long moment did he glance at the 'Indian.' "The men will follow you when they respect you. How you earn that respect is your problem, but you'll have to earn it before I think any differently about you."

"Craps?"

"That's your decision."

"Then good day." I saluted, turned, and followed the shadow of Borglum's 'Indian' across Washington Park toward the fading hope that I might yet retrieve my winnings.

***

We heard what happened in Houston at the end of August. It shocked us—some to silence, some to drink, and some to rage—and in the late summer heat, our own temperatures rose in empathetic fever. We all remembered Brownsville and knew Texans for a particularly egregious breed of racist. We all had felt the desire to kill a white man for his prejudice. And we all understood how easy it might be to unleash that anger hidden in the bowels of a mob. But for all our gall, it would be months of frustration before we learned all the facts. Till then, we only knew what the paper said: ARMY RIOT IN HOUSTON COST 17 LIVES; NEGRO TROOPS ORDERED OUT OF STATE; CONGRESS WILL TAKE UP RACE QUESTION.

***

We found Private Huggins' body a mile northwest of Wharton, on the east bank of the Rockaway River, about a hundred yards north of the closest tracks. He lay on his back, his stockinged feet submerged in the water, his body rigid in the rocks and gravel. Whatever killed him ripped gashes in his cheek and temple. Cold to the touch. Tiny grains, like rice, populated the corners around his eyes and mouth, and along the edges of his torn flesh. The white eggs harshly contrasted against Huggins' coal-colored bruises. Footprints tracked in the mud at the river's edge, north, toward Lake Hopatcong and Hurdtown.

"Couldn't be dead more'n a day," the local sheriff muttered.

I stood to the back of the group, Major Spencer and Captain Little in the front, with the pale-skinned sheriff.

"This looks like he was bludgeoned," Captain Little said.

The sheriff, a lanky fellow who wore his hat high to reveal a long brow shrugged and kicked a rock into the water. "Probably got himself caught on a mail hook from a passing train, threw him out here when it finally let go."

"How is that possible?" Major Spencer said. "It couldn't throw a man like this, not this far."

"Seen it happen before."

"It's preposterous."

"You never know what's possible till you seen it."

From upriver, Napoleon Marshall walked toward us, his steps sliding in the mud along the bank. In one hand, he held his pacing stick, in the other, he balanced a hefty branch.

"Gentlemen," he said as he approached our little group. "I believe I've found the murder weapon."

"What'd you find there, Sam," the sheriff said.

Marshall ignored the sheriff and lifted the branch for our inspection. Closer now, we could see red stains on wood, blood seeped into the grain, bark specked with brain.

"The killers must have beat him here where we stand, stolen Huggins's boots, and then ran north. They dropped this not fifty feet upriver. Their tracks continue north, along the shore. Get a bloodhound down here and I bet you'd run them straight to their front door."

The sheriff turned his back on Marshall and hooked his thumbs in his belt loops. "This *was* an accident. Your soldier got too close to the train and got clobbered, knocked him right down here. Probably hit that branch on his way down, broke it from a tree with his head, and it floated away."

"Upriver?" Marshall said.

"I'm sorry," the sheriff addressed Little and Spencer. "That's what's going in my report, accidental death due to carelessness. You all can take care of the body, I presume."

"Yes," Little said.

"Godspeed, then."

The sheriff stepped around me and worked his way downriver, back past the tracks to the road. In the stunned silence left behind, we heard the echo of displaced rocks roll into the Rockaway—*thwunk, thwunk, thwunk*—sounding as a watery gavel.

"We can't just—"

"Lieutenant," Little said. "We're going to take this body to headquarters and report to Colonel Hayward. We will abide by any decision he makes. If he chooses to pursue this investigation, or take legal action, or do nothing at all, you and I and all of us will be content."

"But Huggins was murdered. We can't—"

"Yes, we can," Little said. "Huggins may not get justice, at least in this life, but his sacrifice will be in service of a larger good."

"Murder is murder, sir."

"If you pursue this, and Colonel Hayward will tell you the same, if you pursue this and make a to-do about it, you may get justice for poor Huggins, but you will have put one more obstacle between this regiment and France. As long as there's a murder investigation pending, the army's not going to send us across the Atlantic. So, if you want to keep your two thousand brothers from the front, then go ahead and make a to-do."

***

Dear T Hall,

As per our agreement, I have observed the goings-on among the members of the Fifteenth New York. I have participated in every aspect of the regiment's activities and done my best to befriend the men. I am always vigilant and aware of the sober responsibility which I have assumed. In fulfillment of which I apologize for not writing sooner, but only today have I discovered something worthy of correspondence.

This afternoon, a member of my platoon was discovered murdered several hundred feet from his guard post. He was beaten severely over the head and left by his attackers. When we summoned the local police, they attributed his demise to the fault of carelessness and the nature of his duty; that he was responsible for his own death and that there was no foul play involved. This conclusion, so painfully false in light of the evidence, prompted me to seek redress. A desire which my superior officers did not hesitate to stifle.

Captain Arthur Little, the regiment's adjutant and close friend of Colonel Hayward, as much as ordered me to take no action in this matter. I am to say nothing to the authorities and do nothing beyond what I am told through the chain of command. This 'request' was repeated later in the day by Colonel Hayward himself when we delivered the body to his headquarters in New York. Both men couched their orders in sentiment and in a desire to improve the regiment's chance of combat duty. I believe, however, they may share some less altruistic motive.

If I see a chance to convert this information to immediate gains, I will pursue such an opportunity. In the meantime, I will remain alert. If this letter does not reach you presently, I apologize, as I cannot send it directly for fear of the army censors. I will post it soonest upon discovery of an alternative mailing method.

Sincerely,
R Ayers

***

South of Ferry Street and around the corner from St James AME, I found a pub that served Negro patrons, and far enough from camp, I could hide from the men. The place served West Indies cuisine. I ordered a plate of yams and a Pabst Old Style Lager—they brewed the stuff across town. A handful of drinkers, ironmongers, barbers, and laborers lent the place an impression of life. Most sat at their own tables, a pair at the bar. A group near the back debated the effects of Mrs. C J Walker's hair straightener on their women. One of the men outlined the process with an enthusiasm disproportionate to his subject.

The door opened. Jodhpurs, hat, pacing stick. The man stepped inside and marched across the floor. Thud, thud, and thud some more. Napoleon Marshall pounded his old man's legs to my table, stopped, and appropriated an empty chair. He waved at the bartender, pointed to my glass, and lifted two fingers.

"You followed me?" I said and took a long swallow of my beer.

Marshall rested his pacing stick against the edge of the table. "I didn't follow you, I had someone else do it."

"Figures."

"I'm not watching you," Marshall said.

"Appearances to the contrary."

"I'm not watching you."

The bartender brought our lager. I finished my last and gave up the mug. The man retreated behind his bar.

"You're concerned about me," I guessed.

"I don't give a damn about you."

I pulled my mug, full again, toward me and watched the foam sway. "Leave me alone."

"You followed orders," Marshall said.

"I followed orders."

"That's what I said."

"How does that equate to you—"

"It's what I wanted to say, face to face, without the others to eavesdrop. I wanted to express my appreciation."

"I see."

A phonograph sat behind the bar. An old crank model that still used Edison's cylinder technology. The bartender set an Edison Blue Amberol in the mechanism and gave it a few good turns. Clear as crystal a horn blew the first, plaintive notes before a larger band joined in and the singers hit their cue. 'Roll Them Cotton Bales,' by the Premier Quartet. A plucky call and response number about a man gone to harvest cotton to raise money for his sweetheart. *Gonna roll them cotton bales for that gal of mine, for that gal of mine...cause I'm just working, gal, for you. Lindy Lou, it's all for you.*

I took a drink of my beer. Marshall did the same.

"I appreciate that you didn't say anything."

"To show you and everyone else in the chain of command to be a bunch of lying—"

"That you didn't contradict the official story."

"The official story is shit."

"He did his duty," Marshall said.

"According to the official story, he did it badly. When in reality—"

"He died doing his duty."

"He died." I took another drink, downed half of what remained, and set the mug down hard. "I feel like a traitor. I didn't sign up to conceal a murder."

"You signed up to kill Germans."

I stifled a burp. "I signed up…I signed up for the same reasons that everyone else signed up. I want—"

"And what you did, this is mutually exclusive?" Marshall huffed, dislodging beer foam from his mustaches. "Our people are forever cursed to be second class citizens because you kept your mouth shut. You are a traitor."

"That's not fair."

"Starting a riot is not going to help your cause."

"So, we should lie to our men."

"If we didn't—"

"The only possible reaction is, of course, a riot. These men can't possibly react with reason and logic. They are a bestial race after all, prone to violence and lustiness. Tell them the truth, tell them that one of their own was murdered by unknown white men, tell them this and the only thing to do is to run riot in the streets."

"With the news of Houston still fresh, yes, that's a very real possibility."

"It's a fucking farce is what it is."

"You're intoxicated."

"Intoxicated? Of course, I'm intoxicated. How else would I think such things, that direct communication and disclosure is possible, nay, preferable to lies and subterfuge? Our men can't handle a frank conversation. No, we have to protect them from the harsh realities, they're too fragile."

"That is enough, lieutenant."

"That is not enough, captain."

"Go home," Marshall grabbed the handle of his pacing stick. "Go home now and I'll forget this conversation."

"Yet you appreciate my complicity."

"Go home."

"You're quite welcome, captain. Let me know if you'd like me to perjure myself in the morning. The good of the regiment takes precedence any day, after all. Yes, sir."

"Lieutenant, now."

I hoisted my mug, threw back the last of my beer, and rose to my feet. Marshall's hands gripped his pacing stick, pale. I ignored his glare, an easy task after half a dozen drinks, and left fifty cents on the bar. The phonograph no longer sang about cotton bales in Georgia, but about a man who wooed his sweetheart's love to the beat of an army on the move. *Hup, hup, hup*. Inspired by the martial strains of 'In the Evening by the Moonlight,' I tipped my hat to the bartender and swayed drunkenly from the pub.

***

The man from Tammany found me at the end of September. Black as Africa, this one, who I'd met once in the city. He snuck through the darkening day, that time when the sun isn't quite down, but its warmth has passed and caught me as I emerged from temporary barracks in Newark. He slipped next to me, a ghost on the sidewalk, and put a massive arm around my shoulders, a muscular eclipse, so I could feel his bicep press into my neck. The heavy touch enough to scare me until I managed a sideways glance. That terrified me.

"Morton sends his best," the brute said. He spoke as thunder, a voice that shook glass panes with its bass. It gave me to believe that the integrity of my femur depended upon the respect I gave it.

"Thanks," I said.

"The boss is curious," the brute said.

"Curious?"

"Why he ain't heard from you yet? And how come you ain't shown no results neither."

"I see."

The brute squeezed my shoulder. I felt the pressure down to my groin. I would have collapsed against the nearest wall but for the weight of the bruiser's arm. Its terrible pressure held me stiff, upright. The slightest weakness and I knew I would crumble beneath it.

"It's what I'm to do," the brute said, "to make sure, you see, see real good how's you can't make no deals with the boss and not think to keep 'em."

The brute reached inside my uniform coat. He searched my pockets until he found the envelope addressed to *T Hall*. It was wrinkled and torn in one corner. The brute must have pegged a connection because the pressure on my shoulder eased.

I breathed deep against the gathering gloom. "We're likely transferred south. I'll find means then."

"Means?"

"Means."

"What the fuck is means?"

"Means. The method of accomplishing the desired end. You have something you want to be done and that's the way of doing it. It's how things happen and, like I said, I'll find means soon."

"I'm not sure soon is enough."

"It'll happen. It'll be easy. A little push and your boss'll have his own personal scandal. More than enough to make him happy."

The big man squeezed my shoulders hard.

"Make sure of it," the brute said before he disappeared into the darkness.

***

First of October came the order. Official. Change of Station. Headquarters and Supply Companies, 2nd and 3rd Battalions to Camp Wadsworth. Machine Gun Company and 1st Battalion to follow.

Harlem, Manhattan

New York, New York, USA
Thursday, November 27, 1919

Mrs. Freemaid served a full spread: turkey, chitterlings, potatoes, yams, stuffing, and a heaping salad. For her efforts, another dollar added on my rent, but one I did not begrudge. We sat together, those of her boarders without family or friends, and ate in silence. Occasionally, Mrs. Freemaid commented on the state of her own gratitude, grateful for good company, a sizable apartment, and for a husband whom she loved and who had loved her in return, at least until his death from influenza. I smiled and continued to eat my food, which, despite all Mrs. Freemaid's efforts, tasted of army rations, bland in my mouth.

***

Sometimes, I sat on a bench, cold stone or iron, and felt the vibrations of my past. When it happened, I grabbed the hard edge of the slab and tested reality. I stared dry-eyed around me. Felt the sharp corner bite my palm. The pigeons remained bunched, their beaks pecking on some bit of crust, gathered around an old woman. Mothers with their children hurried on their walks, unaffected. Lovers hand in hand. Hormone dripped youths walking in proper courtship under public eyes, untouched and untouching. Everyone…everything was ignorant of the memories that rocked me and caused my hands to shake.

I breathed, then, and considered Fifth Avenue. Victorian facades rose as monuments to a white elite, a separate class: intellectuals and robber barons. My nostrils smelled of acrimony. It was in those towers of opulence where lived the men responsible for my seizures. Not specific individuals, *per se*, but the class. Callous, rich, blind to those less fortunate, immune to the horror of the daily casualty rolls.

I wanted nothing more than to relinquish control and loosen my instability, the violence in my heart, on those unworthies.

I spat.

A weak gesture. Enough, though, to break the grip of my phantom passenger.

I claimed no expertise in phrenology or the work of alienists, but from my symptoms and their nature, I had deduced a possible origin. I surely suffered from a form of dormant sympathy, like the overtones of a string plucked, my body an instrument upon which the war played a series of sustained notes, my episodes the final coda of some harsh dissonance. Too many possible performers to know with certainty which one struck the chord. So, I spat and I wrote and I tried to live, a sad and uncounted victim of a war I never wanted to fight.

***

In two months, Prohibition would be in effect. It was an unfortunate victory for the forces of 'progress,' and one which I found unfair. It was a measure imposed upon men by a lonely population of women. While we fought in the trenches of France, they thought to punish us for our bravery. In conspiracy with old men and invalids, our wives and girlfriends and daughters and mothers stole our greatest comfort, our escape from reality, and our solace. It was a betrayal, and it hurt.

I drank whiskey. It was a sin by all accounts. The devils drink. Father Adam Powell, Sr of St Philips Episcopal, a man who was, in many ways, open-minded, agreed most vehemently with the Anti-saloon League on this point. He preached a frequent sermon in which he damned the whiskey drinker to hell.

He was a hypocrite, but a preacher of God.

The story was told of how his son discovered several empty bottles of gin in a dresser drawer. During the confrontation that followed, Father Powell confessed to the libations but insisted that for all his words against whiskey, he had never said a thing against gin.

I disliked gin and therefore remained a sinner—in the eyes of Powell—a whiskey drinker. I bought my liquor from a shop down the street, a shop which would close in January, and carried the bottle home in a bag. Mrs. Freemaid didn't approve of alcohol, but she allowed it. I was quiet about it and didn't make a racket. When, as had happened now and then, I drank too much and sobbed in loud gasps that surely echoed through the apartment, Mrs. Freemaid made no comment. I do not know if her tolerance was for my service in the war, or whether she had known the pain…whatever her reasons, for her tacit understanding and patience, I was grateful. I was alone in this thing and to know that she stood, if not as an ally then, as a witness was more than some small comfort. Her simple act of silence enough to remind me of my own humanity. And more, of the reason for the booze.

My restitution.

Camp Wadsworth, Spartanburg

South Carolina, USA
October 10–24, 1917

Camp Wadsworth. The Fifteenth assigned to a mostly undeveloped plot of land, given either side of a line that divided cotton field from pine grove.

A few wooden buildings dotted the field: bathhouses, latrines, mess shacks. Around these rose tents, eight men per, in row after row. The tents squatted, lines of canvas pyramids, great khaki-green monuments to the military's objective to end the war before more permanent facilities became necessary. Tents cheaper than wooden barracks, but not so good in cold weather. Almost every cantonment located in the south. Anything below the Mason and Dixon line plenty warm to house soldiers in tents. Never mind that southern trees were most likely to carry the load of a good old-fashioned lynching.

***

A hill rolled a gentle break in the horizon. A short hike across the cotton to the crest revealed eight miles of dug defenses, entrenchments in depth and width, built to familiarize the soldiers with the narrow lanes sunk in the earth. A down-home approximation of European reality. Learn this here and now. Drill in the dirt. Two days in and then out. Go again for three more. Repeat. Evade the flares, barbed wire, flying ammunition. Sneak through the dark until you can threaten the enemy's position without detection. This is it. After you finish here, you're on your way. Climb on board and sail to France to defeat the Boche. Learn to get it right because once you're over there…

***

Parade rest.

"Can everyone hear me? Company L, in the back, can you hear me?"

"Sir, yes, sir."

"I need everyone to hear this," Colonel Hayward said. "In the back row, if you can hear me, wave your hand in the air…good, thank you."

Flat roofed, the bathhouse formed a solid stage for the colonel. He marched back and forth upon its wooden heights, his arms raised, lowered, and raised again as he spoke. He kept his voice loud, but not monotone, and changed the pitch now and then to make a point or to emphasize one. Hayward, a lawyer, addressed the full complement with ease. A masterful speaker, a toastmaster, a great debater. Marcus Antony to his Negro plebes.

"I know you've all read about Houston. I won't bother to repeat the particulars. Nor will I repeat the substance of Mayor Floyd's letter to the *Times.* I know we've all read that, too, or had it read to us. What I will say is that my disgust, and Captain Little's disgust, and your disgust, and all the disgust in the world is not enough to justify reprisals. No matter how despicable the actions of anyone here in Spartanburg, he does not deserve our ire.

"Mayor Floyd and the people of Spartanburg are ignorant. They are ignorant of who and what *you* are. They cannot understand the distinction between you and the Negroes they keep on their plantations. You are colored men of New York City, not farmhands.

You are different in education, different in social, business, and community status. You are different in your bearing and your sense of responsibility and obligation to civilization. You are different in so many respects that Mayor Floyd and his ilk have no idea who you are or how to react to your presence here.

"We are presented a great opportunity at this time, you and me. We can compel the people of the south to recognize that you are different, that you are special and thus deserving of different treatment. You can help the people here in Spartanburg accept the very behaviors and beliefs that your northern neighbors have already adopted. You educated men of color, you northern citizens, you can prove your moral worth. How do you do this? How do you overcome the racism of Spartanburg? You refuse to meet the white citizens of Spartanburg upon that same undignified plane of prejudice and brutality. You show yourself better than the men of Spartanburg.

"This opportunity, this great opportunity, belongs to you, to all of you, to the entire Fifteenth Regiment. This is a chance for you two thousand men to win from the whole world respect for the colored race. If you can show here how strong of morality and self-control you really are, you can usher in a change that will someday sweep our country. You are good men, and true, and I would be pained to learn that anyone of you betrayed himself and his people.

"Don't go to places where you know the local white men don't want you. Don't even try. You know their prejudice; you know their tactics. You know Jim Crow's strength and you can't beat him, not all of you combined, not by direct assault. Your best strategy is a flanking action. Avoid him, show him humility, and by so doing, demonstrate the injustice of his rule."

"You will be physically abused by the white men of Spartanburg. I urge you to stand such abuse with fortitude and avoid retaliation. If something does happen, tell me, give me the full particulars, and I will share your outrage. The good Lord asks us to turn the other cheek. I ask no more than he. If a man strikes you, don't strike back. If you do, the press will take any such act and twist it against you and all of us. See to it that if violence occurs, if blows are struck, that all of the violence and all of the blows are on one side, and that that side is not our side. If wrong by disorder is to occur, make sure and doubly sure, that none of the wrong is on our side.

"I am finished but for one thing. I ask you all to make a promise. Promise me, your commanding officer, before God, that you will refrain from violence of any kind under every condition. I know this will be difficult, maybe even more difficult than fighting the Boche in France, but I ask you to promise me. Promise me to stand it, stand beneath it now so that you don't have to in the future. I want every man to raise his right hand, raise it high, and promise me, no violence. No violence. No violence."

***

Southern belles with their arms linked, dresses broad, and parasols high milled about the edges and watched from the stands. Others, from the Twenty-Seventh New York, shared the lawn. A fountain and a statue stood guard. Daniel Morgan, Revolutionary War general, bronzed and elevated. From atop his pedestal, a silent sentry, alert to the crowds every surge.

Bandleader Jim Europe stood in front, his baton in motion, his arms pumped, and his back unmoved. His free hand came up, palm down, and slowly dropped toward the ground. *Decrescendo.*

Noble Sissle marched to the spot, adjusted his glasses, and raised his head as the band introduced his solo.

The crowd murmured. White reaction to the Fifteenth. Whispers behind fans held aloft by society women. Men grunted to match the percussive blasts of the band, angry at a new threat to their virility.

Awful how they smell. Their hair, their posture, their faces. They look just like my house nigger. They all look alike. Uppity northern niggers.

Outrage, disappointment, agitation, race hate. Emanated from the local whites like an alcoholic's stink. An addiction to racial superiority, unable to quit, unable to admit, unwilling to try.

Negroes on the lawn.

Every officer in the Fifteenth mingled among the men. Hayward, Spencer, Little, Fish, Payton, et al. Familiar faces available, white commanders on location, ready. Poised to take control should the assembly turn to chaos. Every private within sight of an officer. Pale faces in the dusk.

For I doan' know what I'd do
If it wasn't jes' fo' you,
You's ma purty little black sugar ball;
You's a little bit o' honey
Dat da bees ain't foun',
You's ma own pickaninny—dat's all.
Little bit of honey.

I saw her on the fringe, apart from the rest, a beauty, a mirror of my one-time love, perfect. Skin the color of a summer custard, eyes that sparked fire in the hearts of men. Her face descended from Greece and Rome, a sculpture gave life. Her hair loose in curls, corkscrewed to her breasts, fibers meshed, cotton smooth from there. A different mold. Black and sleek from shoulder to ankle, a woman's form revealed, seductive, vital, erotic.

My eyes, no longer concerned with the men or the band but with this lusty doppelganger, lingered over the crowd. My heart matched the drums. My feet marched. Jazz soldier saluted. Uniforms, dress suits, ties, and bolos passed. The sticky warmth of autumn in the south another layer. Tactile anticipation oozed through my pores; sweat, sex, and sensation. Yellow Jessamine in the air.

I was a man consumed.

Words pushed at the door of my thoughts. Phrases to break the tense, quiet moment of introduction. Do you have relatives in New York? Are you alone? Come away with me and let's escape this spectacle. My heart is yours and I will throw myself on my bayonet if you so desire. Foolish words. Thousands in a moment. Each discarded in turn and pushed away. This beauty, not one for premeditated consideration but the surprised narrative, heartfelt, spontaneous.

Closer, closer, closer still. So close the lantern's light sparkled in her eyes and I could see. Damp illuminated her face and neck, her brow and arms, her visage. An angel of southern gentility, a hallucination surely, yet my senses otherwise intact, their only failure this singular vision.

Forward, again, another step.

I could smell her, rich womanhood, taste her.

"Ayers," a voice.

She was my existence.

"Ayers," this time accompanied by a hand, tight-gripped, on my arm, "don't be a fool."

Spun around, images clashed in quick succession: supernal beauty, black soldiers, earth and sky. Nausea struck in the form of Napolean Marshall's face. I grabbed his shoulders, gasped deep breaths of air, sucked, cursed.

Marshall leaned close and whispered under Sissle's song, "One word to that and you've as good as started a riot."

"She's—"

"Yes, she is, but you have a duty."

"If I'm to die doing my duty, I'd rather do it as a man."

"You gave your word to the colonel, the same as every other *man* in the regiment."

My head moved and I started to turn, her beauty a siren's call in memory, my muscles unbound by reason.

Marshall grabbed my ear. "You and I are going to march over to Captain Fish and have ourselves excused."

"The band."

"The band be damned—"

"The men—"

"We're going to talk to Captain Fish and then we're going to have a talk of our own until you've straightened yourself in the head."

"I'm fine, and even if I weren't—"

Marshall tugged my ear and swung his pacing stick across my thigh. The sting shock enough to pierce my delusions. I followed, docile. My body still tense with the memories.

***

Captain Marshall boarded a trolley, paid his fare, and took his seat. A white man of questionable parentage viewed Marshall's uniform and recognized him as a northern Negro. The white man complained that Marshall's very presence on the trolley was an insult, an unseemly assault on the white man's masculinity and ability to pleasure his woman. Hearing the white man's complaint, the trolley man ordered Marshall off. Marshall, aware of his rights and the full extent of Jim Crow, knew the order baseless in law and a product of prejudice. *C*onscious of his promise to Colonel Hayward, Marshall ceded his seat and removed himself from the trolley.

***

Private Henry Johnson strolled along downtown Spartanburg, his easy smile visible and his hands plunged in his pockets against a cool breeze. Two white men crossed his path and decided the sidewalk too small for themselves *and* a northern Negro. They informed Johnson of their decision by way of a shove. The private took their act into consideration and landed in the muck of the unpaved street. Johnson swallowed his embarrassment, picked himself and his hat from the ground, and informed the white offenders of his promise to Colonel Hayward. "I done promise my colonel that I wouldn't strike back if you all goes to licking me." Satisfied he had fulfilled his promise, Johnson turned and shuffled off.

***

The truck was black. A stripped-down Model-T, bodiless save the cab and a chassis that extended behind. Sidewalls constructed from wooden slats, assembled by the owner, wobbled and made an awful, banging racket. A pale arm rested along the door of the cab to signal any who might distinguish that this truck belonged to a white man.

The driver slowed to a stop as dust drifted around him and his vehicle.

I rested my rifle in the crook of my elbow.

The white man spat in the dirt, "You hear the news, nigger?"

I shifted my gun, wrapped my fingers under the stock.

"Two of your nigger chums got whooped. Thought they could take one of our police. Last thing they did, too, 'cause they got a noose 'round both their necks."

My other hand wrapped around the barrel.

"Swinging right pretty now, them nigger friends of yours. Right outside police headquarters. You should go see, it's like one of them—"

I lifted my rifle and stepped toward the truck, raised the butt toward the man's face. Imagined blood gushing. Stopped myself short. A direct violation of Colonel Hayward's injunction unwise…a course that would truncate my aspirations.

"Get the hell out of here."

The white man laughed, spat again, and bounced his truck down the road. I watched smoke billow from the back end, gray-black cotton that misted the air with acrid pollution.

***

Reveille. Fall in. Morning roll call. All present and accounted for but two. A pair of twenty-four-hour pass holders absent beyond their approved leave. Two men. Two soldiers. The same number reported hanged by a white bigot in a truck. Two corpses dangled lifelessly at police headquarters.

***

The incident started after breakfast. Morning mist still clung to the hills, a gray blanket that covered even the sassafras. Smoke rose from the mess huts, cooks finished with breakfast began preparations for lunch. Explosions echoed from the practice trenches, mortars and gunfire cracked. Soldiers eased into their routine, unexcited at the prospect of ditch-digging. Others gathered for lectures, instructions, and assignments.

In the midst of function, thirty, forty, fifty men gathered to rebellion. Tight packed and set for battle, ready to avenge their fallen comrades.

I watched from the shade of a lone black oak, a big bush of limbs and twigs stretched high, its leaves browned by the onset of cooling weather. I watched as the leader, a non-commissioned officer, shouted orders to the men. He didn't say much. Every man in formation knew the reasons.

Rows of soldiers squared, then, left, right, left march.

One more valiant soldier here,
One more valiant soldier here,
One more valiant soldier here,
To help me bear de cross.
O hail, Mary, hail!
Hail! Mary, hail!
Hail! Mary, hail!
To help me bear de cross.

I watched from my perch, the oak on a rise, as they turned toward town. Soldiers of the Twenty-Seventh passed. The NCO saluted and the officers returned the salute. Situation normal. Men on drill. Nothing to fear. Left, right, left, right. No one the wiser. No one suspicious. No one to report that fifty soldiers had gone AWOL and marched to Spartanburg, armed with rifles, ammunition, and a determination to avenge their lynched brethren. This was not a drill. This was a riot.

***

An hour passed, quiet, no news from the front.

***

Hoe work. Backbreaking. Nigger labor cheap when available. Men stretched across the fields, hoes and rakes and spades in hand, bent backs exposed to the sun. One group clears drainage to a stream, another digs a trench, a planned extension of the training grounds, one more erects a hut. Work, work, work. If you labor hard enough, you won't have time to think about the race hate that flew off every white man in Spartanburg.

Across the field, Captain Little directed the drainage efforts. Colonel Hayward was closer to the road, his group tasked to clear the brush gathered by last night's wind. I was with the trench diggers. Hoe, pick-ax, and shovel. Loosen the dirt and rocks for the shovels to dig. Quick. Double time. Not a minute to lose. Sooner you finish here; the sooner our white boys can practice for the front. I'm sure glad we've got you Negroes here to take care of the heavy lifting. Wouldn't want the Seventh to break a sweat.

A dust cloud billowed. A car stopped amid a billow of dust. Sergeant Leonard jumped out and sprinted to Colonel Hayward. Hurried conversation, arms gestured, fingers pointed. Hayward dropped his rake and hobbled after Leonard, his run turned limp by a bum heel—as fast as he could into the car. Tires spun, dust rose again, and the car screeched away. Fast, faster, faster still.

***

My stomach disliked the idea of food. My chest, too, felt as if it would squeeze shut and stop any meal well before it reached my belly. Even the smell.

Spaghetti noodles, marinara sauce, meatballs, bread. A military feast.

Torture.

I had no choice, though, lest I raise suspicion.

I hurried through the line and found a seat in the corner, close to the door, alone. I leaned to the window in search of a breeze. I needed to escape, leave this endless assault on my olfactory nerves and disappear into some darkened tent, cool and quiet, where I wouldn't have to pretend.

I swung my leg over the bench, ready to dash through the door, and stopped short. Napoleon Marshall stood in the space between wall and table, a plate of spaghetti in one hand, his pacing stick in the other.

"May I join you, lieutenant?"

Trapped. I slid my leg beneath the table.

Marshall set his plate next to mine and rested his pacing stick against the wall, an old man eager to serve his country, unaware of how badly his presence aggravated my stomach.

I forced a deep breath, four counts in, six out. I took another and another. Utensils clattered. Men spoke and the sum of their conversations raised a mid-level hum.

Marshall cut his spaghetti with a knife.

My stomach turned over and over. Would that I could conjure some excuse to slip behind Marshall and out the door.

"I wanted to apologize," Marshall said between bites of diced noodle. "I was too harsh with you the other night."

"Hmm."

"For my opinions and my beliefs, I do not repent, but there are better ways for a man to persuade his fellow."

I stuck my fork in the pile of spaghetti. The mere thought of lifting the flaccid noodles to my mouth caused bile to rise in my throat. I swallowed and again. I couldn't do it. My stomach too strong-willed to bow to my brain's command. I pushed the noodles across my plate and marched the green beans in a flanking maneuver against the bread.

"This is good," Marshall pointed with his knife. "Nothing like my Harriet's, mind you, but for army rations."

"Yes."

"You aren't hungry?"

I put a fist to my lips and swallowed hard, my will barely enough to halt the enemy's action. A matter of time before it overpowered my weakened defenses.

"I think I need some air," I said.

"You're not well."

I stood, then, and the back of my thighs pushed against the bench. I stepped over it and then behind Marshall. A short sprint to the door. I made it, barely, before I retched. I staggered, my back against the mess shack. I slid to the ground, my head between my legs. My body, in disgust, had rejected my actions. I closed my eyes and settled into oblivion.

***

"Influenza," the doctor said. "You need rest and liquids. In a day or two, you will either recover fully or die. There is little else I can do."

"Am I free to go, then?"

The doctor slipped his stethoscope over his head. "You're infectious. You'll stay here in quarantine."

"What if it's not influenza? What if it's…something I ate?"

"Then you'll remain here until we know for sure. I'm not going to be responsible for an outbreak." The doctor lifted a clipboard from a counter and tucked it beneath his arm. "You're confined to this tent until I tell you otherwise. I suggest you take the opportunity to rest. You may not get another chance for a while."

"What does that mean?"

"You're in the army."

***

Silence thickened the administration hut. Captain Little, the regimental adjutant, sat behind his desk. Green flecks of paint fell like snow around us. A private, tasked to headquarters, stood guard on the other side of the door. Little and I remained alone. I watched water condense on the sole window pane, fogged by the heat of our bodies.

At close quarters, Little's jaw looked square, more so than on the parade field, and it bobbed toward his chest in time to the clock that ticked in the corner. He wore his coat unbuttoned and it parted either side of his waist into twin pools of green wool. His hair was cut short, his face shaved clean, and his uniform starched crisp. Impeccable.

"I will be direct," Little said.

"Yes, sir."

"I do not believe you should continue as lieutenant of K Company."

"Sir?"

Little moved a notebook to the center of his desk. Small, with a sewn binding, the pages of uneven size, it bore scuffs on its cover and the corners were bent. He pulled it open to a page some distance in, a third of the way, maybe.

Little thumbed one more page, then said, "The local press agreed to keep quiet about what happened."

"I don't follow."

"One thing came of it, at least. The incident seems to have persuaded General Phillips that we should be transferred."

"The incident, sir?"

Little flattened the book against his desktop.

"The incident."

I sat at attention, my legs closed at the knees, my hands on my thighs, back straight, and butt on the edge of the wood. I kept my eyes forward.

I had no doubt of my position. Captain Little must surely have discovered the cause of the *incident* and determined to drum me from the service. Dishonorable discharge at best, court-martial at worst.

"I done heard it from Lieutenant Ayers," Little read from the open page in front of him, a transcribed confession, "the lieutenant said he'd heard the police gone and done lynch up two of our boys. And with two men missing from reveille…"

Silence again, this time an accusation.

"Three other men gave your name."

My military career would end in humiliation. I would be unable to find decent employment or position. I would be unelectable. I would be worthless. Tammany would forsake me, and my efforts on their behalf would be worth so much coal in the currency market of politics.

"Tell me what happened," Little said.

The clock ticked and kept time. One count enough for two heartbeats, at least of mine. Nervous, uncertain, trapped. Intense. A high rushed through my body. I could smell the mildew in the hut, the smell of bodies cramped, sweaty, moist, and humid. The troops in the distance marched, swore, trained. My mind filled the camp, or the camp filled my mind, and I realized that I wanted to be here. At that moment, it became…real.

It was all I could do to keep my thoughts ahead of my mouth. "Sir, thank you, sir. Thank you for the chance. Thank you for listening. It's big of you, sir. It shows magnanimity, sir."

"What happened, Lieutenant?"

"On guard duty," I said, "was where I heard it. I'm walking along just outside camp when this truck pulls along. The man inside tells me 'bout two soldiers who'd gotten in trouble with the police and been lynched. Now, at the time, I didn't think anything of it but some troublemaker's talk, but next morning when there're two men missing from roll call…"

"Why did you decide to tell it about?" he asked.

"Concern, sir," I finally said. "I was worried for those men, so I asked some others about them. I thought maybe, just 'cause I didn't know where they went, someone else might. I never meant to spread a rumor, but when they wondered why I was asking, I couldn't tell them dishonestly."

"That's the truth from you?" Little asked.

"Yes, sir," I said, "God's honest."

Little closed the notebook and lifted it in his hand. I had the feeling he would write our conversation in its pages the moment I passed through the door. This exchange would enter regimental history complete with the phonetic misspelling. He hefted it, weighed it, and put it back in its corner. "I don't think someone who would make such an error in judgment should continue as the lieutenant of K Company. It was a foolish thing you did. With a little thought on your part, the entire incident could have been avoided, and a great deal of stress taken from off Colonel Hayward and myself."

"Yes, sir."

"I, however, cannot fault you for your honesty, only for your lack of discretion. When the information you possess is sensitive or seems as if it might produce a detrimental effect, you should consider saying nothing. It is sometimes better for a soldier to be left ignorant than to be given piquant and titillating news."

***

We stood on the curb next to a sandwich stand, two dozen soldiers, waiting for cars back to camp. Most of the men coming fresh from evening services at the local Negro church. I'd come into town to escape the camp, and to maybe catch sight…

Three of us stood in a loose triangle, Jim Europe, Noble Sissle, and I.

A big man, Europe stood over six feet tall with shoulders that stretched wide. He had a large smile, the kind that caught hold and spread to those who saw it. When he smiled—and when he didn't—his eyes bugged out, frog-like, from behind round-rimmed glasses. He exuded friendliness, but also competence.

Sissle, on the other hand, was smaller than Europe, shorter and skinnier. His face was narrow and he wore a thin mustache on his upper lip. I didn't know much about his past, only that he was a singer with the Clef Club before he signed up and that now he sang with the band.

"You think Eubie regrets not signing up?" Europe said.

"Eubie?" Sissle said, "He's the only show in town with us gone."

"That's true," Europe laughed, "but he best not get used to it. I'm going to make this band of ours the greatest music maker France's ever seen. When we get home, we'll be so popular, Eubie'll never catch up."

"Won't stop him from trying," Sissle said.

"What's he going to do, climb the Woolworth Building and shout his name over the roofs?"

"Maybe he's already done it," Sissle said.

"We need to get some New York papers," Europe said. "See if the man's that crazy."

"Where can we get them?" Sissle said.

Europe glanced at me. I shook my head.

A local Negro, dressed in black pants and a white shirt pointed across the street. "Why you can get New York papers right over there in the lobby of the hotel."

We looked over. Across the street stood a small, family-owned hotel, a three-story affair with a restaurant on the ground. We could see the dining room from where we stood, white men in uniform seated at cloth-covered tables, the room well lit. The entrance not a hundred feet from us.

"Is it a white establishment?"

"Yes, sir, but it's quite all right to go in there. The colored people here in town go in there for papers. In fact, some of your boys were in there today to buy New York papers."

Europe turned to Sissle. "Go on over, Sis, and get every paper that has the word New York in it."

Sissle didn't move.

"I'll go get them for you if you're afraid," the waiter said. "I wait tables there and you can take my word it's quite all right."

"I'm no coward," Sissle said. "I'll go."

An army car pulled up, then, empty but for the driver. A Model-T with army modifications, the cushioned seats replaced by wooden benches and jerry-rigged handles, every expense spared in the name of increased capacity—enough for one, maybe two more soldiers than a factory production unit.

Europe hopped from the curb and into the car. He called after Sissle, "Hurry up, we'll hold this one for you."

I joined Europe in the car. Two other sergeants climbed in. Room enough for one more if we squeezed. Knee against knee, thigh to thigh.

"Take us up to that hotel so we can get Sis," Europe tapped the driver on the arm.

"Yes, sir."

The Model-T shook beneath us and then lurched forward. I sat in front with the driver and another sergeant. As we moved past the crowd of waiting soldiers, I stared at the passing faces. I recognized some of them from the march on Spartanburg, but didn't know any of them personally.

"There he is," one of the sergeants said.

The car rolled to a halt.

Sissle stepped through the door of the dining hall and stopped on the sidewalk. He adjusted his cover and brushed his pants. Under his arm, he carried a short stack of papers and he handed them through to Europe before climbing into the back seat.

"Everything okay?" Europe asked.

"No problem," Sissle said.

"Let's get going," Europe tapped the driver's shoulder.

The driver pushed the throttle and again, the car jerked forward. We moved slowly at first and then picked up speed. Behind me, paper rustled. I turned in cramped quarters. Curious for home, for news of it at least.

I never saw it.

Instead, I saw a mob forming behind us. The soldiers of the regiment were no longer on the sidewalk by the sandwich stand. They were on the move. Two dozen men pushing across the dusty road. They moved with purpose but without control. This was not the organized movement of the march to Spartanburg, this was haphazard. Some men moved faster than others, an uneven front, rushing toward the hotel. Words rose from the men, though I could not understand them for the car's engine, I could hear them. Shouting. Anger radiated from those men and crashed against the hotel. In a matter of seconds, they would be at the door.

"What's going on with them?" I asked.

Europe, Sissle, and the other man twisted in their seats.

"Hold up," Europe tapped the driver's shoulder.

"Truth be told, I had some trouble inside," Sissle said.

The car stopped and we all climbed from the car.

The mob was ahead of us, and by the time we reached its trailing edge its leading edge was inside the hotel. Only stragglers, a few slow soldiers, hung back. The rest clumped green on the sidewalk, a mass of angry, noisy, riotous men. I couldn't see inside the hotel for the wall of green—we were blocked by the mob—but I heard raised voices, shouts, confusion.

Europe was in front of me and hit the wall of soldiers without hesitation. He grabbed the coat of the nearest soldier and pulled him from the crowd out onto the street then stepped into the now vacant space. Europe grabbed the next soldier and manhandled him back. One at a time. Europe moved quickly, confidently. For all his heft making rapid progress. Soldier's unable to refuse the authority of his hands.

White folk crept along the streets. A crowd began to gather. Electricity sparked. Tinder wood lit.

In the middle, Europe reached the threshold.

"Ten-hut."

Every man snapped to their feet, straight, arms at sides, shoulders back, feet together.

Europe turned first to the men on the street. He pointed to the sandwich stand, a glare on his face. His presence stronger than any white officer's. It was enough. The men sulked away from Europe's fierce gaze. A crowd of sullen boys.

Only when the last soldier turned heel did he spin to face the dining room.

"All of you soldiers, leave here, take it in small groups, two or three at a time. This is not your fight. None of you. Now move."

Five minutes out, the lobby stood empty. Only Europe and the proprietor inside, Sissle and myself at the door. The proprietor, red-faced, blubbering, threw a paper to the floor and knocked a dish off a table. Flatware shattered.

Europe approached. "What's the matter?"

"Nothing is the matter," the proprietor, a big-bellied man, said. His teeth snapped.

"All right, then."

"Only that nigger there," the proprietor pointed a finger at Sissle, "did not take off his hat and no nigger can come in here without taking off his hat...now you take off your hat."

Hush.

Europe moved. His arm raised...past the point of attack, to his head. He lifted his cover from his close-cropped hair, green cloth in his hand, and lowered it, deliberate, to his side.

"I'll take my hat off to find out one thing, what did Sergeant Sissle do?" Europe said. "Did he commit any offense?"

"No. I told you he didn't take his hat off and I knocked it off, now get out of here."

From where I stood at the door, I could hear a whistle in the distance. Military police on the way. Europe must have heard it too. He gave the proprietor one final glare, whirled, and marched from the lobby. Sissle and I followed him to the street.

"Another two seconds and I'd have smacked him and undone all the good," Europe said.

"You didn't," Sissle said.

Europe nodded and put his cover on his head. "What did he do, sis, that so damn near caused a riot?"

"Well," Sissle rubbed the seat of his pants, "he, um, kicked me in the backside...once when I grabbed my hat from the floor and twice more on my way out the door."

"Let's hope that bastard just kicked us to France."

Harlem, Manhattan

New York, New York, USA
November 28, 1919

I remember the way Europe looked when he said that. The relief that was evident on his broad face. He seemed to be relaxed all of a sudden, his ability to handle the situation situational itself, thus passed, and no longer needed. He took a breath and wiped his brow, and his hat and glasses seemed cocksure on his head and face. I wasn't sure what he meant at the time, but soon we traveled. Soon we transferred. Soon we found our way to France.

It wasn't my first exposure to Europe. I'd met him before, briefly, back when he first conquered Carnegie. It had been a meeting of a moment, his white tuxedo flashy and crass among the other men and women on the street dressed in evening wear.

He was late.

That much I remembered. I had my father's Elgin in my pocket and knew it was the way in, only I didn't know that yet. It wasn't until the crowd convinced the policeman guarding the door that the man in the white tux was indeed the conductor of the orchestra that was to perform, that the crowd gave way and let Europe through, that was when I knew my efforts to slip past the cop without a ticket would bear fruit.

As soon as Europe passed, and he patted me on the arm as he did so, I dropped my Elgin on the ground at his feet. I picked it up and feigned shock and alarm. He dropped his watch, I said to the cop who, spent and underpaid, waved me through without checking for my ticket. It was enough and I swept through the door, past the crowd pressing for entrance, and found myself in Carnegie Hall.

Perhaps it wasn't much of a meeting, I don't know, but Europe's fame spread. When I was working, canvassing San Juan Hill for Tammany, a useless and wasted effort as no self-respecting Negro would abandon the party of Lincoln, not yet at least, and I heard the stories I knew that Europe would become something. He was smart, and savvy, and knew business. He crossed the color line with the musician's local. He organized the performers who had scattered their efforts from one bar to the other, waiting for a call to perform, and started a club.

The Clef Club. He rented space and installed a phone and bought a pool table so the men who played horns and brass and piano and drums could hang out near the phone, and the white folk could know the number to call should they need a band. It was professionalism. That was the word for it, and Europe brought it in spades. He organized the performers, the musicians, and the artists into a professional troupe. He formed orchestras and would skip from venue to venue, conducting the orchestra for one or two numbers, long enough for the thing to be called Europe's Clef Club orchestra, and then flurry off to the next club to conduct the next orchestra.

Yes, I heard the stories. Europe was everywhere. He was the biggest thing. Composer and conductor for Vernon and Irene Castle, traveling with the dancing duo, the couple of stars that fixated the world on their feet. He ran shows, traveling Broadway, and even flirted with the Great White Way itself. Though he never actually stood on the stage, not unless you counted Carnegie, but that was on 57th Street, not Broadway, so the later claims to fame that some of the press seemed to make about his successes on the street were false. But it didn't matter, the perception remained, and for all he did do, he should be recognized.

But the look on his face, the way he glanced at Sissle, and then at me, the bright eyes behind his glasses, recently recovered from goiter surgery, struggling to stand even, and then he had cleared the hotel lobby of black and white together. It was a startling revelation of power in one man, and I knew then, like I know now, that he was a great man, and if only I'd seen it sooner, before I made a fool of myself in Spartanburg, before I reported to Tammany and confirmed my deal with the devil. If only…

I thought of what came next, my pen poised, and I wondered if I should continue. The story of our passage to France, the long nights on watch for submarine wakes, for the signal that would presage an attack, cold and frigid in the North Atlantic, this was what awaited us. And then there was Marks. The poor farm boy from Idaho. I wondered at his sin, for his sin was akin to my own, only in degree different. I had betrayed my people, and I had done so when there was such good in them, for Seaman Marks, his sin was something else, I'm not sure what, but it was enough to harm his heart. And in hurting him, it hurt me, for I had come to identify with the man, though he was white and ignorant. He had the chance to confess, I was there, in the room with him, him and his Bible, but he chose to forsake me, and he forsook his repentance.

That was why I must continue, for I could not forsake myself. I must find a way of confession, I must write it all, and tell it to the next generation, that the youth now running up and down the streets of Harlem, standing on the corners next to their daddies, and smoking narrow cigarettes would know that in power, there is only pain.

December, 3 1917 – January 1, 1918

Onboard the *USS Pocahontas*
North Atlantic

We stood assembled at emergency evacuation stations for an abandon ship drill. One at dawn and one at dusk. Everyday. Two thousand and some Negroes, five hundred plus whites, crammed shoulder to shoulder on deck as the sun peaked the horizon. Keep eyes peeled for periscopes or the tiny white wake that might betray the presence of an enemy vessel. If you see something, tell a sergeant, better one in blue than green, hold on to your life vest, and pray.

When Captain Kalbfus sounded all clear, I joined some men at the rail revisiting what remained of last night's rations. I watched green gobs splash the hull and ooze toward the North Atlantic.

"I pukin' blood now," a soldier beside me said. "I can taste it."

"Like iron."

"Hell yeah."

I wiped drool from my chin. "It's rust. Comes as part of this godforsaken ship."

I stood just fore of the paired funnels that rose from the top deck, massive cylinders that angled back so they looked windswept, or maybe a little drunk. My heart ached. My muscles felt the soreness that comes with a regular retch. I hung my head between my elbows and waited for the next heave. Get it over and done so I could climb down to my bunk and curl into myself.

"It's the damn Germans."

It came from a teenager. His face freckled so I couldn't distinguish the acne on his cheeks. He wore the uniform of someone who worked in the engine rooms: scuffed boots, denim trousers with rolled cuffs, a jumper, and a white cap. Oil stained his knees and sleeves. He wore no insignia that I could see, but the uniform itself marked him as an enlisted man. When the boy saw my gold bar, he snapped a salute.

"Seaman Apprentice Marks, sir."

I returned the salute and tried to hide the green around my own gills. I adjusted my service hat and took a deep breath lest I disgorge myself on the boy's boots. "For what do you blame the damn Germans, seaman?"

"Sir, I meant no disrespect, I just thought as you being a Negro—"

"I couldn't possibly be an officer? Is that it?"

Marks looked at the deck. His face flushed and turned an impressive shade. "Somethin' like that, sir."

"Are you normally a racist seaman, or are you simply ignorant?"

"I'm from Boise, sir, Idaho," Marks puffed his chest, "don't see too many Negroes in Boise."

His callow mien supported this last statement. What I knew of Idaho, too, suggested a base ignorance of the race question. I judged Seaman Marks' error an innocent one.

"Walk with me, seaman," I said.

I led Marks forward. I kept close to the starboard rail and stopped every few feet to rest my stomach's discontent. Ostensibly, I took an interest in the nearest ship of our convoy. Another transport; one of six ships that plied the sea in two columns of three. Each ship in the column trailed its guide-on by a mere hundred feet. Ahead of the lead ships, situated between them so every captain could watch for instructions, sailed a destroyer, its guns a bristle, its towering forecastle followed by four sleek funnels and a low-slung aft deck.

As darkness fell at night, the destroyer would signal the convoy coded instructions using hooded lanterns. During the day, it stalked the water in search of the elusive periscope, the tiny wake, the U-boat.

"What do you know of the Twenty-Fourth Infantry, seaman?" I skirted a lifeboat.

"I don't know, sir," Marks said. "I know the Seventh, with Custer and all, but I can't claim much learnin' 'bout history, sir."

"Negroes. One of two infantry of Negro soldiers. The Twenty-Fourth and the Twenty-Fifth."

"Yes, sir."

"They led the charge up San Juan Hill, on foot, and secured it in time for Roosevelt to huff up the slope and claim the glory," I said. "After they proved their worth in battle, the army tasked them to Siboney and two months of exposure to yellow fever. The Negro is immune to the disease reasoned bigots in Washington, or wherever. Never mind that eight other white outfits refused the assignment before them. They're not heroes, they're Negroes. Thirty men dead and hundreds more afflicted. And after all that, after they charged into enemy fire and selflessly sacrificed themselves to care for their fellow soldiers, do you know what they returned to, Seaman Marks?"

"No, sir, I don't rightly know."

"Jim Crow."

The ship's deck dipped toward the water. A starboard turn. I held fast to a rail. Every ship in the convoy listed to follow the destroyer's instructions. Zig-zag, zig-zag across the Atlantic, each zig spaced at random intervals from the last zag.

"Salt Lake City," I said. "Even as far west as Utah, Jim Crow loosened his hatred on the soldiers of the Twenty-Fourth. Merchants and restaurateurs refused them service and watched with suspicion as they passed in the streets. Police arrested them for infractions a white man wouldn't be scolded for. These men fought and suffered yellow fever for their country."

"That's Utah for you, sir."

"In Idaho, too, and for doing no worse than any outfit of white men has done."

"Idaho, sir? Like I said, we don't have many Negroes, not so you'd know if anyone prejudiced against them."

"Is your daddy a union man, seaman?"

"He ran a livery, sir. The best in Boise."

"Ran?"

Marks blew into his hands. "He had a mare was foundering. Tried to ease her pain while I fetched a gun, but she got scared n' kicked his skull in."

"I'm sorry."

"Surgeons fixed him up best they could, but he's never been right in the head since. We sold the stables, but with him, my ma, and two kid sisters to feed, things got thin. 's why I signed up. I figure it's a guaranteed pay, you know. Not like farming or mining or other things a man could do."

"And what would you do if you could, other than the Navy?"

"Mine most like."

"You know the business?"

"Owners always looking for miners. I'm healthy, young, and willing. It don't take science to swing a pick, even underground."

The sun was up now. I crossed to the port rail and held my hands in its rays. Feeble light. Too cold for my army standard wool coat to ward off the chill. Too cold, apparently, for the distant sun to do much about it either. I mimicked Marks, blew into my hands, and hid them in my pockets; my stomach the last obstacle between me and a retreat to warmth.

Marks hugged his chest. "Aren't you cold, sir."

"As a prostitute's heart."

"Shouldn't we go below decks, then, sir?"

"Five more minutes for my stomach to make a decision and I'll build you a fire that'll burn this ship to the waterline."

"I think Captain Kalbfus'll have words to say 'bout that, sir."

One of our convoys sailed in silhouette against the sun, its profile shimmered by yellowing light.

"By order of President McKinley, back in ninety-two, the Twenty-Fourth transferred to Northern Idaho. The Western Federation of Miners had all but declared war on some recalcitrant owners. Over a thousand miners hijacked a train and blew up a condenser. Your governor declared martial law and requested federal troops. McKinley sent the Twenty-Fourth. They arrested and detained every miner they could find while their white officers interrogated the prisoners to determine who should bear responsibility for the attack. When the miners got uppity in their bullpen, the soldiers called them out. 'Get back you white sons of bitches.' 'Understand that we are the bosses.' One soldier went so far as to point his gun at an uncooperative prisoner."

"It was Negroes did this, sir?"

"Exactly," I said. "If a white soldier did the same to a Negro, it would earn him a drink at the saloon. Even a white soldier to a white prisoner and it would pass without comment. But should a Negro say words to a white prisoner, he's out of line and warrants punishment. The press vilified them, called them 'imps of darkness,' 'hyenas,' 'black beasts,' and a 'rapscallion horde of thieving, lecherous, drunken soldiers.' One reporter suggested the episode would 'leave a blot upon the page of our nation's history that has no parallel.' I counter that any such blot comes not from the Twenty-Fourth, but from the bigots who applied their double standard to heroes simply because they happened to be Negroes."

"Not heroes but Negroes is what you said, sir, before."

"It's why I'm here, seaman, and it's why this entire regiment is here."

***

For two weeks on board ship, black and white co-habituated, but rarely integrated. Our colors juxtaposed in short cycles of twenty-four hours. Day and night. Enlisted and officer. Jim Crow, a subtle institution in the newness of this modern transportation. The officer's dining salon with its padded chairs, wood-paneled bulkheads, and fluted-glass fixtures daren't admit but a small handful of Negro patrons while the white light of day still shone. When the blue, hazy nights settled over the decks of the *Pocahontas*, however, it mattered less the color of your skin than the timbre of your voice or the dexterity of your digits.

I found myself below decks when the order came to darken the ship. Every light was extinguished and the only illumination dim blue bulbs at the base of each bulkhead. Dusk came early to the North Atlantic and most nights the men filled the space between dark and sleep with song.

Steal away, steal away, steal away to Jesus
Steal away, steal away home.
I ain't got long to stay here.

It started with a voice, a tenor in the blue. A natural talent that resounded from hull to hull with its rich beauty.

My Lord, He calls me
He calls me by the thunder
The trumpet sounds within-a my soul
I ain't got long to stay here.

New voices joined the song, raised in a familiar spiritual, a prayer for deliverance not from the harsh realities of slavery but the invisible threat of a German submarine. Unsaid, I heard their pleas in the perfect harmony and sober melody that floated in the azure dark.

Green trees are bending
Po' sinner stand a-trembling
The trumpet sounds within-a my soul
I ain't got long to stay here.

When the last note faded from silence to longing, I turned from the hatch and made my way above decks. I passed not a hundred steps before another voice rose to lead the choir. *Didn't my Lord deliver Daniel* ushered me upward until I heard nothing but the movement of the ship as it cut through the waves. Full-steam from dusk to dawn to take advantage of the cloaking blackness. I kept on and soon a lively improvisation filled the quiet and led me to my destination: the officer's dining salon.

I stopped short of the actual salon. I had arrived late, and I detected lumped figures reclined on the stairs. Relaxed officers, white and Negro, soothed by the syncopated melody that plunked from the piano on the upper landing. Even had I desired, a climb to the salon would be futile. Every officer not involved in the night-time operations of the ship sat up there to listen to the Company K Quartet, Noble Sissle, and Jim Europe.

It was Europe who struck a chord as I settled against the railing at the base of the staircase. "Captain Fish, if you please."

The quartet had a tenor, a plaintive voice, and a baritone, whose combined register and crooning tones blended harmoniously with the resonant voice of the bass as he softly counted the beat in his vocal depths. Sergeant Stout led the group, his pure, lyrical voice a beacon to our hearts.

I am dreaming of you, day by day,
Dreaming when the skies are blue, when they're gray;
When the silvery moonlight gleams,
Still I wander on in dreams.
In a land of love, it seems, just with you.

Underneath the barbershop harmony, the engines pounded out their revolutions. Another turn of the massive blades, another mile between us and home. Mothers, jobs, lovers, booze, and Harlem. Silent reflection of all we had to lose settled over the assembled as the tenor faded the final note: *I'm in love with you.* I held my own image sacred in those moments of contemplation, a woman of pale skin and passion who had taught me so much. My heart ached whenever I thought of what could have been between us.

Jim's piano broke my reverie. He played softly, a melody of minor chords to match our solemn mood. He vamped an étude, a waltz, an invention. He mastered the ivory keys and subdued them to his will. I am Jim Europe and you will play for me.

"Captain Fish, which chord please?"

"C-sharp, Lieutenant Europe."

Jim played the chord and the quartet resumed its flight. Their voices intertwined, rose, fell, and led us home again to those noisy nights in Harlem.

"Sis, you got this?" Jim's voice boomed down the stairs. "If you need help, I know Jerry's part faring well."

"I'd hoped you would sing Trixie."

Jim laughed and answered with his fingers.

Most everybody, has made a study,
Of how to play the role of lover.

Sissle sang with a vaudevillian's confidence. His tenor voice filled the salon and skipped down the stairs. I could hear a joke in it, too, something I hadn't heard from the quartet. Jim slowed then, in anticipation, as Sissle took a breath so deep it was audible from where I sat. When the next notes emerged, they were in a piercing falsetto. Here was the joke. A Trixie no lover could ever love.

It's my impression, you know each lesson,
There's nothing left you can discover.

The laughter that met Sissle's punchline, his feminine styling, almost shook the ship. I joined in easily, eager to forget my mistakes and not alone in the forgetting. We were a hundred novices at war elated by a moment of humor and unconcerned whether it came from black or white, just happy to laugh away the memories.

I did till you came, and brought a new game,
That put me in the kindergarten school.

And Trixie again.

You were the smartest, old loving artist,
I thought you understood each lover's rule.
I never knew what love could do,
Till your love met with mine.
I never knew what hands could do,
Till our hands met one time.
I never knew what eyes could do,
Till my eyes met with thine.
I never knew what lips could do,
Till your lips met with mine.

***

"Watch your step there, sir," Seaman Marks shouted over the dinning of the engine room. "You don't want to lose an arm."

I appreciated the warning, but it was superfluous.

The engine room was filled with wheels and valves and levers that connected each to a vital energy. Here, hidden behind white-washed pylons and steel casings, Herculean forces produced the drive that propelled us across the ocean, a fact reflected in the purposed movements of the place's inhabitants. Elsewhere on board, we moved with the casual velocity of those blessed with too much time. We exercised, studied, and ate, for the only appointment we had to keep came when the sun dropped below the horizon.

In this, the life center of our transport men walked quickly and sometimes ran to prevent the next crisis. A sailor with a clipboard in hand-marked pressure readings with a stubby pencil. One with oil smeared on his cheeks climbed a ladder and yelled profanities at some unseen colleague. Another cranked a wrench, muscles popping until the bolt refused to move any farther. In some hidden chamber, I heard the *shlunk* and crash of shovels as men stoked the fires, fed coal into the boiler, and nourished the pressure that displaced massive pistons up and down and up again. Even Seaman Marks, off duty, kept his eyes wide as we moved through the few feet of clearance deep into the maze.

The farther we traveled, the more I felt like Theseus, trapped in this labyrinth without a clue. Only when I'd lost all hope of retracing our steps did Seaman Marks stop, crouch low, and point to a truncated cylinder as big around as a small skyscraper. "Look here at this moony blemish, the way it dips at the floor. Can you see it? The Germans did that."

Metal sagged in a semi-circle of melted steel and looked so much like a giant candle, half-burned, with wax dripped down the side. I tapped Marks's shoulder. "Can I touch it?"

"Sure thing, sir," Marks said. He reached his own hand to the steel and pressed his palm against the droopy sliver.

I hesitated.

"Don't worry, sir, it's cold. Navy engineers finished this up long before we sailed. Come on, it's okay. Any heat you'd feel comes from inside. The piston rubs against it, creatin' friction. No problem for you, sir. Just put your hand on here like you'd touch a lady's tits. Nice and smooth."

Down the room, a pair of denim-clad Navy swabs watched us, soiled rags in hand, suspicion in their eyes. They stood with their legs set in a bulldog stance, ready to protect their territory. I'd seen it before, every Negro has. It was the universal body language for: get out, nigger, before I feel it necessary to help you out.

"Let's find somewhere more suitable to conversation," I said.

"You don't want to feel her up, sir? It's almost as good, you know, she's the closest to a woman you'll get till we make landfall and from what I hear about those French girls...I don't want to take somethin' home I can't get rid of, you know what I mean."

"Thank you, seaman," I said. The swabs hadn't moved. "At the moment, my stomach's the more troublesome part of my anatomy."

***

There is no specific behavior I can pinpoint from memory that provoked my agitation. The cooks dispensed our meals with the same dazed apathy that marked each scoop, whether the kit be held by hands black or white. No one pointed a finger or spoke askance. A pair of officers even wished us a Merry Christmas on the line, nothing doing, as if our green uniforms hid the color of our skins. It was inchoate, a feeling, an instinct that refused to dissipate in the pleasure of our unusual holiday celebration.

"It's not whether she's fit to be a mother, it's that she's a confessed murderess," Captain Napoleon Marshall said. "Bianca De Saulles is a killer. She said she was glad of having done it. She brought a gun in her car, brought it to the step, and pulled the trigger. It was cold-blooded, premeditated murder. The jurors were distracted by her youth and her pretty looks and forgot their duty to judge the facts as presented."

"Is your turkey dry?" I said.

Marshall took a bite. "It's fine."

"What of passion?" Fillmore raised his own fork. "Her unfaithful husband refuses to let her visit her son, her baby. I have never met a mother who wouldn't bare her fangs to save her child."

I pushed my turkey across the tin. "They were divorced. He violated the referee's order."

"The law prefers less *terminal* remedies," Marshall said.

"Yet for the poor mother who kills to protect her blood, you seek a Mosaic judgment," Fillmore picked gristle from between a pair of molars. He flicked the bit of fat to the floor. "What do you think, Ayers?"

"Sir?"

"What do you think about the verdict? You're an intelligent fellow, you know the facts, what do you think? Is De Saulles guilty?"

I remembered a sketch in one of the papers, back before the murder, when the couple returned triumphantly to Long Island after their nuptials in Paris. The artist rendered her profile, a striking woman in furs, well-lit, smooth-skinned, perfect, and innocent. Beneath her, shadowed and aging, the artist drew her husband face on, his head bowed to accentuate the lines, the light cast to suggest some nefarious intent. A surrealistic accusation of crimes uncommitted by a newspaper hack aspiring.

"That she killed him, I have no doubt," I filled my fork with potatoes. "That he did not deserve to die, I am less certain."

Marshall wielded his utensils as orator's tools, his fork a straw man to disguise the fatal thrust of his knife's logic. "The husband's guilt justified his execution?"

"Not justified, but perhaps mitigated the culpability of his executioner."

"Explain."

I looked at Marshall. "Imagine yourself a slave, a strong man toiling in your master's fields. You have a lover, a woman for whom you would do anything and it tortures your soul to know that you are not the only man to share her bed. Your master likes her looks and frequents her abode of a lazy summer evening. Each morning, your master comes to the fields, carrying his cat o' nine and his musket and wafting the scent of your lover in his loins. There is nothing you can do as day after day of humiliation and abuse slowly mounts and your anger and hatred grow apace.

"Now, imagine you arrive at your lover's dwelling place one day to find her dead, bloodied from a violent rape committed, no doubt, by your master. Would you not be justified in seeking vengeance upon that man in the heat of your passion?"

Marshall rubbed his nose. "Assuming the law allowed such emotion to a slave."

"Yes," I nodded, done with my turkey. "A hypothetical where master and slave may kill with an equal cause. Now, you would seek this man's death at once, yet he carries his musket at all times and is rarely alone. He has succeeded in removing opportunity yet in such a way that your passion cannot dissipate for the daily reminders of his crime. So, you wait, and endure the abuse, and wonder if your chance will ever come."

Marshall stabbed his knife in the air. "Is the justification diminished because the opportunity presents itself only after the passage of time?"

"Precisely. The slave's passion remained unexpressed, though undiminished, until such time as he found his owner alone, or incapacitated, or drunk and, recognizing the change in his position, chose to act out and kill. The original passion thus remains to justify the eventual act."

"But how does this *theory* justify De Saulles exoneration?" Fillmore said.

I turned to face Fillmore, a man almost thirty years my senior with silver hair and mustache, and said, "A theory, as you say, and one which I cannot apply fully to the facts as given. The defense counsel failed to explore the possibilities, or the newspapers to report them, of any abusive relationship that may have existed. We know Mr. De Saulles was unfaithful, he was an athlete, strong and powerful of build and potentially intimidating. These facts suggest, though do not prove, a dynamic of hidden passion."

"So, you agree with the jury's verdict?" Fillmore said.

"No," I forked a cranberry. "The defense failed to explore this theory and in no way submitted evidence sufficient to exonerate their client. Ms. De Saulles is guilty. She should hang for her crime."

The ship listed beneath us for its scheduled forty-five-degree zag to starboard. I put a hand on my kit to keep it from sliding off the table and wrapped my foot around a table leg, just in case. Captain Fillmore followed suit. Fifteen minutes or so before the next zig to port.

Marshall stabbed his kit with a finger. "I saw him play once."

"Sir?"

"De Saulles," Marshall said. "He was a Yale man, their celebrated quarterback. They touted him as the king of the gridiron. Said the man could run like the wind."

The ship leveled.

Marshall shook his head, "You put the two of us side by side, let us go man to man, and I'd whip his scrawny white backside from here to Monaco any day of the week."

"You're almost as old as I am," Fillmore said, "and he's dead."

"He was slow," Marshall said. "Ran the hundred in nine or ten seconds or something similarly sluggish. It wouldn't be a fair contest."

"And Ms. De Saulles," Fillmore grinned.

"She has the misfortune of being a woman, otherwise I would do more than challenge her to a footrace," Marshall said. He targeted Fillmore with his knife tip. "I am a gentleman, however, and an officer of the court. As such, I am bound. Ms. De Saulles, although adjudged guilty by this esteemed body, will remain free because twelve men saw her beauty and fell in love."

"May we be so lucky," I raised my tin cup.

"No German could ever mistake you for a Chilean heiress."

I shot Marshall a look, "So as to avoid an untimely death."

"And Merry Christmas," Fillmore raised his cup.

Marshall looked between us and scratched at his mustache. After a huff that ruffled the hair on his lip, he raised his own cup. "May we all live to see another."

"Here, here."

Cold coffee never tasted so cheerful.

***

The next day, we entered the danger zone. Constant vigilance. The top deck sprouted lookouts like a child stricken with the pox. No sooner would one sit than another filled his place. Fifteen degrees of the horizon at thirty-minute intervals. Constant alert for every hand on board. No one was allowed to sleep below decks. We bundled in full uniforms, overcoats, and life jackets. Grouped by evacuation assignments, we slept on deck, some in the lifeboats themselves, and nestled in the sway of the ship. We lay on our backs and stared at the sky, saw the stars move through the clouds, felt the wind swoop low and the ocean rush past beneath. During the day, we moved quickly about our business, ate, exercised, and ate again. We filled the empty hours by watching the pack of escort ships, come from France, circle our convoy, naval wagons to protect us from the German wolves. Time passed on edge. When we heard shouts from another transport and saw men point to the horizon, we spread whispered rumors of a periscope sighted only to see gray-green cliffs coalesce in the haze.

***

Landed at Brest, right side up.

***

Despite our anticipation to set foot on European soil, the army left us in the harbor to watch the snow drift down the Penfeld and dissolve our world into a cauldron of whitecaps, steel, and ice. A bitch of a storm. At first, it seduced us, large white flakes that floated from the sky and coated the rust in a crystalline blanket, a winter cocoon that damped the noise of the docks, not a quarter-mile off. Alone in nature's majesty, we opened our mouths and laughed as tiny tingles of ice melted on our tongues and reminded us of Harlem and how it snowed there the same way it did here off the shores of France. But it didn't last. It transmogrified. A changeling. Beneath her wrath, the *Pocahontas* wrenched its lines and every army man scurried below decks. We were land soldiers impotent against Neptune's choler. What could we do? What could we offer but our faith? We formed a circle, wide eyes in black faces and some held hands. A tenor led us, his voice raised first in prayer and then in song. Prayer that the anchor held, and song in case it failed.

***

"Used to be that my daddy' would read from the good book of an evening, this big leather thing he'd pull off the shelf, like three books glued together. We'd gather around and listen as he called out the expositions of Jesus, thou shalt not and you know. When he got kicked in the head, though, he couldn't do it no more, and Momma made me learn how. I knew how to read, I'm not saying I couldn't read, but she made me learn how to exposit the Bible, the way Daddy did. There's a trick to it, she said, the way your voice should go up at certain places and then plow deep. It's an art she said. I never understood it, but when she'd shush me and tell me to do it over, I'd change the way my voice went and then she'd lean back and fold her hands in her lap and sigh this happy contented sigh like she was caught up into heaven or rapture or something like that. I don't say I believe it at all, but the way she felt the words when I read, it makes a body think there might be something, you know, up there maybe."

Marks sat on Lieutenant Reid's bunk and rested his feet on a wooden trunk. He'd pulled off his boots and draped his jumper on the foot of the bed. Relaxed. I looked at him in the fuzzy light from the porthole and saw someone older than the boy I had first met, more mature, though unchanged to see him. It was the way he held himself—square shoulders and straight back that suggested newfound confidence, wisdom that hadn't been there before, and the faintest glimmer of manhood.

"You ever read the Bible, sir?"

"Parts, yes."

"You think it's right, sir, with its talk of heaven and Jesus and angels?"

"I don't know," I said. "It would be nice to believe, but…"

We sat alone in my stateroom, the one I shared with Europe and Reid. Because of our color, the Navy had bunked us in separate rooms. Too many for one, they split us up, three apiece, which meant more spacious accommodations than those enjoyed by the majority of the white officers.

"Tell me something, seaman," I said. "Why does my opinion matter to you?"

Marks folded his hands in his lap. "I wondered, sir, that's all. I know you're a smart man, smarter than me, and I wondered if you'd thought on it."

"And?"

"Well," Marks dropped his foot to the floor and leaned forward. "I thought if you believed, what with all you and your people've gone through, then maybe it'd be true. Maybe if God can forgive like the Bible says, maybe there's hope. You know."

"There's always hope," I lied.

"But is there hope of forgiveness?"

I looked at Marks again. It wasn't maturity that showed in his visage, but the stoicism of one scarred by faith. The straight back and square shoulders those of a man who carried the burden of doubt, and guilt, in solitude, prideful. I stared at my young friend and wondered what had moved this boy from cheery naiveté to tragic remorse.

"If there's no god," I said, "there's no need of forgiveness."

"But if there's a god?"

"Then I don't know.

Marks put his hands on the bed and rolled on the edge, forward and back. "What do you think, though, sir? You've surely thought on it, and I'm interested in what you concluded, sir. It would be a mighty big help if you could, well, enlighten me."

"Enlighten you, or forgive you?"

"What about murder, sir?" Marks said, deflecting. "Don't that need forgiving whether there's a god or not?"

"You didn't murder someone, did you?"

"No, sir," Marks pushed up on the bed so his back rested against the bulkhead. "I know a guy, works in the mess. He talks about some things, sir, and he seems to think forgiveness is a matter of color, kind of the way you talked before. If a white man does something, he's more like to forgive than if a Negro does it."

"It's not uncommon," I said.

"But if there's a god, why'd he care about color? Seems to me it doesn't matter if a man that kills another is black or white, he's still got to pay whether you believe in god or…like them soldiers you talked about, that regiment in Cuba. Why does it matter who does wrong, so long as they take an equal lashing?"

The word connoted blood and screams and anguish without cause.

"What do you want to know, seaman? You spoke of God and the Bible, of forgiveness and prejudice. What is it in all of that, what is it that makes you ask?"

Marks lifted his jumper from the bed. He reached to a pocket and retrieved a small black book marked with a cross, stamped in gold on the front cover. I watched him open to a dog-eared page and run an oil-blackened finger along the text. He stopped midway and read a verse in silence to himself before he closed the book again. It took him some time, his face turned down, before he set the book aside. When he looked up, the muscles in his jaw clenched—twitchy bunches of sinew—and he met my eyes with a determination that belied his callow origin.

"This book," he said, "it isn't true, is it?"

I shook my head.

"My mother gave this to me. She starved herself for near a month to save the money for it. She insisted, though, that I needed god's word on my person if I intended to go to war. Said the family Bible was too big to carry. She gave it to me as she's cryin' and made me promise to read it, kissed me on the cheek when she said goodbye."

I closed my eyes against the knotted mass that churned my stomach. Every movement of the ship beneath me translated into a surge of bile and acid. I refused to budge, however, for I felt that to interrupt Marks, no matter how desperate my belly's protests, would disrespect our friendship and would destroy the attitude of confession that hung in the air between us.

"What I did ain't no crime."

I said nothing as Marks threw the Bible across the room. It hit the bulkhead and dropped to the floor. Bent pages forced the book open on its spine, its arms wide, resigned, a lamb to the proverbial slaughter.

"I'm sorry, sir. This isn't something to bother you with," Marks stood and donned his jumper. "I'll leave you be, the way I shoulda done."

As I watched him cross to the door and reach for the latch, I felt a surge of compassion, an emotion I'd thought long foreign to my constitution, and though I did not know what sin he had committed, Marks was a white man who possessed a trait most often recessive in his race: an open mind. For this, if not for any other reason, I decided he deserved some measure of comfort.

"There's more to the story," I said.

"Sir?"

"The Twenty-Fourth Infantry," I said. "There's more that I didn't tell you."

Marks kept his hand on the latch.

"I want to tell you the truth, seaman, for what that's worth. I want you to understand."

Marks dropped his hand to his side. He didn't move to the bed but remained at the door, a skinny boy on the brink and wary—oh so wary—to step out. Scared and alone.

It was not that my story, or rather the story of the Twenty-Fourth, would help Seaman Marks, it was that he deserved to know. He had entrusted me with an intimate secret, a private portion of his soul, and it was my turn. I would do the same. I would bare my pain and lay vulnerable. My jugular exposed. It was the way of friendship, they said, to risk a little in turn, take a step farther into the unknown, and hope the other didn't break your heart. It was the way of friendship, or so they said.

"Shortly before we embarked, the army condemned thirteen Negroes to death," I said. "A fair exchange for the fifteen civilians left dead last August, almost one-to-one a black for a white…it started in Houston. A pair of local police, rednecked bigots…two officers detained a Negress. They beat her some, the papers reported, and a passing soldier from the Twenty-Fourth Infantry interfered—intervened. For his trouble, the officers turned their batons on his head and dragged him to the nearby lockup.

"Another soldier, Charles Baltimore, heard tell of the morning's fracas and went in search of his fellow. None too shy with their weapons, the officers felt Baltimore's questions out of place for a properly subdued Negro man. They beat him for his uppity manner. When Baltimore ran and hid, they found him and locked him next to the first soldier."

"I've heard this," Marks said softly. "The Houston riot."

I folded my hands between my knees and looked to the steel deck beneath my feet. Shamed by my race. "A hundred and fifty soldiers took to the street, armed with Springfield rifles, enraged. The police had killed Baltimore, they thought. The whites had formed a lynch mob and were marching to the fort, they thought. If we don't do something, they'll kill us all, they thought. They thought. They didn't stop to check. They didn't bother to ask. They just grabbed their guns and marched on Houston and let loose their ire. One hundred and fifty foolish, frightened men who happened to be Negroes. Reaction without reason. They killed nineteen people that afternoon. Four soldiers. Fifteen civilians. Nineteen people dead."

"Thou shalt not murder," Marks whispered.

I looked up at Marks. He faced me now, and his eyes met mine. Blue eyes. It is rare, if ever, that I have seen eyes as blue as his, so blue that you wanted to look away but couldn't bring yourself to do it. They entrapped you. An ocean raged in their depths, a sky and eternity, too.

"Who murdered? The soldiers of the Twenty-Fourth who killed, mistakenly afraid for their lives, or the army who kills them back? Who murdered whom?"

"It doesn't matter," Marks said. "It's not true."

"No, it's not."

Marks' gaze shifted, away. "Good luck, sir."

Before I could respond, he lifted the latch and stepped from the room. Behind him, the door swung closed.

I waited for him to open it again, a change of mind, all a mistake, and retrieve the book from its place on the floor. When he didn't, I crossed the room and knelt at the wall. I lifted the small Bible in my hands and returned to my bed. I felt the mottled leather with my fingers and flipped through the crumpled pages. King James. Except for an occasional dog-ear, the book bore little evidence of Marks's ownership. On the front page, though, an inscription:

Jonas,
I love you, and God loves you too. If you remember that, He'll keep you.
Love,
Mom

I closed the book. This belonged to Marks, not to me. I would keep it safe should he change his mind. I owed him that, my friend. Yes, I would keep it safe should he find me someday and ask after it, that little Bible his mother had given him and that he had thrown away in a fit of doubt. Silly, he would say. Silly to throw it out. And I would agree and laugh as I pulled the, by then, tattered tome from a pocket. I knew you would change your mind so I kept it safe, for you, my friend. Across Europe and back just for you.

New York, New York, USA

December 1, 1919

A watch sits on my desk. Early Elgin, the casing is crimped, the cogs clogged and the time it keeps progressively late. When closed, you can see a scene in the gold, a sky with half-moon and stars.

The pocket watch sits atop a book on my desk. The book is a Bible. The leather cover is ripped, the pages stained brown by mud. The gold leaf is gone. I read it once, over there, but I don't anymore. I can't stand the smell of blood and death and waste that emanates from the pulpy pages. It is a reminder of things I'd rather forget, and of things I never will. It is become a keepsake, nothing more, a bequest for an heir undetermined, the remaining detritus of a life so far wasted. The failure of accomplishment not in the effort, but in the goal, adrift without a properly tuned chronometer.

***

Dear Mr. Ayers,

Thank you for your kind words about my son. It is too infrequent that a mother hears good things said of her children. I wish in return I had good things to say to you, but I am afraid the good Lord has seen fit to make life otherwise. You inquired after Jonas and I wish more than anything I could tell you good things about his fate, but the war consumed him as it consumed so many others, too young and too innocent.

After you met him on the Pocahontas, *he made one more crossing before he transferred to St Nazaire. There he worked on repair teams and fixed ships in port. I'm not sure how long he was there before he made his decision, but sometime in February or March of 1918, he left his post without permission. Somehow, he made it to Paris. The army found him living with a group of young men there, in someplace called Marais. The army men who spoke with me seemed to make a big deal of this, but I didn't understand and I wasn't prepared to ask more questions, not after what they told me.*

When the army found him they sent him back to the United States for a court-martial. They put him on a ship called City of Athens *with a group of Marines and some French sailors. Before the ship arrived, though, it was struck by a French ship called La Gloire and it sank in a matter of minutes off the Delaware coast. Over sixty people died in the accident and, according to the military men who came, my Jonas was counted in that number. He died within miles of home on May 1, 1918.*

I'm sorry to be the one to share this unfortunate news. You seem a good man and I hope you have fared better than my Jonas.

Sincerely,
Josephine Marks

***

"It's a matter of honor," I slapped the bar.

The girl next to me wore her hair straight and her dress curled. A red sequined number that clung to her shoulders and traced ample breasts. She came with the bar, and so long as I carried her tab, she'd sit close and whisper agreement. Any more than that would require a down payment and a discreet exit, ten dollars.

I pointed to my glass. "Not a year gone by and the entire country's forgotten what we did. It's all about the Reds now. As if we need another enemy to fight. You would think the bastards would take a moment and reward the men who fought before casting them into another godforsaken war."

"Gosh, you'd think so, wouldn't you?"

I watched the keep grab a bottle and top my scotch-liquid anesthetic.

"It's not even a real war. It's about ideas, ideologies, religion. It's a cold war led by the likes of Mrs. Stuyvesant-Fish and her four hundred. And you know why? It's because they can't be bothered to look out their gilded windows and see what life looks like for the rest of us. They agitate against labor unions at the same time they squeeze workers for every last cent. We can't give you more pay or better conditions because then we'd lose our precious profits. And when the man on the street gets upset because he can't afford food for his family, the high and mighty worry about their stock dividends. It's their own fault this country's up in arms. Bull, is what I say, bull.

"It's not even about me," I said. "I'm no one, a mistake really, but I know of others who deserved more."

"Oh?"

I tipped more scotch down my neck. "I served with some of the best men this city could offer. I watched them charge across no man's land, hell, I..."

"It's okay," the girl said.

She put a hand on mine. It was soft, like silk, and I felt a thrill of memory run straight to my loins. I looked at her face, saw harsh lines and the frozen gaze that filled my nightmares. The dead and dying, the casualties, the victims. Everywhere. They followed me even here, dead soldiers staring from the vacant eyes of a taxi-girl.

"I'm writing a confession," I said. "A book of sorts."

The girl ran her fingers up my arm. "What about?"

"One of the men I knew."

"Was this man as handsome as you?"

I pulled away.

"Hey, it's okay, I'm sorry, really, I didn't mean it."

I grabbed my scotch and crossed to the back room where I could watch the couples move about the floor, their bodies bopped and swayed in imitation of the Castles, or whomever else held the public's fancy. A skinny Negro sat at the piano. He rolled his hands up and down the keys, shrugged and nodded, and tapped his feet to the beat. It *was* a foxtrot, one of the castle's dances. I didn't recognize the music. It sounded like something Will Cook would write, but I wasn't sure. It wasn't Europe.

"What gives?" the girl said.

I felt her hand on my arm.

"We're done," I said.

"But—"

I retrieved my wallet and one of my last Hamiltons. I handed her the bill and rushed to the door. Down the rickety stairs, past the Chinaman, out to the street. The fresh air hit me, then, and everything came out at once. Chop-suey and booze in the gutter.

Brest, France

Tuesday, January 1, 1918

Parade rest, stay in formation, wait. Rows of black men spewed from the tender onto the quay, green uniforms with flappy pants and chevrons on their sleeves crowded on concrete, solid ground, unswayable. Fall in. Don't dawdle. Ignore the Mademoiselles, they'll give you the clap as sure as red-blooded American cunt.

One of the few horn players, a trombonist, warmed his mouthpiece under an arm. Short, squat, and ugly, he glared at the men as they marched past.

Cold. Brest in a word.

White buildings rose in the distance, three, four, five stories. Big boxy things with ornate iron grills, carved crowns, balconies. Each one a city block, pause, then another. A view of a street became one unbroken building diminished to the vanishing point. Perspective on the horizon. As if the government saw Caillebotte's impressions and contracted the military to build his *Paris Street; Rainy Day*.

French soldiers lazed about on the quay. They stood, tasks abandoned, some with containers at their feet and watched as the Negro troops disgorged, companies unending, a stream of black manhood never before assembled on European soil. Harlem has arrived, the 15th New York Infantry, colored, come to France. A few civilians taking their morning strolls stopped at the interruption and gaped from the cliff top at the spectacle below.

Cacophony as the band tuned.

Jim Europe joked with Noble Sissle.

Colonel Hayward, Captain Little and the command staff, white men all, watched from the side, not sure yet whether to smile or glower.

Unloading continued.

Le Chateau de Brest towered either side of the River Penfeld, ramparts erected to guard against invaders. The bulk of the structure set on the east. A red bridge extended to the west. The water that flowed beneath it looked as cold as the ocean. Icy blue. Nothing warm about this place.

"Pretty here," a voice said behind me, one of my men.

"Cold though," another, Private Horace Pippin. "Enough to freeze."

The first, "Damn right. Make you wish for a New York winter, with the mist and snow and all."

"You think there're Germans like they said?"

"Won't know less you hear a shot."

"Like that?"

"Like that, boom, Boche bait."

Welcome to France and happy New Years—now prepare. 1. Keep your eyes and ears open. 2. Keep your mouth shut.

"You think it's that bad?" Pippin now.

"We're in France, aren't we?"

"But for all you know, the Germans could be—"

"Like I said, we in France."

"Don't mean we near no fighting, damn, look at the Frenchies, they don't seem to mind."

"Snipers, sappers, undercover."

"You think they'd look out of a morning, dressed normal, and wander the streets if they had reason to think a bullet could find them?"

"Think what you like."

"But."

"All I'm saying."

"But the Boche."

"All I'm saying."

"I don't think you know better than me."

"We're in France. All I'm saying."

"Lieutenant," Pippin called. "What you think? Them Germans come to meet us?"

I gave it a moment's contemplation, rolled my shoulders, and looked to the sky. "Not today, private. Tomorrow maybe, but not today."

"You sure about that, Lieutenant?"

"Sure as any man recently arrived in France," I said. "Which means about as much as you want it to mean, Pippin."

"Thank you much, sir."

"You're welcome much, Pippin."

A trumpet called attention and faces turned to see Jim Europe, his cover slipped back off his forehead, his round-rimmed glasses aglint in the angled sun, his teeth bared in a grin of anticipation, swing his baton up. Down. Go in three-quarters time. A syncopated anthem. Europe led the band with enthusiasm, a joy, that I had never myself experienced. His eyes opened wide, his arms rose and fell and, in so doing, moved him down to his feet. At times, his grin grew, his smile wide across his face, at others, it would fade and a thoughtful expression settle into place. Jim Europe, bandmaster. Today become the first black man to lead an all-black band on French soil in a ragtime rhythm.

My foot moved *tap, tap, tap* unbidden to the beat. Infected. Stricken by the music.

Ba da ba ba ba da ba da ba.

The melody rang familiar, a classic hidden in the syncopation. White, red, and blue. Up and down and all around. Fast the drums, tight the guitars, mellow the horns. Magic.

Men in the band danced as they played, quick steps, stomp, stomp, their shoulders dipped left and right, grooving to it. Others shouted or sang out, their vocal cords an instrument of invention between played notes. Hard now. Soft now. Music moved, an institution transformed, eighty soldiers now, eighty performers alive in their avocation.

Maybe halfway through the song, the French tripped to the tune. The Marseilles. Their national anthem. It started on the tender. A French swab caught wise and saluted smartly. Men on the quay saw it then and stood straight, mouths wagged, salute. Up to the cliff at last, where locals, unbound by military strictures, pointed and whispered, and shook their heads. What have the Americans done to our…then it was over. Silence but for the distant ships in the harbor.

Jim Europe lowered his baton to his thigh. He turned to the scattered audience, lifted his hat, and bowed low. When he stood upright again, the cheers fell from the heights and catcalls echoed over the quay. Europe smiled and spun back to *his* band. He called a tune. Sissle repeated. Memphis Blues hit the air.

Forward March!

Left, right, left, right we stepped up the quay and past the Chateau. The wind cut through our uniforms and threatened to freeze our toes. On up the hill, past white blocks of apartments, glimpses of a cathedral in the distance. Follow the harbor to the Gare de Brest—a low slung building inadequate for this sudden inundation. Ignore the facilities, men. Load up. Forty to a car, or eight horses, if you've got 'em.

"Where we bound?" Pippin said.

"To kill some Huns," his friend.

"More likely to dig some ditches, right, Lieutenant?"

I laughed. "Military, Pippin. We go where they tell us even when they don't tell us."

"True enough, sir, you think they'll have some hot joe when we get there?"

"Like I said, military."

The whistle sounded and wheels squealed, and the train lurched forward. Where we stop…only Pershing knows.

Harlem, Manhattan

New York, New York, USA
December 7, 1919

Sunday. The last time I set foot in a church was on Armistice Day, a day filled with speeches and remembrances and arguments against Bolshevism. It was a day of war when the people who had already fought wanted nothing more than to remember their lost friends and pray that war never came again. But my church isn't an edifice or structure built of stone and brick, of wood and glass, no, my church is the holy communion of whiskey. I drink it down straight, sometimes sour, but mostly a hearty burn to the throat and a warmth in the belly.

That's my church.

And my confession…that's what I'm working on now. Mrs. Freemaid is kind to me, and my peccadillos and she lets me drink in my room and cry. It's a thing with her, a thing that allows me to forget the sins of my time in the 369th, that thing ineffable yet concrete, liquid in form, and foreign in interest. I know it for my drunkenness. And whenever I feel a moment of pain, of remembrance that feels to overtake me, I think of my confession and my church. Between the two I plan to erase all that happened and all that I did. That is enough, isn't it?

St Nazaire, France

January 2 – February 12, 1918

The train creaked to a stop sometime in the hour before dawn, lanterns cast their light through the slats and illuminated bodies asleep, forty men slumped over bags, kits, and straw rolled forward and back again. I retrieved my father's watch and squinted to see the face of it in the checkered light. Oh, four-thirty. Eighteen hours on this iron horse and nothing but the threat of frostbite to show for it. The frozen air that swept through windows and walls chilled the bones. Only a song, and only in fits, survived our passage through France.

My Lord done smite them Canaanites,
My Lord done smite yon Jericho,
My Lord done smite ol' Gomorrah, too,
So I gotta live'a the good news,
Lest my Lord go n' smite you know who.

Shouts echoed from the front of the train. Boots scuffled, jumped from the sidings, weight shifted and shook the cars. Men coughed, cursed, and whistled.

"We're here."

"Where's here?"

"Hell if I know. Here's here."

"They got coffee."

That moved me, and most of K company too. We scampered to our feet, gathered our gear, and jumped to the wooden platform. A group of soldiers stood close to the station next to a table. They held out kettle pots, dark metal canisters filled with warmed coffee. We extended our cups eagerly and downed it fast, as soon as it reached the brim. Lukewarm plenty hot enough to dull the chill.

"Where we land?"

"St Nazaire," one of the men pointed to a sign.

"Where the hell's that?"

"France."

"Good God."

"How close?"

"They wouldn't put us on the front without warning, would they?"

"It's the army."

"Yes."

"Shit. Give me a gun at least."

"Shoot me if it means I can dream without moving."

"Solid ground."

"I could sleep for a week."

"Amen."

"I just wanna get where we're going."

"'s anticipation."

"Think we can get seconds on coffee."

"Form up."

"Shit. We gotta march."

Two miles, gear in tow, through a muddy swamp to camp. To ward off the chill, they said, like a pack of horses just galloped. Up a steady slope to our new home. Barracks. Fallout quick. Oh five-thirty. Late reveille at oh ten hundred. Get as much shut-eye as you can 'cause you're on Uncle Sam's time now and he's got plans for you.

***

Not until after breakfast, groggy and wet, did it sink in, our designation. Line of Communication. Hard labor. Gruntwork. Pick and shovel. Slogging. Ditches and dams. We had escaped Camp Wadsworth and survived an ocean crossing to work, not to fight. Less than twenty-four hours on the continent and morale took a dive, Olympic deep.

***

St Nazaire is silent, now, in my memory. I know this is a lie, for I know what sounds should populate that portion of my past. Songs and music, the attempts of men to keep hope; mud sloshing, slurping, mucking; metal's ring against concrete and stones; laughter, anger, frustration; rain. I know what should exist, and for the knowing, miss it. I cannot explain its absence, only acknowledge the gap and fill it with other details.

I'm on a hill, maybe two, three miles northwest of the village proper. This is where the hospital will be, its facilities still under construction, wood and plaster, and steel that clasp the sky in half-formed fingers. The completion of which, vital to the war. Necessary to Pershing's plans. A base for injured Doughboys, a way station before the crossing. I stand on the edge of the worksite and stare down at St Nazaire below and see a town evolved from the sea. A crescent of life at the mouth of the Loire. Churches, apartments, offices all grown from the beach. This is a gradual slope that sweeps from the ocean to my hilltop. No cliffs here, no châteaux to guard the coast. Only a port wide open to the waters of the Atlantic.

***

The engineers in charge of 'fixing' St Nazaire assigned us across a swath of territory nearly the size of Manhattan. Some helped with the construction of the hospital, others dredged a swamp at Montois, others laid rail to expedite the movement of war materiel. Storehouses, too. We erected miles and miles of storehouses. And the dam. A diversion three kilometers upriver from our barracks. Every morning, we trudged to our assigned posts, spent the day up to our hips in mud and at night, trudged back.

After washing away the muck, we spent an hour in drill, stiff and depressed, under the watchful eye of Colonel Hayward, Adjutant Captain Little and the rest of the headquarters company. They organized a competition and offered a daily medal to the winner: the soldier with the cleanest, crispest uniform. I never won. I didn't care. I knew better. The crease in my uniform pant would not matter if we, by chance, saw action. The only thing that really mattered was the one thing we weren't given, experience.

***

The band played us home. Each night, they marched to the dam and played us back to our barracks. Each morning, they would escort us out again. In between, they wandered the worksites in an effort to cheer the regiment and help us forget the war we would never see first-hand. An upbeat tune, always an enthusiastic beat; *Army Blues*; the music lively enough to hide the band's own despair.

"We did good today," a deep voice boomed from behind, Jim Europe.

"Sure," I said, unconvinced.

I heard his heavy footsteps accelerate, *slish slosh* in the mud until he drew even. Each step would slide a few inches until the heels of our boots grabbed hold and kept us upright. It wasn't raining now, though it had earlier, and the gray clouds remained to diminish the sun as it sank beyond the waves.

"Why do you do it, each day?" I said. "You could stay with the band."

"I'm not going to shirk my duties."

"Your duties are to—"

"I've got a command to consider. How would it look if I took the easy way out? No. I'm not going to let my men see their lieutenant shy from a little manual labor. Besides, wait a minute, do you see Sissle?"

I looked through the mist at the band, tried to see through the rows of soldiers and instruments. Searched for the narrow frame of Europe's friend. Found nothing. Sissle was not in his place as drum major.

"Sissle's not there," I said.

I followed Europe round the edge of the band. No more *Army Blues*, but now a ragtime piece, something by Will Cook, or the Johnson brothers. Europe moved close so he could talk to Sergeant Thompson—Sissle's stand-in. I stayed to the side, marching on the shoulder, keeping pace as Europe spoke with the drum major.

"Influenza," Europe said when he re-joined me. "Sissle's got the flu."

***

"Hello, from a friend," I said.

Sissle hadn't heard me, his fever too strong to allow something as energy-consuming as alertness. I touched his arm, shook his shoulder, and raised my voice, "Sissle."

He jerked in his bed and slowly turned his head. Not a big man, Sissle swam in the sheets, drowned by antiseptic recuperation. His cheekbones, always prominent, jabbed at his skin. His chin jutted toward his chest and his eyes clawed at the sky as if to escape their sockets, skin receded, flesh consumed by sickness.

"Ayers?" he said and struggled to free his arm from the sheets.

"Don't," I said.

Sissle looked at me, then, and took a breath. Sweat beaded his brow and dripped from his cheeks. His eyes glazed and he seemed half-mad from fever. "How…why…"

"I caught your bug in the south. Medics figure it's safe for me to visit. Some talk of immunity and physiology and such. Don't ask me more than that because it's not my specialty, just be glad of the company."

"Jim?"

"He says hello."

We were alone, effectively, despite the rows of beds filled with men. No one noticed us, each man immersed in his own suffering, sick from the crossing, from the mud, from malnutrition.

"Why did you?" I said. Stricken by a sudden melancholic curiosity. "Why did you sign up?"

Sissle coughed and leaned forward. "Could you?"

"Of course," I adjusted his pillow.

"Jim," Sissle said.

"I'm sorry?"

"Jim. He's the reason I joined. Fucking Jim Europe talked me into it with his ideals and his ragtime and his passion."

"You speak as if you resent him."

"I'm sick in the middle of a swamp a thousand miles from home. I'm going to resent."

"Yes."

"The man is a genius and he's right. I'd follow him from Harlem to…hell, I have followed him from Harlem to Hell. It's just—"

"The fever."

Sissle pointed to a glass on the bedside. I handed it to him and he drank deeply, emptied the glass.

"Let me."

I wandered down the ward until I found a sink to refill the glass. The pipes clinked as I opened the tap and the water sputtered. I waited for the flow to come smoothly before I slipped the glass underneath it. When I returned, Sissle followed me with newly alert eyes, sipped his water, and gave it back.

"It was September," Sissle said. "I'd just returned from a gig in New Jersey when Jim storms through the door, all excited to tell me he's just signed up, and that I'm going to sign up too. I give him this look that says he's got some damn fool idea in his head and to turn back and rethink his thoughts before he tries again. Doesn't do me any good. He sits down and proceeds to launch into this speech of his and he won't brook any interruptions, so I listen. Listen to a good man say some important things, and when he's done…I agree with him. I go down and sign my name to the rolls and commit myself to this misadventure."

"How? What did he say? What could he say that would change your mind like that?"

"It's a grand speech."

"I've got time."

Sissle took a moment to consider himself. He took several deep breaths, adjusted the sheet against his breast, and stared for a moment to the window down the ward and the gray mist visible through its drooping portal. After all of this, he spoke, but not as himself. His voice lowered and his back straightened and his entire demeanor became one of authority. It was as if, in his sickness, he had become Jim Europe.

"Now some of the most influential men of our race in Harlem are going to join the regiment, as they realize the moral effect it will have, being promoted, financially, by the biggest men on Wall Street. It will eventually mean a big armory where the young men can have healthful exercise, swimming pools, and athletic training and it will build up the moral and physical Negro manhood of Harlem. But to accomplish these results, the best and most sincere energetic men in the community must get in the move, as there will be a lot of money spent. And you know, the wrong type of persons generally get in the front ranks of these kind of organizations.

"There are always some smart, dishonest fellows, who have plenty—yes, too much time, who hang around and get in some important office where they can graft for money—and those of us who would have too much principle for such, stand back and say we haven't time to spare. Consequently, what happens? The wrong class of men, by their dishonesty and misappropriation of funds, will so disgust those who are contributing financially to the organization, that they will withdraw their funds. And then who would be the sufferers? Nobody but the younger generation. The grafters will have the money, the benefactors will be probably turned against ever contributing any more funds, and who will be to blame? Men like you and me, who sit back and say we have not got time. No, New York cannot afford to lose this great chance for such a strong, powerful institution, for the development of the Negro manhood of Harlem."

"That did it, huh?"

"Apparently," Sissle said. "I think…I think the stronger argument was Jim himself."

"You mean?"

"I think because Jim signed up, I think I joined up because of our friendship. I think I joined up because I wanted to stick close to my friend."

I stared at Sissle, at his gaunt visage, "That's a strong bond."

"Jim's a good friend."

***

Dried mud flaked from my boots and shattered against the planed wood floor of the regiment's makeshift headquarters. A simple hut converted for the use; less well accoutered than the tent city of Camp Wadsworth, or Dix, or any before. Not even a closed door able to ward the damp chill of St Nazaire. I envied the band their escape from this swamp, this hell hole, but failed to understand why Colonel Hayward felt it necessary to inform me.

"There's more," the colonel said.

"More?"

He pulled the order from my hand and folded it carefully into an envelope. "It's not written, but I've been told."

"Told?"

Colonel Hayward wiped his brow, damp from the constant humidity, the chilled mist that inflicted the worksites and their surrounds. "This came from important people, lieutenant and I'm not one to make light of such…requests."

"Thus."

"You're to accompany the band to Aix-les-Bains, Lieutenant."

"I'm sorry, sir?"

"You're to accompany the band," the colonel returned the enclosed orders to a pile of papers on his desk then stood to his feet.

I jumped to mine.

"Once you arrive, you're to find a man named Martin, Tuts Martin. You are to report to this man and comply with his orders."

"Tuts Martin?"

"Do you understand, Lieutenant?"

"Yes, sir."

"Very well," Colonel Hayward rubbed his hands together. "The band is scheduled to embark on the morrow."

"Make any necessary arrangements with Captain Little. Good day, lieutenant."

"Sir."

Harlem, New York

New York, USA
December 11–12, 1919

"I'm working with Eubie on a project."

"Musical?"

"A show," Noble Sissle said. "We've heard interest from some people with connections on Broadway."

"Congratulations," I said.

We sat at a small deli down the street from Hammerstein Theatre in midtown. The deli, run by a Jewish fellow from Germany—a fellow whose kin fought in the Lost Battalion—was one of the places that never appeased prejudice, and we ate comfortably amidst white and black patrons, a friendly lunch between old colleagues.

"What's it about?"

Noble adjusted his glasses. "I'd rather not..."

"Sorry," I said. "I don't mean to pry...."

"It's not that, it's—"

"Don't worry about it," I said. I lifted a pickle from my plate and sucked cool vinegar.

Sissle, I still thought of him as Sissle, hadn't changed much in the year since the war. Thin and angled, he still wore the bushy mustache and wire-rimmed glasses. He dressed better—anything a step up from army uniform—and seemed healthier. Otherwise, he was the same man I knew in France, and a good friend of Jim Europe, perhaps the best friend.

"I was jealous of you," I set the pickle down. "I was jealous of the relationship you had with him."

"I knew him longer," Sissle said.

It was a throwaway line, a white lie. One I accepted. "He was a good man."

"He was."

We ate in silence and remembered Jim Europe. He was a legend who would never be given his due, not by most people anyway, not the way he should. Instead...

"You got my letter then?" I broke the silence.

Sissle nodded. "It's commendable, what you're doing."

"It's nothing really. A memoir. If it helps someone remember."

"Exactly."

"But I doubt it will do much."

Sissle placed an envelope on the table. "I wrote this a while back, in France. My impressions of how things...of our trip from St Nazaire to Aix. I don't know if you're writing about that, but you're welcome to use it."

I slid the envelope toward me, hefted it, and slipped it in a pocket. "Thank you. I'm sure it will help."

"I might write something about it, someday."

"You should," I said, sincere.

Sissle pushed his plate to the center of the table. "You'll let me read it when you finish."

"Sure," I said. "I'd be honored."

"I best be off," Sissle said. "I'm meeting Eubie to go over one of our songs. He wants to call it 'Harry Mania,' but the lyrics don't go that way."

"What do you want to call it?"

"I want to follow the lyrics. 'I'm just wild about Harry, and he's just wild about me.'"

"I'm Just Wild About Harry?"

"That's what I'm after."

"I'm sure you'll figure it out."

***

Trinity Park, third of the church's cemeteries on Manhattan Island, was a two-block swath of grass and death and flowers in the mid-50s, uptown. Just off the Hudson, it served an elite clientele, white and wealthy, the only Negroes allowed caretakers and mournful servants. The cemetery cum park harked more to Victorian gardens rather than the dour graveyards of early Protestant America. Appearances important even in death.

I moved slowly among the headstones, monuments, and tombs. I read each name and the inscriptions left by survivors. My silent invocations enough to revive the memory of the dead. Loving mother and wife. Exemplar. For eternity, we remember. Love. A noble in the eyes of God. Goodbye for now. We shall meet on the last day. Etc. Etc. I shuffled west, toward the Hudson, searching for a name, knowing full well where to find it.

"Reuben?"

I looked up at the voice, distracted from my momentary communal with Iris McGeogh, *Taken before her time*. Two rows up, a lanky brunette hunched beside a tombstone, flowers in hand. She wore a fur coat against the chill and the thin layer of snow that had brushed Manhattan just before dawn. Her cheeks were red, her face unchanged, and her body…I could only imagine.

"Allie?"

"Reuben Ayers," she set the flowers on the grave and stood to her full, not inconsiderable, height. "I haven't seen you since—"

"You haven't changed," I said.

"Thank you."

I moved closer, awed by her presence though she stood still a dozen feet distant. She stood nearly as tall as me, and the fur coat did little to hide the curve of her thighs. I felt my loins stir and fought the memories of our time together. She was still beautiful.

"It's your…" I pointed to the headstone.

She smiled, a sad little upturn of her mouth. "The anniversary, yes."

"I completely forgot," I stepped closer. "I'm sorry."

"It's not your fault."

I pointed over my shoulder, vaguely. "I have a friend from the war, he…"

"I'm sorry."

"It's cold. What do you say we find somewhere warm to sit down? I'll buy you some cocoa and we can—"

"I'm married," she raised her hand to display a simple gold band.

"Friends," I said. "That's all. I'm curious about you, about what happened after…you know, and I want to hear about this husband. Make sure he treats you better than I did. Come on."

Allie took a moment more at her father's grave, whispered something I couldn't hear, then looked me in the eye. I held her gaze, unflinching, and smiled.

"Friends only?"

"Nothing expected, nothing at all. Hell, if it'll make you feel safer, you can buy your own cocoa."

***

I blew on my coffee, "You still have a sweet tooth."

"Insatiable."

I smiled. It had been too long since I'd sat like this, in a quiet place, alone with my girl.

"You still like those caramels with the nuts?"

Allie brushed a lock of hair from her temple. It was short, bobbed in the style, but still long enough for her bangs to fall forward almost to her eyes. I didn't like the bob on every woman, but on Allie…it worked.

"Chocolate sprinkles."

"Always the chocolate," I said.

"You know what I like."

"I did," I set my mug on the table. "But that was a few years past. What you like now, that's what interests me? What did it take for this fellow to marry you?"

Allie took another sip of her hot chocolate. When she pulled the cup away, it left milk on her upper lip and her tongue snaked to lick the froth away.

Her tongue…

The thought was enough to affect me physically and I felt the pressure between my legs. I shifted in my seat and pulled the coffee close. I took a breath and tried not to think of Allie naked beneath me, trembling, skin aglow, flesh warm.

It didn't work.

"He's a mason, a member of the local. He works hard but he's a good man and, I think, he loves me."

I focused on her face, on the shape of it, the curves, the body. She was sensuality in full, every part of her enough to excite me, to push my grasp on civility, to arouse my animal self and consume me.

Another breath, heavy this time. "I'm glad for you."

"Thank you."

A pan fell in the back and uncooked pastries splattered on the floor. The baker cursed and kicked the pan, clanking and skittering, into a counter pylon. I glanced over my shoulder. It was the same man who had sold us our drinks, a pudgy fellow who waddled more than walked. On his knees, his hands busy gathering his spilled dough, he looked up and saw me. For a moment, we held the connection before he offered a chagrined smirk, his pebbled face turned sour in apology.

I thought of Allie's husband and wondered if he deserved her the way I deserved her. I had been a fool to let fate have any say in our relationship, but that was who I was then, a fool untouched by war and given to the whims of others, those men who held my future in their hands. This had been a mistake, I knew, but not one I could easily remedy. Though now…the same fate that had stolen Allie from me once, now felt to change its fickle temper and bestow one chance more.

"I'm sorry," I said, my voice caught up in the thought. "I'm sorry for what…happened."

"What happened, or what you did?"

I sipped my coffee. "For what happened."

Allie nodded, her lips pulled tight and her cheeks receded into the red blush of winter. "I'm glad for you."

"I didn't understand, then…"

"And you do now?"

"Yes."

"You've learned so much from your time in Europe, your fighting and your war."

"It's not—"

"I'm glad we had this chance to visit, Reuben," Allie touched her cocoa cup. "I need to be going."

"Wait."

"Look," Allie said. "I appreciate the apology, but I can't give you what you want."

"What do I want?"

She didn't need to answer. She knew it, I knew it. So, she stared at me, the lines of her face taut and lean.

I broke off and looked at my half-drunk latte, the milk still mixed unevenly, cream and brown streaked in swirls of caffeine, symbolic juxtaposition. I felt my blood surge. Black and white spots flashed in my sight. I took a deep breath. It did nothing. I took another. Still, the pulse thick and steady in my head. Pounding, pounding, pounding on. I lifted the mug to my mouth, the muscles in my arm strained so tightly that my hand shook. I took it all down, my coffee, and ignored the threshold of pain that grew ever nearer as the liquid threatened to burn. I needed the pain, the reminder of my humanity, of the things I couldn't control, no matter how much I wanted to.

Finally, I let my voice creak from my throat in a low growl that verged on subsonic, "Fuck you."

"You did, Reuben," Allie pulled her purse to her chest and stood up. She stepped around her chair and then leaned forward over the table, one lithe hand extended accusingly. "You fucked me once and I'll be damned if I let you do it again."

A minute later, I followed her into the storm.

***

She leaned into the snow, a dark scythe through the white blizzard, thin and straight as she took each step, her petite boots sunk in the increasing pack. She stopped at the corner and glanced up and down the intersection. It was empty. Only a lonely cab crunched through the snow, slowed and when she waved it on, kept going.

A block back, I began to wonder if perhaps I should catch up and offer my assistance in navigating the storm, apologize and make good, but when she turned south on Third Avenue, I figured she was on course for the El and would soon find refuge on the station platform. No need for chivalry, in that case. So, I remained a shadow, a black shape trailing behind his prey in the whiteness of the street.

It was her grace which still attracted me. It suffused her every action, the way her hands rested on her lap, the way she tilted her head to listen, the way her hips bounced just so when she walked across a room, and the style with which she attired her physicality. I could see it even now, bundled in her thick coat and hidden from sight.

It was jealousy that drove me to follow her. Jealousy that she had recovered from my mistakes and found her way to happiness. Jealousy that she had found a husband who somehow made her happy when I could not. Jealousy that a white man stole this gem from me and kept her chastity to himself. What I intended to do with this jealousy, I did not know, but it motivated my efforts and gave me the power to brave the storm.

Just north of the station, she stopped to let a trolley pass, empty of all but a pair of brave vagabonds, before she hurried across the otherwise abandoned intersection and climbed the platform, three stories up, to the el.

The 149th Street station had two island platforms where patrons waited for the trains. The station house was small, and of more importance, closed. Only the two islands remained open for patrons in the storm. These platforms were narrow, only a dozen feet from rails to railing, and were covered by an equally narrow wooden pavilion. A handful of signs stood along the edges, farthest from the rails, with handbills and schedules and maps.

I maintained my place on the landing below, a half dozen steps from the platform's edge, to wait for the train to arrive. I didn't dare move closer lest Allie spy me and catch me out. I was not a stalker, but I couldn't think of another word to describe my actions. I had followed her several blocks and intended to follow her on the train, to discover her new home and maybe…

Not for the first time, I contemplated the possibility that I was a fool and that my foolishness verged on stupidity. If Allie caught me, she could cry the alarm, and in a moment, I would be surrounded by angry white men happy to lynch a black man, especially one who was stalking a white woman. The realization did little to deter me, though I waited alone and huddled against the cold, I looked up through the steps and saw the back of Allie's head and knew that I would continue in my…foolishness.

I slapped my cheeks—not to break my concentration but to revive my circulation. I was cold. The walk through the frigid streets numbed my extremities, though I could still feel the urgency of Allie's presence, the desire that drew me in her wake. Not even the frozen streets of a Manhattan winter could bank that fire.

I could see up the line, now, and saw four cars in the approaching train, not as many as I would have liked, but it would do. The train jerked, still yards from the platform, slowed, and continued at a crawl. Allie and all the others moved closer to the platform edge.

I allowed myself a tentative step, not ready yet to rush forward, wary of Allie's every movement. It was not too late for her to change her mind, turn suddenly, bolt from the platform. My excuses perched ready in my brain, an easy lie on my tongue should the worst happen. The Third Avenue el ran through Harlem, after all, and I would only ride that far, perhaps chat harmlessly for a few moments and then bid Allie adieu. She didn't, though, do any of these things. Instead, she stood quietly as the train came to a halt and the conductor emerged from the front car.

He wore a double-breasted wool coat and a hexagonal cap on his head. A burly Negro with a hardened belly that pushed the wool into a neat melon shape. He wore a mustache and held an oversized pocket timekeeper in one hand, a chain dangled back to his pocket. He stared down the platform and then rolled his head back, "Third Avenue El, southbound."

It was then I noticed the bolted doors. Only one was open at the front, the same one through which the conductor had emerged. He must have shut the rest against the inclement weather. The discovery froze me where I stood. There was no way to slip on board the train without Allie noticing.

I would not board this train.

I watched her move into the first car and walk through to the second until she found a bench to her liking and eased into it. The shade at her window was open and, as she reached up to close it, her face turned to the platform. Our eyes met.

Even from the distance that divided us, I noticed how her mouth opened slightly and her eyes widened. We stayed locked together, two people in a slow, awkward exchange, as the conductor shouted all aboard and the train squealed its way into sluggish motion. As the cars accelerated away from the station, her head turned back to watch me, her hair matted wet against her forehead, her cheeks flushed, her eyes unblinking. Only when the train turned away and broke our line of sight did I realize that the confusion and fear in Allie's expression gave me a great deal of satisfaction.

***

That night, warmed against the chill by half a bottle of whiskey and accompanied by the memory of Allie's hips ground tight against my own, I opened my trousers and made love with my palm in a solitary haze.

February 15 – March 17, 1918

A E F Savoie Leave Area
Aix-les-Bains and Chambery, France

Not even a week of stale air, stuffy with the funk of men living, sleeping, and eating in the same cramped conditions could quite extinguish the lingering smell of horses that stippled the slats of our rail cars. Day after day the odors intermingled and settled into our nostrils until everything smelled the same. Nearly a week of saturation left even the strongest perfume smelling vaguely of manure and body odor, senses deadened by the overload.

As the last jerking release of steam left the train spent and silent, men rushed to open the doors and breathe the fresh air—to replace the stench of the cars with the fresh, though cold, air of France's mountain resort. Stinging, it quickly filled our car and lifted our spirits. I shared the car with Little and Europe—all of us officers—and we all shared a smiling relief to have finally arrived.

Europe stood at the door, his frame dark against the dimming light. "It's a magnificent view. You two should see it."

Little didn't hesitate, and in a moment, stood beside Europe at the door.

"It's gorgeous. Snow-capped peaks—more than capped. The snow's practically into town."

"You think that's the casino? The one Sothern mentioned?"

"Most likely, lieutenant," Little said.

Europe nodded and retreated into the car to retrieve his pack. "That's a sight to see after a week on this iron monster."

"Lieutenant Ayers, your eyes would benefit from the view."

"Thank you, sir," I said and grabbed my pack. I lifted it onto my shoulders and walked to the door. The train was parked on a siding, away from the platform, and I could see a blue-suited man huffing toward us with a wooden step in his hands. I didn't wait for the step. I bent down, put a hand on the edge of the car, and hopped to the gravel below. The small stones crunched beneath my feet and I started across the yard toward the platform, my eyes down to avoid tripping on a rail.

From the enlisted car, where the band had suffered the week more crowded than sardines, a growing number of men had already emerged. Some of them held their instruments, some their packs, and some both. Many of them wandered in vague circles, carefully stretching their legs and waving their hands for balance—unfamiliar with the task of walking on an unmoving surface, terra firma an almost forgotten experience.

A pair of suited men stood on the platform, smiling figures who, for all the world, appeared overly pleased at our arrival.

"Lieutenant Europe," one of them called over my head. "You've just barely arrived in time."

"You shouldn't be surprised Mr. Ames," Europe said from behind me. "I was late to my own concert at Carnegie Hall."

The two men laughed and I heard the sound of Europe's feet crunching gravel. I stood aside as he passed and then followed to the platform to meet the reason for our trip to Aix, Winthrop Ames, and E H Sothern.

The two men had been tasked with organizing entertainment for the Savoie Leave Area—both of them professional entertainers back in the States—and in the middle of scouting for talent had heard tell of an exceptional musical organization just arrived in France. They promptly visited the regiment in St Nazaire and auditioned the band. Ecstatic at the quality of performance they encountered, they hastily sent a telegram requesting the band be sent to Aix to open the leave area. The posting was to be for two weeks and temporarily placed the Fifteenth Regimental Band under the command of these two thespians.

"Thank god, you've arrived. We've been worried sick."

"Thank you, Mr. Ames," Europe said.

"You'll forgive Winthrop some agitation," Sothern said. "He's been practically fuming that you wouldn't arrive on time. He kept cursing the French railway system. Something about merde and frogs."

"You're our main attraction," Ames said. "And you were equally anxious Ed."

I had seen the two Broadway men from a distance at St Nazaire—when they scouted the band. In New York, Winthrop Ames was a wealthy director who ran his own theatre in midtown. He held a reputation as something of a perfectionist and his current appearance in starched collar, mohair suit, bulged tie, and matching kerchief—not a speck in sight—bolstered that reputation. He stood erect as a stick and spoke with the barest trace of Eton in his voice. He gave the impression of control and left no doubt that all questions should be asked in his direction.

Sothern was a different matter. I had seen his picture in Playbills and advertising on Broadway. I had seen him dressed in simple attire as Hamlet, ornate ruffles as Petruchio in *The Prisoner of Zenda*, and full Elizabethan formal wear as Romeo. Now, he stood distinguished, at nearly sixty, with gray-silver hair waxed in a careful part either side of his head. His face was not terribly distinctive to look at it, though it possessed an eerie talent for expression. It was said he could transition from animated humor to serious contemplation in an instant. With only a minute flexion of the tiniest muscles, he could portray anger or sorrow, terror or pain, tenderness or loss.

"We've put the band in the Hotel Exertier," Ames said. "You should all be quite comfortable there. You'll be spending most of your time, though, in the Grand Cercle Casino Theatre—"

"The domed building?" Europe said.

"That's right."

Over the roof of the Gare de Aix, I could make out the golden dome of the Grand Cercle Casino. It sat atop a grassy hill that was cradled in the midst of the city. On any side, the neoclassical buildings of Aix rose three, four stories, lined up on sloping streets to overlook the bejeweled casino. And as if to emphasize the importance of gambling to the city, even the towering Bugey mountains seemed to focus their white-capped attention on the golden dome, carefully rising above the city like a series of guardians set to protect a gambler's money.

"You'll have most of your work there," Sothern said. "But we have scheduled a few trips down the lake at Chambery."

"The lake?"

"Your train's in the way, but just the other side is the Lac de Bourget. Its waters are rumored to have healed the Caesars. You'll see it soon enough, but first, there's the question of..."

Ames picked up what Sothern dropped. "The parade."

"Yes, the parade."

"At noon tomorrow," Ames said, "the first troops are scheduled to arrive. We have a parade planned. We've a local band who will play first, but after they finish, you'll open the Savoie Leave Area."

"Where's the hotel?" Europe asked.

"We've someone to escort you," Sothern said with a smile. "We're housed there as well."

"Maybe it's best we all rest then, so we can do our best for the troops when they arrive."

"You and your band will determine the success of this venture, lieutenant," Ames said, serious. "I'm sure we don't need to impress the importance of this upon you."

Europe set his glasses a fraction of an inch further up his nose. "There is little I care more about than my music, Mr. Ames. You can expect my…our best, surely the same that I gave the Castles."

"Excellent," Ames said. "Perhaps you can hold a practice in the morning that we might have some idea of what you'll play?"

"You'll have a practice, Mr. Ames, but only if you show me and my men a cup of coffee and a bed that don't move first. I think we'll all be most appreciative for it."

"Consider it done."

***

The Grand Cercle Casino dominated Aix-les-Bains. Not the tallest nor most impressive, it towered by placement, a domed retreat, squat and marble, set upon the central hill's crest. A straight shot from the train station, a gentle slope, rounded hump, fountain, decorative gardens, and then. A grand casino. Play place of Europe's wealthy few. Here was opulence. Stained glass, mosaic-ed, interleaved with gold and precious gems. Baccarat tables, men in tuxedos, roulette. All amplified by gilt-framed mirrors. Chandeliers dangled. Though the ambiance, I imagined, belonged in such a place could not survive intact the meddling hand of the US Army. The tuxedos now were uniforms. Army sanctioned dealers divvied cards, counted chips, and collected on soldiers' bad luck. The glamorous women were absent, the mystique of disgusting fortune gone. Stripped down glamor made functional despite the fit-out.

Crowded now, the first trains arrived and the parade marched, five hundred nay a thousand Doughboys tussled for position, some already despondent, broke and prepared to rely on a comrade's charity for the next seven days. A few sang a verse of *Hinky Dinky Parlez-vous.* Others filtered, wobbly, toward the casino theatre for the evening's main event.

"Fucking amazing this place is."

"But no dames."

"It ain't Paris."

"My uncle served in the Philippines, said they had all the pussy they could get."

"Nice."

"Small gook women. Wild, he said."

"I'd give something to have me a French lady. I don't care if she smells."

"Your girl—"

"We're an ocean away. What she don't know…"

A sudden rush of sound, note upon note, as the trumpet blew assembly faster and jazzier than any trumpet had the right. But more, too, followed as the entire band picked up the refrain and within a measure's distance expanded the daily signal into one of Europe's masterful compositions. A jazz army ready for battle, orders called in ragtime. The inaugural concert of the Savoie Leave Area was about to begin.

***

The theatre felt the clash of green more than any other part of the casino. Ornamented proscenium, gold-leafed garlands, vines carved in wood; curtains that looked dense enough to suffocate a body; gilded newels, banisters, and railing. Three balconies, private boxes, and ample stalls. Nine hundred soldiers; a sea of green uniforms.

I climbed to the highest balcony, to the highest row, and sat in the center to look down at the miniature figures below.

Winthrop Ames marched to the center of the stage. He spoke some words, welcomed the soldiers to the leave area, thanked them for their sacrifice and service, and introduced Sothern. He, in his inimitable theatricality, recited a pair of poems, 'The Highwayman' and 'You Shall not Pass.' He droned, it seemed, in the darkness, but he too passed, and quickly. Ames returned to introduce the 15th New York Regimental Band, Jim Europe conducting. Enter Europe, dressed in his best uniform, clean and crisp, starched razor sharp. He moved with ease, his long legs taking long strides, and raised his baton to silence.

The theatre seemed to contract.

Europe held the baton aloft.

And down.

Music poured forth in a torrent of unfiltered jazzification. One note multiplied sixty times until it filled the theatre with a ragtime exuberance. "Johnnie, get your gun get your gun get your gun." The extra notes filled in by Europe's orchestration drove an excitement through the soldiers. Within three measures, the entire room jumped to its feet. Shouting and hollering and singing. "Johnnie, show the Hun you're the son of a gun. Hoist the flag and let her fly, Yankee Doodle do or die." Energy emanated from the gathered throng. Electric. Power. Jim Europe's military band. "Over there, over there, send the word send the word over there." Mandolins and guitars and percussion boomed with unified intent, not an instrument alike yet together one animal, alive on that stage.

"We'll be over, we're coming over, and we won't come back till it's over, over there."

The last lyrical melody faded and the shouts of the soldiers drowned any remaining notes. Europe's orchestral exit wasted on the ear-shattering fomentation of military might. Soldiers stood on the backs of chairs, covers flew in the air, whistles, catcalls, some even jumped off their chairs from row to row. Green clad monkeys, no longer men. A great arousal of patriotic fervor flowed forth from Europe's baton to enliven the gathered men, galvanize a tired and beaten force, into some multi-vertebrate mob beast that refused to yield until Europe played the song again.

And again.

And again.

***

Bright lights filled the evenings, an hour, two, three in the Casino surrounded by Doughboys. Slap on the back. Chummy. Some from the south brought Mason and Dixon with them, remembered Jim Crow too well and when they saw black…I avoided those as best I could, tried to avoid as many soldiers, found it difficult to succeed completely. Morning and night, I supported the band, towed the line, obeyed Little's orders. Between, I pursued my own agenda, though this too entailed regular exposure to green-clad racists. Problem, this, because my man Tuts Martin worked for the Military Intelligence Division and I knew of no other way to find a military man than by querying other military men. My fate sealed, then, I continued.

"Excuse me."

"Nigger."
"Pardon me."
"Whadda ya want?"
"Do you know a man named Martin?"
"Never heard o' him."
YMCA set up shop, multiple locations, spread across the city. My black skin forbade my entrance so I loitered, arms wrapped tight, breath condensed, hopping, outside the tents, shops and temporary establishments. Snow fell in the mountains. "I'm sorry, sir, do you know a man named Martin."
"Yeah."
"Tuts Martin?"
"Hell no, my man's Carter."
Move on.
At each step, I kept my eyes wide, not for Martin, I didn't know what he might look like, but for women. Thousands of other men had the same idea, I know, and my chances remained slim. My dick, though, not theirs. A few women walked the streets, those who lived or worked in Aix. The army, prior to opening the Leave Area, evacuated any pair that smacked of loose morals. Only three old hags, one whose udders hung to her waist, served a man's needs, at least explicitly. More than once, I sauntered past, saw them seated in aging couches, slack skin, balding, painted. This was the pleasure allowed by an all too puritan country, band performances and sagging breasts. God bless America.

***

Two o'clock. A.M. Rollover. Blink. Wonder why Europe is at the desk, hunched, pen scratching. Don't wonder enough. Pull the pillow over my head. Go back to sleep.

***

Frontpage, front and center, *Stars & Stripes*. Some nameless Doughboy clad in steel-rimmed pan, arms extended, one back, coiled, ball in hand, prepares to pitch. The caption: "The outfield is a-creepin' in to catch the Kaiser's pop, and here's a southpaw twirler with a lot of vim and hop." The image, blurry at best, bled across the pulpy paper.
He's tossed the horsehide far away to plug the hand grenade:
What matter if on muddy grounds this game of war is played?
He'll last through extra innings and he'll hit as well as pitch:
His smoking Texas Leaguers'll make the Fritzies seek the ditch!
I read the lines out for Sissle who laughed easily at the stretched rhymes. Bright laughter, a musician's laugh, filled with meaning and color. Leaned over, he pointed, not to the picture or the poem, but the story to the left, a more important, more personal, more relevant tale. The last headline of four subs, COLORED BAND LEADS TROOPS THROUGH STREETS. I devoured the story in a minute, but disappointed, found only reference to our band twice, and neither time but to say they played. A newspaper indeed. The Fifteenth New York's band was the highlight, the showstopper, the marquee act, and because it consisted of Negros, it was relegated to a mere mention, a passing thought, a clause in a sentence in a two-column story.
"You'd think Jim'd get a little more exposure than 'The colored band, almost at full strength, and led by Europe, repeated its Broadway successes.'"
Sissle crossed the room and grabbed the paper from me. "We've never had any successes on Broadway. God willing, we will, but—"

"You assume journalistic credibility."

"I do."

I gave Sissle time enough to read and continued, "This is, what, the third issue by the same army that refuses to let us fight."

"There should have been something," Sissle said.

"This is a white man's army, Sis," I said. I had long since adopted Europe's familiar nickname for Sissle. "You know that as well as any of us."

"I'd have thought…"

"Thought that America might credit a race that would risk life and limb?"

"They wouldn't ignore us completely."

"This is the United States Army."

"Do you think I should show Jim?" Sissle said.

"He's a better man than I am. He'll see it as a blessing to be mentioned at all."

"It's just."

"He's a good man," I said, "too good sometimes."

Sissle folded the paper. His hands shook, his face red, and tossed the army issued rag on the floor. No disrespect, no hatred, just resignation and disgust; emotions all too familiar. I made no move to retrieve it.

"It's what he wants," Sissle said after a moment. "He wants to use his music to bridge the gap, to bring white and black…to do what Lincoln and Douglas and Washington haven't."

"It's admirable," I said.

"Quixotic."

"I didn't say that."

"But you thought it," Sis said. "Your silence, your pause, suggested as much."

"Perhaps, but not quixotic. Naïve, maybe, intentionally naïve."

Sissle closed his eyes. "Something has to bridge the gap. Something has to bring the races…if not together, then closer."

"Something," I said.

"It's a matter of perspective."

"Desire," I said.

"You think Jim might be right?"

I shrugged, "I can only hope so."

"Me too."

***

Army officials convinced of the band's effectiveness. Extension announced. The band to remain in Aix two more weeks. Standby status until further notice. Continue under command of civilian authority: Over There Theatre League.

***

Chambery, city of cathedrals. Impressive spires mounted the sky, enough to put a man in mind of Rome or some other holy city. A horde of gold thrown at their construction, generations of workers trodden beneath their passage, gone to time as the stone and iron and glass grew into what remained. In the midst of this holy construction, an orphanage. Straight lines, four stories, square, and simple; more beautiful in its practical good than any cathedral spire yet accomplished. Real results for real people, in this life.

The band had set up outside the orphanage, playing in the street where adults and children gathered in excited expectation. Orphans leaned out windows and stood on tiptoes. Some sat on the shoulders of the larger men in the crowd, their bodies swaying softly six feet above the earth.

It was chilly, here, in Chambery, but not like Aix. There was no cold breeze off the lake here. I was cold, but not mortally, my body familiar with cutting winds, snow and all kinds of winter weather. New York preparation enough for the coldest. The cold didn't stop the band, either, and they brought the same enthusiasm as when they played in the warmth of the casino.

In the middle of Sousa's *The Stars and Stripes Forever*, a chubby orphan waddled into the street behind Europe and started waving his pudgy arms left and right, up and down, in imitation of Europe's conducting. The audience chuckled and pointed and watched as the boy spun around, arms in the air. Europe noticed the commotion and stole a glance over his shoulder. He saw the orphan boy but did nothing, his concentration on the performance, on the band. Only when the song drew to its inevitable end, a march in crescendo, big, bigger, biggest, until the cymbals and drums and horns and every instrument cried out in utter unified harmony, did Europe allow himself to react.

As the audience burst into applause, Europe spun around. Sudden and swift. He grabbed the child lightly by the hand and led him to the conductor's post. Confused at first, the child soon yielded to Europe's patient guidance. Europe, unable to speak to the boy in French, made do with body language. He positioned the boy so he stood facing the band and then placed the baton reverently between the boy's chubby fingers. The boy stared at the white stick and slowly realized what was happening. A broad grin spread across his face and he faced the band, baton gripped in his hammy fist. With a smile on his face, Europe stepped back and nodded to the band. As the first note sounded, a clear trumpet call, an excited little boy, red-faced, raised the baton. The band crashed flawlessly into its rendition and the boy waved his arms about gleefully, if not so much meaningfully, as he conducted the performance.

I noticed Jim's foot tapping out an exaggerated beat from where he stood behind the child. Perhaps the band followed his foot, or they simply knew the song well enough to play without Europe's guidance. Either way, they played through, flawless.

Another crash, high horns, finger-snapping good. The child got into it quick, waved his arms wide, imitating flamboyance, uncontrolled enthusiasm. The audience sang along. Caught in the heat of it. The children made a surprising soprano section. And then, in the thrill, some of the rhythm section, deep bass vibrators, joined in, scatting and jibing with all the energy of Harlem behind them. It became an orchestra, a symphony of art, conducted by a child. Once through, twice, three times the band played and the child led, until finally the music reached its last bar and faded into the afternoon's charmed stillness. But only just. A second, two and then cheers and whistles and shouts. A city enthralled. This was a master performer at work—Europe, not the child—to conduct such a spectacular thing with his foot.

When the song ended and the audience burst into cheers, Europe patted the boy's head and retrieved his baton. He then squatted down and gave the boy a proper, eye-to-eye, handshake. Personal congratulations aside, he turned the boy toward the crowd and presented him to the audience. The act elicited another round of cheers. Finally, Jim led the boy back to the edge of the audience and left him there to return to his post before the band. Conductor *de facto* once more. French musical legend born.

***

"What are you doing?" I asked.

Europe blinked, rubbed at his eyes with a fist and turned from the desk. "Writing."

I pushed back the blanket and dropped my feet over the bed. I was stiff, achy sore, the days of hiking interspersed with solitary nothingness took their toll. Plus, the wine. Sissle snored on the carpet. I took a moment to gather myself and stepped over him. Unconscious still, his chest rose and fell in the dim light from Europe's desk lamp. "Why the hell are you writing now? It must be two in the morning."

Europe held several loose sheets of staffed paper in the air. "Arranging. There's this woman, she asked."

"So?"

"Her son wrote it before he went to the front."

"He died."

"And she asked me if the band might play it."

"You said yes."

"How could I refuse."

"You've done this before," I said. Remembering the other late nights. "How many of these?"

"I don't know how many songs. One a night, maybe more. A rough guess is I've written almost three million notes in the last three weeks."

"Three million?"

"It takes a lot of notes to write a score for fifty-plus instruments."

"Shit."

"It's all right."

"But why?"

Europe set his pencil down and rubbed his eyes again. I could see the red irritation of sleeplessness, the bloodshot, the slumping hesitation, drag. I wondered if he could survive this another week, maybe more if the army re-upped our assignment.

"Because I can't not do it," Europe said. "These people…they've accepted us. Welcomed us. No one here knows about Jim Crow or cares. They only know we've come to help and they welcome us. They see us as equals, entertainers, men…and they've lost so much to get to this point. I dare you to look into the eyes of a widow and tell her no. It's impossible. These people need this and I'm going to do what I can to help. If this is all I do over here, I'll go home with a clean conscience and I'll know I made a difference. If nothing else, our race will be remembered in this war for its music."

I stood silent. My eyes wandered across the pages, saw the notes as foreign symbols, alien markings undecipherable. I knew not what the notations might represent, only the results, the music that came from the band day after day. I had heard the dedications, Europe noting this or that person's lost child, this or that sacrifice, but the realization never dawned that to make such music happen required Europe to make this kind of personal sacrifice, to prepare the music for a band of instruments. It was striking, impressive and humbling.

Europe cared enough to give his all for his music, and through his music, for the people of France, for the soldiers and for his race. Here was a man who would give everything to see his music in service to his race. To better all mankind with his gift. A man far better than I could ever claim to be, unabashedly giving while I…while I pursued less lofty aims.

I put a hand on Europe's shoulder. "There's surely a bar still open somewhere. Let me buy you a drink."

***

"It's not that I think classical music isn't important or beautiful, but there's other legitimate art. What we're doing here, for instance, is moving more people than any Mozart symphony…because people have access to it. It's something they can feel and something that affects them. I love Mozart, I was raised studying, but the truth of it, jazz is more fun. Every time we finish a song and I turn around I look out at that audience and I see their enjoyment. It's on their faces. You look out at a concert hall filled with gala dresses and tuxedos and you get stayed boring looks. This music moves people, it moves people in ways that classical music isn't capable of."

Champagne was the only drink available, but we'd already finished our first bottle. I did most of the drinking while Jim sipped at his drink. A man of moderation, another admirable trait.

"I saw the performance at Carnegie Hall."

"Exactly. You saw how black and white sat together in that audience. It was the first time that's happened there. We're crossing the lines drawn by Jim Crow and we're doing it with music."

"You really think."

"The best way, really. Sure, there are other things that need to happen, laws need to change, politicians replaced, but it's the heart and soul that must meet. Laws can only do so much before people's attitudes get in the way, and it's the attitudes that music can change," Europe said. "When we get back, I want to take the band on the road. I want to show the country what we can do with our instruments, with our music. We'll play to desegregated houses and we'll show them. We'll take the country by storm and they won't be able to stop us."

I looked at Europe, at his red eyes, at the hollows beneath, at the determination still evident. "I believe you."

"Not that I think classical music isn't important. I would love nothing more than to lead an orchestra of black men dedicated to the performance of Negro music. It's what we started at Carnegie. It's what our race deserves. There is so much heritage. Spirituals, folk music, ragtime turned jazz, even the classicists have something to contribute. There's more than enough music to keep an orchestra busy."

"What if you…"

"Then so be it. I'll miss my son, and his mother, but I'll have died in a just cause, I'll have died fighting for my race and for my country, and I'll have brought happiness to a lot of people with my music."

I emptied the dregs into my glass and ordered another. A moment later, the French waiter arrived with a bottle and uncorked it into my glass.

"I didn't know you had a son."

"My wife doesn't either," Jim grinned a little, not boastfully, but confidentially, a shared secret, a skeleton let out of the closet for a comrade at arms. "Don't tell her."

I raised my glass. "Not past my lips."

"He's still a fat little thing, just turned one last month. I take care of them both, him and Bessie. Thank God this work has brought in enough money to do that."

"Good for you."

"You know Sis tried to talk me out of this at first, this army gig. Said it was crazy to risk death for a country that wasn't about to do anything for us."

"He actually told me."

"Really?"

"He was feverish at the time. Don't hold it against him."

"I made him join too, he say that? Told him that he couldn't beg off like Eubie. But it's turned out all right. So far, at least. It's been good to have Sis along. Wouldn't be the same without him."

"I imagine."

Europe took another, slow sip.

God, he was taking his time. "You don't drink much, do you?"

"I try to avoid it if I can, at least in large amounts. I've seen some of the things it can do if you let it take control."

"You're a stronger man than I."

"Perhaps, but more likely, it's just experience."

"Maybe," I took a gulp.

Europe smiled, weary, "You'll figure things out."

"If I don't screw things up first," I said. "I've done a lot I'm not too proud of and I hope that maybe, someday, the ends will justify the means."

"It's rarely so."

"That's what worries me. I'm afraid I've started on the wrong foot and now it's too late to go back and start again."

"Change."

"It's not for the weak of heart."

"If you want to enough, you can do it."

"You're a credit to your race, Jim Europe."

"Thank you," Europe finally finished his drink. "And for the drink."

"My pleasure."

"It's an early morning and I've still got some work on that score."

"You're serious."

"I am," Jim stood, "I gave that mother my word."

***

March 14, 1918. Telegraphic Orders. Upon completion of tour in Aix, 15th New York N G Band to ship to Connantre, Department of the Marne. Rejoin parent regiment. Prepare for tasking to front, attachment to French 4th Army, General Gouraud commanding.

***

Grand Cercle Theatre. The band arrayed on stage, the stalls and balconies filled with soldiers, civilians, performers. This was it. The last night for the 15th New York. The final performance of the evening complete. A performance worthy as finale. A band in precision, Negro soldiers, musicians, men on the move. Chests puffed a little more, backs a little straighter, heads a little higher. Tonight was the last night. The last night before we moved, before we became fighters.

As the band lowered their instruments, a man stepped forward, Gerry Reynolds, one of the YMCA representatives in charge. He waved an arm in the air for attention, failed to get it as the applause continued.

A gunny sergeant off stage shouted, "Ten hut."

The majority of the room, already on their feet, snapped rigid, fully alert now. The sudden rush of military discipline spread quickly to the civilians and the room fell quiet.

"As you were."

Reynolds waited for the audience to resume their seats and then spoke, his voice projected to the roof, a veteran of this stage, if not *the* stage. "Ladies and gentlemen of Aix-les-Bains, men of the army, it is my sad duty to announce that we have listened to our last concert by the Band of the 15th New York Infantry. Orders have been received for them to re-join their regiment. Tomorrow, these men, who, for a month, have given us so much pleasure, proceed to the front lines, to serve in the trenches against—"

The bedlam that ensued neared riot proportions. Not a single person in that theatre stayed in their seats. Men jumped up. Louder shouts and applause had yet to reach the rafters of the Grand Cercle Casino Theatre. Whistles, stamped feet, yells from men atop seatbacks. A few intrepid soldiers climbed the balcony, where flags hung as decorations, and tore them from their moorings. These flags, both French and American, then waved back and forth, carried by the soldiers, unfurled as a patriotic witness to the men on that stage. One of the civilian bands who had participated in that evening's entertainment struck a tune, though I only knew this from the puffed faces of the horn players and the frantic gesticulations of the conductor. I could not hear them for the cheers.

Looking back, now, I find myself misty-eyed to think that a handful of musicians could in such a short time earn sufficient respect to prompt such an outpouring. It is heart-wrenching to me, and I wish I had done something to merit inclusion, to have been one of those men on that stage. Not a musician, necessarily, but a man worthy of such adulation, perhaps even just to be an untried yet ready participant in the regiment, unsullied by my sins. Yet, no amount of revisionism can force my way on that stage, or make me worthy to be counted. No, I was not one of them. By their very innocence, they escaped my punishments. Eighty some-odd Negro soldiers, each with a grin on his face that spread from Harlem to the Marne.

***

I was the only one who heard the knock. Europe, exhausted from a month of sleepless nights, was unavailable for conscious considerations. Sissle, always a heavy sleeper so long as the ground didn't move, snored on ignorant of the waking world. I sighed and eased from the bed. The light showed beneath the room door and I carefully moved to open it.

"Reuben Ayers?"

I stared at the man in the hallway. Big. Very big. Really that's the best way to describe him. He reminded me of a secular Santa Klaus, a round mass with legs and arms. His chins extended well down his chest and folds at his wrists sagged almost to his knuckles. Red-nosed, red-cheeked, red all around. This man outdid even the celebrated girth of Taft's belly. It would take two, maybe three bathtubs to heft this fellow. And the yards of linen required to clothe him. I blinked a couple of times, still confused by sleep and not sure of my senses' veracity.

"Who?"

"My name is Tuts Martin."

"Tuts," a moment of thought, forced recognition. Sleep chased away by the name. "Let me get my boots."

***

We walked the streets of Aix. It took only a second of exposure to the chill before my mind cleared and I came fully awake, the last vestiges of sleep gone now, able to consider the possibilities of this surprise interview with Tuts Martin.

"You know I'm with the MID."

"I've been given to understand."

"Then what intelligence do you have to give me?"

I breathed out, let the air crystallize and drift away, watched it melt again. "I'm not sure you know me."

"Reuben Ayers, Lieutenant of the 15th New York National Guard, Tammany crony, social climber, thinks he can trade for influence and support in the organization. Loner."

"As I said, you don't—"

"I don't give a shit what you think or who you are. I have a mission and that mission involves the expected report from you. Now, I've spent the last two weeks undoing the damage you've done here by spreading my name around. Clumsy and crass is what you are. If you'll just tell me what you've found, then maybe we can part ways and forget each other."

"This gets back to Tammany?"

"Everything gets back to Tammany. So long as Wilson's in the White House, the Democrats get a hold of it and waft it Murphy's way."

"Then I get credit."

"I told you, I don't fucking care about your pathetic grasps at power. Tell me about your regiment. What's the situation? Do you comprehend the situation? Or are you too dense to know how to gather useful information."

"Dissatisfied. The men are dissatisfied."

"Why?"

"We've been treated like men by the French, but whenever we run into American troops, they pull Jim Crow. We know the government doesn't care about race issues, but we're here fighting to try to change that. You want to know why they're dissatisfied, tell the military it's because Wilson won't speak up about lynching."

"Endemic?"

"Same way as the color of our skin."

"Anyone in particular who stands out as problematic, more vocal, revolutionary?"

"No."

Tuts Martin stopped a moment, breathed hard, turned toward the lake and the reflections of the mountains cast in the moonlight. "What about Napoleon Marshall? He's created problems in the past."

"He's a hard ass, thinks he's better than everyone else. Not a revolutionary."

"Making trouble?"

"He respects the law. He'll work inside its bounds. No revolutionary there."

"Jim Europe?"

I stopped, then, and stared at the strained face of my contact. He was breathing hard, though we walked downhill. He seemed to have lost color in the chill, though his cheeks now flushed red.

"What about him?" I said.

"What kind of talk does he make?"

"Positive talk. He believes that music is the way to unite the races. He's not violent."

"Socialist?"

"No. No socialism there at all. He's a capitalist for sure, only wants to change people's attitudes on race, not their financial situation."

"I think there's a misunderstanding," Tuts grunted. "You are to give me a report of problems, not a patsy campfire story about how you all get along. Now, tell me what the problems are."

"We're not fighting."

"Excuse me."

"You heard me," I said, growing impatient with the arrogance of this fat white man. "We've come over here to fight the Boche and we've been digging ditches. We're beginning to think that Black Jack's afraid we might actually show him up."

"Black Jack isn't in this."

"He's all about this."

"So, you're saying the regiment is ready for a fight. Like in Spartanburg?"

"What the hell? Are you trying to discredit this regiment?"

"From what I understood, Lieutenant Ayers, that was your job."

"I'm not sure I want it anymore."

Tuts shrugged, maybe, I couldn't tell under all the fat. "We'll be in touch."

***

Little was high on champagne by the time the parade started. Two bottles he'd shared with the proprietor of the de l'Europe, another with the landlady of the Hotel Exertier before we took our first step from the hotel on our march to the train. A wobbly step it was, then, as from nearly the front door, there, to the Gare de Aix-les-Bains, our journey was accompanied by the entire city. Phalanxes of old men, women, and children. Little led, followed a few paces behind by his orderlies, followed fifteen more by the band itself, marching and playing, working its way slowly through the throng.

A squad of police stood ready as we approached the station. Strange hats they wore. Flat-topped affairs. They cleared a path to the train and we marched through it, careful not to tread unknowingly on an innocent's toes until we reached the platform. Ready to depart, though our train was not. The cars—preloaded and prepared for our departure—had yet to be attached. So, the band turned and Jim Europe poised. One last time for the people of Aix-les-Bains.

And then, the clank of connections, the hiss of steam, the noise of yet one more train. We boarded slowly as Little kissed the cheeks of babies and the rest of us looked out at the faces of a city. We had seen these faces over the last month, entertained them and been appreciated by them. For some, the first taste of true equality, a condition we left with difficulty, yet flush with pleasure. Not for the friendship we left, but for the opportunities we approached. After six months of delay, frustration, and stalling, we were for the fight. We would have our chance to prove that Negroes could take it to the Boches as well as any white man. This was our chance. The 15th New York's chance to prove that Negroes can be heroes too.

Manhattan, New York

New York, USA
May 2, 1920

I sat on a bench in Little Italy, off the corner of Carmine and Bedford. I sat with the paper—though I didn't read it—and watched the brownstone apartment catty-corner down the street. From my bench, I could just see the thick oak door of the apartment, the steps and the walk and the windows covered with curtains. It was the apartment of my love, it was the apartment where Allie lived with her husband.

I had yet to catch sight of the man. But I did not sit on a bench so far from Harlem to catch sight of some stranger, no, I came to see Allie.

For months now, I had known her address. A simple task really, to track her down. It took a few days in the library where I trolled through already yellowing back issues of the newspaper in search of the specific announcement: the wedding of so-and-so and Allison Romano. Upon discovery, I took the man's surname, Esposito, and consulted a directory. Her location was easy enough to track down after that.

But I'd done nothing with the information.

Since Prohibition began. It had grown ever more difficult to locate the whiskey I so desperately needed to calm my nerves, nerves that seemed to be overpowering my extremities. I could barely write; my fingers shook so to hold a pen. Several times, my feet caused me to slip down the narrow steps from my room to the main floor below. I was weak. I did not want to see Allie, or for Allie to see me, in such a state. I was a strong and confident Negro and I needed her to see that, not the shivering fool I had become.

Two days ago, I awoke from a nightmare to uncontrollable shaking. A seizure so fierce I nearly bit my tongue in two. It terrified me. I had no idea what was wrong with me and I feared that—if I did not act quickly—I would never be able to see Allie again. So, I rummaged her address and marched here. This bench was as far as I got, though. I was too big a coward to confront her to her face.

Instead, I watched and waited.

In the afternoon, a cab pulled to the curb. The passenger, a thick man with a mane of slicked black hair emerged and entered the apartment. Two minutes later, he returned and stood beside the cab, waiting. A moment later, Allie appeared. I glimpsed her from the distance, her beauty undiminished. Her hair had grown several inches, her dress lost an inch at the hem, and her figure remained as ravishing as I remembered.

What shocked me was the third person.

He emerged from the apartment with his hand in Allie's, his head and body mostly hidden behind her skirts. I watched in curiosity as they reached the sidewalk and began to cross to the cab. Only then did the boy jump ahead. Allie released his hand and the youngster shot forward to hug Esposito. At that moment, when the boy passed between Allie and her husband, I caught full sight of the boy. I could see his skinny frame, his smiling face, and his curly black hair. He looked perfectly normal and happy, except for one thing, he was a Mulatto in Little Italy.

***

I walked slowly, carefully, my eyes focused on the sidewalk beneath my feet. I felt uncertain about my ground as if it might shudder and crack open beneath me. My muscles trembled, tiny tremors that caused me to twitch and jerk with each step. At every intersection, I took my time, stared down at the gutter and the pavement beyond, and saw those six inches as an almost insurmountable chasm. I knew much of this existed in my mind, winding vertigo that had grown over time and made me into a new and uncertain being. Part of it, too, was the realization and the shock of discovery. That boy at Allie's hand, that boy maybe four or five years old, was mine. I did not doubt it. He was my child and Allie…

She kept him secret

It shook me to the core to know this. To think my love could keep this secret so long and so completely. I had a son. True, I had never wanted a child, but the fact, the reality of progeny created in me a sense of responsibility and appreciation that only minutes earlier would have been incomprehensible. My heart ached. My heart ached to have missed his life, to have missed four years of my child's life.

And suddenly, I was angry.

Allie had stolen from me the opportunity, the great opportunity to do better what my own father never did. I had no illusions about my abilities as a parent, no thoughts that I might be the kind of person who would perform his duties impeccably, but to not even be given the chance. To be denied. I wondered what she intended to tell the child. How would she explain his color and my absence? Would she tell a story of a war hero, a man who served his country and died during the war, or would she tell the story of a man who left her in the cold, who refused to love her because of something inside him, a broken piece that prevented him from doing what most normal men could do?

An Austin Twenty turned the corner ahead of me, its long hood and narrow tires bouncing loosely over a pothole. I could hear the engine putter inside its silver cowl, the cylinders firing like bullets from a Chauchat. I watched its progress, the driver behind the windscreen bareheaded and enjoying the late spring air. I turned slowly to follow the car, my mind fixated on the *bang, bang, bang* of the engine, my thoughts enthralled by the memories of Champagne. I continued to stare as the Austin Twenty rolled down Fifth Avenue and changed lanes. When it moved across the street in a left turn, the engine backfired and sent a cloud of smoke and black exhaust from its tailpipe. I froze. I couldn't move. I was in France, literally in the trench, surrounded by men, gun in hand and facing a Boche assault.

March 21 – April 14, 1918

Connantre, Givry-en-Argonne, Noirlieu, Remicourt, Herpont, Auve and Maffrecourt
Champagne Region, France

In the month we'd been in Aix, away from the regiment, Pershing had traded four American regiments to the French Army, a patch on the leaky front to give the French eight thousand men. Instead of compromising his prized First Army and its lily-white pedigree, he sent four Negro regiments. And in some spiteful rage, traded not only our chain of command but our designation as well. No ceremony, no consultation, no consideration. One day, we bore proudly the colors—given us by Governor Dixon—of the 15th New York, the next, we were burdened with some ungodly number, unrepresentative of our volunteer status. It stung, this re-designation. It stung and it baffled and it created in us, in me, a feeling of sudden loss, as though un-numbering disrespected some monumental effort as if Negroes weren't good enough to claim ownership of something so basic as the regiment, the number fifteen too much honor for those dark-skinned niggers.

Thus, weighted with the loss, we stood in a field just off the train, arrayed in neat rows parallel to the tracks. Half a kilometer away, Connantre's barren infrastructure rose from the neglected fields, a clump of buildings constructed from abandoned lumber, pieced together with baling wire, tacks, and military stubbornness. A minor outpost surrounded by mud. The wind blew strong enough to bend what weeds grew in between. Dark clouds poised. The train behind us still sang and croaked as its warm iron shrank in the cool of Northern France. Otherwise, the fields were silent, but silent in an eerie way, filled with menace and waiting to witness a million deaths…to testify of those already passed.

In my mind, I could hear the bombardment of shells and strafing machine-gun fire of the front, but in reality, any noise here translated into a feeling. A stirring of the earth. A tectonic rumble that passed just so into one's toes. Not as much reality as haunting whispers, phantasmagorical hallucinations that might prove tangible come the fall of dark.

Captain Little's figure emerged from the clustered constructs of Connantre. We watched as he marched through the mud. His strong steps and square figure seeming not to struggle in the slightest with the sucking muck. He grew larger and larger and the sloshing of his boots became audible.

"We're part of the Sixteenth Division of the French Fourth Army, it would seem," Little said. "We're to ship to Givry-en-Argonne then march to Norlieu where Colonel Hayward's established regimental headquarters…about ten kilometers they said."

"Sir."

"We're almost there. We may be fighting under a French general, but at least we'll be fighting," Little said.

"The fighting three hundred and sixty-ninth."

"Doesn't quite have the same ring to it, does it?"

***

"I understand you are partially responsible," said Colonel Hayward.

"Sir?"

"For this new posting."

"I'm not sure I…"

I stood in front of Hayward's desk, regimental headquarters an abandoned bakery, an oven to one side. Flour mixed with dirt and charcoal dust.

"This is what I was told."

"That I…"

"That your report, whatever it was, influenced—"

"You were already here before I talked with—"

"I did not say I understood the chronology of it, lieutenant, only that this is what was told me. This I repeat for you because I have been so ordered."

"Sir."

"I don't care if you influenced our new posting here…in fact, I find it somewhat despicable that you are engaged such as you are."

"Sir, I—"

"Let me finish, Ayers."

"Sir."

Colonel Hayward leaned forward in his chair, his physique bursting over the edge of the table. "Every soldier here has their reasons for volunteering. Some of them are here to serve their country, some to serve their race, some for glory, and some for money. I don't know your motives, but from what you've done, I judge them less than altruistic. With over two thousand men in my charge, I cannot afford for you, an officer, to not stand as an example. If you confuse yourself and act in a way that puts my men in danger, then believe me you will face a reckoning and it will be severe."

"Sir."

"Find the quartermaster and report to your Battalion commander. Third Battalion's stationed in Remicourt. You should be able to make it before dark."

***

Springfield Rifles, gone. Hefty knife-like bayonets, powerful and versatile, gone. American canteens, gone. Mess kits, gone. All of it gone but for the uniforms. American Army green allowed to remain, though the helmets…gone. Replaced with French issue. French kits. French Lebel Rifles. French ammunition. French bayonets, long rapier things that looked as if they might stick a man and never come loose. French issue. Now, a French unit our supply chain also became French and our equipment, thus, required compatibility. The hand that feeds now held a baguette.

***

Four days later, the regiment moved north to Herpont, in the advanced zone.

***

Zero five thirty hours, "Réveillez-vous, réveillez-vous, réveillez-vous."

Zero six thirty hours, we gathered for mess.

Zero seven hundred hours. To the fields. Abandoned trenches, winding things, become our home. Hunker, duck, crawl.

"The trowel is your best friend. You will use the trowel to strengthen your trench. You will use the trowel to dig new positions. You will use the trowel to reinforce. Love the trowel. Make love with the trowel. The trowel is the most beautiful woman in France. Treat your trowel with more respect than you would she."

This French Bootcamp bore little semblance to our time in South Carolina. There men spread out, maybe one every four or five yards, a weak line of defense against charging Huns. Here, men watched in groups, patrols, squads, enough to repel a raiding party and the spaces between stretched to reason's limit.

The trenches in France meandered like drunken men, never straight, never in a line. A line created vulnerability. One break, one incursion, and a single enemy soldier with a single gun could decimate defenses for hundreds of meters. The shorter the sightline the better. The enemy could kill only what the enemy could see.

Frontal attack is suicide. We have learned this, we French, from years at this game. A raiding party, a few men in the dark, can do more damage than a daylight charge by a dozen regiments. Strike fast, strike light, come back alive.

Always keep your gas masks ready. You can tell the difference between a gas attack and an explosive mortar by its sound. Learn the difference. Prepare your bomb shelters.

Secure your kits. Rats will eat anything not in metal containers. Rats will eat dead bodies. Do not be shocked to find your best friend with rats in his skull. This is normal, this is the war, this will soon become old news.

Death will soon become old news.

***

General Le Gallais raised his canteen, took a sip. Deep red lips came away from the metal, stained with wine. He smiled across the gathered officers. He was an impressive man, graduated second in his class from the Artillery School at Fontainebleau, first in his class from the Ecole Superieur de Guerre. A colonel in charge of the 40th French Field Artillery by the outbreak of the war, he now served as Division Commander, Brigadier General, thrilled to have American soldiers in his command. "The farthest north, I am certain of it."

"It is a great compliment," Hayward said, and sipped his own wine, though from a tin cup rather than the canteen of the French. "We are greatly honored to be here."

"You ought to be, I'm a grand man to work for," the general grinned. "But my dear colonel, I have to ask you a serious question. You have undoubtedly heard of the new drive which the Germans are starting. We are hopeful that the enemy may be stopped before they gain any important success. It is doubtful, at any rate, if they spread over as far East as our sectors. But, we must be prepared for all things. We must guard against surprise. If they should come through here, we must have our defenses ready. Now, colonel, what I want to ask you is as to just what we may look to you for, even before you complete your training. What could we count upon your regiment doing right away, in the event of the Germans piling through here? What could we count upon the 369th doing in, say, four or five days?"

Colonel Hayward took a moment and glanced around the room. The Regiment's officer corps sat arrayed before him. Men both black and white in one of the few integrated corps in the Army, maybe the only one. Aware of his men, aware that his words would influence French attitudes toward his men, Hayward straightened his back and lifted his head. "We can be counted upon to do the best we can, and that, of course, no man can do more."

"Bon."

"General," Hayward said, then, a smile arranged smartly on his face, "we will do everything in our power."

"With that reassurance, dear colonel, I must be on my way. The duties of a division do not allow a man, even as grand as myself, to tarry."

"Sir."

General Le Gallais raised his canteen once more, took a sip, and took his leave. Hayward followed.

In the brief silence of their departure, one of the other officers turned about, his white face painfully emphasized by his words, and said, "What could we do if the Germans should attack here at once? Why if the Germans should come piling through here this very night, in four or five days, the 369th could be counted on to spread the news all through France."

***

"You'd think after six months."

"You'd think."

"After six months, you'd think they would, they would fucking figure it out by now."

I kicked a good-sized rock down the path in front of us. The impact hurt my toe, but the pain, brief flare, clarified and focused.

"Not every man can understand."

"No, he goddamned cannot, can he?"

Europe walked slowly beside me, two soldiers in the dusk. In the distance, preparations bombarded the line, whether ours or theirs too far to tell.

"That's the point, though, isn't it?" Europe said. "That's why we're here."

"If you say."

"I say, and Sis says, and half the regiment says."

"But isn't enough—"

"It should be."

I breathed a sigh. Listened to the night, the distant front, imagined Europe's music in the relative stillness of Herpont and wondered what good it might do when the German offensive, the very offensive that General Le Gallais mentioned, materialized. Europe's music a boon, but by no means a shield against bullets and shells.

"Are we really ready?"

"Hell no," Europe said, his voice suddenly loud in the village street. Louder than the laughter of soldiers gathered behind a stone wall, dice in hand, craps their distraction. "We're not ready in the slightest, but that doesn't mean we won't fight like hell. We've got something to prove and we'll prove it."

"But is it proof enough?"

Europe grunted at that, a thoughtful grunt, a grunt of contemplation. "If I thought our fighting would be enough to force congress to overturn Jim Crow, I'd be a fool, and so would you. That's not the point. Yes, DuBois may have folded and yes, everyone else got in behind, but that doesn't mean a single man here truly believes it.

"This has never been about proving anything to the white man and it never will be. The white man can only give us so much equality before the entire system breaks down. If the Negro wants it badly enough, then he'll stand up straight and tall and he'll make the white man respect him. That's the only way it's going to happen, and that's what this is about. This is about the Negro showing himself that he's every bit the equal to Arthur Little and William Hayward and every other white man in uniform. This is about us…this isn't about them."

I thought of my meeting with Tuts Martin back in Aix, of my shame in Spartanburg, of the countless little betrayals that plagued my memory.

"In a couple of weeks, in a few days, hell, you heard the general, maybe even tonight, we'll see action. We'll be the first Negro Americans to fight in this war, the first Negro Americans ever to fight in Europe. That's something. There will never be another first like it. It's on us. We owe it to our own memories to make it mean something. If we make it mean something to us, then there's no way it's not going to mean something to our people. It's the way of things. We're going to make this regiment famous, and we're going to show our people what a Negro man can do…what two thousand Negro men can do."

***

Every night, Europe and Sissle and the band would gather in the central square and play tunes for the men stationed in Herpont. It was a rousing time. The band, improved tremendously from a month of intense practice in Aix, wowed the regiment and the French *en repos*. It made the hard days of training all the more manageable to know that, come evening, we would be given the chance to enjoy the rejuvenating syncopation of the band's music.

One night, I don't remember the exact date, we were honored to receive General Henri Gouraud, the Lion of France, in our ranks. He came to visit his first American troops and to review the situation on the ground. I remember the first time I saw him, that night, this man who was our commander several tiers removed. He was not tall, but he was powerful. He had lost his right arm in an earlier war and received an injury to a leg that caused him to limp. He wore a massive beard and mustaches, black and twisted, hung low enough to cover his neck and touch the top button of his uniform coat. His hair was well-trimmed and coiffed. His uniform immaculate as he moved haltingly up and down the line; I did not know what the medals on his chest represented, but the stories proved them deserved. His face was weathered, tanned, and lined from four years of war. He was a man who, I felt when I saw him, deserved respect for he had sacrificed as much as he asked of his men. And more, he cared for his men, the men of the French Fourth Army, his command, his responsibility.

When Gouraud finished his review, the band began to play. Sissle had learned the words in Aix and had perfected the melody.

While you are sleeping,
Your France is weeping
Wake from your dreams,
Maid of France.
Her heart is bleeding; are you unheeding?
Come with the flame in your glance;
Through the Gates of Heaven,
With your sword in hand,
Come your legions to command.
Joan of Arc, Joan of Arc,

Do your eyes, from the skies, see the foe?
Don't you see the drooping Fleur-de-lis?
Can't you hear the tears of Normandy?
Joan of Arc, Joan of Arc,
Let your spirit guide us through;
Come lead your France to victory

Joan of Arc, they are calling you.

Alsace is sighing, Lorraine is crying,
Their mother, France, looks to you.
Her sons at Verdun;
Bearing the burden,
Pray for your coming in
At the Gates of Heaven, do they bar your way?
Souls that passed through yesterday.
Joan of Arc, Joan of Arc,

Do your eyes, from the skies, see the foe?
Don't you see the drooping Fleur-de-lis?
Can't you hear the tears of Normandy?
Joan of Arc, Joan of Arc,
Let your spirit guide us through;
Come lead your France to victory;
Joan of Arc, they are calling you.

After Sissle fell silent and the band concluded, I would not venture to say that Gouraud had tears in his eyes, but there was a visible emotion about him. His stately manner, military mien, seemed shaken, almost broken by the haunting melody of Sissle's rendition. It was a passing moment, a revelation of humanity in a great man, but I would later remember this revelation. It was a distinct attribute that our French commander did not share with the Americans, especially Pershing. Yes, that was the time. I remember thinking that if Gouraud, or men like him, were in charge completely, there would be no such thing as Jim Crow, no such thing as discrimination between men. There would only be merit; the means of advancement results; a new and strange concept that the American forces were far from recognizing in their ranks, and, I recall thinking, one that perhaps the French had already adopted.

***

Sleepless night. I lay awake, my eyes closed, sometimes open, vacant, staring at the ceiling plaster of some farmer's hut above me. After a time, the sound of distant battle faded; lost explosions meaning nothing. My thoughts floated away, fading memories, images of another place, another time, another world. I thought of Harlem, of Allie, of the things that passed between. I thought of Ishmael, of the smiles and jokes, of the meaning he gave to senselessness. I thought of my dealings...my devil made contracts...Tammany a looker in horns and a tail. I thought...I asked myself...what the cost, the cost so far I had paid? Was the cost of so much worth the gain? But the cause—the cause of my insomnia not so much the question, but the answer. What gain?

***

"You will be arranged in combat groups of a few men in number. Each combat group will be placed strategically throughout the trenches. Some will be posted for observation or listening. Make sure your combat group is located so as to command a clear view of the field of fire-meaning, make sure you can see No Man's Land clearly from the combat group on your left to the combat group on your right. Do not allow yourself to be caught in a position where you cannot see your battlefield, so you cannot see what is approaching. You may at times be stationed as far as half a kilometer from the nearest combat troops. Be aware, always aware, of the men on either side of you. These men protect your flanks. You will find this not too terribly difficult a task, once you see the layout. Our trenches are designed for this, for ease of control, for ease of command. You will find that each combat group is located at the tip of a horseshoe…like this…and that the trench curves back behind you. Within this great sweep is a land covered in barbed wire and pits and all manner of mechanical impediments designed to trip up the adversary. If the Boche are dumb enough to venture between you, between you and your flanking combat group that is, they will find themselves outflanked, trapped and under fire from both sides. This is the beauty of the trench, you see. With this, you can hold off an army with only a few dozen men. You will learn variations, of course, once you reach the front, but here, here is the primary design."

***

"These bullets are funny looking, you ask me."

"They are," I said. Hold one up to the light and, in profile, they seemed little different from our Springfield ammunition. Closer inspection, however, revealed a strange double primer cupping at the base, an insert section, a receptor. I took one, from a loose pile between us, and set it carefully in the tube magazine, one after another, until eight sat firmly, nose to ass, all in a row. It was a strange design for sure, one that, despite all assurances of our French sergeants, caused me concern, as the design seemed conducive to accidental concussion and subsequent in-gun explosion.

"Ten total, is that right, sir?"

I glanced at Pippin, at this private under my command, narrow-faced, long-nosed, eager-eyed, Christian. "That's right, Pippin, eight in the magazine, one in the loader, and one in the chamber."

"Watch out for the top of the barrel."

"That's what they said, the Poilus. If you get too close, you'll burn your arm all to hell."

"Heavy, too."

"It's not the preferred weapon, but these bullets, strange as they are, won't fit in our Springfields."

Pippin nodded and quietly threaded eight bullets into his magazine. He was a good man, quick and dedicated, a true believer. I found it interesting how the truly religious more completely converted their zeal into patriotism. It was as if they, in some unknowable fashion, moved their faith in God and heaven to the president and the cause. Personally incapable, it awed me, this simple faith, this belief that because the president so ordered, it must be right. Not blind faith, really, but close. *Misplaced*, I thought, but still. I was in no position to judge, my motives even less clear, less justified, less pure.

"You scared, sir?" I looked away, Pippin's gaze too intent, and considered.

I had heard stories, the Poilus sergeants are more than happy to share their experience, tell of the sheer horror of the trenches. Mud-soaked, powder blind, gassed, and concussed by endless shell fire; Germans left and right and in between; no news of reinforcements, only your combat group between the Boche and Paris; yet despite the stories, I remained clueless to the reality.

"I don't know," I said, honestly. "Not yet, I don't think. Maybe soon, maybe when we get closer, but now…now, I still don't know for sure what…"

"To expect."

"Yes, what to expect. I don't know. I imagine I should be, scared that is, but I'm not there yet."

"Me either," Pippin said. He touched his chest where most good Christians carried Christ's cross. I lifted my rifle, shoved the magazine in place, and locked it tight. I lifted the gun, heavy for sure, maybe ten pounds, and sighted down the barrel at a nail in the doorframe. I held the target for a full five count before I lowered the gun and set it, lifeless, in my lap.

"You're a good man, Pippin, I hope neither of us has anything to be afraid of."

"We don't," he said.

"No," I said. "I suppose we don't. Either we live or we die. Not much to it, I guess."

"And if we die…"

"If you die."

"You too, sir, even if you don't believe."

"Well, private, I'll let you worry about my soul. I'm going to spend my time worrying about those Bush Germans and what I can do to kill more of them than they do of me. We got a deal?"

"I suppose so, sir."

***

"The bayonet is your last resort weapon. The French bayonet is different from the American bayonet. Rather than the shortened, knife-like bayonet you may be familiar with, the bayonet you have to affix to your rifles is a stiletto, long and needle-like. This obviously requires a different strategy and must be used for different purposes. Where you are familiar with a slashing motion, here you must use a stabbing motion, like this. You will learn to be familiar as we practice through the next few hours.

"The attachment is a simple ring that you slip over the end of your rifle's barrel. There is a slot and stud in place with which you may secure your bayonet, like so. Now that you have secured, or affixed, your bayonet, you are prepared to face the enemy. A few helpful suggestions. Do not aim directly for the center of the chest, like so, as the bayonet will stick in the enemy's breastbone and become very difficult to extract. Also, avoid the groin area. Strikes to the groin are nonlethal but cause excruciating pain. A man's first instinct is to grab the bayonet and pull it out and to do so with a powerful grip. We have found that the only way to escape this grip is often to remove your bayonet completely, thus disarming yourself. Remember, the bayonet strike should be quick, in and out, and allow you to move swiftly from one enemy assailant to the next."

***

First and Third Battalions to Maffrecourt via Auve. From there to take position *en repos* for further tasking in *sous secteur*. In Trench training to commence under 131st French Infantry. Preparation for assuming full duties.

***

After six months, we were finally for the trenches.

Manhattan

New York City, New York
May 2 – August 12, 1920

Bellevue. Home to criminals, drunks, aged seniles, and other untoward rejects of society

"Name?"

"Don't know."

"Identification?

"Guy don't got none."

"Where'd you find him?"

"The Bowery. Was yelling at some phantom Germans and charging traffic like they was tanks."

"Money?"

"Not but five spot on him."

"Thank you, gentlemen."

It was the rule for places like Bellevue, for the asylum on Ward's Island and Roosevelt before that, only the worst, the violent, the ones who posed a threat admitted. And even then, if you came from money, you went private, took care of it quietly behind closed doors. Violent and poor. That was the winning combination.

***

Like so many of my brothers' in arms, my mind had disappeared into the quagmire of confusion endemic to the World War.

Shell shock.

I knew men who suffered from the ailment. I had seen men on relief break into quivering heaps at the thought of returning to the front. I had seen men in hospital. I heard of a man who jumped out of a trench and threw himself into the path of a German shell just to end the constant fear.

But to possess it…

***

"Shell shock is a condition that is not new in form. Its various incarnations have appeared for ages. God knows how long. You are lucky, too, in a way. Although the advancement of the disease makes treatment difficult and lengthy, the treatment itself is more certain. We have studies from England, France, and even Germany outlining the most effective treatments proven scientifically through countless experiments."

"I don't know if I like that word," I said.

"No, no worry at all," the doctor said. He was of Gallic descent, tall and lanky, with dark hair and a stooped back. "The treatment is nothing so dangerous as that might sound. You are also lucky, I must say, to be brought to me. There are many other doctors, less enlightened than I, who might ignore the international findings and resort to tried and true—medieval—solutions.

"Please."

"As I was saying. We must re-educate your mind. You have developed a mistaken belief that you are crazy, when in fact, your mind is simply attempting to cope with tremendous stresses… so all we must do is convince your mind that you are not, in fact, crazy and that there is no longer anything to fear."

"That sounds too easy."

"It will take some time if it will happen at all. You have lived quite a while with this problem and like any habit, the more ingrained it becomes, the harder to break."

"What does this…re-education entail?"

"Psychotherapy."

"I'm sorry."

"Perhaps some hypnosis, but primarily, we'll talk and attempt to shed light into the dark recesses where your mind's misconceptions lurk."

"Psychotherapy?"

"It's all the rage in Europe."

***

"I assumed you were part of Henry Johnson's regiment, not the…not one of the other regiments. You see, even in the height of your delirium you spoke with an educated tongue and held yourself with an intelligent manner. I did not think a man such as that, particularly a man from Manhattan, would have fought as a draftee, but rather would have joined the volunteers long before."

"Are you a student of war?"

"Not so much a student, but an observer, and occasionally, a casual inquirer."

"Why do you know that the 369th was a volunteer regiment? It doesn't bear the designation of a volunteer unit."

"I have an ancestor who fought with Rochambeau and the Negro regiments during the revolution. Because of that, I have cultivated an interest in your people." The man shook his head and picked up a notebook. "More than that I think improper to discuss at this time. I think there are certain things that should best be kept out of a doctor's relationship with his patient."

***

After the first month, I was allowed to wander the grounds with an escort, only during the day and only for half an hour. I would step through the door and march straight to the edge of the wharf and stare out at the East River. I would look north toward Hell's Gate, Ward and Randall's Islands, Ishmael's burial ground. I thought of Jim Europe, of Horace Pippin, of all the rest, the entire regiment. And I stared at the cold water as it rushed past before me. Brooklyn on the far side. I could feel the rain on my face, soaking my uniform, dripping into my boots. The orderly would stand a short distance away and, after thirty minutes passed, politely clear his throat and escort me back inside.

***

"What do you think about when you go outside?"

"Aside from the heat?"

"You can think about that inside—I'm interested in…"

"My orderly tattled," I said.

"You're surprised?"

"Not surprised but…I'm curious about your great-great-grandfather if that's who it was. The First Rhode Island and Rochambeau's troops spent the better part of a year in close quarters. He must have spent a lot of time—this ancestor of yours—with those Negro troops."

"That *is* what I said…and I also said there are things you don't need to know…but as you bring it up, you seem to know a great deal about your people's history, more than an average Negro. Why is that?"

"I learned to read at an early age."

"And you read a lot of literature on the subject…who taught you to read?"

"School teacher."

"But who introduced you to abolitionist literature?"

***

"Ishmael, his name was Ishmael."

"Whose name?"

"Who I think about when I go to the river. He's buried on Randall's Island and whenever I look toward Hell's Gate, I think of that and then I think of him."

"Ishmael was a friend?"

I thought for a moment, rapped my fingertips on the arm of my chair, kept time with the *tick tick-tock* of the clock that sat in the corner behind me. "Yes, he was a friend."

"You have a lot of friends?"

"I've sacrificed many things to get to where I thought I wanted to go."

"Do you have a lot of friends?"

"No, I don't have many friends. Two of those who I might count—who at one point I considered being—are dead, and the third, I don't dare talk to because she…"

"She what?"

"I don't want to talk about that now."

"Okay, maybe we can come back to it later," my doctor, his name was Caraman, glanced at his notepad. "How did Ishmael—Ishmael and your other friend, how did they die?"

"Ishmael shot a cop who had sent me to the hospital. He got shot in return."

"He died avenging you?"

"He was dead anyway. A carpenter without an arm might as well be."

"Yet the immediate cause of his death…the act that precipitated it. He died for you."

"Because of me."

"It sounds like he thought a lot of you that he would consider your welfare with his last act on earth."

I said nothing.

"To my mind, someone who gives their life for a friend truly loves that friend. You must have inspired something in Ishmael that you never understood. You have an ability to make friends, very deep connections, despite what you may think to the contrary."

"But I've only ever had two…two people who I would…who I would try to…who I ever cared about losing…and both of them—both of them, they're dead."

"What about your other friend, how did he die?"

I shook my head and stood to my feet, "I think I'm done for today."

"When you go to the river today, and you think about Ishmael, try to imagine what his life would be like if he hadn't…done what he did. Think of that and then think about how you would feel about him. Would you still remember him if he were alive now? Would he be happy? Think about it."

***

It took me a long time, a lot of talking before I could address it. Doctor Caraman in his chair, a notebook opened on his desk, a stack of books on the floor beside him—banished by the encroachment of patient files, paperwork, and the minutia of hospital management.

He had met Freud. This he told me one afternoon, unprompted. He had met the revolutionary doctor and watched him sit in session. The Austrian sat in an armchair with his notepad in his lap, one leg folded over the other. The patient reclined on a lounge. According to Caraman, the reason Freud used this set up was to avoid eye contact. He didn't want to be stared at for hours on end by deranged lunatics.

He told me more too. Titillating my curiosity in hopes of luring me into his trust. But despite all his teasing, what really needed to happen for me to trust was the passage of time.

"And you think you don't deserve it?"

"Not in and of myself."

"Why is that?"

"I've done nothing to warrant—"

"So, your intrinsic worth is…"

"Diminished."

Caraman paused. I could hear his pen scratch across the page. "You believe you have done things that make you less deserving? Less a man? What?"

"I've done…"

"In the war."

"Yes."

"What?"

"In the war, I've done things…things for which I'm not proud."

"And this causes you to think less of yourself?"

I stopped then. There was so much, so much I now regretted. I had lived to see my entire life based on incorrect assumptions, goals, and intentions. I had sacrificed so much, so fucking much for a mistake. I was a failure who had no hope but one, a new hope, one that made me think I might yet find my way to some sense of peace, to some level of contentment with the actions of my life.

"I have a son," I said.

"A son."

"There are only three people, three people in my life, who I have connected—who I cared about."

"You draw a link between your son and these three?"

"One of the three…his mother."

"And the others?"

"Redemption," I said.

"Your son."

"I've been unable to do anything, to save anyone, to make up for—"

"You've wronged someone?"

"I've wronged—" I stopped, started again, quietly now. "I've wronged my people."

"So as to feel you must atone?"

"Yes. I must do something. I can't let my life continue like this. There is no balance."

"Balance?"

"I don't believe in God, I don't believe in religion, but I've come to believe in balance—in justice of a sort, maybe it's something imposed by the universe or from each of us, each person. It's the hole I dug I have to refill."

"Why? Why can't you build a mountain somewhere else? Why do you have to refill this same hole?"

"Because of the third."

"The third person you cared for?"

I nodded. The silence again caught hold my tongue. I wanted to say the name, I wanted to outline my betrayal, in all its particulars, to unburden my mind and my heart. But there was no method to enact my desire. My chest and my throat and my tongue all refused to play their parts. I was frozen and terrified. Was this the reason for my ailment? My mind turned the years of self-deception and duplicity into a trap, steel-jawed, grasping claws.

"Let's go for a walk."

***

The sun was high and heated the air. I started to sweat almost immediately. We took the same route reserved for me and my orderly, from the hospital, along the wedge of shade cast by one of the additions, to the wharf and the river's edge. The gray water raced past us, constant unwavering, frigid. I let my eyes wander across the current, taking in the ripples and eddies, the unerring course of inevitability. I closed my eyes and felt the cool water rush over me, around me, consume me. I floated in its unchanging bosom, my heart finally comfortable in the ice.

"Up there," I pointed. "Randall's Island."

"Ishmael."

"Across the island, behind us, Allie. Allie and my son."

"What do you think about your son?"

"I hardly know," I said. "I only just learned he existed. He's, he's maybe three, maybe four years old. I saw him from a distance."

"How do you know, then?"

I thought back, pictured that fleeting glimpse between skirt and cab, saw the bronze skin, the black hair, the smile.

"He has my coloring."

Caraman pointed upstream and started to walk again. I followed as we moved toward the northern boundary of the hospital grounds. Maybe a hundred feet from the fence, we stopped and Caraman turned to the river and stared into its depths. We stood side by side for a long moment before he shuddered a sigh.

"This is my spot. This is where I come to think. If you crane your neck and squint, you can almost see the immigrant ships sail into the harbor."

"You're not—"

"No. I was born here and my daddy and his daddy and his mother and her mother too…but not her daddy."

"Your ancestor, the one who fought under Rochambeau."

"He fell in love with a woman, a girl from Rhode Island. He didn't marry her as he should have, he was a coward…he admitted it later, but that's not important."

Caraman looked back to the river, drawing strength from its constancy. "He sailed with her to France after the war was over. I don't know if he intended to keep her as a mistress or to marry her there. He never divulged his intentions on that front. It didn't matter, so much, what he wanted with her in France, though, because they never got there, at least she didn't.

"The authorities stopped her at the port and detained her, held her in prison for months. He called in every chit he had. Talked his case up and up and up. To no avail.

The policy was policy and she would be returned to the colonies. It tore him in two, to choose between the woman he loved and the land he loved. In the end, surprisingly, she won his heart. He sold his properties, said his goodbyes, and accompanied her back to Rhode Island."

"He still never married her, did he?"

"They did have children."

"And you're one of the descendants."

"I'm one-sixteenth," Caraman sighed again. "My daddy passed too, moved away from his parents and started a new life, here, as a white man."

"Why would you trust me with this?"

Caraman shrugged. "I want you to trust me with your secrets. Perhaps I shouldn't, but I feel certain you won't betray me."

I laughed. "You are foolish."

"Why?"

I shook my head. "I would not be so willing to divulge such sensitive information to mental patients if I were you."

"If it gets you to open up."

"You want to know about my secret, about what I've kept from you."

Caraman nodded. "That seems to be at the center of your problems. If we can talk through that, help you understand how it relates to everything else, maybe…maybe we can cure you."

"You would risk your career to help me?"

"That's another point. You just might be worth saving."

"I'm not so sure."

"You are. You're a very intelligent man who's gone through war. You may have done some things you're not proud of, but there's no reason that should stop you from being a good man in the future."

"It's all roses, then?"

"No, but we won't know until we see what happens."

"My secret?"

"It's the thing that's holding us up."

I took a deep breath, let the slight breeze off the East River fill my lungs. Was I ready to divulge this? I thought of all the things I had done, of the politics I'd played, of the secrets I'd betrayed. I thought of my regiment, of Horace Pippin and Noble Sissle and…I thought of Allie and my mother and everything that burdened my life. I thought of my son. Perhaps the only thing worth the pain. If I ever wanted to meet him, if I ever wanted to help him, I had to get through this now. I had to tell Caraman about my secret.

For my son.

"I betrayed my regiment," I said. "I betrayed my people. I betrayed my friend. I betrayed Jim Europe."

May 1 – May 21, 1918

Sous-Secteur Afrique/US, between Ville-sur-Tourbe and L'Aisne Champagne Region, France

A match flared in the darkness. Someone lit a cigarette. I glanced over from my shelter hole, saw the glowing ember at the tip light a familiar face. Pippin.

"You're not on duty right now."

"No, sir," he said. "Not now."

"Then why aren't you sleeping?" Pippin took a puff of his cigarette and held it in the air several inches from his face.

"I like to smoke, sir. Not that I smoked much before, you understand, but now, now that my nerves are like to shake me to pieces, I find it helps."

"You can't sleep?"

"I know I'll get used to it. I'm not worried about the long term. Get used to it or go…in the short term, though, I guess you could say, no, I can't sleep." A shell dropped somewhere not more than a hundred yards from us. I was still too fresh to the front to distinguish the sounds, to identify the weapon from its pitch, warble, and woof. Rocks and dirt tumbled to earth and made a thudding sound, put, put, like oversized hail. Someone grunted in the trench, someone else laughed. I could hear a craps game a few posts down the line. I itched to wander over.

"You're still awake too, I notice, sir."

"I am," I said. "Astute."

"Thank you, sir." Pippin threw the last of his cigarette into the darkness and squatted against the far wall. He slid slowly down the rough dirt until his ass landed on the firing step and dangled his arms between his legs. "I heard we're going to be on the receiving end of a Boche push come not too much longer."

"I don't know," I said.

"Maybe we are then," Pippin said.

"Maybe."

"You're not married, sir." I blinked at the missing segue and stared at Pippin in the pitch.

"Neither are you."

"I'm gonna."

"You have a girl?"

"No, but I want one."

"If you're determined, then."

"Oh, I'm determined. I think God's determined too. He told Adam and Eve to go multiply on the earth. He's the kind of guy, I figure, I figure God's probably a guy who gets any girl he wants."

"I didn't know he was into that."

"I'm not saying he sleeps around, I'm just saying he could, you know, if he wanted to."

"I imagine you're right," I said.

"You don't sound too convinced."

"I'm not what you might call a believer," I said. "If God existed, to my way of thinking, this world should be a lot better place." Pippin made an unintelligible ah-hah noise, this half moan half eureka that rose and fell like a Negress caught by the spirit of revival.

"The Lord's put those trials there for us to learn from them. Least, that's what I was taught."

"And you believe it."

"Why not?" I shrugged and felt a clod of dirt shift under my shoulder. Damn trench. Damn French for digging in. Damn Germans for invading. Damn Wilson for joining. Damn it all.

"You should try at least."

"Try, sir?"

"To sleep. Try to sleep or you'll go crazy sooner than you'll acclimate."

"Sir."

"At least I'm gonna try to sleep."

"Sir."

"Goodnight, Pippin."

***

We sat on crates in a bomb shelter off the line of resistance, playing cards. A small pile of cigarettes and other sundry valuables between the scattered cards. I preferred craps, but Jim didn't play.

"Hit me," Jim said. I slid a card from the top of the pile and across the crate. I flipped it over.

"Jack. You bust."

"Damn." I grinned and flipped my own card over. A two. I was still far from twenty-one, but I'd already won. I folded the cards together and dropped the stack in front of Europe. Tonight, we played Blackjack, yesterday go-fish, tomorrow rummy. It was a rotating monotony that helped us weather the passage of time in these godforsaken trenches. We, all of us, wondered when the real fight would begin; each man a tender ready to be lit. When would the order arrive, or the enemy attack, and when would we be able to level our rifles and pierce the German bastards with our bullets?

"I worry sometimes," Europe said, his big hands busy shuffling the cards, "that I'm becoming immune."

"Immune?"

"I saw a rat this morning, it was a big sucker, just sitting on its haunches, paws pulled up to its mouth. It was chomping something in its teeth and didn't notice me. It just sat there, content, secure in the knowledge that I would do it no harm. What's the point? I saw it thinking. If this man kills me, I will only be replaced by a dozen more. And I thought, staring at that hairy rat, how right it was to think such things. But what worries me more, as I stared at this rodent occupied with its morsel, I began to see in this rat a certain appeal. It began to resemble its cousins, the hamster or squirrel. This rat, at that moment, ceased to be a nuisance and became a pet. A cute and cuddly animal whose presence did not annoy me but provided a tiny thrill of kinship and comfort. This, this is what worries me. That I can look at a rat and see in it a thing to adore rather than despise."

Europe shuffled the cards one last time and set them on the table. He slid one to each of us, face down, and flipped the second. We each checked our hole card and then began to bet. Each of us considering, calculating, making a show before we threw in a few more cigarettes, a bit of chocolate bar.

"I'm thinking about writing a song, you know, about the rats. Something along the lines of how they drive you bats. Maybe the need for a few more cats…or some such."

“That would work,” I said, ignorant of how Europe crafted his music but keen on the rhymes.

“Or how they look in top hats.” Europe shrugged and flipped a card for himself.

“More like how they eat through top hats.” He grinned then and flipped his hole card.

“Blackjack.”

“Damn.”

“So, this French lieutenant in the position on our left flank, he’s got the best stories.”

“Anything interesting?” I said.

“Better believe it. This man seems to have single-handedly turned the tide at Cambrai. But I’ve asked around a little bit and my friend lieutenant was nothing more than an observer there,” Europe waved his hands in the air and adopted his best French accent. “It was glorious, the way the tanks routed the Boche bastards. To see these great big metal carriages plunge through their ranks. It was…it was, how do you say, *Magnifique*,” I laughed.

“That’s wonderful. This fellow, I think I might have to meet him.”

“The French weren’t even involved at the battle. He was attached as an observer. But the way he tells it, you’d think he was in charge of half a dozen of the things.”

“He’s at least seen action.”

Europe nodded, then, and passed the deck. He seemed to withdraw into himself for a moment before he said, “I think we’ll have our fair share soon enough.”

“We will,” I was in complete agreement, “and when the time comes, I hope we live long enough to tell tales the same as your French lieutenant.”

“Amen to that,” Europe said.

***

Pick and shovel work. Dig the ditch, clear out the bayeaux, make sure the latrine is covered, secure the duckboards. Another group, sometimes ours, built new trenches, rerouted existing lines for greater effect, built barbed-wire gates. Our drudgery now a different kind; where once we performed this manual labor on our native shores, then the hills of St Nazaire, now we struggled to entrench ourselves against a foe that daily watched our progress through the sights of their guns. Though no different in nature, this work seemed somehow more noble, more human.

***

The last night of our battalions’ first forward rotation I leaned against the wall of an abris, my eyes half-closed, exhausted but not quite able to sleep. I could hear a couple of soldiers standing outside, their voices low, smoking. It was quiet, as quiet as a front can be. In the distance, either the Boche or us were fighting and I could hear the explosions, shells dropping and machine gunfire. It had started raining and the cold mud of the trenches made each moment we remained miserable torture. But not so much longer before we could escape, rotated back for three weeks off the front line-though still at relief.

“Ayers, you in here?”

I opened my eyes fully, then, and saw a large shadow in the door. Only the glint of some distant light off the shadow’s eyeglasses gave me to realize the man before me was Jim Europe.

“Jim?”

"Come out here, I've got to tell you."

"Tell me what?"

"Out here, I don't want to wake those other men."

I sighed and heaved myself to my feet. I grabbed my rifle and helmet and stumbled over a pair of sprawled legs before I reached the entrance to the abris and joined Europe in the damp night air. The pair of soldiers that I had heard talking was silent, now, puffing on their cigarettes.

"This way," Europe said and led me along the trench away from the silent watchmen.

He turned a bend in the trench and led me down a bayeaux toward one of our forward observation posts. We moved a little way along before Europe stopped and turned to face me.

"I've done it," Europe said. He reached up and removed a cloth cap—not his helmet—and wiped it across his brow. "I've made a mess of it, of my own chances I did."

I looked at Europe's face, at the pale features, the normally frog-eyes now almost so big as to burst clean from his face.

"What happened?"

"Yesterday afternoon, I was visiting one of the French officers and, as we were drinking wine, they commenced to tell of their experience in the war. Every one of them had been in the service four years, and all were veterans of the slaughter at Verdun. I thought that a word expressed on my part, as being desirous of wanting to witness some of the thrills of modern war-fare would boost my stock, and being an American soldier, I also thought I should uphold the valor of the American Army, so I up and said: 'One thing I wish to do, and that is to go on a raid.' What did I say that for? Listen, I hardly got it out of my mouth before one of the officers jumped up and patted me on the shoulder and said: 'Bravo! We are going on a raid tonight, and you can go with us. Get permission from your colonel.'"

"The only chance I had to escape was for the colonel to forbid it, but when I went to him, he was only too glad for me to get the experience."

"Aw, aw!" As Bert Williams said, "I speck, I'm gone before I go."

"Seven o'clock that night I was in the French officers' abris. I was given a Frenchman's old uniform and all my personal belongings and everything that would identify me were left off. The thing that made my head swim, was when they gave me a little cloth cap instead of my helmet.

"We drank a bottle of wine and all the Frenchmen were as happy as larks, just as though they were going to a picnic. I was trying to laugh and smile, but the best I could do was give one of those 'no good' grins. I was thinking of the Band—how sweetly they could play—then I would hear the quartette singing 'Sweet Emelina, my gal!'—then the scenes of dear old Broadway passed by. I could see myself standing before my old favorite orchestra in 'Castles in the Air,' and as I stood there, wielding my baton to those jazzing strains of 'The Memphis Blues,' I imagined I once again saw all those old familiar faces tripping by. When I came to myself, one of the officers touched me on the shoulder and said, 'All right, lieutenant, the time has come to go.'

"Those words were just the same as my death sentence, but I came to in time to cover up my dreaming—braced up, and forced the old grin again. 'There's an automatic for you, lieutenant,' said one of the officers, handing me a little pistol. I looked at it and wondered what good would it be shooting at one of those Boche Berthas, ten miles away—but the Frenchmen had them, and as I was with them, I thought I must just as well.

"Silently, we filed out in the darkness. Not knowing the ground over which I was trudging, I was constantly stumbling in the darkness. Every corner of the trenches I turned, leading down to the front line. I would pass the dark form of a member of the patrol, huddled up beside the trench, and not a word was spoken. It seemed to me that if someone would just clear their throat, I would have been relieved. First place, my throat was too dry to even make a sound—for a while I thought I was having a terrible nightmare and kept trying to wake up.

"We finally reached the 'jumping off' place, which the officer with me whispered was just opposite the place that led to where we were to cross No Man's Land. As we hesitated for a minute, I noticed how beautiful the night was. Every star seemed as bright as a shining silver light. It seemed they were mocking me the way they winked their eyes at me, and how I wished I could change places with them. At the same time, I wondered why such a bright night had been chosen to go on this detective job. One of the officers with me explained that as there was quite a bit of brush growing in front of our trenches, we were able to get through our wire, without being detected and the bright light would make our observing easier in the enemy's trenches. It sounded logical, but to me, it was all wrong. I thought that if it was darker, it would be hard for me to see a German and it would be hard for them to see me, and I knew I was not over-anxious to see any Mr. Fritz, and I was certainly most anxious that none would see me.

"'Step one side!' an officer whispered in my ear, and as I did so, one soldier after another of those that we had passed in the trenches, began quickly but quietly, going 'Over the Top.' Each one of the thirty men was checked as they went over, but when the last two came along they were carrying a stretcher. *There now,* I said to myself. *I know I'm coming back on that thing. Oh, Lordy, what did I invite myself in this mess for?* I thought if I only had the wings of a dove, I would have flown away. But it was too late.

"'Let's go over, lieutenant,' said my French friend, and blankly I struggled 'Over the Top,' and crawled on my stomach quietly, till I reached the hole that had been left in the wire, in front of our trenches, and before I was really conscious of the fact, I found myself in 'No Man's Land.' I followed, the lieutenant with me, still crawling, on past the soldiers, who were lying quietly in a straight line parallel to the wire, and finally, we reached the enemy's wire, where I found one of the French patrols, the night before, had cut an opening. Through this passage, a soldier crawled, with a large ball of white tape in his hand, and my comrade whispered that he was going to lay that to the Boche trench, so as to mark the shortest route, and it would also serve as a guide back to the hole. That's the part that interested me, mostly—then getting back to the hole. He made the round trip, undetected, and he was no sooner back than I heard the boom of several of our light artillery guns, and like a thousand pheasants, several shells came whizzing over our heads and burst about forty yards in front of me. I knew my time had come. Now, they came thick and fast. All up and down the front they were pouring—all calibers—and were sweeping the enemy's trench. Talk about hugging the ground. Boy, no sod ever hung as close to Mother Earth as I was. You see, some of the shells would burst in the air and shrapnel whizzed hither and thither. Seemed mostly hither. After about two minutes of this—which seemed two hours—a gun cracked right by my side and up whizzed a red flare from the Verey pistol of the officer by me. Every man jumped to his feet—that is, in a crouching position, ready to run—and one by one, each slipped through the hole in the wire and formed a skirmish line a short distance from the wire. The shells had then begun to advance and at another crack of the pistol, every man leaped up and made a dash for the trenches.

"'Come with me, lieutenant,' whispered my companion, and I slipped through the hole in the wire, following the tape, and jumped over in the enemy's trenches, right where the white tape ended, and there I remained. By this time, all kinds of pretty lights were filling the air. It looked and sounded like the 'Forty-fourth' of July. All this time, our artillery was sweeping the back areas of the enemy's trenches, ahead of our men's advance, and amid the din of the high explosives, could be heard the excited yelling of our men, as they darted first up one trench, and down another, bombarding every nook and corner, with hand grenades. For three minutes, this continued, and then a green rocket was sent up by the lieutenant with me, at the place where the white tape marked the way back to the opening in the enemy wire. One by one, the soldiers came scampering back, some carrying pieces of paper in their hands, some with a German coat, helmet, or anything that might convey information, but to my disappointment, with no prisoners. The thing that caused me to hit the trail, right away, was when I saw the stretcher-bearers bringing back one of their men, wounded. Right along that tape I tore out for the wire, and by that time most of the men were on the same route. Well, the whole time since the bombardment began, hardly took over five minutes, but it seemed ages to me.

"This morning, I heard four of the soldiers were caught in the German barrage and seriously wounded. Next time I go, they will have to read orders to me with General Pershing's name signed and re-signed on them."

Somewhere in California

Feather River Route, Western Pacific Rail
April 16, 1921

I sat the Feather Valley Line in second class, the first-class passage for a black man. I was unhappy with my seat, the wooden bench barely upholstered and the service dismal. I wasn't allowed in the dining car and had to rely on the handouts from the trolley lady who came through every six hours. Eating cold sandwiches when my white coevals dined on steak and chicken freshly cooked by a world-class chef. It wasn't fair, but then, what was? Life for a Negro in the United States nothing like that in France. I remembered the way the men in France treated us, not like the white men who came transplanted across the ocean. It took a moment of consideration before I understood my own thoughts and knew that the white man in the United States would never see the black man as an equal.

But what about a mulatto?

Many of my thoughts over the last several months had been for my son, a boy of only a few years, and whose name I didn't know. All I recalled the brief glimpse of brown skin, thick black hair, and burly shoulders that I'd seen behind Allie's skirts. It was enough to drive me crazy. Hell, it had.

After leaving Bellevue and Caraman's care, I'd traveled to San Francisco. It had been the good doctor's recommendation. Leave everything behind, leave the world, the memoir, the family. For family they were despite all that had happened. The boy possessed my genes, and for that, I would forever be grateful. A father, no, a deadbeat.

I was little more than a donor of genetic material. The possession of the title father reserved for that white man who was in my place. But I had sacrificed that, hadn't I? I had given Allie no hope of reunion. I remembered her sitting in my front room crying, mourning the loss of her father, the one man who seemed to understand and, at least, not judge too harshly her love for me. Judging by the size of the boy, by the way he stood nearly to his mother's waist, he must be four or five by now. That meant he was born by the time Allie had come to me searching for solace.

And I had rejected her. It had been the whiskey. I'd been drinking in her memory even then, knowing how much I loved her and how much I had betrayed her for my hopes and dreams. My dreams…

I looked out the window of the clacking train and saw the rocks of a mountain rise up across the narrow creek that ran along the tracks. They were climbing. I wasn't sure where we were, though I was certain we remained in California, the trip not nearly long enough yet to warrant a transfer to Nevada. It was the Silver line, express, though only second class.

Again, I wondered what it would take to make the likes of this world equal, if not for myself and Allie than for our son. What must happen before the likes of a mulatto boy could find his way into the highest ranks of power? War? No. I'd fought a war and there was no difference. In fact, it was worse. Because in France they saw the way to equality, the friendship and camaraderie of the Poilus. Hairy, bearded Frenchmen who didn't care about the color of your skin so long as you drank the same wine and shot the same Boche.

What would the world carry for my son? Would the French way of thinking prevail or would the United States with its lynching and its anti-miscegenation laws and its Jim Crow mean more to the world? I didn't know, and now, as I sat on the return trip to New

York, I had to wonder. Would there be a way for my son to find his way without the burdens of race?

I doubted it and doubting I rose from my seat and walked back through the moving train. I'd smoked before the war, sure, but it hadn't been a habit. Now, after my time with Pippin and the other soldiers in Maffrecourt, in Champagne and all the other areas where the 369th patrolled and fought, I was an addict. I reached into my pocket and withdrew a cheroot. Turkish. I'd been hooked by the acrid smoke of their enemy tobacco. It had been the most easily accessible cigarette on the front, at least my front, and now, now I tasted the paper and lit a light.

I stood on the caboose. My hand curved around the match as I raised it to my mouth. It was something I didn't understand, something that most people didn't care about, but I felt that if I was to smoke, it was a private thing, not to be shared with the likes of civilians who would never understand the privilege of lighting up in the face of a trench bombardment. I remembered Pippin handing me a light, my ration sacrificed for the men or lost in gambling, as I didn't smoke at the time, and Pippin willing to grant me that much of a concession to my rank.

What kind of man would my son become? I had to wonder that, too, raised by Allie and the ham-fisted brute—for I knew nothing better than that the man had looked Italian—which was what I called the man who married Allie. It should have been me. It should have been me. It should have been me.

***

I took a bite of the cold sandwich, turkey, but canned turkey, the kind of thing that reminded me of the bully beef I'd tasted in France. It was a British concoction, that, but it served one and all alike, and I had the bad fortune to eat it more than once. Though the 369th's mess tent more evolved than bully beef, including fresh baguettes, cheese, and the wine so indicative of France.

Another bite. The bread was stale. I was paying for a first-class passage but knew there was nothing to do for it. I was black, and as a Negro, a nigger to the white man, I was left with a second-class seat.

We'd left the mountain valley by now, California perhaps in the past, and traveled along a dense plain, with orange wildflowers and a green brush that reminded me of my son's hair. What little I'd seen of it.

I imagined the white man, whatever his name, ham-fisted brute, as a metaphor. No longer a simple replacement, a man willing to take Allie and the child despite their obviously tainted experience, but a man who had no reputation of his own to taint. That must be it, for no man would take a woman who bore a mulatto child, not for his loins to break bread with a Negro's.

I finished the sandwich and washed it down with cold coffee. There were at least two, possibly three more days left in my journey. Perhaps I could pass the time with a book…or even my memoir. I wiped the crumbs away from my pants leg and wiped my mouth on the back of my hand. I set the eating utensils to the side—for the trolley lady or some other porter to retrieve—and withdrew the notebook in which wrote my memoir.

***

I had begun my memoir as a quest for forgiveness, a vaunted image of colored glass and light through the vestry. A confession of sorts, a way to remember what had happened and to mold it to what was happening in my life. But I had come to no conclusions, only that I knew one thing, I must meet my son. It was imperative that I do so, to become a part of his life, to enter into his consideration. I was his father and I had nothing left but him.

Him and Allie.

But she refused me. She would not accept me now, not even if I tried. She was married to a white man, and thus, I was not the one to save her. But what needed saving? Her or my own soul?

I jot these notes as the train rumbles through the salt desert outside Salt Lake. It will be a short while yet before I transfer lines, from Salt Lake to Denver, and then from there to Chicago. It is a criss-cross of lines made of iron and wood, traveled by a great herd of iron horses. It is a marvel of technology, something that was missing so much in the front across the ocean, but something that I will forever recall with pleasure—at least what I have experienced of it.

The train rocks back and forth as it moves along the track. I'm not sure how legible my hand is at this point, but I will endeavor to make it last. I know only one thing now, I must see Allie, I must meet my son. It is the one thing on my mind as I prepare myself for my return to New York. My sabbatical in San Francisco has been nice, but with each passing day, the months combined, I found myself in a terrible depression. Not like before, not shell shock, no, but a malaise that stretched across my consciousness. It was not for me, either, that I felt this, but for my son. How could I let him live a life unknowing of his past, of his roots?

I would see him, as soon as I settled back into a hotel or lodgings, I would find him out. I knew where Allie lived. I knew where the ham-fisted brute lived and slept. With her. And wondered how he treated his mulatto son? My mulatto son?

There is still snow on the mountain peaks here in the west and I wonder what it would be like to play in the snow with my son. Would he laugh, his bright voice a reminder of the love I'd known, or would he cry at the pain of a thrown snowball, his eyes piercing with their teary stain? I did not know, and not knowing was perhaps worse than the possibility of dying.

I would see him, I would meet him, and I would save him.

Champagne Region, France

June 22 – July 15, 1918

South. We traveled south, away from Maffrecourt, away from the front lines, away from the clockwork bombardment of Boche shells. We travelled in silence, for a time, along the side of the dirt road that led first to Braux Sainte-Cohiere, then cut west to Dommartin-Dampierre and on to Orbeval, before it cut south once more to Gizaucourt. Ten kilometers, six and a half miles, through the bitter remnants of once beautiful fields turned to mud and death from four years of war. It was June, now, and summer's warmth blazed down on our progress, catching our every step in its blessed comfort. What a change from the cold, dismal places we had lived in for the last month and a half. Drenched and muddy for ten days at a stretch. Time off for good behavior between duties not enough to remove the chill and the memory of it. But this, this summer day walking through the fields of the Champagne, this was restorative.

Two of us, Sissle and I, journeyed alone. We passed the occasional platoon on the march, supply truck, or other random army personnel. No civilians, though, this region now evacuated of all its former inhabitants, too close to the front to exist in hopes of safety. A light breeze blew down the crest of a hill and across the dirt track on which we trod. I loosened my collar and held my arms above my head to enjoy the simple pleasure of it. Breathed in the hint of wheat tramped into the barren fields, the smallest grain left despite the destruction. It was the smell of spring, the smell of rebirth and hope, the smell of something that might again claim the earth as its own and grow into fields of gold to be scythed down and converted to flour and bread and countless products of unimaginable value and flavor, economic virility renewed, a war-torn country resurrected to some semblance of normalcy. The thought of it made me salivate, a fresh baguette, not the hardtack of army rations.

White clouds scudded across the sky, high, miles above us, wispy tendrils. "You've known Jim for a long time?"

"Since nineteen sixteen. Two years and a little now."

"Not so long a time then."

"No, not when you think of a life."

"In New York?"

"Anywhere, really."

"No, you met in New York?"

Sissle nodded. "I was with Bob Young's sextet at the time, been singing down in Florida with Eubie and that group during the winter, entertaining all the best blood gone south to warmer weather. E F Albee organized a 'Palm Beach Week' at the Palace Theatre and brought us up to participate. I'd impressed Mary Warburton somehow, either in Florida or at the Palace and she gave me a letter of introduction to Jim. I took it straight to him and he practically gave me a job on the spot. He knew the Warburton's through the Wanamakers and, with their reputations, saw me as a fairly stand-up kind of guy."

"You worked with him."

"A lot, yeah. He brought Eubie north, too. Figured he could use more men who understood what it meant to be a professional musician, how to wear proper clothes and how to keep dignity about you on the stage. Not that either he or I would speak bad of William and Walker and the like, just that we think it's time for us, as a people, to move beyond the minstrel. You know, show people that we truly are a talented race who has and will continue to contribute to culture and society."

"Sounds a little like Booker Washington."

"No sir," Sissle said. "Jim doesn't believe in accommodation-ism, not in the slightest. He believes that music, jazz music, can bridge the racial divide. That's why he started the Clef Club and put together the performances at Carnegie Hall. That's why he's here in this war. He's here because he's intent to use his music to show the white man what the black man can do. And he's convinced, that when the white man hears the beauty and the passion that comes out of our musicians, that he can't help but admit—admit that nothing short of a man could produce such a sound."

"Ambitious."

"No, not ambitious. It's…it's a kind of faith with Jim. Maybe I'm drawing from my childhood—my daddy was a reverend—but with Jim, he believes that racism, that hate, it's not something we're born with. He sees it as a conquerable enemy and he believes that if he works hard enough, if he just keeps fighting, he can win."

"With jazz, his sword and shield."

"Exactly."

A plane flew overhead, one of ours, heading to the front. It swept past in a low buzz, a biplane, keeping low to the earth for now. We stopped and followed it with our eyes—hands to our foreheads against the glare—until it disappeared to the north. We didn't know what its task might be, though it could only be a few things: reconnaissance, a bomb run, or maybe to clear the air of a Boche bomber. Or there was ranging, as well, if an artillery unit called in support, it may need assistance to dial its solutions.

"What about you?" Sissle asked as we turned south again. "What's your story?"

"My story?"

"Yeah."

"I met Jim outside Carnegie Hall, the first time. I was trying to get in when he showed up all dressed in white, late and had to bluster his way past the guard."

Sissle laughed. "I remember that story. Some folks spoke up for him, testified if you will."

"Yeah, I slipped in after him, pretended like Jim dropped his watch and I needed to give it back to him."

"The guard bought it?"

"I really had a watch," I said and pulled my daddy's Elgin from my pocket. "This one, in fact, but I think it was more that the guy didn't care, not by that time. Too many people and not enough help, you know."

"Can I see it?"

I handed Sissle the watch. He hefted it in his hand, felt the gold case, ran his fingers across the stars and moon, felt the rough scratches on the face, held it to his ear to hear the mechanics, rough and off time as they were, *tick-tock*, clockwork.

"It's a nice piece," he handed it back. "Or at least it could be."

"Thanks."

"To be honest, it sounds like a drunken tap dancer."

I smiled. "I imagine my daddy like that."

"It was your father's?"

"My mother tells me so."

Sissle said nothing, and we continued to walk in silence for maybe half a mile. An ambulance passed us, from the front, its horns silent as it sped by. I could only imagine the injured soldier inside, jarred by every rock, rut, and pothole. I thought of the Bible in my pocket, that small volume, kept close to the Elgin. Something about the two artifacts linked in my mind and my soul. I felt as if I should speak, explain myself, explain the unique horrors of my upbringing, but I could not find the words, or perhaps I was unwilling. An air raid siren sounded in the distance. We ignored it and kept walking, alone in the plains of Champagne.

"I've never met my father," I said, blurted really.

"I'm sorry."

"So am I," I said.

Our boots ground dirt and gravel underfoot, crunched, and took us inexorably closer to our destination. Somber, our mission serious, we hesitated with each thought, each possibility, before we dared launch ourselves into yet one more commitment.

"I don't know why I keep it. Maybe I think it's a link to my past, or maybe it's the one thing I have that says I'm a man, born of a man, but it's all. There's no other evidence, nothing to prove my father…"

"My father was a preacher, a reverend in Indianapolis."

"Pious."

"Yes, pious and strict. I do not begin to compare, only to say that sometimes, sometimes an absent father is not the worst thing he could do."

"You and your?"

"We are on terms. He never abused me, and we speak cordially, but like most sons…I found my way into certain inadequacies. He would have preferred I pursue medicine, or law, or some other worthwhile profession, though he understands my love of music. It is an amenable relationship, strained at times, but livable."

"You're lucky."

"Sometimes, I think so."

We fell silent. Two men alone in the middle of France. Two soldiers marching together in step, trained to keep time, heading south. What we would find at the end of our journey, unknown and unknowable until we arrived. Prisoners. Prisoners to our own ignorance. Our worry, our uncertainty, driving us to reveal secrets and histories that were best left uncovered, hidden in our normal, ordinary procedures. That I would let Sissle know of my father, that I would reveal and expose, struck me as the most naïve of mistakes. How could I let this man, this soldier, know something so basal, so primal inside me? If he saw into my soul, what would stop him from seeing into my reason?

"You think he's okay?"

"I hope so," Sissle said. "I don't know, though. I've heard stories about the gas. How it will turn a man's insides out through his mouth."

"Painful."

"That's what I've heard. Unfortunate, the man who."

"Of course."

"We've been lucky, you and I, not to have—"

"No, you're right."

"We've been lucky," Sissle said.

"Yes, I don't look forward to it. I practice, the way they tell us, put the mask over my face, secure the straps, breathe through the filter—but it still, it's not natural. It's wrong, you know, the way the Boche are bombing us with poison."

"We do it too."

"I know, but it's different, not as bad when we do it to them. There's a distance and a sense of right. We're the good guys, or so they say."

"So they say."

Another spell of silence. We turned west, then, and we could see the village of Dommartin-Dampierre this side of the horizon. A few buildings scattered along the road, a hamlet, a gathering of souls. This was no city, hardly worth mention, a few homes, a few barns, and a pub. Of course, there would be a pub. No one could survive like this without alcohol. To live so remote a life, removed from contact with any but a handful of close neighbors. Growing up in a cloister, forced to wander across the horizon to find a mate, perhaps experimenting with relatives for lack of better, more distant options. No, this was not the way to live, and especially not without the benefit of some kind of chemical damper, a depressant, a way to escape the hell of reality.

"What about your mother?"

I stopped. I stood still, incapable, unmoving, and listened to the faint echoes of shell fire to the north. Each distant explosion rocked me minutely until I swayed back and forth in time to the bombardment. It informed my breath too. Control of such basic functions no more my own but now pledged to this war. My mother's memory…or rather my memories of her yet unbanished by any analgesic available. I began to fear that death alone might salve my guilt and that the explosions, distant though they were, marked some little loss. Some minor destruction of my soul. I could only hope that with my soul's vanishment went my culpability as well. If it only would, I might find redemption yet, short of my own demise.

"There are issues," I said, finally. "I'd prefer not to—"

"I'm sorry."

"I appreciate it," I said, and my feet resumed their march. "When did you start, to sing that is?"

Sissle shrugged. "I learned in church. As I said, my father was a minister and I sang religious songs there. I was destined for the ministry myself until I discovered a way to support my education through music. I sang with a dance band through school and a reader on the Chautauqua circuit. It paid the bills and, as I wasn't reliant on their money, my parents had no more say in the matter."

"So, you've always sung?"

"I guess," Sissle said. "Not that I think about it much. It's something that I do to survive and something I enjoy."

"And you'll always do it?"

"Until they stop paying me, or until it's not fun anymore."

"So, you do it because it's fun?"

"One reason. I really do it because I don't know anything else. It's always been me, and I've always been it, I guess you could say. There's no separating the two. If I didn't sing and make music, I wouldn't be me, at least not the me anyone is familiar with."

"You and Jim and Eubie…"

"We're a team, I guess. Good friends. We enjoy each other's company and we have similar ideas about our role in the world, though Jim is so far ahead of either Eubie or me. It's amazing, really, when you consider what he's done, what he's going to do. I wouldn't be surprised if, single-handed, he brought about the demise of Jim Crow. He's already broken through the musician's local, opened the doors of New York's most distinguished and made a revolution in the way we do business. Before Jim, no one wore a tie to a gig. Hell, before Jim, no one called it a gig. The man is a genius of organization…"

"And he's formed the best damn band the army will ever see."

"And he's formed the best damn band the army will ever see," Sissle repeated.

Silence again. Though this time, a mutual contemplation. Each of us, in his own thoughts, wondered what might happen to the world if Jim Europe had never been a part of it; or if he were to suddenly cease to be a part. It was a possibility that I did not care to entertain seriously. Jim had become my friend, for whatever reason, and I saw him as a force for good, someone who could unite people with his talents and do so without compromising himself or his ideals.

"I wonder…" I said. "I wonder if he could really do it."

"Do what?"

"Change the world with his music. Bring black and white together."

"He's already done it, in a few places."

We walked through Dommartin-Dampierre and all the way through Orbeval in silence. When we turned south again, it was but ten more minutes before the little village of Gizaucourt peaked above the softly rolling hills. A row of ambulances lined up beside a low barn, converted space, now a hospital. We slowed as the buildings grew larger and we began to smell the death and decay now so familiar to our senses. This was a place where soldiers died, a place where men came with little hope. Some passed through alive and well while others, too many others, never passed anywhere again. Here it was we came to visit Jim Europe, unsure of his injury, unsure of his condition, unsure into which category he would fall.

***

Tents the hospital. A low grouping clustered around a barn. Separate facilities near a well. Reliable water a necessary constant for treatment of shrapnel, gunshot, and gas attack. Triage the order of the day. Outside the tents, a few orderlies flitted. A surgeon—obviously so by his blood-stained apron and plastered hair—smoked casually and watched a distant cloud bank loose a deluge.

"Which one?" I said, to Sissle.

"What you lookin' for?" the doctor said and flicked the butt of his cigarette to the ground. "Amputees over there, GSW's right there, poison gas in that one. I think we even got a bearded woman stashed in that one there."

"Gas victim," Sissle said.

"That one, like I said," the man pulled another cigarette from a pack. "Steel yourself, god, you'd think the amputees would be worst—at least they're clean—those boys got the gas…"

"He's my best friend," Sissle said.

The doctor lit up. "For his sake, then, he got a light dose. It happens."

I put a hand on Sissle's arm and pushed him toward the right tent. "No point in worrying when we can soon enough know for sure."

Inside, we understood. The dimly lit tent was crammed with rows of cots—not even separated by sheets—and each cot bore a victim of Boche chemistry. One moaned quietly, his hands tied to prevent him from touching his eyes, or rather, the gaping holes where gas had corroded his skin and tissue. Bloody ichor dripped from the site. Several men lay with mouth open as they breathed gasping, hoarse breaths. They couldn't close their mouths for the mass of boils, blisters, and soars inside. Other men lay with their arms raised in slings. Gas had attacked the rotting moisture and sweat under their arms and left scarring wounds behind. Others gulped air through constricted lungs, nostrils, and throats burned raw—unusable—by the gas.

The doctor was right. Here was hell.

***

We found Europe awake. He sat with his back against a tent post, his knees drawn toward his chest so he could perch a notebook on his lap. He scratched in the notebook with a pen. He wore his trademark glasses, big, shell-rimmed things and his eyes seemed to pop from his head as he looked at us.

"Sis, Reuben, gee, it's good to see you guys," and then without a breath, "Sis, I have a wonderful idea for a song that just came to me, in fact, it was the experience last night during the bombardment that," he waved to his throat then, "nearly knocked me out."

"That's great," Sissle said. "Let's hear it."

Jim lifted the notebook from his knee and read:

There's a minnenwerfer coming,
Look out! Bang!
Hear that roar! It's one more,
Stand fast! There's a Vary light.
Don't gasp, or they will find you all right,
Don't start to bombing with those hand grenades,
There's a machine gun! Holy spades!
Alert! Gas! Put on your mask,
Adjust it correctly and hurry up fast.
Drop! There's a rocket for the Boche Barrage,
Down! Hug the ground close as you can,
Don't stand! Creep and crawl
Follow me, that's all.
What do you hear, nothing near
Don't fear, all's clear,
That's the life of a stroll
When you take a patrol out in No Man's Land.
Ain't life great out in No Man's Land.

"It's wonderful, Jim," Sissle said, his narrow face truthfully impressed.

"It's just some ideas for the chorus yet, I've got to flesh it out and put in the verses, I've got kind of a melody in mind already, too. I'd play you some, but I don't have anything…"

"I'm sure it'll be great," Sis said.

Sis moved closer to Jim and gestured for the notebook. Jim handed it across and for a long minute, the silence was only interrupted by a fit of coughing.

"It really is quite something, Jim. This's going to be a classic, I'm sure of it." Sis handed the notebook back.

"I'm glad you guys came. This place is depressing."

"I believe it," I said.

"How are you doing?" Sis finally asked.

Jim shrugged. "It's seared my throat, they say. Not so bad as it could have been, but not good. They're talking about transferring me to Paris for a little bit, but only for a little bit. I mean, aside from my throat I feel fine, just restless like I can't wait to get back to the front."

"Still, after this?" Sis asked.

"We came over here to do a thing, Sis, and I intend to be part of accomplishing that thing. I don't want to wait out my service in a hospital bed in Paris. I want to be on the front, fighting the Hun, doing what I signed up to do."

Sissle lowered his head, "All right, just don't get so excited you come back before you're healed."

"Is there anything we can get you before we head back?" I said.

"You mean something from the mess they won't feed me here?"

"That's about all we can offer, isn't it?"

"No, I'm fine. It's been all soups and puddings so far. Soft stuff that won't irritate my throat. I ask for chocolate, strawberry, and vanilla, and they bring it. You know, it's not hard service here, just slow and your mind gets to thinking in the quiet, thinking what might be, what might have been. That's the problem, really, is I'm just bored."

"The YMCA—"

"Don't let us in, remember," Sissle put a hand up. "We could ask one of the nurses."

"It's all right. I've got my notebook. By the time I'm healed up, I'll have written two dozen masterpieces. Won't Eubie be jealous?"

"Eubie, and Will and everyone else."

"How about you, Reuben, how's your war coming?"

"About the same as everyone else," I said. "I've been lucky, though, haven't been put in the lookouts. Just lots of frontline grunt work. Digging in for some phantom offensive's coming. We've got the cleanest lines you'll find in the entire Champagne region and my hands are as calloused as a field nigger's."

"Then it's not all bad."

"Yeah, I guess I needed the exercise," I patted my stomach.

"The band's going to perform for General Gouraud on July fourth," Sissle said, suddenly. "I guess he's going to make some big speech to everyone, try to build them up before…"

"So, you've really got a battle coming then?"

"Sounds like it, from everything up and down the line."

"I've had to find my own battles," Europe grinned.

Sissle and I both smiled, both in the joke, both aware of Jim's midnight raid.

"You'll have some yet."

"Like with my nurse."

"A battle you're not likely to win," a woman said from behind us.

We turned to see a short woman, stout, with a pair of elbows that could flatten a forest. "Time for you gentlemen to be leaving the lieutenant alone."

"But we just got here."

"Half an hour ago," she said, a slight Irish brogue underneath. "You'll be gone with you for the moment and if you'd like to come back, you can come back tomorrow."

"Hardly likely on a day's leave."

"Then you'll not be coming back."

Sissle and I glanced at each other. Sissle shrugged. No fight here.

"Feel better, Jim," I said.

"I'll write to Eubie and everyone, let them know you're okay," Sissle said.

"Thanks for coming, guys, it was really nice to see you two. Tell everyone hello."

"We will."

***

July Fourth. Chalons-sur-Marne. The French Fourth Army headquarters. We arrived shortly before noon and disembarked to find the American Red Cross canteen not far from the train station.

The train station was on the west side of the Marne, a bridge connecting it with the main body of the city. There wasn't much to the place, a Cathedral or two, a park, a city hall—or Hotel de Ville—and half a dozen streets arrayed in the French order. I do not know the figures, but nothing in my memory suggests a population greater than a few tens-of-thousands. The Cathedral—and it was big enough to warrant the appellation—did the place justice, a beautiful erection of holy stone, fit for the most devout to exclaim their undoubted humility and limitless righteousness. Otherwise, the place seemed common, a French village grown large, streets filled with pedestrians, a few automobiles, horses and carts. A quaint place for army headquarters.

***

The band played a successful set. French and American officers gathered together in the Red Cross tent, the makeshift performance venue. The assemblage listened appreciatively to the band, jazz tunes ringing in the quiet air. They played well if not brilliantly without Europe. Eugene Mikell took the bandmaster's place, a functional conductor, and led the boys through their paces. For the French in the crowd, and even for the few Americans, it was a stunning display of jazzification, rhythm, and music united in perfect form to cause feet to tap and shoulders to sway. They didn't know the difference. They hadn't heard the band perform at Aix, or at Nantes, or in Harlem. They didn't know the heights to which Europe could carry the music, and not knowing, they applauded just as loudly. For me, it was a disappointment. Europe's absence—in Paris to recover from the gassing—stole a vital element from the performance. Jim Europe was the vibrant heart of the organization. Without him, the beats didn't pop, and the rhythm didn't jibe quite the same. Nothing came off quite right without him in charge.

But the show must go on. And so the band played.

Sissle sang.

A dog fight in the sky above Chalons interrupted the program, the proximity of the airplanes sending the band and audience both running for cover. A momentary break, though, as the German airplane plunged to the earth and the American flew back to its base, victorious.

Sissle sang again.

General Gouraud arrived at the final moment to express his appreciation and to exhort the troops to excel during the upcoming Boche offensive.

***

"You've nothing to report?"

"That's right," I said. "Nothing to report."

My contact was a rodent. His eyes were set too close together, his nose turned up at the tip—a small nose at that—and his hand seemed incapable of descending below his belt. He fidgeted incessantly, tugged at his uniform—which was too large and wrinkled—and, because of his miniature stature, took two steps to my everyone, even at a relaxed pace. It took less than twenty seconds for dislike to set in. At least real rats had fur.

"The leadership at CID won't be happy. Tammany won't be happy."

"It is not my fault there is nothing to report," I said.

"It is, it is," the rodent—who went by the name of Tomlinson—said. "Your mission, it was two-pronged remember. You were to report on any suspicious and subversive activity, and you were to take any opportunity to subvert the purpose of the—"

"Shut up," I said.

"Excuse me," Tomlinson gasped. He spoke with a touch of nasal, too quickly, and with a tendency to repeat certain phrases. "You have entered a contract with the—"

"What if I'm not interested in fulfilling my side of the deal any longer?"

"What if? What if you're not? You're not interested?"

"That's right," I said, a smile creeping over my face. "What if I don't want to be Tammany's henchman anymore? What if I'm done with the CID?"

"That was anticipated," Tomlinson said. He raced beside me as we walked, now, a hundred yards from the train station. "From your previous reports, we suspected—or the CID suspected—that you might have a change of heart." Tomlinson squeaked and did a little hop. "We have other assets, we have other men, that is, who are moving in place. You are no longer, or so I understand, you are no longer the only eyes we have in the 369th. If you chose, that is to say, if you decided to breach your agreement, that would be unfortunate for you, but we would be able to maintain our positions, and perhaps, perhaps do better by them, than by you. That is…that is if you were no longer interested."

The train whistle sounded.

"I'm overdue."

"You will let us know, won't you? You will tell us if you decide that you feel, that you feel you are no longer capable of fulfilling your side?"

I glared back at Tomlinson. "I'll be sure I do."

***

Everyone knew, and when I say everyone, I mean everyone from General Foch to Private Pippin, that the Boche intended to attack. Initial suspicions placed the date for the assault on July Fourth as an effort to catch the American's off guard. When the fourth passed without incident, the military planners quickly changed their thoughts to Bastille Day, on the fourteenth. They figured the Boche would view the day as a day of celebration. Soldiers and staff would be drunk. A sweeping victory launched on such a day would also carry considerable symbolism, to land such a blow against the French on such an important holiday. Not only was the date fixed, but the location became fairly certain well in advance.

For strategic reasons, both sides saw the Marne sector as an important target. For the Germans, who held a salient that extended in a sideways U, they saw the proximity of Rheims and Chalons—two major rail hubs—as a way to supplement their single transportation center at Soissons. For the Allies, a push to Soissons would cut off German supply lines and force the Germans to retreat from the salient completely. Debate raged, however, as the British command saw signs of a possible attack to the north, in Flanders, and argued that available reserves should be tasked to them. Foch disagreed, citing ample intelligence and quietly began building up troops in the Marne sector.

Aerial reconnaissance revealed increased troop movements and interrogation of German deserters further revealed that the Germans had moved heavy equipment and war machinery into a line stretching from Chateau-Thierry to Epernay. Under directions from Foch, Petain issued orders announcing the anticipated aims of the German attack.

To draw the mass of our reserves from the region of Paris and the zone of the Franco-British junction.

To affect the fall of Reims and gain a foothold on the Montagne de Reims.

To bring the Epernay-Chalons-Revigny Railroad within the range of its artillery.

As Bastille Day drew closer, we heard increasing rumors about artillery movements and troop repositioning. At one point, we understood that we were to be re-tasked ourselves, though this did not happen. We were told not to smoke in the open for fear of snipers using the glow to target our position. Gouraud himself issued orders on July seventh.

We may be attacked at any moment. You all know that a defensive battle was never engaged under more favorable conditions. We are awake and on our guard.

On July thirteenth, a German officer crossed the Marne to reconnoiter the Allied positions. Before he could return to his own lines, he was captured and interrogated. It was discovered that he carried with him a copy of the German attack orders. Another prisoner, taken by the French IV Corps in a raid the next day, told his interrogators the exact minute in which the German artillery bombardment was set to commence. July 15, zero ten hours. Ten minutes after midnight.

***

"You like those, don't you, Pippin?" I said.

"Keeps me calm, sir." Pippin took a slow drag on his cig. "Never used to smoke, but here, here it's different, you know."

"Yeah."

We stood in silence, then, for a moment. Pippin held his cigarette between his fingers, maybe level with his belly. We stared in the distance.

K Company was positioned in the line of redoubt—the third trench—and acted in support of the First Battalion. The setup was simple. Only a small handful of volunteers remained in the line of observation. They carried with them grenades and their Lebels and nothing else. They were the advance guard, the warning system. When the Boche crossed No Man's Land they would toss their grenades, close the barbwire gates behind them and retreat past the line of resistance. When the Boche moved forward, they would begin to gain confidence. It's easy to deceive yourself into complacency when there's little gunfire directed your way. A few companies were positioned on the second line of resistance with the purpose of luring the Boche further in. They would offer increased resistance, but as soon as the Boche pushed, they were to retreat. Only when the Boche reached the line of resistance itself, dropping into the trenches, would our full forces be unleashed. The line of redoubt would counter-attack through the boyaux and over the hump. The Boche, who would be trapped in unfamiliar trenches, would be confused and disoriented. With proper planning and execution, we would easily push them back across No Man's Land and maybe beyond.

"This ain't gonna be fun, is it, sir?"

"Depends on how you define fun."

"I guess you're right, there, sir," Pippin took another puff of his cigarette and blew smoke into the night.

It was warm, still July, and the ground was not nearly as muddy as it was just a month before. There was still the occasional summer rain, but it would pass, and the sun would return and dry the mud and swamp into hardened earth. It was a thing to see, baked craters in the French countryside.

"I've seen you reading that Bible of yours, sir, lately."

I froze. I couldn't articulate my motives for doing so, but I had been skimming Seaman Marks' book. I thought I had done it in private, hidden in an abris, behind a tree, or otherwise alone. For Pippin to discover my casual research made me uncomfortable. He was the kind of person who might mistake curiosity for something more…earnest.

"Yeah," I said, in hopes of staving some die-hard Christian testimony. "I've never read it before."

"It's a good book, sir, you'll like it."

"It's interesting," I admitted.

Pippin shrugged; a gesture barely visible by the light of his glowing cigarette. "I've only read parts, I suppose, but it seems to be something good to live by. I suspect I appreciate it more and more every day goes by. What, living here in these trenches, death only a Minnie away."

"Somewhere to go after."

"That's right, sir. The idea this ain't everything. It's a comfort, kind of like these cigarettes I guess. Though maybe it's more than that."

I didn't say anything. Although I would argue belief with any educated man, Pippin was not an educated man. Once I might have gone on the attack—damn his lack of education—but now, now that I had lived with him—and with all the other men of K Company and the regiment—I could not bring myself to tear apart his beliefs. It was a strange sensation, to hold back, to reserve my judgment and my reason simply because I respected someone as a human being.

Strange times indeed.

"Not so sure myself," all I said.

Pippin finished his cigarette and smothered it in the dirt. "Nice night for it, sir."

"Yeah, nice night."

"We get through till tomorrow, sir, I'll show you some of my drawings I've done lately. There's some really pretty things I've seen, what with the summer in the Argonne and the blooming of things. Not that there's much left to bloom after the last few years."

"I think I'd like that," I said.

"Reckon we best get back 'fore the shelling starts, sir."

***

Half an hour later, at midnight on July 15th, our artillery began bombardment of the German positions. Ten minutes later, the Boche guns, fired by surprised and harried gunners, answered fire. The Second Battle of the Marne had begun.

Manhattan, New York

New York, USA
May 3, 1921

Exhausted and covered in travel, my body scented by the sweat of an enclosed cabin, my back sticky and clothes damped I lifted my trunk, stamped New York to San Francisco and back, and set it on the bed. I flipped the latch and opened the thing. I found a set of clothes, slacks and a shirt, a tie and a vest. Too warm, now, for the thicker jacket or trench coat beneath. I gathered these things, this trusty attire and carried it with me to the water closet I now shared with the other inhabitants of the floor. A cheap hotel, not so cheap as to cause me concern over bed bug or cockroach, but not so expensive either.

Take a holiday, take the cure, he said. Continue the advances made in hospital and grow strong.

Returned, now, I felt strong and fresh and clear and all the things that I once understood. I showered and shaved and dressed and prepared myself in every way a man can. Smelling of soap, I smoothed the trunk wrinkles from my shirt and emerged, thinner than when I left, fit and alive. I took the El downtown, to Little Italy, Bleeker, to the brownstone by the park, the one near the corner, where a little boy and his mother lived, where my son and his mother—where Allie now called home.

I found the bench and settled in to watch. I flipped through a paper though did not read the words. I saw the text, black on gray paper, the type not quite crisp for the bleed. I scanned columns and headlines. Every few seconds, my eyes darted up, over the tip of the pages and checked the door down the street, watched for signs of life. After an hour, the door opened and the thick man with the slicked hair marched down the steps, his feet heavy on the concrete, his body lurching. I could see, now, watching him alone, that he held himself like some doyen, the great man himself, head of a family of vast influence and great importance. He moved with the authority and confidence…the arrogance of one in command.

I watched the man, Johnathan Esposito—Johnathan after the saint, I'm sure—look up and down the sidewalk and turn left, back into the island. I folded my paper closed. I waited to see Esposito walk around a corner before I dropped the paper on the bench and strode across the pavement. I climbed the curb, moved down the street, past two, three, four homes until I came to the one, to the Brownstone, to hers. I took a moment at the walk, where the concrete met her steps and breathed in the scent of it all, the spring flowers that grew in boxes either side of the grasping risers. I took a breath, climbed them and rapped the hardwood door.

Allie appeared in the doorway and my heart stalled. She stood erect, though her eyes rimmed with red and her face streaked with tears. Her hair, her beautiful hair, frayed and crazy, a halo of black electricity framing her face. Her dress torn at the sleeve exposed her shoulder. An angry bruise welled there, on the flesh of her arm…gaunt and haunted, she saw me and retreated.

"You can't—"

"What happened to you?"

She shook her head and tried to push the door closed.

I stepped forward and filled the space. She clasped at her torn dress.

"What happened to you?"

"You have to go. If he finds you here…"

I glanced over my shoulder, remembered the way the man had strutted down the street. Now, I knew it for the strut of power, the strut of a man who'd just beat his woman.

"You have to—"

I placed my hands gently on her shoulders—careful to avoid the bruise—and pulled her close. I felt her heat against me, her breasts pressed against my belly, her body trembling, still in shock. "It'll be okay; I'll protect you—"

"You can't protect—"

"You're my child's mother, how can I—"

She pushed away from me, then and stared into my face. "How did you know?"

I took a breath. Over and over, as I sat on the train and crossed through the fields and over the mountains, I told myself that I must tell the truth. The truth was my only hope…yet, to tell the truth here, to reveal that I still…that I stalked her and that through my stalking I saw…I must.

"I saw from down the street. Months ago, I saw you and the boy…what's his name?"

"You were watching? You—"

"What's his name?"

She shook. I watched her shake, there in her hallway, her body frail and lonely, a new-born calf unable to hold itself up, she put a hand to her chest, to her lips, about to cry. "Why didn't you—why didn't you come sooner?"

"What's hi—wait, what?"

"Why didn't you come? If you knew so long ago, why didn't you…"

I blinked. I had expected anger, frustration, rejection—but this sadness, this sense of abandonment, this surprised me. "I…can I come in?"

"Close the door behind you."

I followed Allie into the house, through a hallway to a sitting room. She led me inside, to the paisley sofa, the polished coffee table, the matching chairs. She took a chair and tucked her legs beneath her. She folded her arms across her chest and withdrew. I sat next to her in the second chair, the sofa unoccupied before us. I felt an anger rise inside, a red rage that touched my heart. The man who did this…

"His name is Isaac, brother of Ishmael."

"Isaac…"

"For your friend…the one you always talked about. Johnathan doesn't know."

"When your father died…when you came to me that night…"

"Two weeks after Isaac—"

Allie caught her breath and raised a hand to her mouth. Her shoulders shuddered and she gasped a sob. I ached to move to her, to hold her in my arms and comfort her, to repent my rejection of years ago. But I…

I stood from my chair and held my hand to her. She stared at it, upraised, a strange offering, and only after—it seemed—an eon, did she stretch her own to meet it. Contact. I felt the electric spark and it raced through my body. I pulled her slowly to her feet, pulled her to me, and wrapped my arms around her. I felt her sob against me, heard her tears, her quiet gasps as she tried to suppress them, felt the damp on her cheeks stain my shirt. I held her close, ran my fingers through her hair, let her cry.

"I'm so sorry," I said. "I'm so sorry I let you go."

"I…"

"It's okay, it'll be okay. We can fix things. We can fix it all. I know that now, I know what's important now."

"Don't."

"I have to. I can't ignore…"

"You have to go," she said into my chest. I felt her stiffen. "You have to go now before he comes again. You have to leave and never—"

"Mommy?"

I felt her tense, every muscle bunched and flexed. I let her go, then, and turned toward the voice, toward the small boy—maybe four now—who stood in the doorway. I stared at the boy, at the wild hair, at the giant eyes, the tiny hands, and feet. He stood shirtless, his eyes dazed with sleep and he didn't seem to notice the awkwardness of his mother embracing a stranger. He saw his mommy and raced across the room to wrap his arms around her legs. She lifted him from the floor and hugged him close to her chest.

"It's okay, honey."

"Who's that?" the boy said and twisted in her arms to point a finger at me.

"That's an old friend. He was just leaving."

"Hi. I'm Isaac."

This was my son. This was our son. If it hadn't been for my painful stupidity, my arrogance to think I could be something, my single-minded obsession…this could be our life. Allie and I and Isaac. A happy family. Together.

"Hello, Isaac," I said.

"What's your name?"

"My name is…I'm a friend."

He smiled and pointed to the floor. Allie lowered him carefully and the second his feet hit the carpet he raced out of the room. I watched him move, watched the little muscles move him with such speed and grace, watched his legs pump and his arms flail the way children do. I watched him until he passed through the doorway. I watched him even as he moved into the house, as he passed through a puddle of light. I watched him in horror, then, for what I saw on his back suddenly exposed. A purple and yellow bruise, mostly healed, in that instant.

"My god, he hits Isaac too."

"You have to go," Allie pushed at me. She turned me around and tried to push me toward the front door. I thought to fight her, to stay and confront this reality, but I knew it would not help.

I let her push me to the hall and to the door. At the step, I stopped and said, "If you'll let me…I'll help you."

"Go. Go and never come back."

"I'm sorry," I said.

"I'm sorry too," she said and closed the door.

I stood alone, then, for a long while. My face a foot from her door. My heart still inside. I couldn't stop thinking of that bruise on my child's back, of the things I wanted to do to the man who inflicted it. I closed my eyes and pictured my son, his smiling face, his wide eyes, his tiny body. I saw it all and I saw, too, what I must do. For the first time, I knew what must be done to save my soul.

North of Chalons-Sur-Marne

Champagne, France
15 July – August 18, 1918

Dirt and gravel rained down, plunked helmets and settled into a fine mist of silt over green wool. Another shell landed and blew shrapnel and mud over our heads. Another shell, farther this time, and another, closer. Shell after shell after shell. Each explosion rocked the earth a little and lit the sky with phosphor and gun powder. Metal shards ripped the air. So much noise and destruction, it got so a moment's calm seemed like an eternity of silence, too quiet to let it pass unmarked, too quiet to leave it unfilled. So, we talked, one man to another, until the quiet passed and the bombardment resumed. Only a few moments, but in their intensity, enough to know a man entire.

"How long before they send men across? I can't wait to see those Chauchats mow down some Boche mothers."

"This rate? Maybe tomorrow."

"What time is it, anyway?"

"Sky's still dark. Can't see no stars though."

"Damn clouds."

A minnenwarfer whined down on a trench not too far from my position. Men shouted and cursed. Only one way for the things to take us out, with trenches as deep and well dug as ours, if it slipped between the walls and dug into the floor. Men died when that happened. Otherwise, the things hit left or right or off the side, they blew dirt and shrapnel past our heads, nothing else. A hot breeze and a rain of pebbles the damage.

But the possibility drove a man insane.

Huge numbers, maybe a thousand shells an hour, landed on our sector. A German war machine loosed on a handful of Negroes. The odds dropped with each bombardment until snake eyes stared down from heaven. Cold bones. Cold bones indeed. *Boom. Boom. Boom.*

"You know; I don't think Fritz is ever gonna show."

"We beat him to the punch after all."

"Yeah, yeah. We all knew this was coming."

"I think maybe we scared him. Took away his surprise."

"One time my girl snuck a party on me. Called my friends over. That was, hell, just last year."

"I wonder what Fritzie looks like in drag."

"Shit, man, that's sick."

Boom. Boom. Boom. Hour after hour the shells fell from German guns. Gas. A whisper down the line. One of the replacement niggers pulled his mask on, gasped for air. The rest of us watched and laughed. Not the right sound. Gas canisters came in high and wobbly, almost like a Minnie but just to the left. This was low, a big gun and a big shell, not gas.

The earth shook.

Boom. Boom. Boom.

"Anybody save their wine? I could use me some now. God awful headache I'm getting."

"This thing's over and I find me a vineyard to drink."

"They ain't something you can drink."

"Lots of wine in a vineyard."
"Grapes in a vineyard, you idiot."
"Grapes make wine."
"Somewhere 'sides a vineyard."
"It's like a saying, eat a horse, drink a vineyard."
"Not the same thing."
Boom. Boom. Boom.

A clod of dirt hit my helmet and rolled to the trench floor. I kicked it at a rat. Damn rats. I don't care if Europe found them cute. I hated the lousy rodents almost as much as I hated artillery preparations. Two ever-present evils, always and forever, shells and rats and rats and shells.

A rat scurried past my boots. A shell landed not fifteen feet away. Fuck it. I closed my eyes and leaned my head against the trench wall. If the rats didn't mind, why should I?

***

0430 hours. Pass the mess kits. Kitchens in the rear. Slop of stew and coffee. Breakfast under bombardment.

***

Sunrise in Champagne. A cool mist settled over the ground. Boche artillery—at least our stretch of Boche artillery—stood down, still. For a few moments, anyway, silence. The mist and dew clung to wool and boots and skin, damped the earth so that every step dug through yesterday's sunbaked crust and sunk into the cool mud beneath. A breeze came out of the west, off the Marne, and through countless hill straddled valleys. It carried a hint of sulfur and ozone, powder and blood. The smells of a long night of bombardment. Endless shelling from both sides. The sudden silence, I'm not sure, added to the chill. Sunshine angled steeply from the horizon, unable to burn it off, another hour or two of early morning shivers.

Not that war waited.

The walls of our trench seemed to close in, closer still, claustrophobic. Over the silence, now, my ears recovered from those first few moments after the guns said good day, I could hear the voices of men. German and English and French. Moans, shouts, whispers. Soldiers alone at dawn, wounded, afraid of loss. Medics and comrades among them, back and forth, bandages and morphine. I could feel their weight on my shoulders, another invisible barrier, a ceiling to close me in completely between the caked dirt and bunched wood. My own guilt already unbearable.

A different thing to enter a battle and come out again, alive. Men beside you become more, a bond forms and they are no longer just men.

But I could not call them brothers.

Collapsed walls, trenches demolished, repaired by intent soldiers. New faces took the place of the dead and injured. Fresh bodies dumped from drafted regiments. Untried and yellow inside, but black on the skin more important. The fallens' Lebels in hand they joined the ranks, huddled in abris and lay wide-eyed through the night.

Across No Man's Land, the Germans licked their wounds.

***

0800, we moved. Back through the trenches, up, out. A silent march to the west. Three miles on the hoof. Left, right, left. Some of our men still behind us, dead or dying, victims of the evening's rain. Temporary station Camp Bravard. No relief movement until after dark.

***

"A cigarette."

"Sir?"

I pointed to Pippin's own cigarette, lighted, in his fingers. "Can I have a cigarette?"

"But I thought you didn't smoke."

"I don't," I said. "But you seem to do well with them so I thought I'd give it a try, see how it relieves my stress."

Pippin grinned, his handsome face alight with humor, "You, sir? What do you have to stress about? You, a lieutenant, who gets told what to do just like a private, what can there be?"

"You, private, are more than enough stress."

Pippin laughed, "I deserved that one for sure."

"So, can I have a cigarette…for my stress?"

Pippin extended a small box packet. I fished a skinny stick loose and set it between my lips before I handed the box back.

"So, how do you do this?" I said.

Pippin handed me a match. "You hold the light to the tip of the thing same time as you suck in just the smallest bit. Enough to catch the flame toward you. No more than that or you might burn yourself."

"Sounds perfectly safe."

"And it is, too, except the stuff it does to your lungs. First time you smoke it, you'll cough for sure. Hack a little. But then you'll get used to it."

I flicked the match tip against a rock. It flashed to life and I raised the tiny flame slowly to the cigarette. I followed Pippin's instructions and puffed lightly until the cigarette caught. I shook the match out and dropped it to the ground. A puff and smoke filled my lungs. I let it warm me for a spot before I exhaled into the air above my head.

"You didn't cough," Pippin said. "You've done this before."

I smiled. "I said I don't smoke, not that I haven't ever smoked."

Pippin grinned again. I liked his smile, it was genuine.

I took another puff and Pippin did the same. We stood side by side for a whole minute, quietly smoking and looking up at the pale gray sky.

"Does it help?" Pippin said.

"Help?"

"With the stress?"

"You're still here, aren't you?"

"That's true," Pippin laughed, "that's true."

I finished my cigarette and ground it underfoot. I thought to leave but stopped myself. For some reason, there was something else. More. More to learn. Something I wanted to know.

"Pippin," I said, "Where are you from?"

Pippin nodded, "Goshen, sir. I'm from Goshen, New York."

"You married—wait, I know that. You're not married but you want—"

"That's right, sir. I'll find a miss and settle down after."

"Good luck with that," I said.

"Thank you."

I thought for a moment, "I assume you have parents."

"Yes, sir."

"Hell, I don't mean to deprive you, but can I have another?"

Pippin handed me the packet. "My pleasure, sir."

"I think you might be wrong," I said. "Strangely enough, I think this might be my pleasure."

***

Slumber. War afternoon sun beamed through thin clouds. Bodies reclined, warmed in the summer heat. No rain, no rats, no shells. Hours of uninterrupted shut-eye. The proximate sounds of the front unheeded. Our lives protected by a shallow outcropping of stone.

Camp Bravard.

Some tents really, not a place of dense population, a waypoint for soldiers in transition. A respite to the weary and shell worn. An afternoon only. By nightfall, we gathered to hear orders, chart marches, and confirm rumors.

The Boche assault broken.

Across the front.

Our new sector, Beausejour, the eastern edge of lost ground. Germans bulged south and occupied front-line trenches…our front-line trenches. Elsewhere, they bulged and retreated, spent, but from Beausejour west, the bulge stayed strong. Tumescent Boche territory.

A hot meal broke the monotony of rest. Stew, greens, coffee. Coffee, the army's answer to water.

I ate slowly, savored the easy eating.

Dusk lasted forever. Dimming skies stretched long by the anticipation of the march. Moments spread thin as men talked of girls and friends and Harlem. For an instant, I closed my eyes and imagined Allie close. Felt her skin against mine. Smelled her scent, fecund and powerful.

"Form up."

I opened my eyes. My vision had not delivered me. The fields of Champagne stretched still. Always the fields. Yellow wheat trod underfoot. Mud and weeds trampled into hardened clay.

Take a march.

I grabbed my bag and joined the ranks. Troop movement in the dark a necessary precaution in active fire zones.

"Forward 'arch."

Left, right, left. After the sun. Regiment on the move. To the west toward Paris. Keep up this rate in three days' time we march past the Eiffel Tower.

***

The night settled uneasily. Fitful dreams tossed and turned and transformed into a nightmare. Starlight hid and the moon stayed away. Boche flares floated softly on the still air, nothing moving, nothing alive. Only the *thwump, whine, boom* of shell fire; a flash across No Man's Land, a sweeping arc and an explosion the only life, the only movement, the only evidence of our existence.

We holed up in shallow trenches, bare depressions, dug in haste and disregarded. We reclined against the earth, our heads not quite fully hidden from Boche view. Tiny blue mounds along the edge of the trench, damn Poilus helmets. I longed for the dark green of American helmets, not the blue of the French, too visible blue, too much a contrast to the earth and grass and weeds and wheat. Too much blue south of the sky.

But that concern could wait until dawn.

A shell hit nearby. Shrapnel and earth blew in tiny arcs from the epicenter. A white-hot piece landed on my uniform arm and burned through to the skin before I could brush it away. Pain bit into my flesh and I blew on the red patch.

Damn Boche.

Either side of me a gap of four, maybe five feet then another soldier, another Harlem Negro crowded close to the ground, humping the earth, desperate to escape the Boche shelling. The shallow trenches here providing no protection compared to the well dug, deep lanes of Ville-sur-Tourbe. There a man could hide from the shells, let the debris and metal fly overhead unheeded. Here, anything too close brought death. Men who once would escape the explosive force of a Minnie died within its destructive radius. Ill-prepared defenses, hasty entrenchments, built on the retreat and pressured by the enemy. I imagined our trenches built by the 161st only yesterday, their bodies tense, aware of the Boche hordes pressing down on their position.

Today's front, half a kilometer south of yesterday's front.

I stared at the man to my right, tried to identify him, but could come no closer than to recall he too came from K Company. I did not know his name, but I remembered once that he fated me and lost. In St Nazaire, I think, as we shoveled through the muck of that ill-begotten hellhole.

"You got a smoke?" I called.

He shook his head and patted his pockets. A shell exploded to the north. "Sorry, Ayers, not until the next allotment."

"Thanks," I said.

I wasn't sure that Pippin had converted me to the habit, but I knew that after one time, smoking beside a man with whom I shared the front line, I recognized some calming influence in a cigarette. It wasn't the smoke or the favor, but the motions. Something in the lighting and smoking of a cigarette that brought a moment's peace and reminded me that I might yet survive.

I turned to the man on my left, "You got a smoke?"

He felt at his uniform pockets and nodded. "Yeah, I gots some."

I waited until he pulled a packet and emptied a pair of cigarettes into his hand. He slid on his ass until he was close enough to pass one across. I grabbed it in my fingers and felt the small stick a comfort against my skin. I fished a match from my kit and lit the tobacco. Breathed in warm smoke and let it fill my lungs.

"Thanks," I said.

"No problem, lieutenant," the man said.

I looked at him more closely and recognized him as a man named Freeman. He liked prostitutes. We'd talked about the Bowery girls and the girls on San Juan Hill. He'd never slept with her, but he remembered Rose and the others. He tended to like the skinnier ladies, the ones who barely carried any flesh on their bones. I was just the opposite. I liked myself a girl with proper curves.

"You find any pussy lately?" I asked.

He grinned and shook his head. "Nah, nothing since we left Hoboken. Only way I've found relief is with my right hand."

"Yeah," I said.

"Not for lack of trying, mind you. I've had an eye on every pair that walked past since we landed, but none of them looked back, not for the amount of money I could spread down. You feel what I'm saying?"

"I feel you," I said. Thinking of the three whores who'd escaped the army's notice in Aix-les-Bains. Not that I'd slept with any of them, but I'd seen them disappear into their flats with plenty of boys in green. Desperate soldiers without a hope of finding pussy before they went home to their wives and girlfriends.

"You think—"

Boom.

A shell landed to the far side of Freeman. Its explosive core vaporized the man before my eyes. One instant, he was alive and talking about pussy, the next a red mist. I felt his warm blood against my brow and closed my eyes. I raised my arm to cover my face and turned to spit in the dirt. My heart raced and my cheeks burned. I felt a fear sweep through me that I'd never known. I knew the stories, but god, right in front of me.

"You okay?" the soldier on my right called.

I lowered my arm and looked in his direction. "Yeah, I'm okay, but Freeman…"

"It's these damned trenches."

"Yeah, tomorrow, I think we'd best do some pick and shovel work."

"You got that right."

"I don't want to spend another night so exposed."

A shell landed close enough to shake the earth. I winced despite myself. I could feel the thin film of Private Freeman on my skin. If a shell landed too close…

***

The front grew quiet, returned to the old ways, as the rest of the line decided a German offensive at the Marne Salient couldn't succeed. We hunkered in our lines, patrolled, watched, and dodged Minnies. The Boche hunkered in theirs, patrolled watched and dodged our artillery. They sent a raid one night, we sent one the next. Variations on a theme. We captured two Boche soldiers. They captured none of ours. One night, though, a close thing. A German raid captured three of ours and was on the march back to their side of the void. One of our observation posts caught wise and opened fire. The Germans scattered while our men fell back. A close thing for sure, but not too close. Live and let live, the unspoken agreement. Quiet action, the only movement between major actions. No one is interested in dying today.

A man lost to influenza, another to infection, a third to dysentery. Hygiene in the trenches a deplorable affair. Pits where urine and feces festered open to the air. Flies and insects and rats.

Rats.

A fourth man, rat bit, fell ill and found himself in the hospital tents behind the lines.

Nuisance, menace, plague. Rats haunted the trenches with their furry hides and white tails, whiskers and teeth. They scurried underfoot and perched in concave ledges behind hurdles of wood. Glowing eyes watched every movement, saw every opportunity, followed every morsel. They were an over mind, omnipresent, horrifying. I hated them. A curse is what they were, a curse sent by the Kaiser on his enemies. The German's secret weapon: rats.

A fifth man to influenza. Half a dozen more in hospital.

We moved off our position, ever so slightly, west again. Assuming a different part of the same sector, resumed the status quo.

Waited.

Trenches…hell…modern fucking warfare.

***

Scuttlebutt said Black Jack was about to play his hand and officially segregate the officer corps.

A new contingent of white officers joined the regiment as if to lend credibility to the rumor.

***

August. It never stopped. The rain fell year-round in this godforsaken place. Only the occasional respite, a day, maybe two in which the clouds parted and let the sun shine on the rolling plains of Champagne. If not precisely sunny, such a day promised to be little more than hazy, with the ever-looming threat of something more substantial in the evening.

***

Training in Les Maigneux. Preparations in battalion-sized maneuvers. The rest of Pershing's black babies arrived now needed to integrate. The 369th joined with the 370th, 371st, and 372nd in liaison and support. When the offensive push came it would be these four regiments together. A sizable length of front in the hands of American Negroes. Some less experienced than others. A division of variable quality. The 369th, the only volunteer outfit in the bunch. Ready to lead, ready to fight, hell, ready for leave. Many of the lessons review. A seasoned group of veterans, we Harlemites, who knew the dangers of the trenches as well as any Poilus could tell.

Training in Les Maigneux. Still within earshot of the front but too far to concern ourselves over a lucky minnenwarfer. Bodies relaxed and sleep came easy. Men joked and roughhoused and kept an eye open for the fairer sex. The lectures and field practice took few resources compared to the front. Easy to slack off. Easy to grow maudlin with thoughts of home. Easy to find distractions. Easier to get in trouble.

Training in Les Maigneux.

***

Dommartin-la-Planchette. A handful of buildings that straddled a dirt path not five kilometers of field from Les Maigneux. F Company posted to guard the village, maybe six men on duty.

The men found a bottle of champagne and shared it around. Nothing too terrible but some white soldier got himself agitated and sent word to regimental HQ a 'drunken ruckus' called for immediate action. Never mind that the men of F Company had already returned to their stations or that the one man truly affected by the wine, Private Roy Shields, had been relieved of duty. HQ reacted to the rumor of drunken Negroes and not the fact of disciplined soldiers. They sent a replacement lieutenant, Emmet Cochrane, in charge of a handful of men from M Company—a white boy to discipline those rowdy niggers.

Lieutenant Cochrane was one of the fresh white officers recently assigned to the regiment. Born in Georgia and grown in Montgomery, Alabama, he bore the hallmark background of a good southern racist…whether his feelings led him to overt acts of prejudice, his suspicions and reactions during the incident suggested the training of a professional white man.

In Dommartin, the arrest of Private Shields put an end to any aborning drunkenness and the men settled into their duty with little more impairment than a sense of well-being and a sweet aftertaste in their mouths. Private Whittaker and Sergeant Thomas Emmanuel guarded the western approach to the town. Whittaker carried two rifles on his back—his own and Private Shields'—neither one loaded.

The men from M Company rode an ambulance cart and as they approached Dommartin they didn't bother to slow down. Taking his duty seriously, Whittaker stepped into the path of the cart and waved for it to stop. Cochrane slowed the horses but had no intention of stopping. He shouted for Whittaker to clear the way. Whittaker, not about to let the cart pass without proper identification, grabbed at the reins of the horse and pulled the cart to a stop.

Furious, Cochrane leaped from the cart and drew his pistol.

Private Whittaker, faced with a red-cheeked officer and a pointed gun slowly removed one rifle from his shoulder and set it on the ground before him. As he removed the second and bent to set it, too, besides the first, Cochrane pulled his trigger. The bullet struck Whittaker in the belly.

Whittaker said nothing but stood straight and stared at Cochrane. Finally, he spoke to the white man. "Well, lieutenant you have shot me. I was carrying out my orders and you have shot a good man."

Sergeant Emmanuel reported that after this statement, absolute silence prevailed in Dommartin for a span of four minutes. During that time, as well, each player in this drama stood unmoving. Only when it seemed to reach absurdity did Whittaker once more speak, but this time to his Negro brothers.

"Boys, if I die, tell all the people a good man is gone."

Then, surrendering to the inevitable, Whittaker sank to his knees and collapsed on his face.

***

A single black fly landed on his upper lip, wiped its legs together, and turned toward a nostril. No move was made to shoo it away, no one cared that a fly landed on a dead man's face. Dirt from the road, picked up in a smear when he collapsed, covered his forehead and left cheek. His skin, waxy now, had turned pale and almost translucent so you could see muscle and fat…or at least it seemed so. His chest was laid bare, tatters from his uniform shirt—ripped open by the French surgeon—lay beneath him. An ugly gash scarred his belly. Harsh sutures held it closed, big looping stitches, the surgeon not worried about cosmetic appeal in a dead soldier.

Marshall bent over Whittaker's body and brushed his mustaches. "In and out?"

"Found it in his—what you call—pants," the surgeon pointed to a small metal bowl on a side table. "Bullet's right there."

Marshall looked up, straight at me. "Make a note of that."

I took note.

"And he died how long after he arrived?"

The surgeon blinked dully, "Excuse?"

"How long before he died?"

"Ah, not long," the surgeon raised a hand, fingers open and spread. "Five minutes, maybe, no more than to cut him."

I jotted the note: dead five minutes after arrival.

Marshall moved counterclockwise around the body. I stepped back, uncomfortable. Not with Marshall, but with the reality Whittaker's death represented, or at least the way I interpreted it. It was this exact type of incident that would please Tammany. A white man acted to discipline some drunken niggers and things got out of hand. Almost too convenient. I wondered. Hadn't Tammany's man in Chalons mentioned other agents. He had said there were others, men who would do Tammany's bidding. Men like Cochrane? Had I caused this by my hesitation and doubt? Was Walter Whittaker's death one more body for me to bear?

"Lieutenant," Marshall snapped.

"Sorry?"

"Note down the location of the exit wound please, right here to the right of center."

I nodded, numb, and wrote the note.

***

A soft glow lit the horizon where the front lay. Occasional flashes burned in the night followed by hollow booms. Shellfire by night. Different at a distance. Almost beautiful in a violent and horrifying way.

A machine gun fired, audible across the miles.

Almost a week now since we'd left the trenches. Training with the other Negro regiments progressed apace. An uncertain future turned monotonous by repetition and rote. The only change in rumors, anticipation, anxiety. We would move soon in preparation for the upcoming offensive, some said. Some claimed that the Negroes would be shipped back to SOS and never see the front again. Others claimed a reassignment of every black officer in the regiment. This last one true. Pershing issued a general order to segregate the officer corps. Either all white or all black but not both. White man's fears of a black officer commanding a white one too trenchant to be ignored. The possibility best made impossible.

Already, Marshall had transferred and half a dozen others besides. My time short, I figured, in the face of regimental whitewash.

A rock turned in the darkness, a figure appeared before me.

"Lieutenant Ayers?"

"Yes."

"Colonel Hayward would like a word."

I nodded at the inevitable. I was to be transferred.

I followed the orderly through the camp, tents rose and fell in peaks either side. I walked slowly and he gained ground, now ten, now twenty yards ahead. I was distracted.

I knew Tammany had other eyes in the regiment, other men to do their work. The man at Chalons had said as much and the murder of Private Whittaker confirmed it. I was no longer needed, obsolete and unusable, an unneeded cog in the machine. I understood that now and understood the precarious ledge upon which I tread. If I could not find some way to proclaim my use, do something to salvage my position, I would be forsaken. No use for a tool. All my work to ingratiate myself, to perform for Tammany would be counted as naught. Perhaps in my new regiment, perhaps there was hope there. I could offer my services and renew my loyalty in some way. I couldn't lose my investment, not now, not after everything I'd done. Because I had no doubt that if, for an instant, I stopped serving Tammany, Tammany would drop me from their rolls and forget all about me. They did not care that I had killed for them, or that I had betrayed my people. They cared that I deliver regularly. I had to contact them, find some way to renew my deal, make my willingness known. I had to make everything count.

I reached Hayward's tent and announced myself.

"Come in, Ayers," Hayward called.

I stepped through the open flap and entered regimental headquarters. Two tables filled the space. One was littered with maps and lists and orienteering equipment—a compass, both kinds, and several pencils—the other was fitted out as a desk. It was behind the second that Hayward sat. A lamp hung from the tent post and swayed slightly so that light moved constantly, shading his face in different ways, changing and shifting. I could see his eyes shine, lit by the lamp, and the muscles of his jaw flex. More detail than that passed too quickly between light and shadow. I was left only with a sense of foreboding as I saluted and took a position in front of the colonel.

"At ease, Lieutenant."

"Thank you, sir."

Colonel Hayward ran his hand across his cheek. "You've heard the order about transferring every black officer."

"Yes, sir."

"You anticipate a transfer yourself, I'm sure."

"Sir."

"It's just as well. Do you know how tenuous your fate is, Ayers? You've painted yourself into a pretty little corner."

I shifted my weight but said nothing. I wasn't sure what Hayward was talking about.

Hayward spread his hands across his desk and leaned forward. "It doesn't take much to figure you've been working for the democrats. The orders involving you always came from liberal officers. The democrats mean Tammany, and Tammany means Murphy. Now, I've expressed my distaste for your actions before—and I reiterate it now. I despise Charles Murphy and any man who works for him."

"Sir—"

"Quiet, lieutenant…I'm going to say my piece and you're going to listen to it because I've wanted ever so much to say it for the last six months."

"Sir."

Hayward sat back, almost casually. The light hovered over his nose and highlighted the day's scruff on his chin. "Now, to work for Tammany is one evil. But I am convinced you've complicated your position by working at cross purposes to the success of this regiment. Ever since South Carolina—Major Little told me about your involvement there—I've kept an eye out. You've managed to gamble with every soldier you met. You talk of prostitutes and liquor and other deleterious activities. You seem keen for opportunities to undermine your fellow officers. And in every other way possible, you've made a menace of yourself.

"I warned you that your immunity would not last forever and that when it failed, I would be here to see you get what you deserve. I'm very pleased to announce to you that as of this morning, Tammany Hall has disavowed you completely.

"What do you—"

Hayward lifted a paper from his desk. "I received an order—very specifically in reference to one Lieutenant Reuben Ayers. This order gives me the unequivocal authority to dispose of said lieutenant however I deem fit. It means, in other words, that whoever used to concern themselves with your placement in my regiment ceased to do so. You, Lieutenant Ayers, have come to a reckoning."

I stared at Colonel Hayward, at his gentleman's ease. Even this late at night, his uniform showed crisp creases. He was a paragon of Rooseveltian manhood, and I hated him. I hated his erect posture, his polished speech, and his behavioral correctness. For all his work as our colonel, I knew, standing before him, that he was a racist, maybe a paternalist with good intentions, but a racist still. Though for all truth that may have resided in my judgment, it was useless. Only in that it allowed me to retain some small degree of superiority as he spoke, as he signaled an end to everything that I'd worked for.

"It is within my power," Hayward continued, "to see you safely transferred to another regiment. I could let you escape into some ignorant commander's graces. I could do this, but if I do, I let you continue with impunity, unpunished, the behaviors that have plagued my regiment. It is needless to say that I will not transfer you—though the thought of ridding myself of your rotting taste has appeal. No, I would leave you here to reap the results of your subterfuge and sullenness."

"But—"

"Yes, Pershing's order. I cannot leave you here, lieutenant. Not, at least, as a lieutenant."

I felt my eyes go wide and an uncomfortable heat warm my cheeks.

"Yes, you see it. I cannot leave you here as a lieutenant, but if I demote you, to a sergeant perhaps, a non-commissioned officer, there will be no conflict with the general orders. You could remain with the 369th and I could be satisfied that you get to see the true side of combat—the side from which you've effectively isolated yourself. Expose you to the full dangers of the front without the support of the men. Oh yes, that's right, you won't have any support. After a while, a man will come to rely on the man next to him. It's referred to by some as the brotherhood of arms. You've not developed those kinds of relationships with the men of this regiment because you've been too busy trying to destroy them. That's unfortunate for you, sergeant. You might find it lonely on the front, very lonely, indeed."

I walked from Hayward's tent dazed, shocked, and confused. I had gone in expecting a transfer only to be demoted and, worse, informed that my life's work had been thrown aside like so much trash.

Tammany.

They couldn't renege on their side of the deal. I wouldn't let them. When I got back to New York, I would find them and make them follow through with their promises. I had done so much for them; they couldn't leave me out in the cold.

Yet even as I reasoned and sought reassurance in logic, I knew that Tammany could do whatever the hell Tammany wanted to do. I had no leverage. No matter how I might argue, I would lose. My deal with the devil just that, an unholy alliance, surely illegal, that bore no weight in court. I had treated with Mephistopheles and lost.

I walked away from the tents, away from the front, away from the men. I walked away until I stood alone. The sky above covered with clouds showed no light. Only the moon peeked through to give a yellow glimmer. Enough to see the way but not enough to comfort the lonely. For I was alone now, and not just in body. I was alone in my regiment, alone in New York, alone. I was alone and I was a fool. A god damned idiot. I had put my trust in politicians. I had done things, shameful things, to gain their ear. Worst of all, I had lied to myself, told myself that in the end, it wouldn't matter what I did, I would be in a position to do more good than all the evil I might commit to get there.

A fool. A damn lonely fool.

I lowered myself to the ground, wrapped my arms around my chest and for the first time in my adult life, I cried.

Thursday, May 5, 1921

Manhattan, New York
New York, USA

I bought the ticket first.

I walked into Grand Central Station, with its vaulted roof, arched stained glass, and bustle. I joined a group of people—some in suits and hats, some with bags and children—and moved toward the ticket lines. I joined one queue behind a woman and a boy. I ignored the boy as best I could and let my eyes rove across the tiles and posts. A miracle of modern transit, this place, where thousands and thousands of people came together only to split apart. Every day the same. A hundred clicks of heel against tile every second.

The line moved. Slowly, but it moved. The boy whined. I tried to keep my patience.

A whistle sounded below, somewhere in the bowels of the station a train's steam blew. The sound climbed the stairs and filled each riser before it leaped up to fill one more. Coming or going impossible to tell. A man, one of the conductors, shouted into the great hall, his voice booming loud and echoing in the vastness, to announce a final call. Four times, once each direction. A couple raced down the stairs, red-faced, yelling to some unseen operator to wait a moment more.

The line moved again.

And again.

I stood in front of the ticket agent, a bored old man shoehorned to fit in the tiny confines of his booth.

"Where to?"

"Philadelphia," I said. "And a day later DC…and a return two days after that."

"Going today?"

"No. In two days' time."

"You like to do things in two, huh, buddy?"

I shrugged.

The agent prepared my tickets, took my money, and handed me the three thick slips of paper. "No refunds if you miss the train."

"No problem."

I slipped the tickets in my billfold and walked away from the queues.

***

Back to Harlem.

I used the time on the El to compose my thoughts and to prepare a few notes. It would eventually go into a letter, but I was not ready to write it just yet. That would come in due course, but the thoughts…better to jot them down then forget them. Especially for a letter as important as this. When the train passed 118th Street, though, I folded my notes and prepared to disembark.

That item on the list could wait.

***

I found the office on 136th Street. A drab affair where Marshall shared his work with another Harlem attorney of which I'd never heard. They shared a secretary, a middle-aged Negress who sported a headscarf and jacket even in the early days of summer.

"I'd like to see the captain," I said. I had heard a rumor that after the war Marshall took to calling himself captain, even though he'd been decommissioned the same as everyone else when we hit American soil.

"Do you have an appointment?"

"I do," I said, somewhat to the secretary's surprise. "My name is Reuben Ayers."

The woman looked askance at a small calendar then huffed—she had spent too much time with Marshall, "I'll tell him you're here."

I assumed one of the wooden chairs against the wall as she lumbered from her chair and disappeared behind one of the doors—the door labeled N B MARSHALL, CAPTAIN 369th NY, RETIRED. I huffed myself at that. Retired. I wondered what a dishonorable discharge might look like through those strange lenses Marshall seemed to wear.

"Reuben," Marshall said from the now open door. "How are you?"

He wore a smile on his face that belied our relationship in the regiment. He limped across the anteroom and extended a weak, but friendly, hand.

"I'm fine. You look the worse for wear though."

"Between the gas and the shrapnel," Marshall pointed to his chest and his leg. "I've been better. But please come in. It's good to see you."

I ignored the lie and led Marshall into his office. I found a padded chair and looked around while Marshall hobbled to his seat. Not ostentatious, the room was—if anything—surprisingly collegiate. A pair of bookcases displayed various legal and historical texts. A reproduction of some French artist's work, a painting of Paris, hung on one wall. On the other, his degree from Harvard, his bar license, and a picture of him in his army uniform, pacing stick in hand, proudly erect and almost distinguished with his graying hair and mustaches.

"What can I do for you, Reuben?"

I looked back at Marshall, now seated across from me. "I'm not thrilled about this, but I don't count too many lawyers among my acquaintances."

"Reuben," Marshall raised his hands, palms forward. "I gave you a hard time over there. I felt a duty to the men, and I wasn't sure you felt the same…but that—"

"What's changed?"

"You stayed behind. You gave up your rank to stay with the men. That changed a lot of things in my eyes."

I nodded but said nothing. I did not feel disposed to discuss the reality of my demotion with Marshall. I had a task to accomplish here today. That was all.

"I need you to draft something for me."

"My pleasure."

I pulled a small pile of folded papers from my suit pocket, unfolded them and laid them flat on the desk between us.

"You'll find there the deed to my brownstone, my account information and the particulars of two individuals."

"Okay," Marshall slid the documents to his side of the desk. "What would you like me to do with this?"

"I'd like you to draft my will."

***

It was getting dark. The Harlem River sputtered a little to my left where it ran past a series of drainage pipes. I walked slowly and listened to the city. I could hear the babble of voices in the approaching gloom. Men and women reviewing their days, scolding children, fighting, making love. I could hear a piano and a party. It sounded like stride piano. Ragtime rhythm in the bass register, improvisation in the treble. A stride party. Two, three, four pianists would compete for drinks and tips and patronage. The winner settled for the coming week until another battle challenged his livelihood. In Harlem, it wasn't about prestige or reputation, it was about survival. Each man for himself in competition for scarce resources: booze and a paycheck. Maybe that's what made the Negroes' music so much more alive than the white man's. Not only did we live to sing, we sang to live.

I pictured Jim Europe at the piano, his glasses askew, his big hands sweeping across the ivory keys, his face alight in one of his massive grins. It was enough I could hear the music. Syncopation. I could feel the drive, the undeniable urge to tap my feet, to move, to dance. Jazz was the new Negro sentiment. Enough of mourning and sorrow. Now, now was the time to hope and to celebrate. Soon, we would be free and stand shoulder to shoulder with the white man. Soon, we would be free so tonight, let's dance.

The stride piano was louder now, its rhythmic beats flooding out the windows and screaming to the street. I stopped and listened and started to tap my fingers in time. I thought about my list and about the music and about everything in between. I remembered that first night at the Club when I heard Allie sing…I remembered it all and I knew it could not last. Nothing could last. But in the narrow window between memory and death, I caught a glimpse of life. Tonight, I would dance.

September 25–27, 1918

Battle of the Meuse-Argonne
Champagne Region, France

The village of Somme-Bionne lies on the north bank of the Rivière La Bionne, a lazy stream that runs north of east until it meets the Aisne at Vienne-la-Ville, on the western edge of the Argonne. For ten days, we'd billeted outside the village, our place reserved to take part in a rumored offensive, a major push that was scheduled for some time in the very near future. The word that was whispered most often among the soldiers was 'soon.' Rumblings from the next village over, Hans, supported the scuttlebutt. There, the 372nd was stationed along with the 2d Moroccan. They were already on the move, north, somewhere.

Smart money said we would follow.

I wasn't excited myself. My new position a punishment. Demoted from an officer of the line to a non-commissioned servant made to kowtow, to scrape and bend, to become, in essence, Major Little's nigger.

"Ayers," a voice from behind me.

I turned in the mud, my feet slow to react in the muck. It was Little himself who stood not ten meters away. Dried mud clung to the lower hem of his greatcoat and a new Adrian helmet tipped forward on his head; a bobbled steel cup inverted for comfort and protection. He held a half-page message in his hand, and he motioned for me to approach.

I saluted and moved toward him.

"Eighteen thirty hours. Second and Third Battalion will move out sooner," Little handed me the message. "Inform the company commanders."

"Yes, sir."

"Ayers," Little said.

I stopped.

He stood tall, a man proud, his shoulder square and his head back. His jaw jutted forward, a do-good progressive and an aristocrat as much as any in America. He stared into my eyes. "Colonel Hayward told me why you're here. I'm not sorry for you and I expect you to get over yourself just as quickly. I need a focused and capable soldier, not a self-pitying lunk. You can either moan about your situation or you can do something to redeem yourself. It's up to you."

"Yes, sir."

"Ayers," he raised a gloved hand. "As I say, I expect you to perform as a dutiful soldier. If you're incapable of doing that then I'll be more than happy to write you up for insubordination right here and right now."

I looked down at the mud between our feet. "Sir, no, sir."

"You're intelligent, otherwise you wouldn't have made lieutenant in the first place, and I need someone who's intelligent. There will be some judgment calls to make and I would like to trust you to make them. But I know all about Spartanburg and I'm certain now that your involvement was far more than an innocent mistake. So, I have to question you because you've demonstrated poor judgment, hell, you've done nothing but demonstrate poor judgment."

"I'm capable of making good decisions."

"Then make the decision to follow orders. If you do, then we'll get along all right. If you remember that your judgment is not a substitute for mine."

"Sir."

"I'm going to lean on you more than I might if you were someone else. But I'll also be watching you more than I might if you were someone else. Now, go deliver that communique."

I nodded and turned away. The low-slung buildings of Somme-Bionne on my left, a collection of farmhouses, a church, and a few shops. Only a dozen buildings, maybe. Most of the villages—what was left of them—in the area were never more than that. Three or four families gathered together for protection at night while they farmed the surrounding fields in the day. Tiny population centers scattered about the miles and miles of field, rolling hills and forests. I wondered what made it worth millions of lives. Did it really matter on which side of the boundary these lonely miles resided? German or French? Or was it simply the principle of the thing. Imperial sovereignty is more important than diplomacy, peace and a few lousy farms.

***

Yesterday, the army sent us a gift: six hundred of the least experienced, least educated, most backward Negro draftees the Army could conjure. Replacements, they said, for those men lost to the casualty rolls. Warm bodies. Cannon fodder. They knew nothing of battle. They were not here by choice. They fled at the first opportunity, tossed their weapons in a field and did their best to disappear into the west, away from the front. But they were black, and so it didn't matter that they came from Mississippi, Georgia, Alabama, Louisiana, and Texas—anywhere but New York—nor that they answered to the draft and were not the volunteers of Harlem's worth. They were black. And so were we.

I didn't blame these men. I held no illusions, no misconceptions about human nature—good or bad—nor the mettle required to withstand a good artillery attack. I had watched through the night as shells fell all around. Had felt my knees turn to mush and my brain to hash. I knew the awesome power of artillery preparation, the way it stole all courage, how it could leave men trembling with its onslaught. I had felt nerves raw in the darkness and jumped at every sound. I knew that artillery leveled the brave and coward alike and I knew that men here from the draft had no reason to stand strong. This all I knew but knowing liked them none the better. They ran. Cowards. Full stop.

***

Large tents served as storage. We stowed our gear there and took only our Lebels, one blanket, and emergency rations. The French haversacks which were first issued us in the spring grew into lumpy piles as each company dropped their gear and formed up. I slipped my father's Elgin into the pocket of my uniform pants, a reminder of the things I had long ago vowed not to become. *The New Testament* tattered and stained, I lifted too from the haversack. I had read most of it now and still felt unable to understand why men believed in something so obviously fiction. But there was a power even in fantasy, I supposed, so I slipped the bible, with all its fantasies, into my pocket next to the Elgin. It was time to march.

***

Traffic clogged the main road to the front. Men and trucks and material; enough to support a division, two even, headed first west to Somme-Tourbe, then north toward

Minaucourt and Virginy. We slogged through it as best we could, stopped, started, stopped again. Making slow progress in the congestion of military logistics. The sun, hidden by clouds, grew dimmer still as the day waned toward dusk. Drizzle pattered our helmets, slowly soaked our uniforms, made anxious men miserable. Stuck half-way to Somme-Tourbe, going nowhere fast.

"Ayers," Little said. "Get Lieutenant Siebel."

"Sir?"

"I had him scout the area this afternoon. We're going to cut cross country. It's the only way we'll reach our assignment in time."

"Sir."

I hurried along the line, past B Company, past C Company, back two hundred men to D Company. Lieutenant Siebel stood on the shoulder, the butt of his Lebel sunk into the gravel, his hand on the barrel, his weight rested against the French issued weapon. He was a man at ease.

"Lieutenant Siebel?"

"That's me," he pushed off his rifle to stand straight.

I snapped a salute as he slung the gun over his shoulder. He was a man of little distinction. Brown hair, brown eyes, average height and build, cheeks that sagged over his jaw, and a face that otherwise reminded one of a bulldog, compact, angry and ready for battle. One of the officers who'd earned a grade promotion after the whitewash orders came through. I'd heard he was a decent fellow and managed some respect for his men.

"Major Little requests your presence, sir. He intends to cut cross-country."

"Splendid," Siebel grinned. "Lead the way…"

"Ayers, sir, Sergeant Ayers."

"Weren't you—"

"I didn't want to leave," I lied, "and Colonel Hayward found it within him to grant my request."

"Interesting," Siebel gave instructions to his Sergeant and followed me forward. "What do you think of this war, sergeant?"

"Sir?"

"I'm curious is all. Do you think this push will be as decisive as scuttlebutt suggests?"

A truck had slid off the road and stuck its front tire in the mud. Half a company of men gathered around in an attempt to pull it out. "We're going to have a hell of a time off the road, sir."

"The offensive?"

"A lot of people are going to die. If that means the Bush-Germans surrender, I don't know."

"What do you think?"

"I think we're going to lose a lot of men."

Siebel clapped his hands. "We're tough, we'll do all right."

"We've got six hundred men who don't know the difference between a Chauchat and a gas mask. Do you think they care about me, or you, or the guy in Company K from Goshen, who's been with us from the beginning? They're going into this with only one thought: how do *I* survive? not, how do *we* survive? To be honest, I'd rather go to the lines without them, sir."

"Sergeant?"

"I don't want to waste my blood on some idiot from Georgia who's going to run for home the first time a whizz-bang lands within a hundred yards of the line. I don't owe those replacements anything and it's a shame we've got them."

"Have you told this to the major?"

"He knows," I said. "He doesn't need me to tell him. He's furious about it and the colonel too. They know what it means, and they know how it could affect us in the next few days. Hell, I wouldn't be surprised if Colonel Hayward were to hunt Pershing down and give him a beating."

"Who'd you think would win that?"

I laughed. I liked this lieutenant. "My bet's on Hayward."

"I heard that he once knocked Teddy Roosevelt on his ass."

"Sir?"

"You heard of that training camp Roosevelt set up a couple of years back before Wilson entered the war, Camp Platt or Patch or something like that?"

"Sure," I said.

Siebel laughed. "Apparently one of the things they did up there was fisticuffs. Figured that if you got close enough to a Boche you might need to know the proper form. Felt it part of their duty to give a bloodthirsty Hun a gentleman's chance. Anyway, Roosevelt was keen to show off and asked for a volunteer, Hayward jumped at the chance and proceeded to run Teddy in circles. Got him so tired the man ducked when he should have jabbed and ended up on the mat."

"That's brilliant," I said.

"So, you see why I'd put my money on our colonel, especially as Black Jack's been sitting in a hotel back in Paris the whole war. I'm sure he'll wind easy and when he does," Siebel punched the air, one, two. "That's a fight I'd pay to see."

"You and the rest of us, sir," I said. "Damned shame we can't organize it."

"Might do something for morale if we could."

"Lots of things might do something for morale, but none of them are going to happen before twenty-two hundred hours," I said, making reference to our orders. Less than three hours more to reach our assigned position, half-an-hour lost already in the confusion of half a mile's distance.

"You think the men will fight?" Siebel said. "The veterans from New York I mean?"

"They'll fight," I said, though I wanted to say *we'll fight*. I knew better, though, than to usurp some non-existent relationship between myself and the men. Hayward had been right when he talked about the brotherhood of arms. I'd done nothing to endear myself with the men—especially not the men of First Battalion. Maybe if I'd remained in K Company I might rely on Pippin, or maybe some of the others, but here in First Battalion—I didn't know a soul but for to take a pile of money from them in a game of craps. I was as much a stranger as the six hundred draftees. So, I said *they'll fight* and left it there. "They'll fight for sure."

"And you?"

I looked at Siebel, and he looked right back. "I'm not in a position to fight. I'm a runner. I'll run, but unless Little changes his mind, I won't be doing much fighting."

"Fair enough," Siebel said.

"What about you?" I said. "What do you think about fighting?"

Siebel shrugged. "It's my duty."

"You don't seem too enthusiastic."

"I think you and I both have seen enough of the front to know better. This battle's not going to be easy and it's not going to be fun. A lot of people are going to die, and a lot of people are going to die needlessly. That's just the facts of it, sergeant, and I'm not too particularly fond of them."

"But you'll fight."

"As I said, it's my duty."

***

For three hours, we marched, a silent host in the darkness, men kept in order by non-coms, the occasional profanity and a guide who possessed an innate sense of direction, a natural orienteer. Aside from one brief moment of confusion, Siebel led us without error. We arrived at our position, the Ravin des Pins, early. Twenty-one thirty-nine hours to be precise. Little ordered the men disposed and sent runners to report: In position.

***

At twenty-three hundred hours, the artillery preparation commenced.

***

At some point, I'm not sure the hour, I roused myself from my sleep-hole and sauntered slowly to the edge of our battalion's encampment. The clouds, nature's camouflage, had parted for a time and revealed the stars that lingered over France, bright specks in the universe—different, still, from New York, but brilliant nonetheless—that shed light upon our position in the hills above Virginy.

Our Battalion was held in reserve by General Gouraud, while the Second and Third Battalions approached the front in direct support of the French 163rd and the French 363rd Infantry. They would see the first action in this new offensive. They would gain the greater glory as we stood in the rear, helpless to act, watching through our binoculars as they threw themselves at the lousy Hun come the morning.

I lit a cigarette and breathed the thick smoke into my lungs. Fatima. Turkish tobacco—although an Alliance country—still the best available cig on the Western Front. I held it inside until the harsh smoke forced me to cough the warm air into the night. Another puff. In, hold, out.

In Hans, there is a gun—I forget the official designation—that rides on a rail. It is so big that when it fires the barrel rolls back a dozen yards before it hits the stops. It takes three men to load a shell. This gun can fire half a dozen kilometers away. It is a marvel of modern engineering—wartime ingenuity—that allows our men to attack with surprise and alacrity.

Tonight, this gun is silent, more conventional artillery of the French military preferred. *Thud, thud, thud.* A gun every thirty meters. Enough explosive power to drive regiments mad with their might. I almost pity the Boche, as I smoke my cigarette and watch the shells descend and explode on their positions. Hour after hour, the preparation continues. All through the night hit by a ceaseless attack only to be followed at the dawn by thousands of angry Africans and Negroes, thirsty for their few feet of No Man's Land. I watch as the shells rise and fall and kill. Tonight, I am safe in reserve. Who knows what the morrow may bring?

***

Exhausted yet unable to sleep, I stirred in the darkness. It was a morning to put Shakespeare to shame. A wet chill hung in our camp, mist and rain undissipated in wayward clouds, silent ghosts that moved across the ground between. Combined with the sounds of war that drifted across the valley, it put me in mind of Birnam Wood and Dunsinane.

I came upon Major Little at his lookout. He stood alone on a jagged precipice of rock, a jutted vantage of the valley and the far-off front. As I approached, he raised a pair of binoculars to his face and scanned the panorama below.

"It's started," he said.

"Yes, sir."

"We'll be in it ourselves before long."

"Sir."

He lowered the binoculars and turned to face the battalion's encampment, a small hollow on the downward slope overlooking the front. "Do you care at all for these men, Ayers?"

"I—I can't rightly say. There are a few I care for, I suppose, but not in First Battalion."

"The truth at least," Little slipped the field glasses in their case, "I've been ordered to take you on, and so I have, but it would help if I thought you might be redeemable, maybe if you possessed some quality I could point to, something like loyalty, or courage, anything that might give you the complexion of a soldier."

"How about honor?"

Little laughed. "I did not think you knew the word."

"I pay my debts, if nothing else, I've tried to do what I say. I believe my word is still my word despite…"

"And you owe these men something? Why?"

"Because I took something from them, or I tried to at least."

Little lowered his binoculars. "You betrayed them."

"I had cause, I thought the results would put me in a position to help my people. I thought—"

"The ends would justify the means."

"Yes. I thought the ends would justify the means. And I figured that this regiment wouldn't be able to do much to change things. We're here and we're fighting, but no one outside the Negro community cares. The white man isn't paying attention to Henry Johnson or Neadom Roberts. They don't care about Negro heroes. We're nobodies to them. And we always will be until someone with enough power forces them to change."

"And you thought you could get that power."

I shook my head. "I thought I could start the process."

"That's unfortunate, but it doesn't answer the question. You say you owe these men and I still wonder, why?"

"Because the only way I can help them now is to stand with them in the coming fight."

***

Airplanes clashed in the skies. Biplanes raked the battlefield, tiny wasps that chased each other through the air. German, American, French. Fokkers swooped low over the front, machine-guns firing on our men, but the German efforts were countered by our own planes in low-flying pursuit; aerial maneuvers to distract and disarm the German attack. We watched from our post as hundreds of planes engaged across the length of the front then soared, twisted and dove until one gained the advantage and dispatched the other. Not far to the east, a dogfight ensued.

One of the few monoplane fighters on the front, the Loening M-8, dove on a Fokker, machine-gun blazing. The Fokker banked at the last minute and climbed toward the sun.

The Loening, with American markings, flew after it. Both planes disappeared in the glare until someone spotted black smoke and the Fokker spiraled to earth.

***

At ten hundred hours, we received our first orders. We struck camp and marched downhill, Virginy on our right. The town had been reduced to a few buildings, the roofs opened to the sky by mortar and bullet. A chapel stood visible among the ruins, its steeple cut off in jagged bits of masonry, bullet holes pocking its face. It looked like every other village along the front, ravaged by the back and forth of the trenches, scarred by German, or French, or British weaponry. A testament to the futility of this war that we fought for the same ground back and forth and in the middle a town like Virginy, destroyed by the men who fought to preserve it.

We passed Virginy and moved through the valley to Vilquin Sector. Familiar ground for us: to our rear Butte de Mesnil, at our front Massiges. Beausejour sector just to the west.

"We won't go up today, I don't think."

I turned to see Lieutenant Siebel's now familiar face, his brown eyes ringed with dark circles, his face haggard.

"What makes you think that, sir?"

"Too easy," he said.

"I'm sorry?"

Siebel pointed north, toward the front, "Our boys are routing the Boche. You noticed the columns of prisoners we passed?"

"I saw," I said.

To the east, a group of prisoners large enough to populate a platoon marched south, their scuffling progress guarded by a handful of poilus. It had been the same all morning, hundreds of prisoners sent back from the lines.

"I think it's the Africans," Siebel said. "The way they scream their way at the enemy. Hell, I'd scream like a girl if I saw a hundred of them headed my way."

"Better them than us."

"Always."

"You said it was too easy."

Siebel ducked his head and squatted to grab a stick. He stabbed the muddy earth and broke the top half away, leaving the lower half stuck in the ground.

"Black Jack," he said.

"I don't—"

"He's afraid you all just might prove yourselves men, right?"

"But we're under Gouraud."

"That's just it. I'd bet you the Lion of France knows full well that Pershing's got issues with you Negroes. There's no way he doesn't know about Jack's time with the Ninth. I think that one-armed Poilu is holding us in reserve long enough for the going to get bumpy."

"And then…"

"Then he sends us in to shove it up the Boche's ass."

"So, he'd sacrifice us—"

"It's a privilege. Think about it. Is there any better way to prove yourselves men than to succeed where no white men could? That's what Gouraud's giving you. A goddamned privilege it is to give Pershing what he's most afraid of. Pershing and the rest of America, too."

***

That afternoon, a convoy of ambulances drove from the front. Converted Model-Ts bounced and sloughed through the mud, over pockmarked fields. Red Cross drivers behind the wheels, crazy. They rumbled south in numbers almost as great as the prisoners before them. Truck beds filled with injured men.

***

As darkness settled over our position, I worked my way back, through a communications trench left by the Germans, to the offal pit. I loosened my belt and unleashed a stream of urine with a splash. It was in this condition, my member dangled in the night air, my rifle slung over my shoulder, my body relaxed by the release, that I spotted the shadow against the setting sun.

Without hesitation, and without bothering to sheath my penis, I grabbed my rifle and took aim. "Who is it?"

"I'm a friend."

"Who is it?" I shouted as my flow shrank to a trickle and then a drip. "Identify yourself."

The voice was slow, slurred by an all too familiar accent: southern, nigger. "I'm Washington, I am. Abe Washington. My mammy done named me after two different presidents. Yes, sir, she did."

"What are you doing, Washington?"

"I was…was wandering a little, s'all."

"You trying to desert?"

"No, sir, never, sir. I wouldn't do nothing like that. I mean…I don't want to go fighting tomorrow, but…I want…I want to see my mammy again."

"You…"

I couldn't finish it; I couldn't admonish this boy from the south with words alone. My frustration and disappointment and anger wouldn't allow it.

I launched myself around the latrine, my pants loose around my waist and my dick flopping free. I charged with the rage that had grown inside. I let it out with a scream and raised my rifle high. Washington cringed and cowered, but still, I attacked. I slammed the butt of my rifle into his face.

The beast crumpled beneath the force of the blow.

On top of him, I slammed the rifle butt into its belly, listened as air burst from his lungs, smelled the beans on his breath, the piss in his pants. I tossed the rifle to the side and straddled him, my fists more than enough to pummel this insignificant into pulp. My rage sufficient to destroy with knuckles alone. Left, right, left. Punch after punch after punch its face deteriorated under my barrage. Blood from his nose gushed. His lip split. Teeth cracked. Blood on my knuckles. Black bruises and lumps of flesh separated in slow motion. Flecks of blood flew from his mouth as he coughed, gagged, and retched. Black rage flared, flickered, and died.

I left it there, then, a bleeding mass of whimpering flesh. I would piss on it if I hadn't already spent my bladder's contents; it was that disgusting. So, I spit a gob of spittle and mucus on its bloodied face. I stood and gave him a final kick in the side. A humiliating onslaught now completed for this inhuman pathetic. The pain in my knuckles happy price for the pleasure of a moment's release.

***

Around two in the morning, we moved into position a quarter-mile behind Second Battalion, a move which forced us to climb over Butte de Mesnil. Muddied by the incessant rain, the hike was unpleasant, but not as bad as that had by the artillery; small groups of men who struggled to move their massive guns across shell holes and trenches, barbed wire and bodies. They would find a stretch of solid ground and pick up speed, their backs would straighten and their faces fill with hope, only for the carriage of their gun to edge too close to a wall. It would start slowly, a barely perceptible arc through the air, accelerate as the mud gave way under the weight, and then it would be too late, the barrel skewed at some odd angle, wheels bogged, and men cursed. Even the horse teams, four steeds harnessed together, did little to move the heavy machines through the slurry. It took two or three teams hitched together, with every wheel manned, for any discernible progress. One, two, three, and the horses' flanks tensed, teamsters swore oaths to god, and the men at the wheels rammed their shoulders against the wood. An inch, two, a foot. More mud. Then a Boche corpse left in the night. Up and over until the guns began to move toward the front, wheels now bloodied by German guts.

My own feet sank in the mud and my boots—a half size too big, per army standard issue—sucked at my socks and threatened to disappear in some gray-brown pool of sodden earth. Barbed wire, once threaded across acres of the Champagne, now disappeared under our march, deeper and deeper with each passing soldier.

Over the Ravin d'Hebuterne, trenches Jacquinot and Bourrasset, down the slope of Butte de Mesnil. Into the position recently held by Second Battalion, now vacated farther north toward Ripont and the Dormoise River. Here, we found the bodies of a dozen men—members of the Second Battalion—their black skin bloodied, some of it charred, by precision shellfire. The one advantage of retreat the ability to fire on the abandoned positions with absolute knowledge of the distance.

We stopped there and spread ourselves along the empty trench, living interspersed amongst the dead, the time required to bury the bodies too long in the midst of such a large-scale offensive. The thought of trying to dig a grave in this mud, too, turned any consideration of decency into farce. A gallon of dirt and rain and water would slide into any hole faster than a trowel could move one scoop of it away. Better to leave the dead exposed for now and bury them later, when the regiment was relieved and time lent itself to contemplation and ceremony; when we would have a better idea of the numbers of the men lost to Boche bullets; after the battle, whenever that might be.

As we settled into this temporary haven—the German artillery pushed too far back by pressure from the front line and thus too distant to attack our present position—the day dawned. Under the cloud cover and drizzle, it came as a soft light, a dim lifting of darkness, puffy delineations to the east. One moment, it was dark, the next, gray clouds glowed and rain continued to fall, heavy drops turned streaks of yellow by the light. I took a position not far from Little, my uniform sopping, my boots like buckets, miserable.

***

The rain eased into a sometimes spit by mid-morning. Little ordered food and we gathered in squads to cook broth and dried beef bits—the army's idea of battle rations—over cans of alcohol. It was salty, thin, and unappetizing, but it was something to fill our stomachs and more importantly, warm.

***

From where we stood, our heads poked above the edge of our trenches, we could see the fighting below. Across the valley lay the tiny village of Ripont. A river wound between Ripont and our position and marked the low point of the valley. The terrain from the north bank of the river to the village rose sharply, maybe thirty or forty feet of elevation, and only leveled out as it approached the first buildings of the village. North of Ripont the ground rose first gradually and then abruptly as it peaked in the summit of Bellevue Signal ridge. This last was a series of hills that jutted from the plain for maybe half a mile in either direction. Unfortunately, it stood directly in the middle of our advance. We would have to fight for every foot of it.

In the valley below Bellevue Signal, the 163rd (French) had already crossed the river. They were holed up with our own Third Battalion on the north bank. The sharp incline proved good cover and they were well protected from Boche artillery.

"The Second Battalion's there, see," Little pointed to our right, at the columns of men who were just marching into the southern end of the valley. "They'll have to cross the Dormoise to support the Third Battalion."

I tracked forward of the columns. A pair of rickety footbridges crossed the river, wide enough for maybe a single man to cross at one time.

"It's almost narrow enough to ford," I said.

"Not with weapons," Little said. "It's deep enough and fast enough, a misstep would land half a platoon in it and destroy the use of their Lebels for hours. No, the better way would be that stone bridge over there, you see it?"

I followed his finger and saw a solid stone bridge not a third of a mile to the left of our position. "I see it, sir."

"Those footbridges there, they increase a column's exposure, forcing them to go single file. That's a bad strategy, dangerous in a situation like this when the enemy has the higher ground."

I nodded.

"We'll send three companies across the stone bridge. I wager they can meet up with the rest of us at the nearest footbridge about the same time the Second Battalion's done."

"Which companies?" I asked.

"Send the Machine Gun, B and C Company by the stone bridge. We'll take D Company and the Headquarters Group across the plank bridges. That way we'll limit our exposure on both routes. Once we cross the river, we'll hole up in that cemetery there, between the bridges."

"Yes, sir," I said.

***

I saved D Company for last, found Siebel lounged against a rock in an arroyo. His eyes were closed. I stopped several feet away from him, searched around my feet until I found a pebble, grabbed it up, and tossed it at Siebel's chest. It landed with a small thud and Siebel, who'd not heard my approach, jumped to his feet, Lebel at the ready as he spun around and dug his feet in, ready for an enemy charge.

"I surrender," I raised my arms.

"Ayers," Siebel growled.

"Can I lower my arms now?" I laughed.

Siebel lowered his rifle, "You're a bastard."

"My parents were married, though my daddy left a little later, when they had me."

"Doesn't change anything," Siebel said. "You figure out how we're gonna organize that Hayward-Pershing match yet?"

I shook my head. "It's going to have to wait. We're moving over the river."

"Damn shame. You let me know when you got a promoter, though, 'cause I'm putting together a pot."

"You got a deal," I smiled, raised my fists to show the cracked skin, said, "In the meantime, I think I might go in for some lessons myself."

"What did you go and do there, sergeant?"

"Accidentally ran into a deserter last night. Me standing over the latrine taking a piss, this fucking son of a bitch goes sneaking past. I figured it was better to give him a few knocks than to shoot him where he stood, might cause an artillery barrage by mistake."

"And you complaining about me calling you a bastard." Siebel stooped down and picked up a pebble. He tossed it in the air and caught it again before he said, "I like you, Ayers, so we can talk like this, but mind your tongue when we're around the men."

"Of course, sir," I said with a grin. "I'm not a complete idiot."

"Little had some words with me yesterday. I guess he saw us getting chummy and thought it was something to end-run. He's not your biggest fan, you know, so be careful."

I gave a short salute. "Thanks for the warning."

"It's given in friendship, mind you, I don't want you thinking I'm all serious of a sudden."

"Never, sir," I said, chuckled. "I'd never think so low of you."

"Good, now, about these orders."

***

As I was a burr attached to Major Little's sock, I accompanied the Headquarters Group across the narrow plank bridge. We crouched as we crossed, a single row of men exposed to a full view of the enemy. Despite the danger, we reached the other side without incident and rendezvoused with the rest of the Battalion, our rendezvous point a cemetery, quiet except for the chatter of soldiers.

"If we were back in the States, you know these dead people be rolling all over the place to see a bunch of niggers stomping on their graves."

"Who says they ain't?"

"We could dig 'em up and see."

"What we ask them if we do?"

"I don't know; you learn any French yet?"

"Hinky-dinky parlez-vous?"

"Don't count."

"Who wants to talk to a dead *poilus* anyway. Hard enough to talk to a live one."

"And you know they all speak English."

"Sure as hell."

We didn't stay in the cemetery for long. The front line moved forward throughout the afternoon at a steady pace, and we moved forward with it, north. Once we breached that quick rise off the river, we found the plain north of Ripont was well-shelled and pocked with holes. When we moved forward, now we could hide in the craters, our exposure limited as we moved from hole to hole.

By five, the progress stopped, though and we didn't move for two hours. We sat still and listened as the sounds of battle diminished and the only thing we could hear became the regular whistle of artillery and the occasional rat-tat-tat-tat of a machine gun—the kind of quick burst that I'd come to recognize as a place marker, a *don't-forget-I'm-still-here-to-shoot-you* message across No Man's Land. The active prosecution of the assault had come to a halt for the evening. We settled in to get as much sleep as possible, harried only by rain, artillery, and memory.

West Chester, Pennsylvania, USA

Saturday, May 7, 1921

The house was modestly situated on a narrow plot that stretched from street to street, the kind of neighborhood where people put their trash outback. Cozy. Suburban. Distant enough from Philadelphia so as to be able to look up at night and see past the distant glow on the horizon to the stars above. In this place, then, Horace Pippin lived. His house, two stories, with a single dormer on the upper level. The yard was not untended, but neither was it polished. The grass was too long, but it was spring yet and perhaps no one had thought to oil the grass clippers since winter. Not that Horace could be expected, not with his injury.

I wonder, now, sitting in my hotel room, writing this, why I bothered to visit Pippin. I understand my pilgrimage to Arlington two days yet distant, but why stop in West Chester, why visit this man for whom I only shared a slight connection and who would remember me as little more than an officer in a uniform. It is the bible, I think then, the one from Seaman Marks, *The New Testament* that sits atop the hotel stationary, scarred and corrugated, but no more opened after a year's return to America. It is the memory, and the questions, that haunt me, which bring me to this extra stop in my itinerary. Why, in my darkest hours did I think to press my fingers against this Bible? There was no faith for me to place in some divine being, yet still, I found comfort. Why? There is no redemption in Jesus, but…

Horace Pippin, among all the men I met in the war, possessed a simple faith. He is a man, I believe, who will listen to my doubts and my questions and not rebuff me for my intellect. Honest, in a word and not plagued by the mendacity so common to those educated pastors and men of god who claim to speak his word, for a fee.

I knocked on the door. Down the street a group of children chased after a boy on an ancient bicycle, their arms raised in the air, cheering. I did not know the purpose behind their celebration, nor did I have time to theorize. The door opened and I was greeted by a hefty woman in a plain gray dress. She wore her hair bobbed with a tight curl at the ends. Straightened, no doubt, by Madame Walker. Thick glasses hid her eyes and made her head, already too small for her bulk, seem even punier. She held a pair of crochet needles in one hand. She was in the middle of making a doily or some other household decoration and I could see the white thread trail from the needles to a pouch hung around her waist. Another pouch near burst beside the first, full of clothespins.

"May I help you?" she said.

"I'm to meet Horace," I said. "I'm Reuben Ayers, from his regiment."

She glanced over my shoulder and shouted into the street. "Get off that contraption right now, Richard. You're liable to kill yourself."

I covered my ear, but too late. My head rang with her maternal admonition.

"But Mom—"

"You hear your momma? You get off that thing right now."

I glanced at the crowd of children and saw the boy, Richard, stop the bicycle and climb off. His shoulders slumped and he stared sullenly at the ground. As soon as his foot hit the pavement, another boy took up the bike and was off and the crowd with him. Richard stayed behind, let them move away. His momentary disappointment was forgotten as the new boy crashed to the pavement amidst shouts and jeers from the other children.

Richard's mother smiled, then, and put her free hand on her hip. "You see what would have happened if he hadn't minded his mother."

"Yes, ma'am," I said, not sure what else to say.

Finally, satisfied by her boy's obedience, she turned her attention to me, this stranger on her step. "Now, what did you want?"

"I have an appointment to see Horace. I knew him from the war."

"Oh, yes. He mentioned…come in and I'll fetch him. I imagine he's fiddling with his woodwork again. Can't do much else with his arm and all."

I followed Mrs. Pippin into a neat little sitting room. A Victorian couch and pair of armchairs filled the room. Day-old flowers threatened to wilt in a vase. Antimacassars—obviously crocheted by Mrs. Pippin—covered the backs and arms of all the furniture. A short bookshelf with glass doors sat against the wall to one side. Everywhere, it seemed, was evidence of her crocheting. Under the vase, atop the bookshelf, on the wall, the antimacassars. Good to have a hobby, I supposed.

"Please, sit," she said and disappeared into the house.

I took a seat in one of the chairs, the one angled slightly backward, so I could see through the dining room to the backyard. I should say dining room with some reservation as, yes, there was a small table that seemed intended for dining, but it was pushed against the wall in favor of a large ironing board, a hanging rack and several baskets of laundry. I noticed the iron lay flat, cold, on the board and that the hanging rack was filled with men's dress shirts, starched and stiff. Through a window beyond I saw wires strung across the yard and hung with various laundry: underthings, skirts, blouses, more dress shirts. It was a maze of multi-colored fabric. Somewhere, I could hear one of the new, mechanical washing machines, its vibrations shook the walls as its drum spun round a batch of clothes.

"The Mighty Thor," a voice said from the stairs, "the washing machine."

I looked up to see Horace Pippin, his left hand gripped firmly on the banister, his right hung limp at his side. He took each step slowly, as if an old man unsure of his knees, and once descended, he continued to move with a similar agony. I stood as he entered the room and crossed to him. For some reason, I extended my right hand to greet him and, realizing my mistake, lowered it again.

"No, I can do it," he said.

His teeth clenched as he reached across his body with his left arm and raised his right arm upward, a stiff simulacrum of its former self, and extended his hand. I took it and felt the barest pressure from his fingers before he let go and his arm dropped back to his side. He sighed, then, and settled into the couch across from where I had taken a seat.

"It's a bitch of a thing, isn't it, lieutenant?"

"It is," I didn't bother to correct his use of the title. I had been a lieutenant, after all, though not for the duration.

He sat relaxed, despite his injury, and I appraised this man who had grown so much during our time in France. He wore a loose-fitting shirt with the top buttons undone. He wore his hair tight against his skull and otherwise no facial hair. He was clean and well-groomed, a good soldier still, and I could easily imagine him in a suit, or a uniform, a distinguished gentleman. There was something else, though, I noticed. A thin dusting of what appeared to be sawdust settled on his sleeve, a few chips of wood, as if he had just come from a workshop and not thought to brush himself.

"You've been married since…"

"November last. Her family lives here and...with Richard and her business, we figured my pension wasn't enough to stay in New York."

"Of course," I said. Twenty-two fifty a month wasn't enough to support a bachelor let alone a family of three. "She's a laundress?"

"One of the better in the city," Pippin pointed toward the various collections of laundry. "She keeps every businessman between Philly and the Lehigh Valley line in clean shirts."

I waved vaguely as if to encompass the house. "This is a nice place you have."

"We have some lodgers, help with the payments. I just wish I could..." Pippin let his head dip and his gaze descend toward his arm. "No one'll hire a man with a gimp arm. Not one without an education."

I remember when it happened, during the Battle of the Meuse Argonne, though I wasn't there. I only heard after, the story, and that second and third hand from other members of K Company. I'd been with Little, then, separated from my men, and unable to help this one whom, I now realized, deserved much admiration.

"I recall you seemed keen on art."

"It's not a living, sir."

During the war, Pippin kept a diary of events. He showed me, once, one of the illustrations he'd drawn, a rough picture of an artillery bombardment, almost childlike in its simplicity, with yellow and red and orange explosions. It was one of several drawings he'd done, all of them breathtaking in their innocent representation of the horrors of war. They were gone, now, though. When Black Jack imposed the race line and all of the Negro officers transferred out of the 369th, one of the new, white officers ordered Pippin to destroy his notebooks. A threat to security, he said, if the enemy got hold of them who knows what information they might contain. It was a shitty justification and showed less a sense of operational security than a sense of idiocy and prejudice on the officer's part. But to his credit as a soldier, Pippin destroyed his notebooks without complaint.

We sat for a moment in silence.

"What about you, sir?"

"Me?"

"What have you done since..."

I thought about that question. I thought about the last two and a half years, about the things I'd done, the alcohol I'd consumed, the things I'd written and thought and felt. What had I done? Written the better part of a memoir and consumed enough booze to drown a platoon. Slept with dozens of whores and stalked a woman I used to call my lover. What useless shit. A waste. It all remained, still, the memories of my betrayals, the sins, the mistakes that weighed on my mind and my heart. Nothing I had done, nothing I had thought to do, had eased the burdens or relieved my guilt. I had failed my men, I had failed Jim Europe, and looking back, I had begun to suspect that this tome was less a confession than braggadocio. The more I wrote about what I'd done, the more I realized how much I didn't regret. The one justification for it all, though, was that it might testify to the goodness of others, men like Horace Pippin.

"This and that," I said, finally. "I've been writing a book."

"What about?"

"The war."

Pippin fell silent again. His head leaned back, and he stared at the ceiling. Mrs. Pippin waddled down the stairs and through the sitting room into the bowels of the house. I watched as her head reappeared through the window and she began to pull clothes off their lines in the backyard.

"Is it made up or are you telling what happened?"

"It's mostly a memoir," I said. "Truth as close as I can tell it."

"That's good, sir, 'cause it needs to be told."

"I think so."

"You remember those journals I kept, sir?"

"I do."

"Well, I had to destroy them, the ones I'd made, but I've made more since then. Wrote down everything I remember as best I could," Pippin pushed himself off the couch with his left arm. He smoothed his shirtfront with his hand and then crossed to the small bookshelf I'd noticed earlier. He knelt carefully and withdrew three small notebooks. It took him a moment to juggle the notebooks and close the doors with his good hand before he rose to his feet and carried them across to where I sat.

"These are what I remember. I even put some drawings in them, too."

The topmost was a green composition book, small enough to hold in the palm of my hand, and I opened the cover to see a nearly illegible scrawl stretch across the page. His grammar and spelling were atrocious. I quickly deciphered the first lines: "I Rimber the day, varry well that we left the good old USA all tho, she were in troble, with Germany." It was a reference to our sailing on the *Pocahontas* back in December of 1917 and I remembered the difficulties, the damaged engine, the fire, the collision. It had been as if some ancient god of the sea had thought to prevent us from our journey, a fleet sent to destroy Troy, and mighty Poseidon determined to prevent it. But Pippin's journal continued beyond those few troubled weeks.

I flipped the page to see a rendering of three Doughboys on the march. Their path followed a well-tended wooden fence that separated them from a hill that angled upwards to the edge of the page. They were dressed in full uniform, with the flattened American helmets, rifles slung over their shoulders. Each one humped a rucksack though with varying degrees of difficulty. The farthest in the image used a pacing stick while the nearest carried one in his hand, parallel to the earth.

I flipped through several more pages, saw other drawings: a barbed-wire entrenchment along the edge of a wood, men in gas masks on patrol in their trenches, an airplane battle above the Argonne, men charging through an artillery bombardment, and a view of the enemy trenches at night. All of the drawings were in the same, simple renderings, and to see these reminders of the war, I wondered what we ever thought to accomplish over there. I shivered, too, at the memories evoked by Pippin's pictures. These were experiences we shared, and to see those experiences from such a naive perspective, one obviously horrified by the carnage, chilled me. An unwelcome and surprising mirror to my own failure of sensitivity.

"Can I borrow these tonight?" I said. "I'm staying at a hotel in town and I'll see them returned in the morning."

"You think you might be able to use something?"

I shrugged. "I'd like to read your story."

"It was a miracle, sir, that I survived," Pippin said. "I tell myself that every day and thank God for it."

I shifted uncomfortably. Here was the very subject I had intended to broach. The idea of god and of forgiveness and of some kind of divine hope. Yet now that Pippin provided the opening, I froze. I could not bring myself to voice my…questions. I knew Pippin was raised in the AME Zion Church, and I knew much of their doctrine. I also knew that my questions could easily be interpreted as antagonistic, when in reality, I was on the verge of honest curiosity, something new to my experience which I lacked the vocabulary to dispassionately express.

"I'm sure it was," I said weakly.

"Make sure I get them back before you leave, if you don't mind, sir, but feel free to borrow them. It's easier, you know, if you read the story than me telling it. I don't particularly enjoy that."

"Definitely."

It was a sentiment I shared.

***

The piece was exquisite. Pippin had taken me to his workshop. It was upstairs in the hallway closet. At some point, he had removed the door from its hinges and constructed a table inside the tiny space. A stool sat in the hall. A lamp, with its cord strung into the next room, provided his light. The entire work area, and immediate vicinity was covered in wood chips and sawdust and smelled of fresh lumber. A small pile of oddly sized chunks of wood towered in the corner. A small saw, three knives of various sizes and purposes, and a pair of chisels laid in a neat row on the table. An iron poker leaned against the door jam, incongruous.

"It's a mixed media of sorts," Pippin said.

He handed me a piece of wood about the size of a large book. On its flat surface, he had burned an image, a scene: two soldiers, one with a cigarette on his lips, lounging in a bunker. Instead of faces, however, Pippin had drawn them as hollow skulls. Death heads in repose. It was chilling and terrifying and all too accurate. A cross lay on the floor, sideways, as if knocked from the wall by a nearby explosion. The haunting power of the scenario was only intensified by the odd medium. From the looks of it, Pippin had taken the iron poker, heated it in the fire, and burned the lines into the wood. After that, he took the knives and chisels to the piece to add dimension: half-etching, half-relief. It was a masterpiece. All the more so considering his handicap.

"This is…impressive," I said. "You've done this with your arm?"

Pippin nodded though he seemed to grimace at some phantom pain as he did. "It's taken me six months to do that. I can hold the poker or a chisel in my right hand and move my arm with my left hand."

"That's amazing."

"It's hard. I can only work for a little while before it hurts."

"And you can't do this with your left hand?"

"Never learned."

"Of course not," I said.

Why would he? Who planned to lose the use of their right hand? I knew that if I ever lost my right hand, I would be useless. What would I do if I lost a limb? I would rather kill myself outright, I thought, than live without my arm. I could say such things from the comfort of myself intact, but should I actually be deprived of a limb, I doubted my strength to act. I was a coward after all, and a coward who enjoyed his life too much to give it up. Thus, to see Pippin struggle on and fight to pursue his passion despite such a fierce obstacle impressed me no end.

And to that effect, I said, "Why?"

"Why do it?"

"Yes," I said. "What makes you do it when it would be so much easier not to? You have every excuse, but—"

"My momma raised me not to waste anything comes from God."

"The art?"

"It's a thing I love, and a lot of folks seem keen on what I can do, so I figure as I never learned it in any official way, it comes from somewhere else."

"What about the cross?" I pointed. "It's as if you're saying god abandoned these soldiers."

Pippin lifted the piece of wood from my hand and set it down on the table. He turned to face me, full-on, uncomfortably close. I was taller than he, and his proximity forced me to step back.

"I'll be honest with you, sir," Pippin said. "There were times out there I wondered. I've been raised a good Christian. I believe in God and Jesus and the Holy Ghost, but out there in those trenches…when I saw that man get vaporized by that Minnie, I think his blood drove the spirit from me. For a long time after, too, I couldn't bring myself to say a word to heaven. I couldn't understand how God could let that thing go on. How could He love his children and let them do what we were doing to each other? I couldn't wrap my brain round it, no sir."

"But you seem, now, to have—"

"During the big battle, when I was laying in that shell hole, and I thought I was going to die, I had a good long time to think."

"What did you decide?" I said.

"That if God heard my prayers, and if I survived, then He must have been the one to do it. And if I lived because of Him, I'd best believe. So, I believe."

"You believe because you survived?"

"Yes, sir," Pippin said. "If I'd died, I would still believe, but I'd be in heaven, then wouldn't I?"

"If heaven exists."

"It does," Pippin said with a simple assurance.

I didn't push the point. It was enough to hear his admission. He believed because he lived. Belief based on debt. Surely, though, his upbringing gave him the knowledge and the faith that he possessed, but the linchpin of Pippin's faith was nothing more than a bargain made in the mud of Champagne. I had assumed Pippin's faith was something more, something deep and abiding, something real. To discover that it stood upon a foundation little more solid than the sands of parable left me…disappointed.

"And now?" I said.

"Now, sir?" Pippin said. "Now…I'm grateful."

***

West Chester was still segregated. I had found a rundown hotel on the black side of town and, Pippin's notebooks wrapped securely in a brown paper sack, I attended dinner in the half-disintegrated dining room just off the lobby. The place was empty, not surprisingly, except for a frumpy woman who served double duty as a waitress and chef. I ordered steak fried chicken and potatoes and waited in silence as she shuffled into the kitchen and set about clattering pans and sizzling oil. When the food arrived, I ate in silence, the package that contained Pippin's notebooks just off my water glass. For some reason, as I forked the lumpy potatoes and overcooked chicken into my mouth, I found an increasing and abnormal eagerness to read the notebook's contents. I was excited.

I paid my bill and carried the notebooks to my room. I sat down and—though now a year and a half into prohibition—reached instinctively for a bottle of bourbon. Not finding any, not knowing where to find a speakeasy this side of Philadelphia, I settled for a glass of water, which I carried to the desk and sipped as I peeled back the paper bag and lifted out the first of Pippin's notebooks. I hefted it in my hand and realized it possessed a weight similar to that of Marks' *New Testament*. A curious coincidence, but not one in which I would bother to seek a sign. I was still, after all, a confessed atheist.

I opened the cover and began to read, starting this time with the title crammed against the top of the first page: *Autobiography of Horace Pippin.* I moved slowly through the narrative, obstructed in part by Pippin's uneven script, but more by his hesitant sentence structure and inconsistent spelling. I quickly noticed two patterns, though, that accelerated my work. First, the way he parsed words by syllable. Instead of writing 'until' he would write 'on tell,' 'another' as 'a nother,' or 'again' as 'a gan.' Second, he tended to add an extra 'e' whenever he wrote a gerund or a verb in the present tense: instead of 'wearing' it was 'wareing,' or 'goeing' rather than 'going.' For someone with Pippin's education, I was nonetheless impressed.

As I read, I slowly became immersed—not by Pippin's powers of description, but rather by my own memories—in our shared experience. I recognized the events, the battles, the missions. I also recognized an increasingly confident soldier, one who grew comfortable with the command of others. I read how he began to smoke, and how he found comfort in the shelter of an overcrowded bunker. I read how he witnessed the direct hit by artillery shell of one of his friends and how the man seemed to vaporize. I read how Pippin took out the sniper during our weeks in the Vilquin sector. Then, ultimately, I read about the battle of the Meuse-Argonne, where Pippin received the wound that had paralyzed his arm, how, separated from his Company and alone with a buddy, he had tried to take out multiple machine-gun nests until a bullet put an end to his efforts.

I picked up the second, and then the third, notebook. They covered much of the same material and added only levels of detail. There was little of revelation between their covers. I was transported, though, to each location Pippin described. I heard the shell fire, felt the rumbling of the earth, smelled the smoke and gunpowder and death, remembered much of what I had hoped one day to forget. I even, in my mind's eye, enjoyed the simple pleasure of a cigarette, the way the smoke filled my lungs and then flowed through my nostrils and past my lips, the taste of the tobacco and the buzz, ever so slight, in my lungs and in my heart and in my head. A forgetting. One moment of relief amidst the hell of war.

I finished the last notebook and set it down atop the others. Pippin had offered their use for my memoir, and I considered all I had read. I would have to modify his grammar and spelling to make it legible to the average reader, but there were sections which appealed to my sense of dramatic narrative. Might I be able to provide a different perspective than my own, perhaps show what I had failed to do during my time assigned to Major Little? Demonstrate my complete lack of redemptive action in those last few days on the front. A symbolic and literary self-flagellation seemed in order. I picked up the first notebook and flipped to the end, reread Pippin's depiction of the Meuse-Argonne and made my decision. I would include his testimony in my confession.

***

Our shell fire was thin now for they were coming closer. At one o'clock, the artillery was in their position and began to fire. The German's airplanes were after us good and strong. By the end of the Day, we got 14 machine guns, 500 prisoners and a town. Then the artillery moved up. Prisoners were coming through our line and going back and it seemed every one of them was happy. They were out of it and they knew that they would see home again.

We only held the line that night. The machine guns were thick and they kept spitting bullets across our line until the artillery came up. Then, that morning, I got in with Co. I.

I had had nothing to eat for 3 Days. The Germans line were strong and shells dropping everywhere. Yet, we were advancing slowly.

I was in shell holes that were smoking and hot. The machine guns were in trees as well as in bushes and in houses. Anything they could get a machine gun in, they had it there. Women, as well as men, used machine guns.

We were facing another hill. Their snipers were thick there too. I seen a machine gun nest and I got him.

My buddy and I went after another one. Both of us were in the same shell hole. I was looking for another hole that would put me in view of the sniper. After I seen one, I said to my comrade, "You go one way, and I'll go the other, and one of us can get him." We could not see him from where we were at, for he was behind a rock. We had to get him in sight and, to do that, we had to take a chance. Both of us left the shell hole at the same time. I was near the shell hole I had picked out when the sniper let me have it.

I went down in the shell hole. He clipped my neck and got me through my shoulder and right arm. I had still not had nothing to eat yet and I only had a little water in my canteen. I began to plug up my wounds when my buddy came to me and did what he could for me. Then he told me that he had gotten the German and the gun. I was lying on my back. I thought I could get up but I could not. I shook hands with him and I never seen him since.

Now the shells were coming close to me, pieces of shell would come in near me sometimes. A German sniper kept after me all day and his bullets would clip the shell hole that held me. This was 2 o'clock in the morning.

Sometime after noon some French sweepers came by. They looked for Germans that were left behind. He saw me laying there and stopped to say something to me. But he never got it out for just then a bullet passed through his head and he sank on top of me. I saw him coming on, but I could not move, I was just that weak. So, I had to take him. I was glad to get his water and also his bread. I took my left hand and I got some coffee, though I had some hard time getting it from him. After that I felt good and I tried to get up again, but I was too weak to do so.

Night was coming on and it began to rain. I tried to get the blanket from my dead comrade. That I could not do and I could not get him off of me. The rain came more and more until I was in water. I was growing weaker and weaker all the time and I went to sleep. I can't say how long I slept, but two boys came and I woke up. They took the Frenchman off of me and then took me out of the shell hole for some distance where there were more wounded ones.

I was left there the rest of the night. Every time I would get in a sleep, I would be woken up by the French troops going to the line. Near morning, four French took me into a dugout and then to another until they found a doctor. I do not know anymore that night.

When I woke up, it was day. I was carried out of the dugout. I seen then that it was full of shot-up men like myself, some worse than I. I laid out there for some time in the rain, waiting for my turn to be taken down to the road to the ambulance.

Over the hill came some German prisoners with a French officer and they took me to the road. It was all they could do to stand up under me going down the hill. They had me over their heads and I thought I would roll off. A shell or two came close to us. But they made the road. I was shoved in the ambulance with 5 others, 6 in all, and shells followed in until we got to the full hospital.

When I got there, it was all I could do to tell them who I was. I pointed to my shirt where I had written down: 101127 Horace Pippin Co. K 369 INF. I knew no more until I was taken to the table to see what was wrong with me. They gave me some dope and that put me away for good. I can't say how long I was in it. After I came out of it, I was not there long. They took me to another hospital base in Leon.

Bellevue Signal to Sechault, Champagne, France

September 29–30, 1918

A wind blew atop the signal and it whistled up the windward side of the ridge and came off the peak. It drove the rain through wool and cotton and rubber. Already wet, it chilled the skin and muscles and bone. It turned the rain into a misery, kept us drenched and shaking. Water in my boots, my socks sodden. Water dripped down my back and mixed with sweat. The wind whipped my clothes tight against those reservoirs of moisture, turned the small of my back to ice, my underarms too. My hair near frozen by the windchill, tiny icicles that collected on my brow.

Down the hill, to the north, the fields stretched no more than half a mile before a village broke the flat. Sechault. The place stood at a crossroads and was nothing but a gathering of a dozen buildings. From on top of the hill, you could see the rough grid—two streets by two streets—that lined those buildings into a box. Straight lines that ran on the cardinals. Beyond Sechault maybe a mile more, and maybe on an angle south of east, a wood spread to the north. It looked thick and gnarly—the same kind of place, the same trees, as covered all of the Argonne. Past the woods a long, long way to the north, the fields resumed and seemed to sweep all the way to our division's objective.

Right now, though, we were in position on Bellevue Signal, just north of the peak.

"Is everyone off the horizon?" Little asked.

"Yes, sir," I said.

Our Poilus guide had stretched us across the spine of the signal. We had lined up along the German's horizon like ducks in a shooting gallery. A quick order sent me running to remedy the situation before the Boche could take advantage.

"If we can find this damn regiment, we can get ourselves into this battle for once and for all," Little said, grumbling.

"You sound eager, sir."

"I know you don't understand it, Ayers, but I'm as eager as the men to see battle. We've been close, but each time we've missed it. We have yet to truly have a go at honest to goodness war."

"Sir."

I had to admit that Little was right. We'd stood guard on the line, sure, gone on raids and laid wire, but a charge across No Man's Land—the true test of a soldier's mettle—we'd not seen the like. In the German's offensive in July, we'd come close, but even then we remained in support. Our war had, so far, been one that was *safe* and *protected.*

"As soon as we finish this relief, we'll be in it. We'll be the men on the front. The decision as to whether the line advances or retreats will be ours. Once we find these damn poilus, we'll be in a place that no one can deny. We'll see war and we'll have the chance to finally and irrevocably prove ourselves men and heroes."

"That's lofty."

"That's what a lot of men are here to do, Ayers, men who enlisted with pure motives."

I said nothing, looked to the plains north of our position. The morning light illuminated them through the clouds in a gray haze. In that haze, though, the future—the field to Sechault and the woods beyond—and I suddenly could see what lay ahead. "There are going to be a lot of dead men before we're through."

"That's true of every sector."

"More true here," I said. "We're in the middle of the French colonials. We're not up against an easy front."

"So, we die. At least we die heroes."

I shook my head. Little, occupied with unfolding a map, ignored me.

At its eastern edge, Bellevue Signal swings north, almost like a scythe, and in the subsequent crescent, maybe three hundred yards from the base, a farm nestled. Bussy Farm.

"We're to angle between the farm and that hook," Little said, comparing the reality to his map. "We're to head northeast from there to Sechault. At least if we can—"

"Sir," A coal colored private appeared from the brush. "We've found Favre's battalion."

"Excellent," Little folded his map. "Ayers, inform the company commanders, we're moving out."

***

The sun hung in the sky, its luminosity barely dimmed by the clouds. German shells peppered the hillside—not so accurate as before, this position passed in haste without a chance to dial their solutions—sending small showers of rock and shrapnel through the bushes. Undergrowth and weeds minimized the mud. Bellevue Signal pristine battleground, too early yet to have been denuded by bullet and men and shell. Soldiers crouched in it, hid as best they could under cover of it. Leaves and branches mean substitute for a trench, though, and did little to keep the whizz-bangs at bay. A semi-regular stream of casualties lumbered up the hill and back to medics on the other side. Men injured in the brush, hiding on the hillside.

Little hardly noticed. He stood behind a copse of trees and watched the lower plain through the foliage. One moment, he squinted past a golden canopy, the next he jotted a communiqué bound for Hayward at HQ. Meanwhile, men died. It seemed a waste to me. To discard warm bodies to no end. Why lose the numbers waiting, why accomplish nothing with their deaths?

Questions of war.

At fourteen hundred hours, Little sent me to gather the company commanders. I rushed through the weeds, running over uneven ground, to carry the message. Again, I found Siebel last and we traveled back to Little's trees together. We ran hunched forward, like giant apes, close to the ground.

I huddled close to Little's conference.

"From our position on this slope, we're at an angle to our designated direction of attack. The cover thins out once the terrain levels so it's going to be a problem to align our approach."

"One you've solved, sir?"

"We're to resume the offensive at fifteen hundred hours. At that time, B Company will go over the top. You'll hit the plain and angle east of north—toward Sechault. Fifteen minutes later, C Company will follow. Fifteen minutes after that, D Company. The idea is for all three companies to be in line angled toward Sechault by the time D Company advances."

Little paced a few steps and came back. "We're to march straight at Sechault and take her from the Germans. I imagine we'll find resistance in the village, and certainly in the woods beyond it. Prepare your men as best you're able to face it. We've never done this before, none of us, so we can only plan so much before it happens. I just hope to rely on the tremendous fortitude the men have demonstrated time and again. They'll follow you, but make sure those lines are straight. Finally, appoint some men as liaison. I want to be kept informed of your progress at every step. Questions?"

I moved away until I could look past the trees at the plain below. I stared at the fields between us and Sechault, at the weeds and brush that had grown where once wheat and corn had swayed. I looked for German entrenchments, for the tell-tale signs of the enemy, but saw nothing. The Germans had fallen back, given up the plain in favor of Sechault and the woods to the north. There was no way to tally their numbers, hidden as they were, no way to know how many men waited—machine guns warmed—for our charge from the hill.

The rain grew heavier. Steady drops of a middling size. This wouldn't turn the world to mud but it would make things slick and miserable. I scratched at my side where lice bit and winced as a shell landed short. In less than an hour, B Company would start across those fields to face the Germans. Suddenly, I felt grateful to be assigned to Major Little. At least I wasn't cannon fodder.

***

"Where's B Company?" Little shouted over the gunfire.

I leaned close, "It looks like they're holed up on the west side of town."

"Resistance?"

"I don't know."

We crouched in a ditch that ran along the road south of Sechault. Behind us, two companies and a third of the machine guns—kept in reserve. Ahead of us, C Company attacked deep into Sechault, fighting house to house, encountering heavy German resistance. To their right, D Company came in on the east side of town, facing some resistance but not nearly as bad as that in the center.

"We're facing heavy resistance down the middle—maybe a machine gun lined up on our men."

"If it's a machine gun," I said, "it's coming from the north. It's gotta be out toward the woods."

"Have we heard from HQ?"

"Not yet," I shouted.

I was growing hoarse from all the yelling. Our situation had gone from good to bad in short order. At fifteen hundred hours, B Company set out from their redoubt on the hill and in fifteen-minute increments, C and D Companies followed suit. They moved slowly down the last of the incline and angled toward Sechault. Progress moved apace. Only snipers and range finders remained in the half-mile between Bellevue Signal and the village. At one-point Lieutenant Siebel presented Major Little with a prize German prisoner. The man, red-haired and bearded, pleaded for his life and apologized for what he'd done—signaled German artillery the range of allied troops. Minor hiccups, road bumps, on the way to Sechault.

I'd followed Little and battalion HQ behind the leading edge of men. I'd heard the first shots as C Company engaged in Sechault. I'd watched men collapse in the streets. But after that Little setup position in the roadside ditch. My visibility dropped to the southern faces of village buildings. My only information, the liaison messages sent back from the three active companies.

Gunfire mostly was the sound that filled the air around Sechault. The put-put-put of our men's Lebel rifles and the *rat-tat-tat-tat* of the six Chauchat machine guns deployed with B, C, and D Companies. There was another chain gun—German—that mixed with it, and handguns and the more poignant sound of men's voices. I could never decipher words, but I could hear the shouts. Deep, gospel filled shouts. Some carried the tones of an order, others cried for help. Still, others sounded as men in pain. I recognized the timbre—that soulful rich bass and the jazzy tenor—of men from Harlem. It seemed to me that the Germans fought in silence. Only once did I hear the guttural animal noises of the Boche, and they were followed immediately by a *rat-tat-tat-tat* that sounded of our Chauchat.

My stomach growled in hunger. I ignored it.

"Do we know where the liaison group is?" Little shouted.

"Still delivering your last message. You just sent it five minutes ago."

"If they don't get back soon, I'll need you to take the next one."

"When the time comes," I shouted.

Little was obsessed with liaison. He sent a message back to regimental HQ every quarter-hour. He had tasked a man to run messages for every two hundred yards between us and Colonel Hayward. He had taken to heart the importance of communication on the line—almost too much. It seemed he was on the cusp of sacrificing performance to liaison, but no matter how many men he kept running messages, the Germans still required more.

"We need to put more men in the center," Little said.

"If there's a German machine gun—"

"You're right. We should get a better idea of its position and call an artillery strike. Damn it. We need more information." A shell landed behind us and we crouched into the ditch. A thin stream of water turned our footing to mud and each step required concentration to keep from losing ground.

"Give it some time," I said. "Siebel reported in just ten minutes ago and the other two maybe ten minutes before that—"

"But there's information…that's it," Little turned and put a hand on my shoulder. He pulled me close. "Go find Lieutenant Siebel and have him send some men to get a fix on that German machine gun. We can be proactive in this."

"Sir," I said.

"Be careful."

I ignored Little's last comment as I ducked past him and headed east along the ditch, toward D Company.

***

C Company captured a German mortar at the southern entrance to Sechault. A nearby ammunition dump almost went up in flames except for a fast-thinking private who extinguished the fire before it could ignite the live ammo. Second Lieutenant Hundley, of B Company, entered the casualty rolls and was sent to the rear. He was followed by first lieutenant Vaughn of D Company. Twenty men from the 372nd regiment, lost from their mother unit, joined our ranks. D Company set up an automatic rifle post on the second floor of a brick building on the north of town. The rest of D Company joined C Company in occupying several ditches on the northern edge of Sechault. An airplane buzzed our position in the south side ditch, strafing the dirt and brush and sending men to the rear with bullet holes in their bodies.

***

"Who're they?" Little asked, pointing across the plain toward Bellevue Signal in our rear.

I turned to see a large group of soldiers—maybe a hundred, maybe more—making their way toward us. They wore American uniforms and French helmets. More, they were black.

"I don't know. Reinforcements?"

"At least they're not Germans."

"We'll find out soon enough," I said.

A few minutes later, a white officer stumbled into our ditch and found his way to Major Little. I recognized him as Captain Eric Winston, captain of H Company. He was a big man, almost as big as Jim Europe, but he seemed shrunken—whether from battle or from death or from some other cause I could not tell.

"Cobb's dead," he said. "Killed."

I stood back a respectful distance, though I could still hear every word of the exchange.

"How did it happen, Eric?" Little asked.

"We were holding in support, positioned on the rear slope of Bellevue Signal, that eastern spur. Somehow the Boche found us and opened up. Heavy shellfire. Cobb got his right at the beginning—almost a direct hit. A piece of the shell took off the entire back of his head…"

Little put a hand on Winston's arm. "Who are all these men coming across?"

"They're our men, we couldn't stay where we were, the Boche had our number. Clark took over command and he decided to move up to you."

Voices sounded up the ditch and Captain Clark appeared in the fading light. "Major Little, Captain Clark reporting. We've about a hundred and fifty men left and we're at your disposal."

"Welcome to Sechault."

***

As darkness settled, so did our situation. The remnants of the Second Battalion had integrated into our force structure. The last German personnel within Sechault had been captured or killed. And the perimeter had been secured.

That is not to say our hold on Sechault was perfect. Boche machine guns on the plains to the north remained lined up on every street in the place. To cross into the open streets drew almost immediate fire. And there was the disturbing discovery that we were very much alone.

On paper, the 369th was to form the tip of a wedge aimed at Sechault. Both our flanks were to be covered by French forces—the 163rd and the 363rd—but repeated attempts to establish liaison had failed. At nineteen hundred hours, we received a communiqué from Colonel Hayward confirming that neither regiment was in position. That meant we were stuck in the middle of German forces, alone, and if they thought to, they could outflank us and cut us off from the rest of our forces. So, it was in less than perfect security that we dug in for the long night ahead.

***

I sat in the darkness, listened to all the noises of the night. Every one of us clustered together—some in houses, some in the ditches—close quarters. Coughs, whispers, mutters and moans. A few men moved about, let their feet crunch gravel and weeds, as they waited out the night. A tattoo of bullets. Shouting. Calming words and admonitions. Quiet whispers resumed. Stomach growls broke the stillness—every man hungry. A shell landed behind the village, its noise like thunder, the mushroomed debris falling like rain. Sounds in the darkness.

I heard Little's footsteps, pacing. He walked back and forth on the wooden floor of the blockhouse. His steps made soft patter despite heavy army boots.

I slipped my own boots off my feet, peeled the socks off sodden skin. I rolled them up and squeezed them out and set them atop my boots to dry. I knew the morning would dawn on damp socks, but I couldn't pass the chance to air my feet—no matter how badly they smelled—I wanted nothing to do with trench foot. Blackened toes and amputation did not appeal.

"Who took their boots off?" someone said.

I shifted my boots between my feet. "We should all take our boots off."

"We ain't got dry socks."

"Should still air out your feet. Can't hurt any."

"Boy but it stinks."

"This war stinks," I said, still not sure who owned the other voice.

"Ayers is right," Little said. "You should all give your feet some air. We can keep the doors open, try to ventilate the place."

As he spoke, he moved to the front door and pulled it open. I saw his shadow move across the space and he stepped outside, his adventure protected from the machine guns to the north by the bulk of the blockhouse. I stayed seated, my feet stretched out, as comfortable as I could get. If Little needed me, he could ask.

The room grew quiet around me and I leaned my head against the wall. I kept my eyes open, though and watched the door. Dim moonlight lit the street outside, and I could see Little's form pacing back and forth, his hands tapped his thighs as he walked, and he looked so much like a man in need of a cigarette. Agitated and nervous—not a good state of mind for a man commanding three hundred men, men surrounded by Hun forces and all alone in the night.

Then gravel crunched and another figure stopped in front of Little. The man was quiet for a moment and in the bare light, I couldn't hope to identify him. And when he spoke, I could only make out that he was a white man, an officer.

"Major," he said, "please don't stay out here. They'll get you, sure, if you do."

I watched as Little seemed to shake in the darkness, his head nodded from side to side and he took several steps backward. "My god. I think that's what I want. What do I know about warfare? What have I done this afternoon? Lost half my battalion—driven hundreds of innocent men to their death. It would be a relief, my boy, a relief."

The second figure moved closer to Little and extended a hand to clasp the major's shoulder.

"Please don't talk or feel that way, major. I can't see you give way to despair, we've been too close these past few weeks. It's no longer the superiority of the age or rank that counts with me, major. It's something deeper. Now, you've just got to come in."

Little shuddered then and nodded. He grabbed the second man's hand for a long spell and when he broke the contact, he turned for the blockhouse. He walked right through the door to the center of the room, turned slowly around a full three hundred and sixty degrees, and sat roughly on the floor. I closed my eyes, then and tried to sleep.

***

I couldn't sleep. No matter how hard I tried, some noise would jar me awake at the last second. After maybe an hour, I gave up, just sat in silence with my eyes closed and let the night wash over me.

Little was in and out of the blockhouse the whole time. He would confer with some courier in low whispers and then he would pull one of the company commanders outside for a quick conference. Once or twice the sound of machine-gun fire drove him back through the door right quick. It didn't matter, though, Little kept ongoing. Occasionally, he would cross over to where Lieutenant Robb sat and exchange a few words with him. He only very briefly sat still and quiet.

Lieutenant Robb made his own kind of noises. He had been shot in the arm earlier in the day but had kept fighting despite his injury. When ordered to the dressing station he had gone only long enough for the medic to patch the hole before he returned to duty. Now he sat on the floor against the wall. Whenever he shifted, he would gasp in pain. It didn't stop there. After he gasped, he would fake a yawn or a cough or make some other noise to mask that he was, in fact, hurting. Not that I begrudged the man his pain. It was admirable that he stayed when he could just as easily have retired the field. Impressive that he would sacrifice his own comfort to stay with his men.

A far cry from my behavior, I thought, as Robb let out a particularly harsh gasp. I would have hit the dressing station then Paris. I had no need for courage. I was content with survival and I would be happy just to get back to Harlem in one piece. No, though I admired Lieutenant Robb, I had no desire to join him, self-sacrifice well above my pay grade.

***

I awoke to a chill, my feet near-frozen in the night, and I pulled them close so I could rub them with my fingers. They felt rough, like hardened clay. I moved my fingers slowly, carefully, until warmth returned—or at least they weren't freezing anymore. It was still dark outside, though the vague lightening that presaged the dawn began to work its gradual hints into the eastern sky.

I checked my boots and socks. Still wet. And now they were cold too. I shivered and pulled them on. I needed to pee and I figured it would be better to take care of such necessaries in the dark instead of in the full view of Boche snipers.

When I returned to the blockhouse, a courier from the northern trenches stood in the room, his outline visible in the approaching light.

"—evidence all across the plain. We're seeing the movement of troops, noises of regiments on the move. We think they're preparing for a counter-offensive, one that, from the looks of it, is going to happen before dawn."

Little gave this news a moment's consideration. "Return to your post. Ayers, notify the company commanders. Everyone else to your posts. Those in headquarters, see what you can find in the way of lookouts and fire positions. We don't have long before the dawn."

The blockhouse burst into activity. Hoarse voices shouted, men collided, and boots clopped on wood—heavy thuds—making the suddenly small space into chaos. I turned back to the door and slipped outside. I didn't have to worry about B Company or the elements of the machine gun company—their commanders had both been in the blockhouse. It was C and D Companies that needed informing, though I suspected they already knew. It was a soldier from C Company that broke the news to Little. That meant my priority became D Company.

The sky was light enough now that I could make out the eastern horizon, a darker line against the sky. Not light enough to spot the outline of a man in the other direction. I stayed close to the blockhouse, all the same, as I slipped around the corner of the building into a north-south street. I held my breath for a long second, waiting for a Boche gun to light up the corridor and riddle me with bullets. Nothing came. The Boche machine gun remained silent. I let my breath out in a rush and gulped new, fresh air to replace it. The chill felt good in my lungs and I let myself breathe a handful of breaths before I began to inch my way forward in the darkness.

I felt weeds and pebbles under my feet. Winced as the sounds announced my presence. I didn't care that the closest Boche soldier was maybe a couple of hundred yards away, I didn't want a clank of stone to spell my demise. So, I walked on the sides of my feet, rolling from heel to toe in slow waves, moving as if I carried some fragile cargo on my back. I kept one finger on the blockhouse—just in case—too far away and I became a separate target, my sole desire in life to meld with the building and become indistinguishable from the wood and brick. When the building ran out, I dropped into a crouch, nay, a crawl, and eased forward on my hands and knees.

Before I'd passed twenty feet, a voice called, "Who is it? Who goes there?"

I dropped to my belly and raised my arms to cover my head. Earlier that morning, a patrol from the 163rd Regiment had approached our lines. Our sentry called a challenge. The French responded, "Comrades," but didn't stand to. Our men fired on the patrol, killing two and wounding several others. I wasn't about to risk my life over a sentry's challenge, so I burrowed in the dirt and cringed like a coward.

"Sergeant Ayers," I said. "Headquarters."

"Ayers? You that fella who wouldn't fate me back in Jersey."

"That's me," I said.

"Well, shit, come on over. I won't shoot you, though most 'spectable folks'd consider me more than justified if I did."

"Much obliged," I said and crawled the rest of the way to the ditch.

Rolling into the shallow entrenchment, I grinned up at the sentry. A small man with a crooked nose and a pair of missing teeth, he just shook his head. "Hell of a way to make an entrance—on your ass."

"I'm looking for Lieutenant Siebel," I said.

The sentry pointed to the east. "He's over that way. You best watch your step lest you roust some angry niggers."

"Thanks," I climbed to my feet and assumed the now-familiar crouch, back bent, knees sprung low, head down. I moved past the sentry and down the ditch. I felt exposed in the shallowness of it. A Boche sniper would have no trouble zeroing my skull. It didn't help that I kept bobbing, either, every couple of steps a pair of legs. I stumbled once and an angry voice—just like the sentry had said—roared at the disturbance. I apologized and moved on. Maybe sixty yards along, I ran into a small group of white men.

"Lieutenant Siebel," I said, and managed a crippled salute.

"Sergeant Ayers."

"I'm to inform you that headquarters suspects a counterattack before dawn."

I couldn't see much beyond Siebel's pale face, and that a blob of lightness in the dark. "We know. We've been hearing movement all over the place. It's like a party—cursing and shouting and clanking about…tell Major Little we'll be as ready as we can be."

"Sir."

Siebel turned back to the other officers, dismissive, proper. He was not about to engage in badinage with a Negro soldier, not in front of other white men. I took the hint and turned west. I walked on a few steps before my disappointment in Siebel gave way to self-preservation. I hunched over and kept on marching. I had no idea how far it was to C Company and I wanted to be back in the blockhouse before the sunlit Sechault's streets. I picked up my pace, double-time, and ignored the cries from sleeping soldiers. My ass was more important than their sleep.

***

The dark turned to light and no attack. The Boche refrained, left us to wonder and cower at their renewed bombardment. Heavy shellfire covered our positions north, some in Sechault proper. Adding their heft to an already lengthy casualty list. Men left either dead or wounded by shrapnel, the shallow ditches no true defense. Soldiers limping past, or helped by comrades, on to the dressing station. Too many, too fast. Like a train, powered by Boche shells.

By the time light edged the horizon, HQ sent orders. Continue the advance at 0700 hours. March to be preceded by an artillery preparation only—no rolling bombardment.

***

Dirt ground against my cheek. Weeds and stones made lumps beneath the weight of my body. My Lebel dug into my arm and did little good where it lay, extended north, flat on its side, waiting for some unforeseen command to spring into action and fire its load of three shots against the enemy, an enemy that lurked somewhere in the brush and settled in the woods beyond.

The line spread from one side of Sechault to the other, its roughly straight edge directed at the enemy and placed approximately half a mile north of the village. Soldiers in repose waited for news. Stayed by a pair of machine-gun nests toward the left flank.

"B Company's facing little to no resistance," Little said to his current amanuensis, Lieutenant Cosgrove. "If we set up a machine gun on the east, we can draw their attention, distract them while Bates takes his men around their flank."

Earlier that morning, Little had pulled the men back from the front line to allow for an artillery preparation. When the last shell fell on the plains north of Sechault, he ordered the men to advance toward the woods. About 0730, the men began to move, slowly and cautiously to advance on the Boche positions. For maybe an hour, the men marched to the north, deliberate steps taken by men hunched low to the earth, before the machine gun nests opened up and pinned C Company to the ground. Once the situation settled into static, Little moved headquarters from Sechault proper—took us to within yards of the line—and began to direct the advance from his new position.

"If B Company gets caught," Cosgrove said. "They'll be butchered."

Little lifted a shoulder off the ground. "We'll have to keep the covering fire constant. And they'll have to advance with the utmost discretion—"

"They can do it if they take the right tack. If they angle too close they'll reveal themselves too soon, too far and the Boche will get suspicious before they can attack."

"Bates is a good man; he can pull it off."

The machine-gun nests were situated on the west side of C Company's front and angled toward the eastern approaches. I had little doubt that B Company could slip behind the nests and clear them out with little more than a semi-regular rifle fire to keep the machine gun crews distracted. It was a straightforward task and like much of the war required only that the men in question perform their duty.

In some ways, I was beginning to be disillusioned with this war. True, I had been protected, but everything great that our men had accomplished came not from some courageous heroism, but from a simple sense of duty. We did what we were told. We obeyed orders and we accomplished our assignments. Before I had thought war a conglomeration of great deeds, a piling together of tremendous valor. I had put the stories of the past as testimony to the greatness of soldiers and viewed them as worthy of stories and monuments. The reality, in many ways, stung with its mendacity. War was not made of heroes. Yes, it made heroes, but only because soldiers did their duty. Courage had become just that, duty. Duty under fire. And to acknowledge the simplicity of it all depressed me. Wasn't this all to be for some greater purpose? Weren't we here to become heroes?

"Let's go for it," Little said. "Bates can move around their flank, cut them off, and we can get moving again…Ayers, get me Lieutenant Bates."

***

An unknown number of machine guns hid in the thick foliage. Artillery and men waited behind the leading edge, a forest in the true sense, trees packed so densely that visibility fell off within feet of the tree line.

A death trap.

And only 1300 hours to boot. A wonderful way to spend the afternoon: throw your forces against that wall—pillboxes and all—and expend the last of your men for a few yards of earth.

Requests for an artillery preparation resulted in a dozen shells, pitter-patter, that fell haphazardly in the trees, nothing like the hours of bombardment necessary to make a dent in the Boche defenses. A tribute to our value, that a dozen shells are all we warrant. A waste at that because the shells signal our advance and remove the element of surprise.

"That's all we get," Little said, his body sprawled in the dirt. "I think that's it."

"Sir," I said. "We can't hope to beat the Germans without—"

"I know, Ayers, but duty—"

"Duty? Duty's worthless here. Duty asks us to advance into those woods without any artillery preparation. Duty asks us to die needlessly. No, duty should not be the deciding principle, not here."

"Sergeant Ayers, you forget yourself."

"No, I think for the first time I am very much in command. We have what, three hundred men left—that's out of all three battalions—and HQ wants us to march into god knows how many machine guns, concrete bunkers, and entrenched positions without showing us the respect of a decent preparation? No, sir, no. I have done what you've asked but I cannot do this without raising my voice. This is madness and I want nothing to do with it."

"Are you going to disobey my order?"

I stared at Little, my cheek hard against the cold ground. I wanted to say yes. I wanted to mutiny. I knew that to attack those woods meant certain death for what remained of the regiment. If we followed orders and marched into those trees none of us would march back. I wanted to raise my voice and tell Little he could go to hell, but I couldn't. For all the reason that screamed inside me, there was something else, something that dwelled in the innermost realms of my heart and revolted at the idea. How could I say no when men far better than I stood ready to advance at the Major's orders? How could I let the cowardice of reason eliminate what chance remained that I might be counted among them?

I could not say I would disobey, but I could not say I would obey. "Sir," I said, "I honestly don't know. I don't want to die, not now, but I owe it to the rest of the men to…"

"That's all I can ask," Little said.

"Sir."

The sun beat through the clouds and warmed my back. My uniform was wet from crawling in the mud, my Lebel slung over my shoulders. All of us in the same position—a line maybe half a mile long—spread across the fields facing the woods.

"Have you read *The Red Badge of Courage*," Little said.

"Years ago."

"The main character was obsessed with courage. He spent his nights wondering what he would do in the face of battle, whether he would fight or flee. When the opportunity first presented itself, he fled—ran into the woods to escape the terror of battle. But he regretted his decision. He came back to the fighting and he eventually was injured. It's called the red badge of courage when a soldier is wounded in battle. That's why the name of the book because the character showed the courage to go back and face the inevitability of injury."

"I'm not sure I understand," I said.

"It's why I don't need a yes or no. It's why your indecision is okay. If you're willing to wait for the order before you make your decision—I'm willing to let you wait."

"Okay."

"Because it is inevitable. If we go in there, we'll be decimated. Every last one of us will enter the casualty rolls. So, if you're uncertain about going forward I understand. I just ask a willingness to try, to risk yourself, to maybe obtain the red badge of courage."

"I don't want to die," I said again.

"Nor do I, but courage is obedience to duty in the face of defeat. If we make this charge then our regiment goes down in history as one filled with courageous men…courageous Negroes."

"I'd rather we be living Negroes."

Little said nothing, then, and let the last of the paltry artillery preparation fall in silence. The last shell exploded, and the air seemed to grow static as if the bombardment had never happened. An eerie stillness settled over our lines as every man pondered on the future, on the machine-gun nests that loomed just inside the trees, nests untouched by artillery.

A scraping sound broke the spell and a voice called from behind us. "Major Little, a message from Colonel Hayward."

The courier crawled forward and extended a folded paper to Little's grasp. Little unfolded the page and read the words in silence. After several moments, he smiled. "We've been reprieved."

"Sir?"

"We're to be relieved tonight. The colonel's told us to hold tight until then. We don't have to advance. It's over. We just have to keep our position a few more hours. It's over. We've survived."

I closed my eyes and felt my body relax. Every part of me felt a sudden relief. I would not be asked to test my mettle. I would not face the red badge of courage, but rather escape intact, unbitten by Sechault and the terrors of this infantry offensive. I was alive and would remain that way. I let out a breath and breathed another in. I could smell the earth close and mixed with the acrid smoke of exploded shells. Black powder. I didn't know where we might go next, only that we would get to go there, the men of the 369th, Negroes, worthies, some of us even heroes.

Arlington National Cemetery

Arlington, Virginia, USA
May 9, 1921

I stood in front of Arlington House, its pillared façade facing to the East, where I could see the oak trees spread about the fields and the rows and rows of headstones that tracked the nap of the earth like corn; neat furrows of green interrupted by ridges of marble and granite. I did not know how many lay interred here, nor did I need to—the enormity of the sacrifice stretched before me, visual evidence more meaningful than any number, any statistic. This was the power of faith and patriotism. A nation filled with men who would stand behind its flag and give their lives for principle, for the commands of its elected officials, academics who couldn't distinguish between historical truth and sensationalized filmmaking. I didn't know whether to cry or scream.

But a critique of Woodrow's policies—and now Harding's—was not my motivation. No, I came for a different reason. A memorial to a lost friend. A memorial to a man who I should have known better.

I stepped away from Arlington House and walked down the hill, aiming east of north. I followed the contours of the land and passed through rows of the dead. This area was filled with monuments and expensive obelisks—phallic stone erected in memory of the dearly departed. I topped a rise to see a path cut the hillside below, a road for hearse, coffin, and family to traverse. Beyond that, just a few rows down, my destination.

I was not alone.

Two figures stood silently at the foot of Europe's grave, a woman and a boy, maybe five or six years old, big but still awkward in his childhood. The woman wore a simple Merry Widow with a single ostrich plume. Her dress was plain, dark brown, modest. From chin to ankle to wrist not an inch of flesh was visible. Her face was round but not fat. In her protestant modesty, she remained very visibly a woman and her features evidenced femininity that belied her stern attire. The boy, on the other hand, was dressed simply, in a shirt and tie and shifted uncomfortably and tried to pull the tie away from his neck and the shirttails from his pants.

I drew closer and that's when I realized…when I saw the boy's face and I knew. The pouched cheeks, the wide lips, the bug eyes…it was Jim Europe's boy who stood there. His mother had brought him to visit his father's grave on the anniversary and to lay a bouquet of lilies at the memorial.

"Hello," I said cautiously as I approached.

"Hello," the woman said. "Did you know Jim?"

"In the war."

The woman accepted this with a nod as if to say that she expected as much and, that with the exception of Sis and Blake, no other musician could be bothered to remember her husband.

"He was a good man," I said, "and I'm sorry."

"Thank you."

"Your son?"

She reached down and grabbed the boy's hand. The boy, who had been busy tugging his shirt completely free, looked up and stared at me as he noticed me for the first time, "Who are you?"

"My name's Reuben Ayers."

"My name's James."

I squatted down and held my hand toward the boy in greeting. He stepped forward and extended his own, straight and manly. I took the tiny hand in my own and shook once, twice, three times. "It's a pleasure to meet you, James."

James smiled and, as I released his hand, he drew closer to his mother's skirts.

I stood up and gave James' mother a small bow with my head. "It's a pleasure to meet you, ma'am."

"Bessie Simms," she said.

I stared at the woman then, examined her fine nose, her delicate lips, and her tastefully rouged cheeks. I remembered seeing her at the funeral. She had not been with the family but had stood back. She had followed with the boy James on her shoulder, a toddler then who had been unable to comprehend the sorrow of the day. And the name I knew, the woman who Europe mentioned now and then in France, was Willie Starke, not Bessie Simms. This was the mother of Europe's child but not his wife.

"I saw you at the funeral," I said, unsure of what else to say. "It was an amazing service."

"I didn't have much to do with it."

"But you should feel proud that so many people cared about your man."

Simms took a long, slow breath. "They cared about him 'cause he made them money. Not no one's gonna remember him in five years."

"You will," I said. "I will. James will."

"No, he won't. He was two years old when his daddy died. He's not going to remember him at all."

I shook my head. "He was too much a part of Harlem."

"Harlem? What good's Harlem? There ain't no use in Harlem less you got someone to go with. Lord almighty. How I miss the man."

I glanced at James who had now managed to conquer the tie knot and was wrapping the tie around his wrist. "James may not remember his father, but you'll tell him stories, you'll tell him all about Jim Europe and how he was the best bandleader of his day. You'll tell him how you loved him and how you miss him and how good a man he was. You'll tell his story and because of that, James will remember. Maybe not the man, but he'll remember what you remember. And in the end, that's all we can really hope for…at least in this life."

"Lord, but Saint Peter don't admit no…"

I smiled. "From what I hear, they don't play jazz in heaven and I don't think Jim's gonna stay anywhere he can't play jazz."

Simms smiled at that. "You knew him pretty well."

The words struck my heart and I turned away. I did not know him, not the way I would have liked. I had only known the surface of him, never really known him as a friend…and now, it hurt even more to know that such a failure of knowledge resulted from my own, poor choices and from…I said none of this, though, only, "I would have liked to know him better."

"Like you said," Simms adjusted her hat. "He was a good man. He always took care of me and James. He treated us proper. He wasn't perfect, lord knows, no man is. But he was more right than wrong, a lot more right."

I smiled a little, then, at the thought of Europe with this woman and their son, a little family, happy. It was good to know that he'd had it good in this relationship. He deserved it. And who cared about the impropriety? The progressives? Damn the progressives. Europe was happy with this woman. No one had the right to deny another man happiness. Sure, it didn't fit in the proper mold or conform to the standards of decorum set out by wealthy dead white people in England, but we were Negroes. And nothing was going to change that. No white man would come along with a magic stick and suddenly transform us into a bunch of pale imitations. No. We were Negroes and we would make our own rules.

"He'll be remembered," I said quietly, turned to read the engraving on his tombstone.

FIRST LIEUT. JAMES REESE EUROPE
REGIMENTAL BAND, 369TH INF.
Feb. 20, 1880
May 9, 1919

It was insufficient, I thought. Europe was more than part of the regimental band. He was an officer, a machine gunner, an inspiration and a friend. He organized and he planned, and he promoted. He brought light into Harlem's music scene and drove a haphazard conglomeration of musicians into an organized army of artists. He broke the color line and he shared his ideals through his music…music that defied any man to stay still. How could you listen to that music and keep your feet from moving? He was a genius, a giant, a man who should be remembered among the great artists of the twentieth century. But he was dead, and his death…it truncated a life that should have burned brightly for decades yet to come.

"He'll be remembered," I said again as if to confirm the truth of it.

"I appreciate you coming," she said, her eyes shaded by the brim of her hat. "He'd have appreciated it too. He was good with friends like that."

I smiled. "It's been a pleasure to meet you."

"Likewise."

I waved at James, nodded once more to Ms. Simms, and turned back up the hill. The boy reminded me of my son, and I wondered what Europe would have done to save his own child.

***

The train moved in rhythmic precision, an iron giant swooping northwards, moving me ever closer to Manhattan. I sat in the Jim Crow car with half a dozen other Negroes. We rode in silence, our shared oppression uncommented, our shared race not enough to bring us together; something more required to unite us in a common cause. It was the kind of thing at which Jim Europe excelled, but that I did not understand.

Two years ago, today, the world lost a great man.

I had been there, in Boston, when it happened. I had come to confess my betrayal and beg forgiveness, but I was too late. I had intended to approach Europe after the band's performance. I would corner him and tell it all. Tell him how I had made a deal with Tammany and how I had almost caused a riot in Spartanburg and how I had spied on the regiment. I would tell him, and I would ask him to forgive me. Not that I had expected him to. I think that was one of the reasons I had intended to tell him. I needed someone to know of my betrayal and I needed someone to hate me for it. It was part of my penance that I chose for that person to be Jim Europe. He was the best man I knew and he would fully comprehend what I had done. But he had died before any of it could happen.

During intermission, the drummer stabbed Europe in the neck. The injury had seemed minor, but at the hospital, Europe had been made to wait as the blood continued to leak from the wound. Before the doctors attended to him, he had lost so much blood that he died before they could do anything to save him.

I had sat through the second half of the band's performance—continued in Europe's absence—and only later learned what had happened when I tried to find him afterward. The news shook me badly. I had placed my hopes of redemption in my confession to Europe only to be denied. I left Boston confused and distraught. How was I to atone for my transgressions against my people? How was I to improve their lot now that politics had been denied me?

It occurred to me a week later. I did not have the musical abilities that allowed Jim Europe to improve race relations. I had no special talent for art like Horace Pippin. The only thing I might be able to do was to write. And at Europe's funeral, marching with the rest of Harlem behind his casket, I knew that was the answer. I would write my confession—the one I never made in person—and I would publish it for the world to read.

***

My list is finished but for one final task.

As I write these final words, I see arrayed before me the small holdings that—in the end—have come to constitute my life. My father's watch, that dented and scarred Elgin, with whatever meaning that may be found therein. *The Bible* of Private Marks, with its mud-spattered and crinkled pages, that traveled with me across the world and—though it did not see me through hard times—accompanied me through the darkness. This manuscript, now a thick pile of pages that is weighted with the burdens of my existence. And the *Croix-de-Guerre*, an honor awarded to the entire regiment—not one which I merited by any action of my own. Four things that I will enclose in a box and deposit with my lawyer, Napoleon Marshall, to deliver, after all is done, and I am gone.

I intend to kill a man, you see, and thus, the final object on my desk. A pistol. Polished and silver it shines in the dim light of the electric bulb. I have spent some time to clean and grease its workings, practiced with its grip in my hand until I have grown confident in my success, and reverently placed six bullets in its chambers. I reached a hand to touch its hilt, felt the chiseled wood cool against my skin. A simple purchase—though not in New York—a trip across the Hudson necessary to avoid the mandatory reporting requirement for any Negro that buys a gun.

I do not intend to kill for a hatred of the man. I kill for Allie. For I saw her eyes, shadowed and dejected, haunted by the cage of her marriage. It is for her and for Isaac. I kill to protect my son, that he may grow to adulthood without the violence of a selfish drunkard and that he might be able to escape the prejudice of that monster. Though in killing I am certain of death, and in dying, I can only hope to be remembered.

For that reason, I leave this manuscript, and all the rest of my possessions, to my son.

***

Dear Isaac,

I suppose the best way to start this is to tell you something about your namesake: Ishmael. I call him your namesake because your mother thought it fitting to name you Isaac after the Biblical character because Isaac was the brother of Ishmael by Abraham. So, Isaac, let me tell you of my brother in life—if not in blood—Ishmael.

Ishmael was my first true friend. He was a carpenter—a fine one—who made coffins late into the night to earn extra money. He had a dream that someday he might save enough to open his own workshop and escape from beneath the employment of a white man. He loved baseball, too, and taught me—if not to love it myself—to appreciate it. And he loved women and he loved to enjoy life. He was a rare man who deserved far more of my thought and respect than I gave him. When I got involved in some unsavory politics and was beaten into a coma, Ishmael pursued the men who beat me and lost his life in the effort. If not for his loyalty, I am confident he would soon have accomplished his dream and opened his own shop in Harlem. I'm not sure which trait I admire more, the loyalty so fierce he gave his life or the tenacity to work day and night to achieve his dream. I am only sorry that your mother—and you—never met him.

You mother is a stunning and passionate woman. I will not elaborate as such comments tend to embarrass the child of such a conversation's object. I will say, though, that she taught me what it meant to give myself to the moment—to a cause—to anything. She moved me to stand for my own people and to invest myself emotionally in…in life. It is a skill I have never possessed and still struggle to exercise, but one which I have always envied in those who wield it as effortlessly as she. Allie, your mother, is gorgeous and sage and considerate. She has sacrificed for me, and you, more than you will ever know and I cherish her for that.

I know that this letter reads like an attempt to impart some digest of fatherly wisdom in a few pages, and for this, I apologize. My intent, I think, is to leave some memory of myself and, knowing that my own life is little worth remembering, I rather would you remember those I've loved and now miss.

Of those few strong enough to touch my hardened heart was James Reese Europe. An accident, really, but a happy one for me. We served together in the war and I saw in him a very great man. He was a hero of our race, talented and capable, who saw an opportunity to change the world with his music. More than that, he acted on the opportunity in an effort to bring people together. I grew to trust and respect him yet…I had already betrayed him. And not only him, but all my brothers in arms and my race as well. He helped me realize the extent of my error—something I have spent the last two years trying to rectify—to cover up my regrets.

That, I suppose, is where this ends. My regrets. I have many of them, many things I have done and many more I have failed to do. I have made a mess of my life, but I have been privileged to change. And in changing, I hope to one day be exonerated. By what or whom I know not, only that in my heart I might be able to assuage the guilt—lift the burdens that, in my life, I have managed to attain.

I do not pretend to admonish you, for I do not know you, and that, too, is a regret I should have. Your mother is a capable parent and I believe she will do better by you than if I were to impose myself in your life. What I will do, briefly, is explain what comes attached in this package and then I will bid you adieu as I do not anticipate a long continuance of my existence.

The account of my life—at least the last several years of it—should be explanation enough for itself. I have endeavored to recount my sins and my efforts to atone—successful or not. This you may read or discard. It does not matter. What matters was the writing of it. The watch belonged to my father and, though I am abandoning you as he abandoned me, I feel that some small piece of him should continue on beyond my life. As such, I bequeath it to you. The Bible I cannot explain. I shared a brief connection with its former owner and, for some reason, carried it with me throughout the war. I took occasion to read its pages, but have not found myself converted or unduly influenced by its contents. Read it, consider it, and do with it what you will.

Finally, the Croix-de-Guerre. This perhaps, more than anything else, is mine to give and to be proud of the giving. It is a reminder of the brotherhood of battle and the camaraderie of war. It is a reminder of the two thousand men who set out from Harlem to serve their country—for various reasons—when it refused to recognize their rights and even their lives. It is the ultimate symbol of the sacrifice of a people, and I hope you can someday come to recognize its value.

I wish you luck. This life is not easy. It is hard. Your parents have not given you an easy start of it either. I only hope that, in forsaking any part I might claim in your existence, I make your life that much simpler. Grow up and be something worthwhile. Make friends. Love. Give yourself to the moment and do the things I was never capable of doing. Be great though no one may know. I go now to my final act. May it influence your life for good.

Your father,
Reuben Ayers

CPSIA information can be obtained
at www.ICGtesting.com
Printed in the USA
BVHW011219011019
559908BV00006B/39/P